Schrödinger's Cabinet

Adam K. Childs

Published by tCeti Ltd.

For Jill who had a helluva year;
May the next be far, far better

Contents

Dramatis Personae

POLITICAL AGENCIES

WHITE HOUSE
"Mogul" (R)   Code name for the Republican presidential candidate
"Achilles" (R)   Code name for the Republican Vice-Presidential candidate

CONGRESS
House of Representatives
Congresswoman **Linda Starr** (R)   Member of U.S. House Committee on Homeland Security

Senate
Senator **Marvin Jäger** (R)   Member of the Senate Judiciary Committee, FBI oversight
Senator **Markos Metaxas** (R)   Member of the Senate Select Intelligence Committee

REPUBLICAN NATIONAL COMMITTEE
Francisco Duarte   Chairman
Dina Accardo   Co-Chairperson

NEW YORK STATE GOVERNOR'S OFFICE
Major **Murray Allard**   Advisor to the Governor, NY Office of Counter Terrorism

INTELLIGENCE SERVICES

CENTRAL INTELLIGENCE AGENCY
Brice Payton   Classified

DEPT. OF DEFENCE, NATIONAL SECURITY AGENCY (NSA)
Morna MacCallum   Technical Analyst

UNITED STATES SECRET SERVICE (USSS)
A sub-department of the Department of Homeland Security (DHS).
The Director of the USSS reports directly to the DHS Secretary.

Ian Croft   Deputy Director

Uniformed Division – Counter Assault Team (CAT)
Lt. **Danilo Stankić**   Counter-Sniper on NY assignment
Sgt. **Luis Gomez**   Sniper-Observer on NY assignment

Uniformed Division – Specialists
Officer-Technician **Jean Byrnes**   Airspace Security on secondment to NYPD Aviation Unit
Officer **Tomas Holgersen**   Airspace Security on secondment to NYPD Aviation Unit

Special Agents
Rusty Wilkins   Assistant Special Agent in Charge, New York

LAW ENFORCEMENT

NEW YORK POLICE DEPARTMENT (NYPD)
Detective Bureau

Chief **Nolan Quinn**	Commanding Officer, Detectives
Assistant Chief **Emery McKinley**	C.O. Manhattan Borough
Lieutenant-Commander **Martin King**	Senior Investigator
Detective **Kasia Pasternak**	Senior Detective
Detective **Eugene Marchetti**	Detective, Second Grade

Joint Terrorism Task Force (JTTF) Counterterrorism & Intelligence Bureau, New York

Assistant Chief **Ross Benbow**	Chief and FBI Liaison Office
Captain **Siobhan Niven**	Commanding Officer

UNITED STATES ATTORNEY'S OFFICE

Alden Saunders	U.S. Attorney for the Southern District of New York
Bill Ngo	Deputy U.S. Attorney for the Southern District of New York

FEDERAL BUREAU OF INVESTIGATION (FBI)
New York Field Office

Rafina ('Rafi') Matos	Assistant Director in Charge
Ivan Biskup	Special Agent in Charge, Investigation
Sharmila Patil	Special Agent in Charge, Communications

Florida

Paul Briggs	Agent in Charge

CIVILIANS

Kino Melki	Syrian teenager living in Brooklyn
Jaffar Saqqaf	Arab teenager, friend of Kino Melki
Bart Sneiders	Bird trainer in the Netherlands
Rostam Alinejad	Bird trainer in the Netherlands
Dr. Lloyd Randall	Personal physician to Mr Trump

'Here you go, Joe; the last of the votes'. The Vice-President and his Chief of Staff were alone in the V-P's office, and after four years of working together, had no need to stand on ceremony.

'Thanks, Steve'. The V-P took the proffered envelope, walked over to the filing cabinet and filed the envelope alphabetically by State. 'That completes Schrödinger's cabinet!'

'What's that, Joe?'

'Oh, just a little joke of mine. You know Schrödinger's cat – the cat inside the box that is both dead and alive at the same time until we look inside the box?'

Still puzzled the Chief replied, 'Sure. Basic description of quantum physics. And?'

'The same thing is happening here. Inside that cabinet are the Electors' ballots for the next President, right?' His Chief nodded.

'But is that person actually the President now?' The V-P continued, 'or is he only the President after Congress counts the votes? A lot of the American people think Trump was elected in November – which, of course, he wasn't – but when is he elected? At the College?'

He carried on. 'Some law professors say the *spirit* of the law means that the President becomes the President when – *if* – the Electoral College casts a majority of votes for him; the Congressional count is simply a public confirmation of a fact. Then there are other professors who cling to the *technical* legal interpretation, and say until Congress count the vote, he's still just a candidate. After all, Congress can reject some of the votes if they want.'

'Still trying to see how this fits with quantum physics…"' Steve said.

'I'm getting there'. The V-P smiled, and gestured to the filing cabinet with a flick of his thumb. 'We can guess how many votes he got, but we don't know for sure if there's a majority of votes for Trump or not until we open the box, and see if the cat's dead or alive.

'As for what Schrödinger's cabinet has to say about my successor as Veep; that's definitely a mystery for the New Year to resolve.'

Three Weeks Earlier...

Day One

November 29, 2016
Assassination

Washington, D.C.

Matt Johnson sat on his couch and watched his wife die on television. Over and over and over.

'What the fuck just happened?' swore Special Agent Rusty Wilkins. He turned to the man dressed all in black at his side. Despite the man being large, Wilkins found it hard to see him in the dark of the rooftop.

Danilo Stankić – "Danny" to his friends, a group to which Wilkins did not belong – lowered his long-barrelled rifle and shook his head slowly. His gesture was felt more than seen by Wilkins and wasn't really meant as an answer anyway, more a shake to clear his head of what he had just seen.

Jean Byrnes, US Secret Service Technical Officer for Airspace Security in New York, stood a few metres away from the two men. Stankić looked over at her but her gaze was locked on a spot thirty meters away in the Garden on the chaos and *all that blood*. Her left hand swung her radio loosely by her side, desperate voices spilling into the night.

Danny looked at her white face and realised with a shock that she was physically shaking... and it wasn't the cold. He realised he was shaking as well, but for a different reason. Adrenalin had flooded into his system but there had been no release; no fight, no flight. He was trained to shoot people – to kill if necessary – not just to stand and watch.

But there hadn't been a person to shoot at. Just a bird. And the bird was dead anyway.

Almost in slow motion he replayed the scene in his head trying to figure out "what the fuck just happened?"

Five minutes earlier, Danny had been slowly scanning the crowd below through his night-scope listening to Gomez over his headphones, telling him where to focus his attention:

'Fifth Ave building, second floor window directly above Teuscher's... come left, one window at a time... OK, other end, scan crowd outside Lego. Short male, blue beanie...'

Danny worked with Gomez a lot; they had both joined the Secret Service, Uniformed Division, in 2010 and now worked full-time as part of the Counter Assault Team (CAT). They didn't get out of D.C. very often so when this assignment came up they had both volunteered – good to get out of the office for a while, and great to get a head start on Christmas shopping.

Gomez' voice was quiet and steady. A constant background of information dripping into Danny's ears. Gomez did the big picture: scanning crowds, buildings, traffic with his binoculars while Danny could focus right in on a face through his 'scope. They were one of six CAT teams scattered around Rockefeller Center that night. Danny had been assigned to the roof of West 49th

Street overlooking the Garden where hundreds of people had gathered to see the Christmas tree lit up for the first time in 2016.

With him on the roof was Jean. Danny had got to know her a little in the last two days: A solid, technical officer and USSS Special Agent Wilkins. *And, boy, was he "special"*, Danny thought to himself. There was always tension between the Uniformed Division and the plain-clothed Special Agents within the Secret Service but in this case there was an additional chemistry issue. The two men simply didn't like each other.

There had been no snow to speak of so far this year but the parapets were cold and frost-slick. All three of them were glad of their winter clothes, Danny particularly so as he had to half-lie on the concrete roof, his rifle on his arms resting on the parapet, the cold stone leaching the warmth out of him even through thick layers.

Meanwhile Gomez was sitting pretty with a grandstand view over the Gardens. Warm and comfortable, he was in an office in the Comcast Building kindly provided by NBC.

'Take a look twenty feet ahead of "Mogul", ten o'clock his reference. Guy in dark glasses. Black coat, could be long.'

Danny complied, and spent a good fifteen seconds studying the man before radioing back, 'Looks Oscar Kilo to me, but nudge an Agent over there just in case. I'll flick back once in a while until they arrive'. Gomez continued his monologue, directing Danny's eye to anything Gomez felt concerned about.

Jean's radio had been relatively quiet all evening; the teams used different frequencies, but it suddenly came to life. Danny couldn't hear the words, but the tone was urgent. Agent Wilkins stiffened and turned towards Jean to listen. Jean nodded, despite her listener being unable to see her, said a few words, and then started to scan the sky to the East towards Saks.

The sun had set two hours earlier and light from a thousand cars, streetlamps, office windows, shop fronts and Christmas lights made seeing anything difficult. Danny let his gaze leave the rifle and flick over to where Jean and Wilson were looking. Seeing nothing he went back to his 'scope and checked out the guy in dark glasses. As an Agent walked away from the man Danny saw him take the dark glasses off and put them in his pocket with a worried and slightly myopic look on his face. *All clear.*

Thinking back Danny remembered that Gomez had gone quiet at that point but Jean's radio – *and* Wilkins' – were full of noise. Even through his earbuds Danny heard Jean talking loudly into her handset.

'Roger that. UAS confirmed. Code Thor. Confirm?'

A brief silence then, 'Understood. Code Thor. Releasing Hedwig now. Standby.'

Jean put her handset down and turned to two large cages behind her in the shadows. One of them was covered by a dark cloth and was barely visible.

Reflected light glinted on the metal bars of the second cage and a shape – a shadow amongst shadows – could just be made out.

Her voice changed from her previous professional radio-chat becoming more musical and soothing, 'Okay Hedwig, we've got a drone down there. Not doing anything too suspicious – probably just an amateur getting a good view of the ceremony with a GoPro – but we take no chances do we?'

She opened the cage and put out her arm at a right angle to the opening. 'C'mon Hedwig, up we go.'

A large owl hopped out onto her arm, its drab colouring making it still difficult to see. The bird suddenly and disconcertingly turned its head one hundred and eighty degrees towards Danny. Two orange eyes caught the lights below and glowed eerily at him.

Jean stood with the owl on her arm and walked to the parapet taking a phone out of her jacket pocket. She looked briefly at the phone, touching the screen a few times before bringing it to her face.

Danny could see her lips moving, and had assumed she was talking into the phone. Now recalling the moment he realised she'd actually been murmuring quietly to the bird not the phone. There had been something touching about the scene; a sense of mutual affection, even love, between the woman and the owl as the two whispered to each other in the night.

Speaking quietly but clearly into the phone Jean said, 'Play record now.'

A high-pitched whirring sound came briefly out of her mobile and the owl stiffened upright. It swivelled its head towards the Saks end of the Gardens. On a soft word from Jean the owl left her arm silently in a shallow glide, swiftly being swallowed in the dark above the kaleidoscope of lights in the Gardens themselves. Jean lifted her binoculars to her eyes. Danny assumed that she had been able to locate and track the bird through the infrared enhanced lenses. This was confirmed seconds later when she said two words into her phone.

'Lightning strike.'

By now Danny only had one earbud in and, while he automatically continued to scan the crowd below, he kept straining to see into the darkness, the festive lights ruining normal night vision. Gomez must have had a better angle with fewer lights beyond the owl.

Over his headphone Danny heard, 'Wow! Gottit!'

Even now, replaying events, Danny could not be sure if he saw the bird or not, silhouetted against bright displays of snowflakes, giant festive bells and golden angels. He knew where it was even if he couldn't see it by watching Jean slowly turning as she tracked the bird over the crowd to the west.

To no one in particular Jean said, 'Where's he going?' and then repeated the question more stridently, 'Where's he going? Where's he going?'

'No!' she screamed. She was now facing the west end of the Gardens. Facing right at the Tree. Right at "Mogul".

'Crap!' exclaimed Danny as he raised his rifle and focused all his attention on the presidential candidate making one more self-congratulatory speech as the lights lit up the tree in deliberate stages from the bottom to the star at the top. Micro-second snapshots of memory played through Danny's head:

Achilles looked up bewildered, then ducked violently.

An Agent pushed Mogul away from Achilles, sending him to the ground.

Another Agent reached towards Achilles.

An owl flew at Achilles following Achilles's movements.

The owl had something in its talons.

The owl went for Achilles' head.

The owl, and Achilles' head, exploded.

Mason Robbins, known to the US Secret Service as "Achilles", Republican nominee for the Vice-President of the United States and running mate of Donald Trump, the winner of the November eighth elections, was dead.

Matt Johnson, on his couch, watched as Special Agent Amelia Johnson – Amy, his wife – reached towards the future Vice-President of the United States as he fell to the ground. There was a blur – a bird of some sort – and then an explosion.

He watched as Secret Service personnel converged on the bodies of Trump and Robbins as they lay on the ground.

He watched as more officers hurried civilians away from the stage.

He watched Amy lying there, ignored by everyone for seconds, and he swore he saw her hand wave, once, at the camera as if she was saying goodbye as she died.

The network replayed the footage six, ten, twelve times before someone realised that this was not appropriate and coverage changed to an interminable succession of interviews with people who obviously knew little more than anyone else.

But all Matt saw was Amy waving goodbye.

Martin shut down his computer, checked that no confidential papers sat on his desk, locked the drawers and stood up. He was a scrupulous man, meticulous to the point of fastidiousness at work but at home he could relax and allow a little disorder into his life - easy to do with two teenagers in the house.

That was that for today; another day of paperwork completed and, if the Gods of Traffic and Accidents were listening, I'll be home in an hour, he thought to himself. *Or not - I said I'd check out that used camera store up Broadway; see if we can get a macro lens for Cecilia's Christmas present, I could walk there and back within an hour.*

Although parts of Police Headquarters would be humming throughout the night, Martin's floor was already quiet. Those who were working had gone to other floors. Those who weren't on duty had slowly trickled out of the door over the past half-hour. Martin – or, to give him his full title, Lieutenant-Commander Detective Martin King – was the last man standing in the office today.

He stretched just as his phone rang. Last minute dramatics were more suited for television than real life – it was probably his wife or one of the kids. Then he saw the number calling and the thought that he might not get home soon crossed his mind for the first time that night.

'King' he said peremptorily into the phone…

He burst into the Detectives' Lounge. 'Quick, turn on the television' half-formed in his mouth, of course it was already on. Some of the dozen men and women in the room were on phones – checking on friends and family, cancelling dinner dates, letting spouses know they'll be late. The others were fixed on the screen, their minds already thinking of the "who?" and "how?" Few bothered to ask "why?" The presidential campaign had been bitter and angered so many people that asking "why?" was pointless at this stage.

King caught the eye of Detective Kasia Pasternak. She was looking at Martin with a slightly sardonic smile on her face… again. Kasia always seemed to be a few steps ahead of Martin. She definitely was tonight. Her slight smile faded into something grimmer as she flicked her eyes to the screen, inviting Martin to watch.

'…the President-elect is in critical condition at Mount Sinai hospital. No further details have been released as yet. Politicians from both sides of the House are lining up to express their sympathies and we hope to have a few of them on the show in a few minutes. Meanwhile, the nation grieves for the death of their new Vice-President…'

Martin turned away; there was no substance in either the coverage or the expressions of grief or sympathy. News desks did what news desks do in times of crisis; fill airtime with words, suppositions and "experts" eager to be seen on television, until such time as real information was available. And that, he reflected, was *our* job.

He flicked his head towards the door, indicating to Kasia to meet him there but, when he turned to look he saw she was already there, waiting. *Always one step ahead of me… literally.*

They made an odd couple. Physical and mental polar opposites, they shared a passion for Justice (with a capital "J") and the desire to untangle the most "tangled of webs weaved by those who practice to deceive".

Martin King: African-American, 45 years of age, medium height, medium build. Tending a little towards middle-aged spread, each year he found the annual physical a little harder. Face somewhat more lined and creased than expected for his age and a small (but getting bigger) bald spot on his crown made him look older than he was.

Kasia Pasternak: Caucasian, 39 years of age, tall, slim build. A classic Eastern European blonde, she was athletic and taller than King by five centimetres. She was classically beautiful; a clear complexion over a model's bone structure. Perhaps to encourage people to look beyond the beauty, she carried a cool, even strict, expression on her face in repose. When she looked at someone the first thing they saw were her pale grey eyes. They were arresting, animal eyes; even King often found himself having to focus more than usual when Pasternak spoke to avoid being distracted. They were a useful feature when questioning suspects; people felt nervous or guilty looking at her even if they hadn't done anything.

'FBI called Quinn. They're expecting us over at Federal Plaza now', King told Pasternak without preamble. 'Fill me in on what you know on the way over. Assume I know nothing; 'bout the truth anyway.'

They started walking out of Police Headquarters over Park Row. The trees in the small park were bare and did nothing to block the traffic noise below them. It diminished a little as they entered St. Andrews pedestrianised plaza.

Kasia took the opportunity to light a cigarette, ignoring Martin's disapproving glance. *Not my father,* she thought. Aloud, she said, 'They called Quinn, not the Chief?' Although Nolan Quinn *was* the Chief of Detectives, for King and Pasternak "the Chief" always meant their boss, Assistant Chief Emery McKinley, not *his* boss, Quinn.

'Yeah. Quinn. Quinn told me he'd call the Chief after he got off the phone with me. He'll be pissed'.

'Who? Quinn?'

'No, no. The Chief. He'll be pissed that he was by-passed'. King was silent for a moment.

'This is going to get a *lot* of people pissed if they aren't involved; everyone's gonna want a piece of this and they're all gonna want their moment of glory'. He shook his head glumly. 'It's already started.'

He didn't need to tell Pasternak what he meant by that – they were already half way to the FBI's offices instead of their own.

'It's not going to be our case anyway', she objected. 'An attack on the President's a federal offence – FBI and Secret Service will be snapping at each other already as to who gets the collar.'

'Yep'. He nodded as they waited for the lights to change to cross onto Lafayette. 'But in the end, who knows the City? Who has the manpower for the hundreds of interviews that lie ahead? Us, that's who. We'll be "asked" to "assist"' his voice heavy with sarcasm. 'Which means we do all the heavy lifting, they take the credit if we get the guy, or guys, or women, or whoever, but we'll take the blame if it goes nowhere'.

Pasternak kept her peace. She knew that once the case got going his cynicism would be lost in the challenge of unravelling the puzzle.

'So…' continued King as they crossed. 'What's the story?'

Pasternak spoke rapidly in her "just the facts, ma'am" voice:

'The President- and Vice-President-elect arrived on the stage at Rockefeller Center around 18:45 with their usual contingent of US Secret Service. Normal security precautions in the area. Loads of NYPD uniformed. The USSS were out in force of course; uniformed and Agents. FBI observers, some CAT and even some CRC folks putting in some pre-Christmas overtime on the pretext of practice-in-the-field'. She used the acronym CRC for the Critical Response Command of the Counterterrorism Bureau NYPD's equivalent of the Secret Service's CAT.

Neither Pasternak nor King had quite made up their minds about CRC – the Bureau had been initiated within the past year. How this new Bureau would fit in with the rest of the Department, especially the Joint Terrorism Task Force (JTTF), hadn't been fully worked out yet.

'At 18:58,' she continued, 'one of our uniforms spotted a drone over the Saks on Fifth building. She called it in and it was confirmed by USSS.'

She hesitated. 'Here it gets a bit weird so don't hold me on this but… seems USSS have been experimenting with a new way of taking down drones. Something the Europeans have been doing. They use a bird – eagles and things, and in this case an owl. It's like the way the K9 guys work with dogs. Yeah, yeah, I know,' she said seeing Martin's frown, 'I said it gets weird. Anyway, this bird is designed to catch drones and then fly them away to safety. Much better than just shooting it down, potentially dropping something into the middle of a crowd. This time it didn't work out like that. The bird caught the drone alright, but then flew directly at the stage. Preliminary reports have it that the bird flew right at Trump, but swerves to follow Robbins at the last minute as he ducks. The drone in its claws – talons, is probably the right word – explodes'.

King was used to her minor digressions for factual accuracy. He was also used to her sometimes inappropriate sense of humour: 'Suddenly, it's snowing! Feathers everywhere… Result: The V-P and one Special Agent are dead. Trump and one other Agent are in critical and three more injured'.

'All of them – including the bodies – were taken to Mt. Sinai. USSS are trying to locate Mrs Robbins but she probably already knows; same for the kids. It's been all over the news'.

As they turned into the FBI building she looked at her boss. 'So that, as you asked, is "the story so far"'.

King hesitated at the door. 'Anyone being held?'

'Yeah. Uniformed Secret Service name of Jean Byrnes. She released the bird. She also trained it'.

'And this drone? Must have been an operator somewhere'.

'Uniform are on it. Marchetti's organising that. He's also got Domain Awareness on board. Got them beginning search of faces and licence plates in the area, but DAS isn't strong in midtown yet'.

King walked into the building. 'Anything else?'

'Not yet, boss. Gonna be a long night'.

Kasia Pasternak and Martin King entered the fifth floor conference room. Already present were Rafina ('Rafi') Matos, Assistant Director in Charge of the FBI's New York office, FBI Special Agent Sharmila Patil and United States Secret Service Agent Rusty Wilkins.

Martin knew this was a small group for such a catastrophic event but he knew it would get bigger, and fast. Kasia, on the other hand, had never been involved in a major case like this and felt even her usual solid self-confidence tested. Although she was a senior detective, these were *senior* people indeed.

'Hi Martin', Rafi Matos walked over to shake King's hand. 'Always welcome, but a shame it's nearly always under these circumstances'. Rafi nodded to his FBI colleague. 'This is Special Agent Sharmila Patil. She'll be in charge of communications. We've got another Special Agent on the way who'll join us shortly and will be in charge of investigations'. Neither Martin nor Kasia missed the emphasis of who was in charge here.

Rafi continued. 'Of course, there'll be a lot of inter-departmental liaison; I hope that we can count on the help of New York's finest?'

'Of course', beamed Martin with a wide smile, 'always happy to be of assistance'. Martin knew that a jurisdiction pissing contest would happen sooner or later but now wasn't the time. Now was the time to be all smiles and cooperation.

'And this is USSS Assistant Special Agent in Charge Wilkins'. Rafi indicated the other man in the room. 'He was on the roof when the owl was released'. Martin and Kasia looked at the man with curiosity.

'You released the owl?' asked Kasia as she shook his hand.

'No, no. I was overseeing the personal protection operation. The roof was a good vantage point, is all. I knew about our new protocols for intercepting UAS – unmanned aerial systems, drones – but had never seen them in action before; I was curious. Guess I got more insight than I needed…' Wilkins stopped himself. He had been about to make a snide remark about the ineffectiveness of that system when he realised that it was, after all, a USSS system and these people – despite their smiles – were going to be looking for someone to blame.

'Hokay!' said Rafi, clapping his hands. Still directing proceedings, he indicated that everyone should take a seat around one end of the long table in the middle of the well-lit, but windowless, room. 'Let's have a quick round-up of where we are, shall we? Martin, do you want to start?'

'Sure. Although I haven't had much chance to catch up with the details so I'll let Kasia take it if you don't mind'.

Without waiting for acknowledgement, Pasternak started. 'Obviously, we had a lot of uniformed in the area. After the explosion they went into crowd control mode, cordoning off the area, controlling civilian egress and doing the usual first response issues. They checked for injured people, called ambulances, ensured no windows or structural items had been weakened and were hazardous, gas leaks, downed electric wires, *et cetera*'.

'We then got the news from one of the Secret Service agents…er…'

'Sergeant Gomez', interrupted Wilkins. 'He was one of our spotters'.

Expressionless, Kasia continued. 'Once we got the news from … Sergeant Gomez… that the attack had been from the air, and possibly controlled from somewhere in the area, we shifted the emphasis onto getting people away as safely as possible. Fortunately, Detective Marchetti was already on hand; he organised perimeter cordons of 610, 611 and 620 Fifth Ave as well as the Rockefeller Center itself, focusing on people who were on the third floor or higher. For those of you who don't know New York that well…' she looked at Wilkins, 'these buildings are home to some of the most prestigious shops in the City – Saks, Prada, Teuscher, *et cetera*. A few weeks before Christmas at rush hour is an easy time for someone to get lost in the crowd, but we had to try.

'Marchetti also contacted DAS – Domain Awareness', she continued, 'to start searching the crowds for any "faces" and pinging all the licence plates in the area from 18:30 onwards. Even with the computers those guys have, it'll take some time before we can be sure we've covered everything.

'In terms of civilian casualties, the blast was relatively small. Doesn't seem to have been a lot of shrapnel. Of course, we'll need to wait until the Forensic Investigation Unit confirms'.

A look from Martin stopped her. 'Or', he said, 'until the FBI Lab does their stuff. May not be our FIU. What d'ya prefer, Rafi?'

'Ah. Yes. Let's talk about who does what after we're up to date with everyone shall we? Although it *is* more than likely that we'll want our boys and girls to do the tech stuff'. Rafi sounded almost apologetic – he, like King, knew that there would be plenty of these flash points in the days to come and wanted to postpone them as long as possible. 'Anything else, Detective?'

'Some. Injured civilians have been taken to local hospitals and/or treated on site. I have no numbers or details, but there are no reports of civilian fatalities at this point. Many of the injuries are unrelated to the explosion; they were caused during the subsequent panic and flight. No other major hazards. Some of the wiring for the lights got damaged, but that was easily isolated.

'We're trying to reach the FAA…', both Rusty Wilkins and Rafi coughed at this, but decided not to interrupt. 'And are continuing with our floor-by-floor searches working on getting a list of CCTV footage in the area, every shop has loads of them for a start, and are working on an appeal for people who may have been videoing events on their smart phones, but maybe that's for Special Agent Patil?'

Kasia stopped her speech having become aware of some impatience in the room.

'OK! Great, yeah', said Rafi. 'Good idea. Sharmila?'

Sharmila Patil: Indian descent, fifty years old (or thereabouts), short with a small build. Her creased face constantly in motion displaying a range of expressions from genial grandmother to severe FBI Agent. Disconcertingly she spoke with a mid-West accent much like Frances McDormand in the Coen Brother's film *Fargo*.

'Yah. We understand that USSS agents are with Mrs Trump and Mrs Robbins now'. She looked at Rusty Wilkins, and received a nod in return. 'Now we're asking for all official communications about the incident and the investigation come through me, if only as a coordination post, and would very much appreciate you folks' cooperation on that'. Nods of agreement, for now, around the table.

'We've already notified the media unofficially that there was an attack, and that the Vice-President-Elect is dead. There's nothing to gain by denying that; there are hundreds of witnesses. We've also confirmed that the President-Elect is in hospital. The White House, I assume the President, but that hasn't been confirmed yet, will make a statement at 21:00. We're setting up a hotline for the public to contact us. Perhaps NYPD could distribute that number when they're out there on the streets?'

It was unusual for the FBI to take the lead on front line activities. After the Boston Marathon bombings, Boston PD ran the hotlines. It wasn't really a question though. Patil was simply communicating what her bosses had already decided. Martin and Kasia nodded, as if granting permission, but actually acknowledging that the FBI had scored the first point.

Rafi Matos ended Patil's summary for her. 'That's about it for us at present in terms of comms – early stages! We don't have any information on Mr Trump's condition. Agent Wilkins?'

Rusty Wilkins was not used to going last. He was also not used to the idea that *his* Secret Service could be culpable in the attempted assassination of a President. He suspected that the other four were being tactful at the moment by trying not to attribute blame right away, but he knew it was coming. None of his anxiety showed as he gave his own brief update.

'Mogul –' *dammit, he was used to using code names* '– that is, Mr Trump, who isn't *technically* the President-Elect as yet'. He was trying to sound knowledgeable, but knew he was coming off as officious. 'Is in critical condition in Mount Sinai. The ward is guarded by the Secret Service. As is the morgue where Mr Robbin' body was taken'.

'POTUS', he didn't bother explaining the acronym for the President of the United States assuming everyone in the room would be familiar with it. 'Has been informed; security around him has been strengthened'.

'We…' Rusty Wilkins hesitated. He wanted to be very careful with his words here. '…have started our own preliminary inquiries into what happened. It's too early to say that anything went wrong with our UAS interception system, but I've had a brief chat with my staff and hope to have a longer talk later. Of course, I'll keep everyone in this room informed of everything that we find'.

All five of them smiled even though they all knew that last sentence to be a lie.

'And on that note', Rafi said, 'I think we'd all like to know a bit more about this "UAS interception system". It's likely to be one of the starting points of the investigation, don't you think?' This last to no one in particular.

'But we're are still waiting for one or two people, so why don't we break for coffee until they get here? Nespresso machine over there…' He pointed to the far end of the room. '…as well as herbal teas and the like, but I think we're all going to need caffeine'. He was acting the jovial host.

'No smoking here, of course, but there's a smoking balcony on the sixth floor for those who need it. Washrooms down the hall next to the elevators where you came in'.

The green awning and modest entrance of the Capitol Hill Club, or the National Republican Club of Capitol Hill to give it its full name, belies the important issues discussed inside. This evening the Club was much busier and noisier than usual for a Tuesday night.

There was only one main topic of conversation of course. However, the business of running the nation still went on so talk of the assassination was scattered with intermittent banalities concerning support for the next vote, arrangements for the next gala dinner and ongoing arguments over the placement of commas and colons in the latest bill before the House.

'Can you imagine the police asking Melania if she "knows of anyone who might want to hurt The Donald?" She'd probably start with most of the people in this room!'

'…awful about Mason. I had lunch with him just last week. I hope his wife - Kim isn't it? - is being looked after. I heard Francisco has organised something on all our behalves'.

'Isn't that Leonora over there? She's been looking really tired since she didn't get re-elected…'

'…this legislation would not only mean jobs in my State, but in yours as well…'

'You heard that Obama's going to address the nation at nine, right? Well, I think we should be ready with a…'

'…sonofabitch was asking for it. I lost my seat because of him; this is going to be one of my last nights at the club for at least four years…'

'Easy, Joe! Someone might think you had an axe to grind; make you a suspect!'

'Well… jest sayin''.

'…taking the boys to see the Capitols beat the Penguins this Saturday…'

'…with corporate tax revenues dropping by three points in the last quarter. We should look at increasing the next tranche of thirty-year bonds by a commensurate amount to keep cash flow steady through the inauguration…'

'…so I said I was a Congresswoman, and she said she was a man!'

'I was never clear on this. When… if… Donald dies, does that mean Paul becomes President? He did in that Harrison Ford movie'.

'I'm not sure a movie should be used as interpretation of actual legislation!'

'It depends if Donald is the President or not when he dies'.

'Who decides that?'

'Well, until we count the votes in January, we do. And, even after we count the votes, I think we can still decide. Not sure about that last bit…'

'I heard he's in critical condition. May even be brain-dead'.

'How'd we know?' Over-loud laughter followed that comment.

Perhaps the commonest questions heard were: "Where's Paul?", and "Where's Francisco?" referring respectively to Paul Ryan, Speaker of the House and Francisco Duarte, Chairman of the Republican National Committee. Both of whom, perhaps wisely, had seemingly decided not to visit the Club today. Mitch McConnell, leader of the Senate, was also absent, but he wasn't in Washington at the moment; no one had expected him.

Francisco Duarte *was* in the Club having entered via a side door, and staying away from the main bars and dining room, had ensconced himself in the small Lincoln room of the Club. With him were other senior members of the Grand Old Party who were having a more practical and focused conversation. The American election system was grand in theory being full of checks and balances, but in practice there were many situations that the Constitution did not fully address. Even the most dedicated political scientists and politicians were unclear as to what should happen in situations such as these.

Although many people in the USA, and most people outside, believe that the American President is elected in the general election in November, this is not true. Those elections determine which *Electors* will attend the *Electoral College* in December. Each State has a pre-determined number of Electors who attend the virtual college (they don't all meet in one place), and in theory each State Elector will vote for the person who won the popular vote in their State. In practice this doesn't always happen. To complicate matters further each State gets to set their own laws as to how Electors are chosen and what responsibilities and obligations each Elector has with regards to how closely they follow the common vote. Individual States also set the penalties, if any, for not meeting those obligations.

'With Robbins dead we're going to need to decide on a new V-P', Francisco stated.

'Do we decide that?'

'Sure. They're our Electors. We just have to tell them who we want'.

'That's not right. The Senate has to choose the V-P; the House only gets to choose the President'.

'No, no, no. That only applies *after* the Electoral College and *if* the college vote doesn't result in a clear majority'.

'What if the majority winner is dead?'

'Well, that's the beauty of it! Once again, we're in charge. We can't ignore the count; the House committee said that we "have no discretion" and "would have to declare the dead person the winner", but we, that is all of Congress not just the House, could argue that the dead person was already in office from the time of the College, therefore the Twentieth Amendment line of succession applies. If both Robbins and Trump are dead that means Paul Ryan becomes President. *Or* we could argue that there was no President or V-P elect in which case we get to appoint anyone we like as Acting President'.

'Doesn't the Twentieth say that the Acting President must be replaced in accordance with the line of succession?'

'Yep. Doesn't specify when though. There's wiggle room in the wording and no precedents. It might also be possible to use Article Five and tweak that amendment, there'd be enough Democrats who would vote for stability'.

'Far be it from me to argue with you, Rory, on the finer points of constitutional law. You know that stuff better than me, but aren't we running away a bit? Trump's not dead, Robbins is. We're ten days out from an Electoral College and no one in the running for a GOP V-P'.

'Aren't some of the Electors required by law to vote for the person who won the popular vote?'

'Sure, sure. There's what? Twenty-nine, thirty States with such laws on the books…'

'Twenty-nine. I know the big ones, California, Florida, Ohio, Michigan, but don't push me to list them all'.

'Thanks. So, twenty-nine States in which the Electors have to vote for whoever won the popular vote *or whomever the Party nominates*'.

'Now, wait a minute, Sam. In some of *those* States the law is clear; the Electors must vote for whoever won the election'.

'Now, Linda, my dear, you've been around as long as any of us; y'all know the law is open to interpretation'.

'Doesn't matter which of you is right or wrong, really. If a few of those twenty-nine states require Electors to vote for a dead Robbins then they have to choose: cast a useless vote or vote for whoever they want. We just want to make sure that "whoever they want" is who we say they want…'

'…and, let's not forget this applies to all States. None of the ballots will have our new nomination's name on it. They'll have to write it in; let's make sure they know how to spell her name!'

'*Her* name? Linda, you tryin' to tell us summat?'

'No, no. Just trying to make sure you "gennelmun" remember it's the twenty-first century'.

'As I saying. Doesn't really matter anyway. Do you know what happens if someone is faithless or casts a vote that doesn't meet State law? Thousand buck fine at best. Spoiled vote at worst. Think we can all dig in to cover any fines any Elector may incur'.

'Whoa, Marvin. You're getting real close to election tampering with that'.

'Fine, fine. Just saying we can always make it up to them. Doesn't have to be cash. Shit. A grand? Take them out to dinner somewhere nice, or show them a good time in Vegas sometime. Not like any of the Electors are on welfare. Time they did something for all those perks anyway.

'Ah jest thought of summat else. What happens if those ballots get spoiled? Could that mean our man, sorry Linda, *wooman*, doesn't win? Could the Democrats get the most votes?'

'Jeesus, Rory, must you always be the pessimist?'

'Jest a realist, Marvin. An' while we're at it, how sure are we that *any* of the Electors are going to vote GOP? We've made a it clear that we're not happy with the nomination. Suppose some of them think this is a "who will rid me of this troublesome priest?" moment and write in, I dunno, Ryan's name or even vote Democrat?'

'Priest?'

'Henry II. Shakespeare. Jeez, never mind'.

'There are precedents to guide us, y'know. 1872. Similar situation. Grant was the incumbent and establishment favourite, but some liberal Republican Electors, a kind of anti-tea party, voted for Horace Greeley. Some Democrats voted for him as well, so it's hard to tell if he was a Republican the Democrats liked or a Democrat that Republicans liked. Anyway, as we all know Grant won handily, but Greeley died before the College. All but three of the Electors pledged to Greeley voted for someone else; there were eight presidential nominations! The three votes for dead Greeley were treated as "spoiled". He didn't get the votes, but they were included in the total when determining what was meant by "a majority". Incidentally, the votes from Arkansas and Louisiana Electors from that same College were all thrown out due to irregularities and *not* counted in the total'.

'So who-all was doing this objectin' and countin' and discardin'?'

'Us. Congress, when they opened the ballots in February 1873. Same as we did in Ohio, 2005'.

'Shee-it. Francisco? Can you have someone prep a new data sheet for us all? Which states have laws requiring Electors to vote for dead people and all? What happens if they don't vote for the winner in their state? Spoiled or abstain? Fines? And, what options do we have when counting. Do spoiled votes get counted in the total? After all, the winner needs to have an overall majority of votes cast not just get the most votes'.

'And everyone: go back and lean on your State teams. Let's ensure that when the Electors vote in twenty, no…', he looked at his watch, '…nineteen days' time they vote the way we want. But let's not forget, in the end, no one knows how the Electors have voted until those ballots are opened in January and counted… *by us* and in accordance with the rules for determining how to count the votes which are also decided *by us*. We need to game plan all the different scenarios especially now we've lost the Senate…'

'And *that* was all that f-ing Trump's fault! Pardon my French, but he cost us the Senate. Almost cost us the House as well! The winning party is meant to *add* seats, not lose them'.

There were murmured "sorries", "hard luck", "you ran a good race", and "not your fault Trump pissed off your constituents".

'As I was saying. We lost the Senate, and we'll be doing a full assessment in the New Year on that, meanwhile we cannot let the Vice-President count be unclear after the count. *Then* the Democrats get to choose, and we won't like their choice…'

'Francisco, we're going to need a formal debate of the Committee tomorrow. We haven't even begun to talk about *who* we want or who would *want* to work with The Donald or… What're we going do if Donald doesn't make it?'

Within an hour of the first meeting, the room had filled up, and Rafi Matos' good humour as the host was stretched. Luckily for Rafi, Ross Benbow had arrived. Ross was the Chief of New York's Joint Terrorism Task Force. The JTTF was a loose agglomeration of personnel from specialised departments of the New York Police Department, the FBI's New York office, and the New York State (as opposed to New York City) Division of Homeland Security (DHS) that was part of the State Governor's office. Ross was also the NYPD's liaison with the FBI; the perfect person to act as co-host.

With him had come Major Murray Allard, Ross' counterpart at the New York State Office of Counter Terrorism (OCT). This was a State level department, and Allard reported to the Governor as part of the NY DHS. Ross Benbow had an uneasy relationship with Allard. The two men often had to work together closely, but on a personal level they clashed; pure and simple.

Complicating matters were the different ways in which their roles interacted. Ross had the authority to pull people away from the OCT to the JTTF on temporary assignments, an authority he used on a regular basis. On the other hand, as the Deputy Commissioner of the OCT Allard was indirectly in charge of the New York State Intelligence Center that was the home of New York's Forensics and Crime Scene Units. Units that the JTTF relied on, but units that supported other departments as well, such as the NYPD, and whose time was always in demand.

From across the room, Martin watched what he called "the dance of power" as Ross Benbow and Murray Allard were joined by Martin's boss, Assistant Chief of NYP Detectives, Emery McKinley. Secret Service Agent Rusty Wilkins was with them. The constant, but subtle, sparring over resources, status and power would be refereed tonight by Rafi Mantos as the host, but also because the FBI would be dependent on assistance from all four agencies to manage this investigation successfully.

Better you than me, thought Martin, happy that he had managed to stay one level below that political in-fighting. *For now. Sooner or later, they'll promote me. Then that'll be me.*

Watching from across the room, Martin could see that Wilkins was persona non grata with the others. *At least until they can figure out how culpable the Secret Service is, they'll keep their distance.* He could also tell that none of the other four liked Murray Allard that much. Martin didn't know why Wilkins wouldn't like Allard, but he did know that Rafi, Emery and Ross still saw themselves as cops. Cops who also had administrative and political responsibilities, but cops first and foremost.

Major Murray Allard, and he made it clear to subordinates that he preferred to be called "Major Allard", on the other hand, saw himself as a politician with law enforcement responsibilities, and was always trying to insinuate himself into meetings with the next line up; Nolan Quinn, Emery's and Ross' boss, and regularly dropped the Governor's name into conversation.

From long acquaintance, Martin didn't like Allard either. When they'd shaken hands earlier Allard had repeated his tired witticism about having come from "Martin's Office". Allard's office was in Harlem on Dr. Martin Luther King, Jr. Blvd.

Martin King gave a wan smile in return and inwardly cursed his parents (but only a little, he did love them…) for being such fans of Dr. King as to name their son "Martin". Luckily, his middle name was Alex, not Luther, and as a teenager he briefly got people to call him "Mak" to dodge the Dr. King comparison, but it didn't stick. Sure as hell, though, Martin was stopping his education after his Master's – no way was he going for a PhD and becoming Dr. Martin King!

Martin thought about why so many people found Murray hard to like. Superficially, he was a nice enough man, but soon his pretentiousness and self-importance grated on people. Moreover, Martin knew why Murray Allard had left the army on half-pay aged thirty-eight. Allard had been told in no uncertain terms that a certain incident had meant that his chance of further promotion was zero. The details of that incident still made Martin uncomfortable and worried that such a man advised the Governor. *None of my business, though.*

The gathering coalesced into small clumps of people on the basis of rank with non-aligned, and junior, personnel circulating between the groups. *Along with Rafi,* Martin noted wryly. *Being the good host, making sure the Nespresso pods didn't run out.*

Martin took some pride in noting that "his" group comprised field personnel; people one step down from the Murray, Rafi, Emery, Rusty and Ross clump. *People who still got on the front line once in a while.* Martin looked at the four people standing around with him and thought, *it'd be easy to cast us in a film; we're such stereotypes!*

There was Kasia with her distant, cool European beauty. Then there was FBI Agent Ivan Biskup, whom Agent Rafi had just announced was being put in charge of the FBI's side of the investigation. Ivan towered above the others. A big man, he had once been muscular, but now carried a few too many extra kilos. A round face, with smiling eyes and cheeks and just a hint of redness that suggested a love of drink as much as a love of life. All in all, a cliché of a Russian émigré. However, if someone ill-advisably said something to that effect, they would receive a loud outpouring of disgust and denunciation. 'My ancestors are Slovaks! Not *zatracené* Russian!' Seemingly oblivious to the fact that his swear words tended to be in Russian…

Next to Ivan was Captain Siobhan Niven. Siobhan was a very attractive, petite redhead with green eyes, almost a clichéd Irish lass, in her late thirties. Like Kasia, she found that her appearance often meant people, especially men, dramatically underestimate her. Unlike Kasia, however, Siobhan played on her looks, sometimes flirting outrageously until, too late, people realised they'd said more than they'd planned. Siobhan was the Commanding Officer of Ross Benbow's JTTF.

Joining the law enforcement officers was Bill Ngo, Deputy District Attorney for Manhattan. Bill was a young, second-generation Vietnamese-American and a very smart and ambitious man. Tall for an Asian, he was second only to Ivan in height, although Kasia could look him in the eyes when she wore heels. Good looking, Bill dressed well, his shoes as black and shiny as his immaculately styled hair. A well-pressed suit and tie (unlike the other two men) and an expensive watch. He exuded an air of decency and professionalism that played well in the courtroom.

He had "married well", had a lovely daughter and lived in the posher suburbs north of the City. Despite all this, he was a very nice man.

Martin smiled to himself. *If we're going to be film stars, who'd play me? Morgan Freeman probably…*

Scanning the room Rafi saw Brice Payton, widely understood to be CIA, but always evasive; no one pushed him on it. Suffice to say that when he needed to he always had sufficient security clearance and the right to be wherever he was at the time. Chatting to Brice was… Rafi had to think for a while as he tried to recognise the woman… *ah, Morna MacCallum!* She was an analyst with NSA, Rafi used the common acronym for the National Security Agency. *What's she doing here?*

Technically, this was a by-invitation-only meeting, but Rafi had let it be known to all the various agencies that a preliminary get together would take place here and anyone who had a legitimate stake would be welcome. It stamped 'FBI' authority over the case early on. These sorts of eclectic gatherings also threw up surprising synergies and tensions that proved useful later.

Rafi nodded to himself. Pressing flesh, making contact, judging the mood; who stood where and who wanted to do what. These were all essential first steps in managing a complex case.

Lieutenant-Commander Martin King of NYPD Detective Services didn't agree. He couldn't wait to get out of this "gab-fest" and start doing some real work.

As his career took its inevitable path he had moved from patrol officer to detective, and then up through the detective grades to first. The normal route would have been to progress to Lieutenant, Captain, Inspector, *et cetera*, increasingly swapping investigative responsibilities for administrative ones with each promotion. King had been able, temporarily at least, to remain involved with solving cases. It was the reason he had wanted to be a detective ever since he'd been a teenager. *Nothing to do with the fact that dad had been a cop,* he told himself unsuccessfully.

The rank of Lieutenant-Commander was a rare one within NYPD shared by only a score of men and women. It gave them the same administrative duties as a regular Lieutenant, but also allowed them to be the lead investigator for some high-profile cases. They didn't get much more high-profile than this.

He was relieved when Ivan suggested that the group move somewhere quieter to discuss details of the case. Siobhan and Bill declined saying that they still had to talk to some people here. Martin followed him, knowing that Kasia would be right behind.

'We can use Rafi's office', said Biskup as he led Martin and Kasia down the hall. 'I've also invited Rusty Wilkins to join us; he'll be along in a few minutes'.

With the lights off, the room even felt a little magical, perhaps romantic, lit by the lights of New York City. With the lights on it was clear whose office this was. Rafi Matos' workplace was subtly appointed to reflect his position as Assistant Director in Charge. A little larger, a better view or a slightly bigger desk would have been seen as reaching above his station whereas anything less would not command the right amount of respect for his position.

Accordingly, none of the four in the room even considered sitting behind the Director's desk when they entered. The two agents, Secret Service and FBI, sat on comfortable armchairs at either end of a modest coffee table while the two detectives sat on a matching couch along one side of the table.

Rusty Wilkins opened the conversation. 'Just like to say thanks for inviting me, Ivan, and to you folks as well', nodding towards Martin and Kasia. 'Good to see interagency cooperation right off the bat, and let me say that the resources of the Secret Service will be made freely available to help the course of this investigation'.

A short, yet distinctly awkward silence followed this declaration.

'Ah. Actually Rusty' began Ivan. 'It's not so much that the Service has been invited to be part of the investigation team as, er, part of the investigation', he finished lamely.

'Meaning what, exactly?' Wilkins' tone had sharpened.

'You have to admit, Rusty', Ivan was still being conciliatory and friendly. 'That the Service, well, the Service provided the...' *don't say "murder weapon"* Ivan thought, '...method of delivery for the device that killed Mr Robbins'.

Martin watched quietly. Although he sympathised with Ivan, this was definitely one responsibility that he was glad the FBI had taken over. Wilkins was silent, but his expression was worth a thousand words. *If looks could kill... we wouldn't need owls!* Martin bit his lip hard to stop himself smiling at his own witticism. *Not a good time to laugh...*

'So', Ivan continued, 'I think it's only fair to say that we'll be needing to talk to your agents to find out exactly what happened. If the bird had simply flown off in an unexpected direction, I think we would all accept the possibility that this new… technology… was experiencing teething problems, but…', Ivan shifted back into his comfort zone of FBI Investigating Agent, '…it didn't. The bird, the *Secret Service* bird I might add, flew directly at a President and Vice-President Elect carrying a bomb. That is not an accident. That is an incident. And an incident that points to infiltration of the Secret Service'.

Now silence all around the room. The conclusion was not revelatory to anyone there, but it had now been said out loud. The United States Secret Service housed a traitor who had undermined the Service's main reason for existing; protecting the most senior Government officials. With the words said ramifications could be denied no longer. This wasn't just a high-profile murder case or even a possible case of terrorism. This could leave the Secret Service, and its oversight department, Homeland Security, fighting for its existence and possibly create the biggest shakeup of the US intelligence community since the creation of the DHS.

Assistant Special Agent in Charge Wilkins was not stupid. He sat still for some seconds while he formulated a response. Deep down he wanted to shout, to defend his beloved Service, to deny these slurs on its, and by extension, his, reputation, but rationally he recognised the truth of the situation. Something *had* gone wrong with the Protection Detail. If he was to be able to salvage anything for his agency he would need to tread very carefully here.

He broke the silence. 'Well Ivan', *no need to get officious yet, keep it friendly and on first name terms,* he thought. 'While it certainly doesn't look good I don't think we should be jumping to conclusions as yet. There could be scenarios that we haven't thought of. So… why don't we', he pointed to himself to show he meant the Secret Service, not the four people in the room, 'do our internal investigations and get back to you?'

'Of course, of course. You should do your own internal assessment', Ivan did not use the word "investigation" intentionally. 'Meanwhile, we hope that the Service will work with us by allowing us to interview your Agents with a minimum of official paperwork?'

'No problem. Perhaps you could start drafting a list of who you had in mind, pass it to me and then I can set up some appointments?'

'Actually Rusty, we've, ah, we've already started talking to some of your people. Lieutenant Stankić and Sergeant Gomez…'

Ivan turned to Martin and Kasia on the couch. 'They were the Counter-Sniper team; Stankić on the roof, Gomez observing'. He turned back to Wilkins. 'They already kindly agreed to give their statements about half an hour ago'.

Seeing Wilkins face Ivan rushed on, 'It's more the, ah, bird-team, that we and NYPD', looking to the couch for support, 'want to interview in a bit more detail, with, of course, you in attendance'.

'It seems *Agent* Biskup, that you have already taken the liberty of presuming upon our cooperation by interviewing my staff without my knowledge. Next thing I know, you'll want to interview me'. Wilkins concluded sarcastically.

Martin King spoke for the first time. 'Actually *Agent* Wilkins, that's exactly what we'd like to do'.

Once again Martin felt valuable time being stolen by politics and interagency bickering. Judging by Kasia's fidgeting she probably felt the same, he thought. Or maybe it was the coffee. Or maybe she needed a cigarette. *Or maybe all of the above*, he thought as she excused herself and left the room.

By the time she'd returned, the wrangling was over. Rusty Wilkins had resigned to the inevitable, and a fifth and sixth person had joined the room; an FBI secretary and USSS Officer-Technician Jean Byrnes. It had been made clear that Wilkins was free to attend any interviews of Secret Service staff or not at his own discretion, but under no circumstances was he to interfere with the interview itself. It was a difficult choice to make. If he stayed he would be giving his blessing to the interviews, and merely by his presence, convey to his staff that they should be as open and forthright as if it was an internal Service investigation. However, if he left he would have no control over the proceedings whatsoever, not even by a look on his face, and would have no direct knowledge of what was said. He'd decided to stay while Ivan Biskup led the interview with Martin and Kasia occasionally intervening.

'Officer Byrnes. Please sit. Make yourself comfortable. Although this is an informal interview we will record it for reference, and it is possible that your statements may be used later to guide more formal proceedings. That said, our goal tonight is simply to find out what happened and how it happened. It's not about assigning blame'. *Yet.*

Jean Byrnes sat on the couch opposite Martin and Kasia, the New York lights behind her. It was an awkward position Wilkins realised, as it meant that she had to half turn away from him unable to see his face as she faced Biskup on her left. She was still dressed in the clothes she'd worn on the roof, minus her coat, gloves and hat. Smart, but casual, function over form. She wore jeans and a white blouse topped by a padded dark blue vest with "Secret Service" in bright yellow on the back, plus the usual paraphernalia of radio, whistle, flashlight, *et cetera*. She looked anything but comfortable.

She started by repeating the facts that were already known. How she had received the "go" signal, released the owl (she always called it by its name, 'Hedwig'), and then watched in horror as it flew towards the podium and exploded. Everything, except the outcome, had been by the book. 'Really! By the book. Not a step out of place. It *should* have been fine!'

Ivan prompted her to continue. 'Tell us what is *supposed* to happen after you release... Hedwig. How does it know to go to the drone? What's it supposed to do when it gets there?'

'Hedwig's been trained for auditory signals', Jean stated. 'She's given a unique two-tone signal. The sound she hears after that is the sound she is to locate. Tom, Tomas Holgersen, my partner, captured the sound of the drone after it was spotted; he has a parabolic microphone. He sent the recording to my phone. I the signal tone to Hedwig, and then play the recording. Which is what I did'. *Everything by the book.*

She paused, and looked at Ivan, Martin and Kasia, but didn't dare swivel all the way around to look at her boss. She quickly looked away from Kasia's impassive face with those grey eyes. *She looks like a cat staring at a bird cage*, Jean thought. She focused on the men and, seeing nothing but encouragement on their faces, she continued a little more confidently.

'I can tell when Hedwig knows what to do. She looks at me, gives a little nod, and then swivels her head around scanning for the sound. She did that tonight, too. Then she flew down towards the east end of the plaza exactly where we'd been told the drone was. At this point, we, I, was confident it was exactly the same as in training. After Hedwig flies off I call Tom to get his return signal ready. Tom has a small speaker system that plays a special sound to recall the birds. Hedwig's signal is based on mice rustling through grass, but amplified and digitised to make it a unique sound that cannot exist in nature. She's trained to home in on that sound once she's caught the target'.

Kasia interrupted. 'There are three audio signals? The first cue sound, the recording of the drone, and then the homing signal?'

'Exactly'. Replied Jean.

'And the bird doesn't get confused?'

'Oh, no. Hedwig's quite smart. Not once in training did she get confused'.

'Ah. Thanks'. Kasia leant back into the couch.

'So, um… right, so, Hedwig flies to the target. I tried to follow her with my field glasses, but she's quite hard to see at night and it took me a while to get the glasses up, but no problem, we have spotters who were watching for her. I know Sergeant Gomez was following her as he said something like "gotcha" over the radio. And, of course, Tom follows Hedwig. We've been debating whether to put an LED on her leg or something, but have been worried that it might upset her balance or night vision or even make her a target. Whatever… we haven't done that yet'.

Jean hesitated. 'I know what's supposed to happen next, but obviously it didn't, and I wasn't directly involved so, well, perhaps you'd be better off talking to Tom? He's supposed to trigger the recall sound as Hedwig leaves me. I don't know why he wouldn't do that, but can't say for sure that he did. I didn't hear it, but then I wouldn't from that distance'.

Both Ivan and Kasia went to talk at once.

Ivan waved generously to Kasia, 'Ladies first'.

'Bunch of questions really. Why have a homing signal? Doesn't the bird get hurt by the rotors? How can an owl carry a big drone anyway; how heavy are those things?'

Jean was now in her comfort zone. 'Well, the guys who first set up these programs obviously had to address these issues, and many others, it took them years to work everything out. Luckily for us the birds we use, mostly Eurasian eagle-owls for night work and White-tailed eagles during the day, have a great sense of body position and can grab the middle of a drone, avoiding the rotors by millimetres. Hedwig also had some small metal stockings on just in case.

'These birds are all really strong. The Eurasian eagle-owl has some of the strongest feet around; they use their talons for killing not just holding prey. All our birds can carry at least two kilos, and can steer something weighing up to four kilos to the ground in a controlled fall.

'The UAS's we use them for are small quadcopters used by small hobbyists up to larger, more expensive octocopters that can weigh up to two kilos, but usually less than that. They're the commonest UAS's in private use'.

'What's a UAS; unmanned aerial something? And what about the homing signal?' Kasia reminded Jean.

'Yeah, Unmanned Aerial System. A drone to the layman. The signal is to get the drone away from an area. The birds will generally fly away from people. Once they catch a UAS they act as if they've caught dinner, and want to go somewhere quiet to eat. In built-up areas those places aren't always available so we guide them somewhere safe. There are other protocols used by other agencies around the world. Some simply shoot down the UAS. Others use "attack-drones" that fire nets at the intruder tangling the rotors and causing it to crash. The problem with both of those is that it can result in explosives or biological weapons dropping onto a crowd. The beauty of using birds like Hedwig is that the landing place can be chosen. Tom can even place the transponder away from himself so he isn't exposed until he's sure it's safe'.

Jean was enjoying herself now, talking to people who were interested in her passion. Martin King brought her back to earth.

'But that didn't happen tonight, now did it? What went wrong?'

Jean reddened slightly. 'No. No, it didn't work. As I said, maybe something went wrong with the transponder, but even if it had Hedwig would have looked around for a quiet place to land not flown the length of the plaza...' She got emotional. The owl had been like a beloved pet to her.

A small silence and then Ivan said, 'Well, Officer Byrnes, you've been very helpful. Just one more thing: who trained... Hedwig?' he smiled at using the name. 'Did you?'

'Oh, of course I was involved in her training. So was Tom. We are, were, her primary handlers, but the main training was done by the people in The Netherlands who have pioneered this method.

Tom and I spent a couple of months in Holland with four other Service Officers before we all brought our birds back here. That's why they're all European species at the moment'.

The interview broke up with expressions of gratitude for peoples' time and continued cooperation, swapping of numbers and goodbyes all around. Jean left the office.

'Agent Wilkins? Anything to add from what you know or saw?' asked Ivan.

'Not really. More or less what I know about the program, and everything she said matches what I saw on the roof tonight'.

'No discrepancies from our preliminary talks with Sergeant Gomez Officer and Lieutenant Stankić who was on the roof with you either. As you said, everything matches up. Give me a sec, will you?'

Ivan pulled out his phone and walked to the window his back to the other three. After a short conversation he came back and sat down.

'That was the other interview team. They've talked to Officer Holgersen. He said he triggered the transponder and walked away about four metres. Said he wasn't really sure if the sound came out, but didn't think anything at the time as it was noisy in the plaza. Our tech guys had a look at that transponder. Nothing wrong with it, *except* the batteries were dead…'

Ivan looked straight at Rusty Wilkins. 'Seems odd, don't you think? Would have been one of the most basic of equipment checks I would have thought'.

'No, you're right'. Ivan held his hands up and dropped his head slightly as Wilkins stiffened, about to say something. 'I shouldn't have said that. Far too early to start finger pointing. It's been a long day and could be a long night, apologies'.

As Rusty Wilkins left the interview room, he saw Major Murray Allard waiting at the elevator.

'Agent Wilkins', nodded Allard.

'How are you, Major?'

'Not great. Everyone', he nodded to the conference room he'd just left where the powers-that-be were still talking, 'is looking at this and thinking how to shaft Homeland Security. There's been enough cock-ups over the years and we don't need another'.

Allard looked directly at Wilkins. 'The DHS Deputy Director called a while ago. He wants me to assure him that this… incident… has no roots in the Secret Service. None. Can I assure him of that, Agent Wilkins? Can I assure him that the Service is squeaky clean? No moles? No subversions? No "technical glitches"?'

Wilkins started to formulate a response as the two men stepped into the elevator when Allard stopped him.

'No. Don't answer that now. Take some time and give me a truthful answer not a wishful one. Take, oh, I don't know, forty-eight hours? And *then* tell me the Service hasn't screwed this up'.

They rode down to the ground floor in silence.

Ivan, Martin and Kasia stood on the small balcony of the FBI buildings third floor. It was cold, but they all had coats on and this was one of the few places that Kasia could smoke which she did, while also wrapping her hands around yet another hot cup of coffee. The men had raided Rafi's "hospitality centre" and poured themselves whiskeys.

The night was clear, but starlight was no contest for the lights of the city. Their three faces were lit up from the lights below, ghoulish. Martin's dark features were especially difficult to see with just the underside of his chin, the tip of his nose and eyebrows a little lighter than the shadows around them. Kasia's pale face was more visible and occasionally flared redly as she dragged on her cigarette.

'So', said Ivan. 'We've got quite a few strings to start pulling on. Someone was operating the drone. Someone, maybe the same person, maybe not, added a bomb to that drone. Someone put dead batteries in the speaker... or failed to check they were working. Maybe an accident, maybe not. And, of course, someone convinced that owl to fly at Robbins. If *that* was done during training we may be looking at someone in Holland. And... I hardly need to say this, but... The Secret Service are up to their eyes in this. Their interception protocols, their protection detail, their batteries for Chris'sake'.

Martin and Kasia's ghoulish faces nodded in the dark.

'Hear the news about Trump?'

'Of course. The PM been told yet?'

'Nah, don't think so. She came straight back from that stuffy dinner and headed to her rooms with a stiff 'un before the news broke. Early start today and even earlier tomorrow. Unless she turned the telly on, she was probably in bed before it happened. You going to wake her?'

'No point. She never liked the bastard anyway, especially after his remarks on Scotland and Brexit. No reason to disturb her rest. I'll draft a quick message; you know, "heinous crime", "our thoughts with the families", *et cetera*. She can read it out in the morning. Let some other bugger figure out what this means for our "special relationship"…

Much of China was still waking up, but the Party was already at work.

Seven members of the Central Committee, dressed almost identically in dark Western suits and white shirts, sat at one end of a long table made for many more people than just these men. Their positions and personal reputations were a nuanced reflection of the importance of the issue at hand. The group was senior enough to be able to discuss issues and ideas beyond the official line and to make final recommendations but junior enough that not implementing those recommendations wouldn't create a crisis.

So these seven men, sitting in a room as the rising winter sun tried vainly to pierce the smog that hung over the city, reiterated current Party positions and perspectives, rehashed the arguments behind those positions and then, slowly, hesitantly, felt their way forward, looking for consensus or censure, and started to discuss the future.

Trump's electoral success had given the Party much to think about. It was clear that Trump's stated position vis-à-vis China was not positive. He wanted the renminbi revalued, trade agreements renegotiated, tariffs imposed, *et cetera*. Yet looking at the long game, definitely a Chinese strength, Trump's vindictive policies could easily be used to demonstrate to the American people the value of good relations with China, not the least of which was to keep consumer prices low in the US. Should a full-blown trade war break out China would be hurt, but not as much as America. To start with, inflation would climb rapidly into double digits as the cost of Chinese, and other, imports swiftly rose. If the US tried to shift to imports from elsewhere while still keeping tariffs high on just Chinese goods? China owns well over a trillion dollars of US debt. Selling large chunks of that would reduce the dollar's value making all imports more expensive and possibly starting a global run on the currency.

The result would be a massive outcry by the American public unable to buy two-cent plastic spoons for their bbqs or a new washing machine every other year. In just four years Americans would kick Trump out and the new government would come begging for trade deals that would be even more advantageous to China than before. Alternatively China could simply seize all American assets in China and turn its back on them. The rest of the world was enough of a market.

Either way China was well positioned financially and socially to ride out such turmoil.

The Central Committee had also concluded that the non-economic ramifications of a Trump-USA provided many opportunities for China. If Trump followed through with his rash campaign promises, the net result would be a US disengagement from the Pacific. This would leave a lot of space for even more aggressive Chinese moves in the region. China would be able to establish itself as the paramount power in the Pacific. It could even leave the door open to a final solution to Taiwan.

Many in the Party saw him as a one-trick pony, or as one wit put it, a one-trick war horse; his unsophisticated bluster boiled down to only one argument: military force. At the same time, his policies of forcing US allies to pay more for their own defence and to equivocate over NATO obligations undermined that military force. Paradoxically, his policies of wanting other countries to pull their weight would isolate and weaken the US, not strengthen it. Even though the US was still vastly superior militarily to China the gap had been closing the gap. By alienating its traditional allies, that gap would close even quicker. More importantly the Chinese had learned from history something it seemed Trump had not done. Vietnam, Iraq, Afghanistan… they all showed that the USA will not accept soldiers in body bags. China would.

On the other hand the one thing the Party valued was stability. Stability enabled slow, controlled change. Changes that suited the Party could be implemented. Those that didn't, weren't. Rapid change, turmoil, global revolution had too many unpredictable factors and outcomes.

Finally there was the nuclear option; literally. Whereas these men could calmly agree that China could lose a hundred men for every American GI and still win the war the question remained: 'How crazy was Trump?' Would he get so frustrated that, like a schoolboy bully faced with not getting his way, "takes his ball and goes home"? Leaving their much-loved metaphors and analogies aside for a moment the seven men asked themselves bluntly: "Does Donald Trump's belligerence and rashness extend so far as to use nuclear weapons?"

For *that* was the war that China would lose.

In the end, to no one's surprise, the group decided to recommend a cautious "wait-and-see" approach. The selling of US debt that had been going on for close to a year and had seen over two hundred billion dollars sold should continue. Public statements should continue to be conciliatory and reasonable ("someone should send their condolences to the Vice-President's family"), but in private negotiations with other countries in the region, especially Japan and South Korea, both the carrot and the stick should be made larger.

Oh, and North Korea most definitely should be sent more support (discreetly, of course). Pulling that tiger's tail was always a good way to remind the world that they needed China.

The West had Donald Trump to scare the world. China had Kim Jong Un.

Outside the room, one of the younger men of the group, he was not even fifty, pulled a more experienced and higher ranking colleague to one side.

'Do you think we had anything to do with this? Directly?'

The older man nodded slowly, 'I really couldn't say'.

He wandered away letting his colleague ponder the ambiguities of that statement.

Fajr, the first *adhan*, call for prayers, of the day usually attracts a very small attendance, but this morning, in Tal' Afar at least, the mosques attracted more than their usual number. Many residents had been woken earlier than usual by the sound of gunfire.

Gunfire was a part of life in Tal' Afar mostly wasted into the air rather than at anybody in particular, but gunfire just before dawn usually signified military action rather than celebrations. Parents had gathered their children and headed into the safest room of the house. A few early bakers covered their ovens so as not to give away their locations by their light. A few had already started work and the delicious smell of freshly baked spread mingled with the burnt pepper smell from the firing of many guns.

Whatever Islamic State's feelings were in terms of non-acceptance of non-Sunni entities it didn't extend to their weapons. It was a veritable smörgåsbord of internationalism that had ripped into the sky. Mikhail Kalashnikov's venerable AK-47 had led the orchestra, but contributions from Colt's M16, the FN FAL automatic rifle from France and Russia's PKM machine gun along with the occasional odd bark of more antiquated weaponry (one IS commander made a point of being idiosyncratic with his 1935 browning high-power automatic pistol) provided counterpoint. Many of which were courtesy of the USA via the Iraqi army.

The firing had started an hour before dawn had even begun to hint at light in the east and now, in deference to the *muezzin* calling for prayers, had mostly stopped. The fighters now wide awake and charged with adrenaline, walked to their mosques. They were joined by young men and teenaged boys from houses nearby.

Most of the older residents of Tal' Afar and all of the women, stayed inside with the lights out.

'A great day, yes?'

'They are all great days, *insh'Allah.*, but perhaps not as great as we think – that Muslim-hating monster still lives. He may yet become President'.

'Allah forbid. Allah will let him die'.

'And which do we want? To have this, this... devil die and be condemned to *Jahannam* for eternity? Or to have him live? To resurrect our recruitment, to rekindle the fear of crusade that fuels *jihad*? With Trump as President even the House of Saud and Israel will become our allies!'

'But... if that is what you think, why did we try to kill him?'

'My thoughts are not everyone's thoughts. Besides, I'm not sure we did'.

Senate Building, the Kremlin, Moscow

Moscow slept under a fresh fall of snow. Its city lights are not as bright as New York's, and a few stars could be seen as the sky cleared and the temperature began to fall.

A hard crust, sparkling invitingly, formed on top of the new snow that had fallen on the square earlier in the night.

Footsteps cracked and squeaked as the man, anonymous in his thick coat and felt hat, hurried across the square. He entered the overly warm ground floor room fuggy with cigarette smoke and air wet from damp clothes and kerosene heaters.

'You heard?'

'*Da. He's* not going to be happy. Not happy at all'.

'We're going to have to contact Matveev. He's going to have to delay the talks'.

'The Saudi's will also not be happy, comrade. From what I've heard, they've been very receptive to our overtures. The war costs are high and oil prices low. They're worried about their own Arab Spring'.

'*Da.* Damn that *mudak* for doing this thing. Let's hope American medicine is as good as they say and they fix Our Donald up so he can go on and make great President. "Putin is a man we get along very well with". Must be one of the few!' The man broke into a coughing laugh.

The second man joined in the laughter, but quieter. '*Da!* But say that softly. The walls have ears. And the floor and ceiling too".

"It will be a good day when Our Donald succeeds to the throne. With Our Donald there will be no complaints about how we treat those *хуёво* Chechens and Muslims'.

'Russia will own Middle East!'

'Our European Soviets will come back to the Motherland'.

'*Da, da, da!* Turkey will leave NATO!'

'And Japan and Korea won't pay American bill and sign up to good Russian defence!'

'But biggest, biggest present is that *He* will be happy. And *He's* never happy!'

They chorused the last line together, 'Donald Drumpovich; Make Russia Great Again!!'

More coughing laughter in the humid, stale air dying out to silence and then:

'So which one of us gets to tell *Him* in the morning that his American *brat* might die?'

The town lay quiet starlight reflecting off the tin roofs of houses and crescent moons atop mosques.

'Papa, Papa', the teenaged girl called softly to her father who grunted querulously as she woke him.

'What is it?'

'Donald Trump has been shot'.

'Who?'

'Trump. The new American President'.

'And?'

'I thought you should know'.

'Does this mean the war is over? That rain is coming soon? That Boko Haram will let you go to school tomorrow? That the desert will stop taking over our land?'

'…um, no, Papa'.

'Then I don't care. Men get shot every day'.

He rolled over and went back to sleep.

Day Two

November 30, 2016
Investigation

By morning, routines had been established, tasks allocated.

Detective Eugene Marchetti ('Gene' to most of his colleagues) was running operations on the street with the help of uniformed officers. This included ongoing crowd control (mostly shooing away gawkers and selfie-taking idiots) around the crime scene and door-to-door interviews. He was also in charge of rounding up all the CCTV footage in the area and liaising with the Domain Awareness people.

FBI Agent Patil, she of the *Fargo* accent, was running public communications. The hotline was a joint NYPD-FBI operation with Patil overseeing it with the phones manned (and womanned) by police officers.

Late night phone calls between Major Allard of the NY State Office of Counter-Terrorism, USSS Deputy Director Ian Croft and FBI Assistant Director Rafi Matos had established that any further interviews with Secret Service personnel would only occur with their explicit approval and would likely be subject to various conditions. The three of them had also formally decided to invite Assistant Chief Ross Benbow of the FBI-NYPD Joint Terrorism Task Force to "observe". He would be fully briefed and could keep his agents up to date with the investigation; it was possible that the case could include a terrorist aspect at some point.

Despite the interagency infighting with the Secret Service and, by extension, Homeland Security, the core of the investigation remained united, not least because of the mutual respect of the two men in direct charge, Ivan Biskup and Martin King. Similarly, Kasia Pasternak's friendship with the Assistant D.A. Bill Ngo gave them an important back-door link to Washington and a voice in the NY Governor's office. The inclusion of Ross Benbow also helped; as the commanding officer of an interagency force he was politically adept and a calming presence.

More importantly the investigators had direct control over the physical evidence. The remains of the bomb, the drone, and the owl had been sent to the FBI lab in Quantico, Virginia overlooking the Potomac River.

At Police Plaza, King and Pasternak had set up their "command centre" in a small room which, despite being deliberately windowless for privacy reasons, was comfortable, well-lit and well-ventilated. Although subordinate to the FBI investigation, they'd still be a lot of paperwork at NYPD. King and Pasternak, along with the rest of the team, would sort and prioritise what the police found, and then share the relevant information with Ivan at the FBI.

The priority questions, and those responsible for answering them, were clearly spelled out on a whiteboard:

Who operated the drone? (Gene)
Model? Homemade? (Ivan)
Who bought it? (Kasia)
Associates? (Kasia)
How did the drone get on the roof? (Gene)
What explosives? Source? (Ivan)
Type of bomb? Made by? (Ivan)
Why did the owl go the wrong way? (Martin)
Who put in dead batteries? Were they checked? (Martin)

It wasn't meant to be definitive, and the list was certainly going to change over the next few days, but it gave them a starting point.

'Any news on Trump?' Martin asked Kasia.

'They operated on his head last night. Seems his hair plugs deflected a lot of the shrapnel…'

'Kasia!' Martin admonished in mock outrage. Like so many people who deal with death on a daily basis they shared a black sense of humour.

With just the merest twinkle in her grey eyes, she continued. He took a big hit though. Multiple contusions all over, but the main damage was to one of his lungs. Seems something tried going through his ribs broke a couple and one pierced a lung, and moderate brain trauma…'

Both of them had voted for Clinton. They both looked at each other seeing if the other would break first and make the obvious joke, but neither blinked.

'So the doctors have induced a coma with propofol. Not sure how long they'll keep him under. Depends on when the swelling goes down'.

'What're the symptoms of "moderate brain damage"? Particularly in this case?' Martin asked, prodding Kasia to be the first to break into a smile.

'Well, it seems that the clinical definition of moderate damage can include the patient being confused, not following commands, and…' her hesitation had a "wait-for-it" feel '…may make the patient irritable and combative'.

Neither could help themselves breaking into laughter at the thought of doctors diagnosing "The Donald" as "irritable and combative".

Martin shook his head gravely. 'Not very professional of us, Kasia. Not professional at all. A man's life hangs in the balance…' As he used the cliché, both of them remembered that it wasn't a joking matter. A man's life *did* hang in the balance, and two people were already dead.

He continued more seriously. 'What of the other Secret Service Agents? One was in critical condition wasn't he?'

'Yeah. They say he's stable now. One of the others was treated and released last night. The other two are still under observation. There've been a couple of other admissions. Civilians hurt in the panic not from the explosion itself, but nothing major that I've heard'.

'How's Gene getting along with the door-to-door?'

'Lots of data, little info. People have either got their "I was there" story to tell or, like long time "N'Yuckers", have a been-there, done-that attitude and "didna see nuttin". He'll get something though, he's relentless. Soon as Ivan gets back to us with the type of drone used we'll be able to narrow down our search on where it came from. I've already got people contacting City retailers, online sellers, Amazon, *et cetera*'.

Kasia's normally calm demeanour shifted as she continued. 'Do you know how many drones have been sold in the past month alone? Two hundred thousand… that's how many. We're talking over two million in this country in the past year. We really need Ivan's guys to get back to us soon if we're going to try and trace this through sales. One thing working for us is it's a fast-moving industry. If Ivan can pinpoint the model it'd narrow the search down dramatically'.

She shifted back into pure professional mode. 'Gene tells me they've got some CCTV that covers most of the doors that can lead to the roof. Mostly maintenance access so the footage is intermittent. His team's working through that'.

'Right'. Said Martin. 'So, young Kasia: "Means, motive and opportunity". Where do we stand?'

'Well, *old* Martin. Sounds like you're getting ready for your retirement as a law professor in some mid-west bumfucknowhere college?' Kasia laughed, and then went on. 'Let's start with the easy part; motive. By my calculations, Trump has pissed off about four billion people. Women, Muslims, Mexicans, Chinese, hell, all of Asia. Plus all our allies, Europe… So motive is both easy and hard. Easy because so many people have motive, but hard because it means we can't use it to narrow our search. It's like Agatha Christie's Orient Express, ever'one dunnit'.

'Uh, huh'. Martin nodded for her to continue.

'Means: The drone's easy. The explosives are harder, and the timing of the explosion even harder still. It seems overly complex and could, even should, have gone wrong…' Kasia's eyes unfocused as she looked at nothing in particular. Martin watched her. Although everyone talks of Sherlock Holmes' "deductive powers", he was actually an inductive reasoner. As was Kasia. Martin had far more experience, had a better "gut", and knew how to play politics much better than Kasia, but when it came to pure reasoning Martin readily admitted Kasia's superiority. Admitted to himself at least.

Those grey eyes refocused on Martin's face. 'That's our starter! There's no way this could have worked unless the perp had control over each stage. Whoever did this didn't leave things to chance. He… she, what the hell… *knew* the owl, what was that stupid name, Hedwig? Was going to be used. He/she *knew* it was going to fly towards Robbins and Trump. They *knew* the bomb would go off when it got there. So who would know the owl was going to be used? We didn't. And who could guarantee it would fly to the podium and explode there? Ivan's right, the Secret Service are up to their necks in this one'.

'Uh, huh', Martin grunted again. *C'mon, Kasia, take this further, what can NYPD do here?*

Seeing his face, Kasia nodded. 'Right, right. So the general *why* is a given, Trump annoyed someone; maybe someone outside politics even, he's been around a long time. Ivan'll help us figure out *how* all this fits together logistically, is he in touch with the Europeans on this yet?'

'Yep. A general, non-specific request to Europol and a much more specific request to the FBI attaché in The Hague to look into the guys who train these birds'.

'So we'll work from the different ends of the string. Ivan looks at whose pulling it. We look at who got pulled?'

'Ah… yeah, sure', Martin said, unsure what her analogy meant, but unwilling to concede the point. 'What you're saying is that Ivan's guys will work on the big picture; we pin down who did what on the night. It's doable. The normal grind just with a lot of political pressure on top. Which, incidentally, is already building. My main problem is how we answer the last two questions', he waved his hand at the white board, 'if we can't ask the USSS?'

> Why did the owl go the wrong way?
> Who put in dead batteries?

'Think I'll go and visit Ivan' he concluded.

Kasia walked Martin out of police headquarters and then went her own way. She was meeting Bill Ngo from the D.A.s office for lunch. This was a common ritual for the pair. There was a park roughly midway between that they used when the weather was nice. It wasn't nice today; they would have to eat inside, and Kasia would just have to wait until after lunch for a cigarette.

Bill was only a few years older than Kasia. They had a lot in common professionally and enjoyed being able to talk freely about cases and office gossip as well as the usual small talk between friends.

Martin joined them for lunch only on rare occasions usually precipitated by an issue regarding a specific case. Although Bill and Martin got along well enough, they never quite hit it off as friends and their relationship, while warm, was not overly personal.

Kasia opened the steamed-over door to the deli. Bill waved at her from a table near the back; whoever got there first was responsible for snagging a table. Lunch passed pleasantly.

The main building of the US Secret Services lies upstream from the FBI lab at the confluence of the Potomac and Anacostia Rivers., but that building is for operations; strategic decisions are made at the headquarters that lie much closer to the centre of power in just another 1970's concrete cube on L Street, just off Massachusetts Avenue.

Special Agent Wilkins had caught the red eye from New York to find himself crumpled and distinctly unshaven waiting in the corridor opposite Deputy Director Ian Croft's office with a lukewarm cup of machine coffee in his hand.

After a long delay, the door opened and Croft, on his mobile, beckoned Wilkins into his office. Rusty entered. It wasn't his first time in the spacious room with its large, walnut topped desk, luxurious leather couch and chairs, but neither did he get invited here on a regular basis. It was rarely for social reasons when he did.

Although Ian Croft was a large man, the first impression of power was not from his size. Everything from his polished shoes and his tailor-made, conservative dark suit to his clean-shaven face and immaculate haircut said "here was a man who walked the corridors of power".

Indicating his phone, Croft said, 'That was Morna MacCallum, NSA? You may have seen her last night at the FBI shindig. She'd gone along to see if maybe there'd be someone to talk to, confidentially, y'know? Seems she couldn't quite find anyone there to confide in'. The accusation was clear; Wilkins had been one of those people she hadn't been able to trust.

Croft continued. 'Seems the men in black have a source embedded, well, in a place where ISIL hangs out... y'know, normal spook stuff... she says there was some chatter a few weeks back about a "second 9/11" and "retaliating against the infidel haters of Islam", blah, blah. No one took it that seriously, but she had a hunch last night and listened to the recording again. May have been a bit lost in translation. She thinks "a second 9/11" could be translating as 2-9/11 or, 29 November in Euro/Arab speak. Says she reported this to her boss, but he didn't take her seriously so she called me, thinking this is too important to leave for a week while people double-check and cover their asses. Interesting, huh?'

'Yeah!' Wilkins relief at seeing a potential lifeline was evident. 'And who does Trump hate? Well, hate most, other than Mexicans... and women... anyway, Muslims! That's who. And where are most of the Muslim terrorists based nowadays? Europe! France, Belgium and... Holland. Where was that bird trained? Holland. And who use birds for hunting a lot... you know, hawking and things? Saudis. Muslims!'

Croft didn't rise to his position by being impetuous so it was a few moments before he nodded, slowly. 'Perhaps. It's a theory anyway. What do you want to do with this?' already distancing himself.

Wilkins didn't catch the shift of responsibility onto his head. 'Who do we know in the CIA that might be able to look into this discreetly? Do some digging into the background of the Dutch trainer, put some feelers out in the Middle East, go back to MacCallum and see if NSA has anything else? That sort of thing'.

'I'll have a word with Congresswoman Starr. Linda's on the Homeland Oversight Committee and she either did something similar with the Agency or knows someone who does. Let me get back to you with a couple of names. Meanwhile, get your boys and girls out of New York, post 'em somewhere quiet and remote'.

'Hi Ivan'.

'Hey, Martin, c'mon in'.

Ivan Biskup's office was definitely not as inviting as his boss's. In fact, it wasn't really *his* office, it was open plan, with six desks loaded with an inbox (invariably full), a phone, file folders, papers, photos, pens, *et cetera*. Along one wall were a row of filing cabinets and a long table on which printers and scanners sat next to a coffee machine, small fridge and a sink, the support army for computers and humans alike.

The room was where ordinary business was done. Confidential work was done in the SCIF - Sensitive Compartmented Information Facility, a suite of rooms in the basement of the building that were physically, electronically and sonically isolated. Biskup had commandeered one of the SCIF rooms for the Trump-Robbins investigation, but avoided it when he could. The ventilation, fluorescent lights and the low humming of jammers dropping in and out of hearing range left people jittery and irritable after a few hours.

Everyone in the office had security clearances at least equivalent to Martin King so he knew he could take Ivan's cue as to when the SCIF would be needed. Until that time, Martin was comfortable talking to Ivan in this office.

'Good timing', Ivan continued as Martin pulled a steel fold-up chair next to Ivan's desk. 'Preliminary results from the lab, they pulled an all-nighter. Everyone knows this case has top priority. They think it may have been the latest model from Parrot, mid-range, decent specs. Definitely not the cheapest, but neither is it an expensive, commercial model. Sales numbers are hard to find, but we've got our Paris office looking into that'.

'Paris? As in France or Texas?'

'France', said Ivan sending a quizzical look Martin's way. Sometimes it was hard to tell when the policeman was joking. 'Parrot's parent company is French. It may take us some time to get data out of them. I've sent a general request for help to Europol on this and the owl trainers in Holland. Given France has been in a state of emergency since the Paris bombings last year, we should get a lot of cooperation from Parrot, so long as we promise to keep their commercially sensitive data confidential'.

'Back to sales. How many are we looking at?'

'That's the bad news. Although it's only been out a couple of months, upwards of half-a-million units have been sold, well over a hundred thousand here in the US. Maybe two'.

'But at least we know the model, I can get Detective Marchetti to start looking at retailers in the New York area; I assume you'll look at online sales?'

Ivan nodded. 'Already got someone on that. More importantly is the operator's range, if they were using the super-duper controller, the operator can be up to two miles away. Would probably want to be much closer, though, so they had line of sight. The explosives were Semtex, the lab will be able to get more info on that as well which will help pin down where it came from'.

'You don't look too thrilled, Martin. This is good stuff this early on'.

'What? Oh, yes, yes. Sorry, my mind was elsewhere. Listen, what strikes me is how many steps there were in the plan, whoever did this had to be very sure that each step would be guaranteed to work'.

Martin ticked the points off on his fingers. 'One, that the drone would work. Two, that it would be spotted. Three, the Service would deploy their owl. Four, the owl was capable of catching and carrying the drone. Five, that the transponder-thing for the recall signal would fail to work. Six, the owl would fly at Robbins. Seven, the bomb would work – and we still don't know what the firing mechanism was – and eight, that the bomb would go off at exactly the right time and place. Now doesn't that strike you as being overly complicated? If all you want to do is kill Robbins and/or Trump one suicidal sniper would be enough'.

Ivan smiled slightly. 'Well… when you put it that way…' Then, turning more serious, '…so what's your theory? The Service has been subverted into killing a guy who is likely to do or say something that ensures one of their own will have to take a bullet for him one day? As actually happened yesterday…'

'Not exactly. Though I suppose we shouldn't discard the possibility. Start with something more basic. Whoever did this had intimate knowledge of how the Service works. Specifically the Protection Detail and…' he held up his finger to indicate this was the important part, '…*access* to their equipment. We can't say, yet, if the bird was tampered with, but I'll bet you anything that those dead batteries weren't an accident'.

Martin thought for a while. 'There *is* one thing that would make someone use such an elaborate plan… there are a lot steps that could have gone wrong, but it also means that there are a lot steps for us to solve. If we miss one, maybe they get away with it. A sniper may have been easier, but they got Oswald within minutes…' He tailed off.

With a brightening of tone and posture, Martin continued. 'Anyway, I'll let Gene know about the drone model so he can refine his search, but I don't think we'll find much there. Hopefully we'll have more luck on the CCTV cameras now we know the shape and size of the controller that would have been carried. Meanwhile, can you step up your investigation into the owl? FBI's got an office in Holland, yeah?'

'Yeah. In The Hague, attached to the embassy. They're aware, but I need to run this by Rafi first. International ops always need approval from higher up, and he's been busy with PR crap, but I'm sure I'll get the go-ahead'.

Martin got up to leave. 'One last thing. We haven't really discussed it, but am I right in saying that we all think Trump was at least a joint target, if not the primary target?'

'Well… yeah. Why bump off Robbins?'

'That could be the question we should be asking ourselves. If this guy's so clever he gets eight complicated steps to all work, why assume the last step didn't? Why do we assume he "failed" to hit Trump? Maybe he wasn't aiming for Trump at all'.

Day Three

December 1, 2016

'King'. He'd answered on the fifth ring, he'd had little sleep the night before.

'Martin, it's me', Kasia's familiar voice on the phone. 'Gene's found the operator'.

The call had come in over the 911 line, not the hotline, at 07:48.

Many of the buildings around the plaza had been partially closed by the police the day before and Ms. Simmons had not been able to get to her office. Although Uniformed had gone through the building, they didn't have the manpower to visit every one of the thousands of offices involved. Especially as most of them would have required contacting the occupants and getting their permission or getting search warrants. The police had spent the day checking corridors, stairwells, furnace rooms, *et cetera* for anything untoward. Nothing had been found.

Anxious to make up lost time, Ms. Simmons had come to work earlier than usual. Other than that, she had followed her normal morning routine. She took the elevator to the 33rd floor. She unlocked and opened her office door. She had been clear about that in her statement to the police, the door had been locked and required her pass card to open it. There had been no sign of anything untoward. She'd opened the door and seen the body on the floor. She'd called 911.

Martin and Kasia stood back from the body on the floor while the FIU officers worked. It had been agreed the night before that the NYPD Crime Scenes Unit would take the lead on working the scenes with the forensics work being done at the FBI lab. This hadn't been the easiest of compromises to reach, but the inarguable fact that NYPD had already been in charge in securing and investigating the site of last night's attack had been a vital factor.

Dr. Turnbull, coroner, stood with the detectives having finished his work before they'd arrived.

'Fairly straightforward. Male. Middle-Eastern descent around nineteen years of age, just a kid…' Turnbull's voice trailed off momentarily, then picked up again. 'Gunshot wound to the right temple. No exit wound. Not a lot of blood. All commensurate with the small calibre handgun in his hand. Time of death round about seven o'clock last night plus or minus my usual fudge factors. Looks like suicide, but I'll give a more definitive opinion…'

'…after the autopsy', the three of them said together. Standing joke, everything useful was always "after the autopsy".

'In some ways', the doctor continued, 'he was lucky. The small calibre, thick bones in the skull and a hand shaking with emotion often means they live… paralysed, blind or otherwise severely injured. Rest of their lives they are tormented with guilt, failure, stigmatised…' He shook his head. 'Maybe I'm getting old, but it seems the cases I see get younger every day'.

He indicated that the body could be moved anytime as far as he was concerned, and left.

Martin wandered over to the window. 630 Fifth Avenue was one of the beautiful art-deco buildings that comprised Rockefeller Center and stood on the north side of the Plaza. From the window of room 3306 Martin could see to his left the rooftop where the drone had first been spotted, and to his right the Christmas tree surrounded by police tape and NYPD and FBI officers. A temporary white tent had been erected over the site of the actual explosion. A good thing given the light rain that drifted from a concrete sky. Altogether, a depressing sight, he thought.

As so often when he was feeling vulnerable or emotional, Martin found the David Bowie song "Heroes" running through his head. Bowie was one of his favourite musicians and Martin had been playing a lot of his music ever since Bowie's death earlier in the year.

Martin wondered if this young man had felt like the hero in the song two days ago; that he could beat "them". Perhaps this is how all jihadists felt; that they could take control if only for a day or two.

He turned back to the room. With the body removed it was somehow easier to focus on the rest of the furniture. It was a typical office. *Typical if you worked for a billion-dollar multinational legal and accounting company as the occupant of this office did*, Martin thought wryly. Said occupant was currently down the hall in another office temporarily requisitioned by the FBI who were taking the woman's formal statement, but King already knew the basics.

A note? Of course there was a note, but not your typical teenaged suicide note. King looked at the sheet of paper inside the clear plastic evidence bag he held in his left hand. The words had been printed presumably from a regular computer printer.

> 'All men dream, but not equally. Those who dream by night in the dusty recesses of their minds, wake in the day to find that it was vanity: but the dreamers of the day are dangerous men, for they may act on their dreams with open eyes, to make them possible'.

They'd elected to take New York Transit despite the drizzle. There was a direct service between the office and Rockefeller Center and most of the walking was through underground shopping malls. Neither wore uniforms and Kasia's firearm was very discreet. Martin preferred not to carry a gun unless he knew he'd be needing it.

'How're you doing?' Martin asked Kasia, a touch too casually.

'I'm fine'. Kasia replied, a touch too frostily.

Kasia had joined Martin's team of Detectives in lower Manhattan four years ago. She'd needed a change in scenery. Two months before the move she had been working uptown when her partner had been shot at close range execution style. The murderer had tied her partner up and then opened a channel on his police radio. There had followed a two minute diatribe against the "fascists who stomp their boots onto the faces of the public", followed by "any last words?" Her partner had tried to keep an even voice, but it had ended in a terrible scream. The murderer had then broadcast, "good night, fuckers". There had been the sound of a shot and then a crash of static as the radio hit the ground.

Kasia had been the first on the scene and seen why her partner had screamed at the end. His nose had been cut off his face, the raw wound still bleeding despite the bullet hole just above it. The murderer had been hiding; waiting for a first responder. He'd hit her over the head with her partner's gun. The same gun he'd used to shoot the policeman. He didn't have a lot of time with Kasia before others would arrive. Kasia never talked about those terribly long minutes as she lay semi-conscious on a concrete floor staring at her dead partner's mutilated face. The murderer had never been caught.

She'd been off work for five months and in therapy for longer. Upon her return there had been talk of putting her in an administrative role. She vetoed that and requested a transfer to a new division so she could get back to work away from sympathetic faces and constant soft voices behind her back.

Martin had been impressed by the young detective's record and demeanour and had no difficulty accommodating her at One Police Plaza. Within the year she was his main partner for the few field cases he took. Martin, and his wife, had gone out of their way to invite her to family and department functions. Helped her fit into her new extended "family". Over the months and years, the tightness of Kasia's expression slowly faded, but it hadn't disappeared.

Despite their close professional and personal relationship the subject of her partner's death was never discussed. The same went for family, at least on Kasia's side. Martin had no idea if she had any siblings, where her parents lived or even if they were still alive. He could, of course, easily find out some of that from Human Resources, but... well, it would feel like a betrayal of trust.

It was an uneasy balancing act for both of them.

Martin felt somewhat protective of Kasia, not quite a daughter, more like a younger sister. He was proud of her resilience and inner strength yet afraid for her. Surely, deep down, there was a still a scared girl who just needed a hug and told that everything would be alright?

Kasia felt Martin was a little too solicitous. At the same time he also made her feel safe; she knew his concern was genuine. She had built up a cool exterior that she knew fitted with her fine features, blonde hair and grey eyes, a typical "ice queen army bitch". It wasn't a suit of armour, she could relax with colleagues and friends, but it served her well on a daily basis. Sometimes, though, she just wanted a hug. A hug which never came.

Bart Sneiders' office was mostly outside. Three white interconnected shipping containers had been retrofitted much like those found on construction sites. The central container had two doors opposite each other on the long side of the box. One door opened onto a gravel parking lot whereas the inner door led to a large netted enclosure. This enclosure bordered, and could open up to, the large forest that sat to the west of this quiet town in the Dutch countryside. A lovely place to work especially if you liked the outdoors as Bart, and so many Dutchmen, did.

He was used to having law enforcement officers visit; they represented the major market for his drone-catching eagles, hawks and other birds. He waved his two visitors to sit in the beaten up couch while he made them all coffee. *Douwe Egberts, proper Dutch coffee, not that watery filter stuff Americans call coffee,* Bart thought to himself, not thinking that maybe, after a few years of living in the Netherlands, his guests may have already acclimatised themselves.

The news of the assassination of the Vice-President elect had been the top news story of the day and, given the connection to his business, Bart had avidly read as much as he could of the event. He knew these two men, who were obviously not regular policemen, were not here to order a replacement for Hedwig.

'Terrible news', Bart said. He waited a split second and then, straight-faced said, 'Hedwig was such a lovely bird'.

He handed the men their coffee as they squirmed slightly to find the least uncomfortable spot on the couch. Sneiders had another office in town for business meetings, but this was a working environment, not made for long sitting, and watched them struggle to respond to his opening remark.

'Hee! Just a bit of Dutch humour. Of course, it's bad news all round'.

Unimpressed, the first man replied. 'Yeah'.

Bart waited.

'So tell us how one of your birds ends up killing the Vice-President?' He said brusquely, the welcome had not put him at ease, but he also knew the Dutch liked straight talking.

'She didn't. From what I know, a bomb did. What I gather you're asking is why did Hedwig fly at the President and not the transponder?'

Poker-faced nods for Bart to continue.

'The only way that could have happened is for another audio signal, more powerful than the proper signal, was played. That second signal would have had to have been identical to the proper signal, just of a greater amplitude; louder'.

The second man leaned forward. 'What about a visual signal or something else that distracted it, a laser perhaps?'

'Nee. Eurasian eagle owls have excellent sight, but only at short distances. Their primary sense is hearing. It's why we use them for low light operations and Bald eagles or White-tailed eagles for daytime. Whatever the signal is, it must be unique, something not found in nature and something unlikely to be generated by humans without intent'.

'What if the first signal failed, but there was no second signal? Where does the bird go then?'

'What we do here is to tap into the bird's natural instincts and refine them. Much like training a dog to herd sheep. There's no point in using a breed that doesn't have a natural inclination to hunt the animals. Same here. Our techniques wouldn't work on most birds. The *Accipitridae* and *Strigidae* families, eagles and owls, are the best we've found. They are hunters. Superbly agile, they have very strong talons and capable of carrying up to three kilos. In the wild, these birds will catch their prey, and then take it somewhere safe to eat. "Safe" for them is away from other animals and birds preferably a bit sheltered, but that's secondary. We've trained them to believe that wherever the recall signal comes from will be the safest place for them'.

'You didn't answer the question. What if there's no signal?'

'Then they go back to their instincts and find that safe, dark, sheltered place away from people. Not into the light and noise. There must have been a signal. Now, if this had been daylight, it's possible that one of our birds could have mistaken *mijnheer* Trump's hair for a bird's nest'.

This time, a slight smile on Sneiders' face told the two men that he was joking. Inappropriately in their opinion. The first man spoke again. 'You said the signal had to be identical to the recall signal. Isn't it possible that the owl was taught to recognise a second signal?'

'Possible, yes. But Hedwig wasn't. At least not here. When Jean and Tomas were here, she was trained with just the one recall sound precisely to avoid any such confusions'.

'You knew Officers Byrnes and Holgersen then?'

'Of course. We worked together for months training them and the birds as a team. They stayed at *de grote Beer* hostel down the road. It is also possible that *they* trained Hedwig on a second signal. They would have had the expertise by then, but it wasn't done here'.

'What does this signal sound like?'

'Each bird has a different sound. We take the natural sounds birds are attracted to and then digitally distort it so it is unique, but still falls within their auditory spectrum. It is a slow process. In Hedwig's case, we started with the sound of mice running through grass and then changed the sound very slowly on a daily basis until we got the sound we wanted. Then we practice with that for at least a month'.

'And can we hear the sound; can you play it for us?'

'No'.

'Ah… no?'

'No. These sounds are, for reasons you can probably appreciate on this fine wintry morning, proprietary and confidential. All recordings are digital and are kept on drives isolated from the internet. We always distribute by physically transferring a USB stick or hard drive'.

'You know we're the FBI, yes? And that this is a murder inquiry of which we are the chief investigators with complete authority?'

'In your country, yes you are. However, this is the Netherlands. I have been cooperative, but I am not about to violate my own contractual obligations to my client, the US Secret Service. Why don't you ask them for the recording? Far easier I would think'.

Deputy Director Croft answered the call from Rusty Wilkins.

'Where are you, Wilkins?'

'Hartford, Tennessee. Middle of the Blue Ridge Mountains. I drove down here last night with Ross and Holgersen. They're going to be doing some wilderness training for the next week. Well away from people, phones, and radios'.

'Good work. Any other thoughts?'

'Yeah. I was talking to them about their time in Holland, how the bird was trained, that sort of thing. The boss there was a guy called Bart Sneiders, Dutch as they come. But they also told me that the main handler, who fed and cleaned the birds, and bought food for them, was called Rostam Alinejad. He's Iraqi. I've got Customs and Border Protection looking at both of them, but didn't really want to involve Europol or any other domestic agencies for now'.

'Understandable. I talked to Linda yesterday. She said that you could be onto something. Suggested you call Brice Payton at the agency, he was at the meeting a few days back'.

'The agency? NSA?'

'No. CIA. Unofficial so do it quietly. Go for coffee or something. You can say you talked to me, but don't mention Linda. She *is* oversight after all; wouldn't be done for her to be seen getting involved. Drop those names into the conversation and suggest there may be something worth looking at'.

Day Four

December 2, 2016

The Professor put his arms behind him and leant back onto the desk.

'The current tragic assassination of Mr Robbins and wounding of Mr Trump obviously raises a number of interesting questions for us. However, as this is the last class before we wrap up this semester, we don't have time to look into the ramifications in detail. Moreover, next semester looks at these issues in more depth anyway so it behoves us to save the discussion on the ramifications of such an attack until the New Year'.

He looked around the class. Second year constitutional law was a small class, but known for its wide-ranging and sometimes controversial discussions.

'However, it is traditional that we end this first semester with a provocative question that you should formally answer in a paper written over the holidays. Let's throw around a few ideas on the topic today; help you formulate your argument'.

He walked around his desk to write on the white board behind him:

> Are there any circumstances under which it is justifiable to prevent a person from becoming the President even if they win the election?

He turned back to the class. 'Not, you understand, justifying the personal side of the attack, personal injury and death is morally indefensible, but what circumstances can we imagine when the results of the November election should be nullified. And what legal instruments exist to do so? Yes, Lisa?'

The young woman put her hand down. She seemed a little puzzled. 'Surely it's straightforward enough, sir. If the candidate or President-Elect commits any of the acts that are impeachable, then they should not be able to take the oath'.

'And those acts are?'

'Um... treason, bribery, or other "high" crimes?'

'Excellent. Who says a person has committed, for example, treason? Mark'.

'The courts do. I suppose in this case, it'd be the US Supreme Court'.

'Again, text book. But note that simply being found guilty of treason or bribery does not equal impeachment, it merely provides the grounds for such. Who is responsible for the actual impeachment?'

'Er... the Supreme Court?' Even as he said it, Mark knew he was wrong. The professor wouldn't have asked otherwise.

'Nope. It's Congress who decides whether the President should be impeached. Part of your assignment will be to explain why it is Congress and not the Courts. In addition, being found guilty of a criminal offence is not a necessary prerequisite for impeachment. Congress can decide a President, indeed, any elected official, to be unfit for their duties for a number of reasons outside of the criminal. Incidentally, Lisa, the actual term is "high crimes and misdemeanours". Another component of your assignment is to discuss that term

57

and the myriad offences that it covers. Penny; would you like to give us an example of potential grounds for impeachment? Ones that have *not* happened historically, so no Clinton or Nixon, please, but something that could realistically happen under a Trump administration'.

The pretty redhead chosen looked thoughtful for a moment and then replied. 'Putting the country into unreasonable risk?'

'Explain'.

'Well, what if Trump were to *become* a "clear and present danger"? The *Economist* put a Trump Presidency in the top ten risks to global security'.

'Interesting, Penny. To be exact, the *Economist* put his Presidency in the top ten risks to the global *economy* while acknowledging that disruption to the economy has a security element. I'll come back to that phrase "clear and present danger" later as it actually only refers to curtailments to First Amendment Rights, not national security. Leaving that aside for now, can you be a bit more specific as to what you're thinking?'

'Well, suppose Trump made one of his more extravagant remarks and it insulted someone like Putin to the point where nuclear war became likely? Or when he says he'll "bomb the shit out of ISIL", but now he has access to nuclear weapons. Surely starting a nuclear war unnecessarily is grounds for impeachment?'

'Hmmm. It'll be interesting to see how *all* of you answer Penny's question in your papers. Surely it is the *responsibility* of the Commander-in-Chief to use the country's nuclear arsenal if needed? Who has the right to gainsay his judgement?'

'Only Congress has the right to declare war!'

'Yes, Mark. And that's why the USA has not formally declared war since 1941. All other military actions have, it can be argued, circumvented Congress and the Constitution by entering into hostilities, but not formally declaring war. Yet no President has been impeached for such an act. So, Penny. Any other arguments?'

'Trump often seems very angry and spontaneous. Supposing he decided just to launch nuclear weapons because someone annoyed him. Could that be seen as treason? James Madison said that a President who "abused the power of the office" could be "fatal to the Republic", that is, put us all in danger. Such an act would play into the hands of our enemies and thus could be considered providing aid and comfort to the enem; the definition of treason?' She stopped, a little red-faced.

The professor chuckled. 'I like your imagination, but fear you may be conflating at least three different arguments. Still, this is an open discussion and I haven't given any of you time to properly formulate your arguments. Run with that, Penny, I can't wait to see your assignment; there's at least one good point in there!

He continued, addressing the class as a whole. 'Let's suppose that Penny's scenario is not so arbitrary. Imagine a scenario where it is clear to everyone that the Commander in Chief is no longer capable of rational thought. Obviously, that would make him "unfit for his office" and lay the ground for impeachment proceedings. In the meantime, while waiting for Congress to slowly grind forward with its intrigues and formally remove him from office, what stops him from launching those weapons? Yes, Mark?'

'He can issue the orders, but the Army doesn't have to follow them'.

'Even before he has been found legally unfit to issue such orders? Isn't that insubordination tantamount to treason itself? Isn't that a coup?'

'It's not a coup to passively resist. A coup needs active attempts to replace the President with a person chosen by the coup leaders so, no, it isn't a coup. And I'm fairly sure there was a ruling about not following orders that "an ordinary man would know to be illegal". That soldiers aren't obliged to follow illegal orders'.

'Indeed there have been. *U.S. v. Keenan* and *Little v. Barreme* come to mind. The problem we have today is the term "illegal". Is waterboarding illegal? Is Guantanamo? I suggest you all do a Google search for Michael Hayden, the former CIA director who recently – that is, just a few months back – said "if Trump ordered troops to kill the families of terrorists, as he has said he would, the American Armed Forces would refuse to act". What components of the Constitution permit them to refuse the C-in-C? And, in your opinions, do you think an active military commander in the heat of war rather than a retired officer voicing his opinion on a talk show, actually have the gumption to "refuse to act"? Reference section 892 that describes the penalties for disobeying such an order and ask yourselves, "Would I be willing to take the risk? Do I really believe that my judgement is better than the President's?" Anyway, that'll do for now, have a wonderful holiday, people. See you in January'.

As Penny packed up her books, Lee-Ann whispered to her. 'All of that was for a *sitting* President. Trump isn't. Not yet. Maybe that CIA guy just doesn't want to be put into that position in the first place. Wouldn't be the first assassination the CIA's done!'

Republican National Committee, Washington

Congressman Francisco Duarte, Chairperson of the Republican National Committee, was looking tired. And with reason. Even before Robbins' death he'd had a lot of work to do; there was revolution in the air in the Republican Party.

Typically, Senate and Congressional elections in a presidential year favour the party that wins the Presidency. If 2016 had been like any other year, the Republicans should have consolidated their grip on both Houses. As it was, the party lost nineteen seats in the House of Representatives and six seats in the Senate. That meant twenty-five people, many of them friends with Francisco, were out of jobs and very, very unhappy. Francisco, by being part of the "Let's Unite Behind Our Candidate" movement was seen as being partly responsible for those job losses.

Added to that was the disaster of losing six Senate seats. Now, the Democrats had taken the Senate back from the Republicans with a slim majority. This was going to make things even harder for a Trump presidency; with a less divisive figure as President, compromises on some issues may have been possible. Now it would be payback for all the times the Republicans had blocked Obama's initiatives. Any chance Trump's more bizarre or controversial plans had of actually being implemented had gone out the window. *This is going to be a four-year train wreck for the Party,* he thought to himself. *It'll take decades to recover, and there'll be more jobs lost at the mid-terms.*

The process that led to Trump's nomination as the Republican candidate had exposed deep rifts in the GOP leaving much rancour, and had taken months in the first place. Now Francisco had to duplicate that process for Trump's running mate, and possibly Trump himself, in just a few short days.

For the past forty-eight hours, he had got little sleep. He'd called people across the country, attended breakfast meetings, even pre-breakfast meetings and working late over dinner and post-dinner drinks, trying to get the RNC to reach a consensus on a Vice-Presidential candidate. And then convince that someone to accept the nomination.

His constant companion over the hours had been the Co-Chairperson of the RNC, Dina Accardo. Dina had never liked Trump. She had been outspoken on #NeverTrump earlier, but was now working as hard as Duarte was for which he was very grateful.

As each day ticked away, the chances of mistakes or even defection on the part of the Electors grew. The Electors were morally, and in some cases legally, bound to cast a majority vote for Trump.

Although there had been faithless Electors before, no overall College vote had ever returned a result different from that expected by the number of States won in November. That wasn't quite the same as winning the popular vote as the number of voters each Elector represented was not equal across the country. That scenario has happened four times, most recently when Bush won in 2000 with half-a-million less votes than Gore.

The danger this time round, at least from a Republican perspective, is the possibility that Tim Kaine, the Democrat's nominee for V-P snuck in the back door and won the nomination due to Elector confusion or faithless voting. *Which could happen,* Duarte thought. *The Constitution and the law are ambiguous on what happens now. We may even have to put someone else on the ballot in case Trump dies after the College such that Congress has a Republican option when they count in January. All very confusing; it feels like we're gambling with the highest office in the land and I'm the one rolling the dice.*

'Good evening America, and welcome to this special edition of *Current Affairs*. America, and Americans, are struggling to come to terms with yet another cowardly terrorist attack on our country and our leaders. Our prayers are for a full recovery of President-Elect Donald Trump and for the families of Mr Trump, Mr Robbins and Amelie Johnson, the Secret Service Agent who died protecting Mr Trump in their time of sadness'.

'America is also struggling with what this means for our country. President Obama is, of course, still our President and will remain so until January, but what then? To help us answer this question, we are pleased and privileged to have with us on the show tonight some very distinguished and expert panellists'.

In the control room the producer was directing the show, issuing instructions to the camera crews and occasionally talking to the moderator via her ear piece. *'Camera two, slow pan right and medium zoom as she introduces each guest. Camera one, keep full desk in view'.*

'On my right, we have Daniel MacQueen professor emeritus of law at Harvard. To his right is constitutional expert and author of many books including "Storms on the Horizon: Unknown weaknesses in the US Constitution", Klemens Attwood. Welcome gentlemen'.

'And to my left, we have retired Associate Justice of the Supreme Court, Ruperto Sarto and Antonia Halloran, former political analyst with the Democratic National Committee. Welcome to both of you as well'.

'Get me a camera to stay on Antonia Halloran, I'll ask for frequent cuts to her even when the others are speaking. Three men, one woman and no minorities, what were the execs thinking? At least we got Lisa as moderator'.

'Let me start at the beginning with Klemens Attwood. Klemens, can we just be clear on a few things as they stand right now. Barack Obama *is* still the President at the moment. At what time does he stop being President and when does Mr Trump become the President-Elect? Is he now?'

'Well, Lisa, first, thanks for inviting us all here today, a fascinating subject as I've noted in many of my books…'

'Oh, Christ, a self-serving plug within the first minute, someone talk to that jerk at the next break and tell Lisa to limit her questions to him until we can have that word. Self-centred prick…'

'…to answer your question, yes, Mr Obama is still the President and will, barring any unforeseen tragedy, remain so until noon on January 20th. The Twentieth Amendment is very clear on that point. What is less clear is who succeeds him and that, as you quite rightly asked, revolves very much around *when* the President-Elect becomes the President-Elect'.

'But didn't Mr Trump become the President-Elect when he won the election?'

'Not exactly, Lisa, as he didn't win the election'.

'What? Can you explain, Klemens?'

'Of course. At the election, five hundred and thirty-eight Electors "won" the election if you want to use that term. Only when *those* people cast their votes at the Electoral College on December twentieth, can we say that someone is the President, or for that matter the Vice-President, elect'.

Antonia looks like she wants to interject, Lisa.

'Okay. We'll get back to the V-P position in a second. Antonia Halloran?'

'While it is clear that no one is formally the President-Elect before the College, it isn't clear on what date they *do* become President-Elect. It has been argued that this happens once the College has voted, that is on December nineteenth, but others have argued that it doesn't happen until Congress opens the votes, counts them, and publicly announces the winner'.

'And when does that happen?'

'January sixth'.

'Isn't this just semantics? Surely it doesn't matter when he is declared the President-Elect? Yes, Daniel MacQueen?'

'Thank you, Lisa. And may I say it's a privilege to be here on this momentous occasion…'

'Oh, no… a pontificator. Lisa, be prepared to cut him off if needed'

'…but no, it isn't semantics. Firstly, it is a matter of principled authority. The 115th Congress will be sworn in on January third with forty or so new members plus the incumbents that were elected or re-elected on November eighth. The first major order of business after the swearing in is to count the College votes and subsequently announce the next President of the United States. In this way the new Congress "crowns", if you like, the President thus accepting their own authority and responsibility by announcing that this person will be *their* President. If Mr Trump, or whomever, were to be considered *de facto* President-Elect ahead of the formation of the new Congress, it could open the possibility of the new Congress saying that *they* didn't vote for that President'.

'But, they didn't! Sorry, Lisa'.

'No, no, go ahead Judge'.

'So in that sense, while it may make Senators and Congresspeople feel empowered, it doesn't actually change anything from a factual point of view'.

'So you're disagreeing with Daniel?'

'Not at all. Daniel's absolutely correct in the facts, but, in my humble opinion, the emphasis is in the wrong place. It isn't that important for Congress to feel important; it *is* important, however, to know the exact date when someone becomes President-Elect for the impact it can have if something happens to them, as it has'.

'Perhaps you can expand on that, Ruperto?'

'Certainly. Section three of the Twentieth Amendment says that if the President-Elect dies before his term begins, the Vice-Elect becomes President on the twentieth of January. But if this person, in this case Mr Trump, were to die *before* he is officially the President-Elect then the Vice-Elect only becomes a temporary President "until a President is chosen"'.

'And how is that done?'

'The Amendment isn't exactly clear on that point, but if I were still on the Supreme Court and were asked for my interpretation I would say that the Twentieth gives Congress the power to choose a President. That's why the date of becoming the President-Elect is so important; it determines which Congress, the old or the new, chooses our next President'.

'Klemens wants to jump in, but go to Antonia Halloran first'.

'Seriously? Congress can choose anyone they want as President in some circumstances? Regardless of the popular vote in November? Antonia, would you like to comment on that or what Daniel said?'

'A quick aside first; the November election is *not* the same as the popular vote. Different Electors represent different numbers of voters. For example, in the election just past each New York Elector represents about five hundred and twenty thousand votes. In Wyoming, the number is just over one hundred and forty thousand – not exactly equitable!

'But we have another issue here as well…' Antonia continued, '…not just the date. For the sake of argument, let's say that the President-Elect becomes official on January sixth after the new Congress has counted the College votes'.

'Okay'.

'Well, what if no one gets a majority – two hundred and seventy votes – when Congress counts?'

'How could that happen? There are only two candidates, surely one of them has to get a majority?'

'Let's not forget, there *is* a third candidate, Johnson, who ran as an independent'.

'But he didn't win any States'.

'Doesn't matter, the system allows, sometimes even compels, some Electors to vote for Johnson. Even without Johnson there are many other ways in which no one gets a clear majority. Especially in a tight race such as this one. According to the November election we expect Donald Trump to receive two hundred and eighty-two Electoral College votes, a clear majority. But maybe not all of those Electors will vote according to what they have said, or in accordance with the popular vote'.

'Wait a second, don't they have to vote that way?'

'Well, they're supposed to, but the penalties for not doing so – they're called "Faithless Electors" by the way – are relatively minor; a small fine, potentially expulsion from the party, that sort of thing'.

'Surely no one would do that?'

'Not only would they, they have. There have been a number of faithless electors over the years none of which changed the overall winner, but it has happened. There can also be spoiled votes: even one transposed letter when writing the candidate's name could spoil a ballot. That has also happened before'.

'But spoiled ballots don't count for the other person, so how would that help them get a majority?'

'It's up to Congress to decide if spoiled ballots count in the total. Right now, a candidate needs two hundred and seventy votes out of five hundred and thirty-eight to get a majority. If eight Trump electors were "faithless", then he would still have a majority of two hundred and seventy-four votes. But if another five electors spoiled their ballots, accidentally or not, then he would only have two hundred and sixty nine out of five hundred and thirty-eight votes; not a majority.

'But… Congress can decide at the time of counting, to include or not include spoiled ballots in the total count. There is precedent for that as well. In this case the official number of votes cast would be five hundred and thirty-eight less five or five hundred and thirty-three. And two hundred and sixty-nine *is* a majority of that total'.

'Phew. Anyone want to add to that? Yes, Klemens Attwood?'

'Antonia is right on the money, but there can even be more scenarios'.

'More? It's starting to sound amazing that anyone can get elected! Go ahead, give us another scenario'.

'Assume there are no faithless electors and no spoiled ballots. Mr Trump has two hundred and eighty-two votes. What if, God forbid, he doesn't recover? What if he dies after the College, but before the count? As Ruperto said, this hinges on Congress' determination of when a person becomes the President-Elect.

'It *also* depends on whether his votes are counted as "spoiled" or not. If they are, then the only votes deemed to be cast would be the ones cast by Democrats and *their* candidate would have received one hundred percent of them; a definite majority! With the House still in Republican hands, but the Senate now controlled by the Democrats, watch for sparks to fly and a possible major constitutional crisis'.

'Mind if I jump in? Thanks. The Twelfth amendment clearly states that *all* ballots must be counted, even if the candidate is dead. The House committee on the Twentieth Amendment upheld that'.

'But that was just a Committee reporting before the amendment was ratified; it's never been tested'.

'If I can remind everyone, this isn't wholly virgin territory. The Continuity of Government Commission back in 2003, envisaged exactly this scenario. They criticised the current laws for not having a provision for when the President is wounded and the Vice President killed'.

'But that criticism doesn't hold here, Klemens. The Commission's scenario was for a *sitting* President, not a President-Elect'.

'And the Line of Succession would surely kick in if the President was incapable, temporarily or permanently, from performing his office. The Speaker of the House would resign that position and become President'.

'But we're not talking about a *President*. We're not even sure we're talking about a President-*Elect* yet'.

'Break it up, Lisa'.

'Okay, okay. Let's hold those thoughts for a while. What about the Vice-President? Mr Robbins is dead and the Electors still haven't cast their ballots. So who will they vote for now? Daniel?'

'While it may seem absurd, many Electors are bound by State laws to vote for Mr Robbins even if he is dead. I can only assume that the Republican Party is lobbying as we speak for a new candidate to rally behind, and then try to convince those Electors who are bound to vote for Mr Robbins to vote for the new candidate'.

'Wouldn't that make them faithless?'

'Indeed, but isn't that better than spoiling their ballot?'

'Some of those States automatically invalidate any vote that isn't cast as pledged so for some Electors, it doesn't really matter what they do, either they vote for someone who isn't with us anymore or their vote is discarded'.

'There's an ironic aside here'.

'Yes, Daniel?'

'Remember what Mr Trump said in January? He said, "I could stand in the middle of Fifth Avenue and shoot somebody, and I wouldn't lose any voters." And now, here he is, having been "shot" by an owl very close to the middle of Fifth Avenue and it still won't affect any of the College votes"'.

'Ah... no, it's good; laugh – I think that's our soundbite for the evening! Bit of intellectual humour'.

Lisa laughed as instructed by the voice in her ear. 'You're right, Daniel. That is ironic. Back to more serious matters, though. Ruperto? You look as if you want to add something to what we were just talking about'.

'The Twelfth Amendment tells us that in the event that the Electoral College vote is indecisive, the House of Representatives gets to choose the President while the Senate gets to choose the Vice-President'.

'Thanks for that. Antonia Halloran? Thoughts? What's the likely outcome?'

'The Twelfth also says that the House must choose from the three presidential candidates who won the most Electoral votes and the Senate must choose from the top two Vice-Presidential candidates. Right now, if all the Republican Electors vote for Mr Robbins, then there would only *be* two Vice-Presidential candidates and one of them is dead. That would mean that the Senate would have to choose the Democratic candidate...'

Chuckles all around the panel.

'...which, of course, they would anyway, as the Democrats are in charge of the Senate. There is no doubt that the Republicans will get at least one Elector, probably a non-bound one, to cast their vote for someone else completely, just to get an alternative into the mix that the Senate could vote for on January 6ᵗʰ in the event that the College vote is inconclusive'.

'Wow. And would that person have to be someone who had been a candidate for the nomination?'

'Not at all, Lisa, they could choose you if they wanted'.

Everyone laughed.

'I can't see that happening! Anything else?'

'This means that the Democrats are in the driver's seat for the V-P, but the Presidency is still Trump's. Unless he dies and then, as we've heard, things get quite complicated. I wouldn't be surprised if the Democrats sacrificed a few of their votes and got one of their Electors to vote for a new candidate instead of Clinton just to ensure that an alternative is in the Presidential mix. Then it becomes a game of poker with each party trying to decide how many votes to sacrifice from their main candidate to new candidates on the off chance they can position themselves as numbers one, two and three if Trump dies after the College'.

'Quite cold-hearted'.

'That's politics, Lisa'.

'And doesn't that open the possibility of a Republican President and a Democratic Vice?'

Cut to Klemens Attwood.

'Exactly, Lisa. And the 2003 Continuity Commission also highlighted that as another weakness in our system'.

'And during all of this fascinating discussion, I haven't heard a lot about the right for the American people to choose'.

'Spot on the money again. Other than telling the College what their *preferences* are for the New President and Vice-President, the American people have little input into the process. If their preferences are unavailable, as is the tragic situation with Mr Robbins, the people's preferences don't even get a look-in'.

'Sounds like we're going to have to do another show on what "Democracy" means in the United States of America in the Twenty-First Century! My thanks to our panel tonight and… as for who will be our next President and Vice-President, I guess we all have to wait until January 20ᵗʰ to be sure. Goodnight, everyone'.

And… we're closed. Well done, Lisa, good show, not the most engaging of topics, but I think you were able to tease out some controversial issues. At the very least you managed to confuse the beejesus out of me; who is the President?

Rusty Wilkins had been busy. He'd called Brice Payton who had been perfectly happy to meet for coffee. Which they did. It was a waste of time; Brice was the sort of person who could speak for hours, amusingly, intelligently, yet somehow without revealing anything of substance. Brice did give Rusty a telephone number for Morna MacCallum's and told him that she was staying at the Westin near Grand Central, but Rusty could have got that from Ian Croft.

Rusty called Morna anyway and heard a longer version of the "29-November, second 9/11" story complete with a number of technical details. He found this professionally interesting, but not overly relevant.

He called Jean Byrnes and Tomas Holgersen and was relieved to hear that the numbers were still "out of service range".

Staying on the phone, he contacted a friend at Border Control, and asked him to keep an eye out for a 'Rostam Alinejad'. Yes, this was official and could be done openly. In return, his friend, well aware of Rusty's connections to the attack on the twenty-ninth, told him that the FBI had a photo of a subject they were also keeping an eye out for, could this be Rostam Alinejad? Unlikely Rusty told his friend, but asked for a copy of the photograph to be sent to him anyway. And could he keep Rusty informed of any other FBI requests? No need to bother them with this Alinejad thing for now.

Leaving the most difficult one until last, he went down the hall to the elevators to see Major Murray Allard.

'Ah, good morning, Agent Wilkins!'

In a jovial mood this morning, Rusty thought, *can't be a good thing.*

There wasn't a lot of small talk; there rarely was between the two. Within a few minutes they were talking business. Rusty started with a quick update.

'We've isolated Agents Byrnes and Holgersen for now until we have a better understanding of what happened and we're getting somewhere on that. The owl was trained by an Iraqi, name of Rostam Alinejad'.

'What? I thought it was trained in Holland?'

'The company is in Holland and the owner, Bart Sneiders, is Dutch. We're doing additional background on him, but he looks clean. However he doesn't do a lot of hands-on work; the actual trainer was this Iraqi. The FBI don't even know about him. He recently spent time in Saudi Arabia. He left Holland last month, whereabouts unknown.

'I've got Border Protection looking to see if he's ever been here. And', leaving the best till last and using the royal "we", 'we've found the "shooter". Middle-eastern male, early twenties.

Looks like he initiated the drone, then waited for this Alinejad-trained owl to recognise it and fly it over to Robbins. Job done, he then killed himself, leaving a note about "dangerous men cleaning up". I'm sure you'll get the details from NYPD in a day or two'.

'Hmm. Well that fits with what Ian told me about a Jihadist connection. My guess is that Linda has access to some info that can't be made official that supports that. I'll talk to Allard, the Deputy Commissioner of Counterterrorism. OCT should have someone on this investigation. At the very least let's get JTTF involved'.

Day Five

December 3, 2016

Even law enforcement officers take a few weekends off. This Saturday was not one of those.

Martin King had enjoyed a rare Saturday lie-in. His wife had taken the children Christmas shopping and would probably treat them to lunch. The two teenagers were growing up fast. *Won't be too many more Christmases with them both living at home,* Martin thought a little sadly to himself.

He got up, pulling on his "weekend uniform" of track pants, t-shirt and sweat shirt and an old dressing gown on top. He brushed his teeth, used the toilet, but didn't bother to shave. Then, slippers slap-slapping on the floor, wandered into the kitchen where the low morning sun streamed in. He put coffee and water in a slightly battered macchinetta and put it on the stove. He'd had the coffee maker since his college days, and it only got used on mornings like this.

Martin pulled a stool up to the kitchen aisle, clutching a cup and a plate with toast liberally slathered with peanut butter. The *Times* was on the counter a few sections having been looked at perfunctorily by someone, but otherwise untouched. He loved being the first one to pull the sections apart, and the first to read about whatever was new in the world. He rarely had the luxury. *It's the little things that make life worth it.*

He smiled and hummed a Bowie tune to himself. He was terrible at remembering exact words, but the sentiment was clear enough

> Gettin' out of bed
> Scratched my beard
> Scratched my head
> Coffee in the pot
> Wood on the fire
> Gettin' breakfast while it's hot

Then he remembered the second verse and his smile slipped away.

> Through the window, out of thin air
> Into my head, the nightmare
> Four horsemen of the apocalypse
> As my reality slips
> Away

His work mobile rang.

The call was from his boss, Emery McKinley, saying that it was *advisable* if Martin worked with counterterrorism on the Robbins-Trump case.

There had been some sort of factional in-fighting between Murray Allard, Deputy Commissioner of the Office of Counter Terrorism and Assistant Chief Ross Benbow of the Joint Terrorism Task Force. "What else is new?" Martin's boss had sighed. OCT, as part of Homeland Security, reported to the NY State Governor. JTTF reported to the NY City Police Commissioner.

There was constant fighting between the two lines of command. Emery had done a good job imitating Allard's fussy tone: "someone from OCT or a sub-division, thereof", (probably meaning the New York Intelligence Fusion Center), "be assigned to the investigation". Benbow didn't agree.

Normally these spats ended in stalemate and compromise. This time Benbow called his FBI counterpart, Rafi Mantos; the "Joint" part of JTTF meant NYPD & FBI. Rafi, as lead investigator, had agreed that "OCT's request had merit"; it would be good to have an intelligence and/or terrorism background with local knowledge assigned to the case. He had then promptly asked Benbow if he knew anyone who fit that bill. Benbow suggested Captain Siobhan Niven. She'd been seconded to the JTTF some years back from the Fusion Center.

Niven's paycheques were still signed by Murray Allard. On paper, this meant that Allard's request had been met. In reality Siobhan had been part of JTTF so long that she was considered part of NYPD now.

'So, Martin, if you would be kind enough to brief Captain Niven and bring her up to speed *today*, I'll get the paperwork over to Rafi. Allard needn't be informed until Monday when it would be a *fait accompli*. And I do hope you appreciate all the work we're doing to shelter you from the politics and media attention so you can focus on the case?'

Martin was not sure how much of the last bit was sarcastic – it was so convoluted, he felt a headache coming on. There were only two things the call made clear to him. One, his decision to put off further promotion as long as possible was the right call, and, two he had to go into the office on a Saturday.

I'm getting too old to still be working every weekend. He thought of another David Bowie song as he unlocked his car, feeling tired even before the day began.

> Sure times can change me
> Sure wish I could change time

Kasia Pasternak didn't have to leave Brooklyn as Martin did, but she was still working. Following up on a lead from missing persons, she would spend an emotional hour with the parents of the young man found dead in an office.

Eugene Marchetti was also working. He was doing a final check of the crime scene at 630 Fifth Ave with officers from NYPD CSU. Afterwards, he went to the NYPD Forensics lab (FIU) to find them in a foul mood. FIU officers had just finished carefully unpacking and cataloguing the deceased's clothes when they got an urgent call; the FBI CSI unit was supposed to be the one that did the forensics on this case. The FIU officers had then spent another couple of hours carefully repacking and couriering the clothes to Washington. They had just finished that job when Gene walked in wanting to know how far they'd got with CCTV and other video.

Contrary to many crimes, this one suffered from a surfeit of video evidence. Hundreds of responsible citizens had sent in videos and photos from their smart phones. Practically every shop in the area had CCTV cameras, and there were a fair number of NYPD street cameras as well. There was also footage from the television station covering the event.

Sorting through all of this had meant some overnighters by FIU staff; it was understandable that they would be somewhat irritable on this Saturday afternoon. However, their diligence had resulted in a positive identification of the drone in a number of shots and, crucially, determined that the drone had *not* been on the roof at the time of the last Secret Service sweep.

The discovery of the body drastically narrowed their search. FIU had tentatively identified a young male, same description, same clothes, carrying a black backpack entering the ground floor of 630 Fifth Avenue at 17:26 on Tuesday, November 29th. *That's our boy,* Eugene thought, watching the snippets of footage that had been strung together, catching glimpses of the man walking from the Rockefeller Centre Subway exit to Fifth.

Eugene called Martin to come upstairs and take a look.

In Washington, an FBI agent with CSI had come in early to finish up his report on the findings of the drone, the explosive device and the explosives used. This would be emailed to Rafi Matos and Ivan Biskup by noon at which point, the agent planned on going home and having a nap before meeting up with some friends for dinner.

Not far away from CSI, the ATF's National Tracing Centre (NTC) was quiet. Having determined that the gun was not in their databases, they were dependent on the gun manufacturer supplying the names of the distributors or retailers who could have handled the weapon. The manufacturer was closed over the weekend so the NTC team were the lucky ones who got to take the day off.

A brief five minute walk southwest from the Republican Capitol Hill Club is the National Democratic Club. Whereas the Capitol Hill Club shouts old money, the Democratic Club is far less salubrious from the outside. It's a relatively modern building attached to the Democrat's party headquarters. The front looks out onto a parking lot and commuter trains rattle past the rear of the club at all times of the day. Inside, however, it is just as opulent as its opposite number.

In a room on the second floor room, rain hammered at the windows, but made no sound thanks to the double glazing that had been installed a few years back. The room was warm, heated by a log fire that occasionally crackled and spat; the wood hadn't been seasoned quite enough.

Three men and three women relaxed in high backed chairs upholstered in cream with light striping. All had drinks, but only two of them had opted for alcohol at this time of the afternoon, even on a Saturday. One man had bourbon on the rocks while another sipped Frangelico with his coffee. The six had pulled theirs chairs closer together ignoring the small conference table. This could have been to take advantage of the heat from the log fire, or so they could talk softly, or both.

One of the women asked, 'Whatd'ya think, Frank?'

'Francisco will be shitting himself', the large man with the bourbon answered. 'He's got sixteen days to find a replacement for Mason that the rest of them will back and that's willing to work with The Donald. *Then* convince the Electors to vote for them'.

'That won't be too hard will it?'

'Not if they're smart. He'll look for someone more moderate, more mainstream, like Romney, Paul or even Rubio. Then and the Electors will be happy to break the faith. But if they pick the wrong person…'

'…it opens a door?' Finished a second man; the one drinking tea, not coffee.

'Exactly. If their Electors split, then it could be a three-way vote come January with none of them getting a majority. Then we get to pick which one of 'em gets the job, now we control the Senate again'.

'Hallelujah'.

The third man chimed in: 'I've got some people beginning to whisper in the ears of some of the less convinced electors. A few, maybe even enough, may be convinced that the only way to stop Trump "Breaking America Bad Again" is to pair him with a Democratic Veep. It's a tough sell, but Donald didn't sweep the Electors as much as he did the voters'.

The woman closest to the fire and with her back to the rain-lashed window said, 'And there's always the issue about the votes for Robbins. Some of the bound Electors will vote for him regardless. Question is, will they be counted in the final tally? Maybe our guy will get that majority anyway'.

'Again, depends, depends, depends… there's still a lot of bargaining room. More importantly, what do we do about the Presidency?'

'You mean, if Trump doesn't make it?'

'No', said Frangelico-man, 'he means should we make sure Trump doesn't make it?' He smiled, but some of the others weren't sure how much he meant it.

'Don't even joke about that!' One of the women said.

'Okay, okay', he laughed softly. 'But what if He's listening to our prayers and divine providence has it that Dear Donald kicks it before the Count? There's no point in planning for anything after the Count, that's straight Line of Succession stuff, but before? We'd be fools not to at least have a plan in place. Sid, can you get those whisperers of yours to work on an alternative for the Electors if Trump isn't available in two weeks' time? Or even if he's still not *compos mentis*? Yeah, yeah, "how could we tell?" That joke's too easy'.

'Maybe we can start a back door campaign suggesting he does have real brain damage? Get a few doctors on some daytime television shows, a couple of online rumours? The rank-and-file may not like it, but it wouldn't take too many Electors to switch sides to give us the majority'.

'Possible, sure. What if they do vote for him, but he isn't around on the sixth? That might be our better chance. The House has to vote for us in that case.'

'The GOP would have already figured that out even before that TV show. Let's assume that they get at least one Elector to vote for… I dunno, maybe Romney again or Cruz or even Bloomberg; maybe he could be convinced to come in via the back door? Anyway, assume they put someone else in play in case Trump dies'.

'And?'

'And that means if we had *two* people who both got more votes than their second guy, then we would have top votes one, two and three. One's a definite; Hilary's always gonna have more votes than anyone else if Trump's out of the picture. If we gave two more people with more College votes than a Republican, we're home free'.

'So we convince some of *our* Electors to go faithless? Not vote for Hilary? She won't like that'.

'She won't have to know. Think about it. If Trump lives Hilary's votes mean nothing. If Trump dies and the GOP put someone else in play, they have the House which means they're gonna vote for their guy. Once again, Hilary's votes mean nothing. Either way her votes are useless. So we may as well do something useful with them. They can't afford to take more than what? Half-a-dozen votes away from Trump without taking too much of a risk of him not getting a majority due to unplanned defectors or spoiled ballots? Assume they do go for six.

That means all we have to do is get fourteen, seven and seven, Electors to vote for two alternate Democrats and the House has no choice but to pick one of ours. Make it ten and ten to be safe'.

'And if Congress decides to throw out the Trump votes?'

'Easy. That means there will be a total tally of two hundred and fifty-six ballots of which Hilary would still have two hundred and thirty-six; safe as houses'.

'Unless they have a mini-revolution down the road, and decide that Trump simply isn't going to be presidential material even if he lives. It's not such a long shot that someone who gets hit in the head by an exploding owl and ends up in a coma may not come out of that coma in one piece'.

'Mmmm. If that decision was made, how'd they play it?'

'No use changing votes from the States that have laws invalidating anything that isn't Trump. How many's that anyway? No one? Well, let's say it's about ninety ballots; it's somewhere around there. That gives them a hundred and ninety-two to play with, definitely enough to get their guy into the top three no matter what we do. Then the House picks that person regardless of mind how many Hilary has. Fact is, I think they'd be smart to do that anyway. No one gets a majority and if Trump is back on his feet by January, they can still pick him'.

'And if those votes are thrown out? Hilary would win. Would they gamble on keeping those votes in?'

'Well, we have some precedents, Gore and Bush in 2000, but that didn't go anywhere. More dramatic was 1876 when twenty votes for Tilden were awarded to Hayes, but 1872's the one to read up on. Greeley won the election, but died before the College. Some Electors still voted for him whole most switched to…ah, Hendricks and, um… Brown, I think, plus a couple of others. Tellingly, the Greeley votes were discarded as spoiled, but the so-called faithless votes for Hendricks and the others counted. Didn't matter, of course, Grant won by a landslide. Since then, we've had the Twentieth Amendment which almost, not a hundred percent, but almost, says that the votes would have to stay in. If I was them, I'd take the gamble'.

'It'll be a Committee decision, not just one gamblin'' Southern Gennelmun, Frank. And Committees always play safe. I don't think they'd do it'. There's a lot of potential fall out; we'll survive if twenty of our Electors go against the popular vote especially if we end up winning. But would the Republicans survive if they gave the 'Muricun peepul the finger to the voters by having the majority of their Electors ignoring popular vote?'

The woman who had been quietest then said, 'And would our Democratic system survive? It is possible, ladies and gentlemen, that a major deviation from tradition – even if legal, even if our system allows these things to happen – a major deviation from two hundred years of history… there's been an increasing ground swell about distrust in our systems recently: "Black Lives Matter", "Occupy Wall Street and the 99%"… I'm not sure how the public would react if we were to give them a full-on, cold-water wake-up call telling them that their votes actually have no legal value… It sounds a bit like the boy who said "the Emperor has no clothes". If I remember my fables correctly, that led to the downfall of the Empire'.

A minute's silence punctuated only by sips at drinks and the crackle of the fire.

'Still, it's not us that would make that decision, it's them across the road. We just need to be prepared for any eventuality including that one. Keep up the whispers and let's put two people into play as presidential candidates. There's still a chance we can put a Democrat in the White House'.

'And who might you be thinking of for those people, Frank?'

'Well, now, I'm glad you asked…'

The room was dim lit only by the fire and some grey light filtering through the window as the sun set. No one had turned on any lights, but the man and woman who were left in the room knew each other well enough to talk without seeing each other.

'Do you think we, I mean the Democratic Party, may have had something to do with the attack? Even if they hadn't thought the whole thing out there's a lot of angry people out there. Angry that Trump has "subverted" the political process by out and out lies, by pandering to emotion beyond what's right?'

'I think… I don't know what to think. It's possible that some people saw political advantages fast enough to put all this together in a couple of days. It's possible someone made a plan years ago, and just blew the dust off it, but it's also possible that Trump made a few people angry enough for them to go that far. There's a lot on the table, and politics can be very dirty'.

The fire continued to spit and snarl even after they left the room.

The conversation in French was made over Skype, rerouted via various VPNs and deliberately distorted. Not enough to arouse suspicion or impede comprehension, but enough to create another hurdle for anyone trying to identify the voices.

The call was monitored of course, as all calls are, but the computers did not alert their human overseers - neither Skype address was on a watch list and no trigger words or phrases were used. The call passed into the ether unnoticed the precautions unnecessary… this time.

'It's me'.

'About time, Black'.

'*Mister* Black thank you, Mister Orange. I wanted to see how the dust settled before calling'.

'Well, it's settled. And it looks like a major balls-up'.

'Let's remember that the plan wasn't all mine. Against my best wishes *you* wanted operational input…'

'…which, for a large sum of money, *you* decided to accept…'

'…and made the job unnecessarily complicated'.

'We can argue all day about how we got here, we're more interested in where we go now'.

'There is another option. It'll cost'.

'Of course it'll cost. When hasn't one of your plans… never mind. Let's talk terms'.

A third voice entered the conversation. 'Perhaps we should reconsider? It's been very… traumatic… perhaps we've done enough to accomplish our goals?'

'And perhaps we haven't, Mister White. Then people will have been… affected… for nothing. Far better to finish what you start'.

'But…'

'No, Mister White, I agree with Mister Black. We agreed on this so let's finish it'.

A fourth voice, previously quiet. 'I don't care how it costs. That bastard has cost me big time. So what about those terms?'

'Later. This call's gone on long enough'.

Day Six
December 4, 2016

Three men and two women sat at a table by a window, looking at pedestrians ducking their heads against sleet, swept by the wind, insinuating itself through every gap it could find. Inside the wine bar, however, it was warm and inviting. It wasn't a large place and only a third full on this blustery Sunday afternoon.

The décor was eclectic-modern, a chandelier of coloured glass globes and small oil portraits meshed with heavy, dark wood furniture. Although the sun was going down – it was almost the shortest day of the year – the bar was bright and well lit; the manager would turn the lights down and put candles out later for a more intimate feel when a jazz trio started playing.

The restaurant was known for its oysters so the foursome had ordered a couple of dozen that sat on ice in the middle of the table. While Ivan and Martin had decided to wash their oysters down traditionally with Brooklyn Black Chocolate Stout, Kasia had opted for a New Zealand Marlborough Pinot Noir. Siobhan Niven, the new member of the group, had gone for a popular Blue Moon *witbier*. Bill Ngo was on soda water, with a slice of lime, just to make it a little fancy…

It was, deliberately, a little out of the way for all of them. No one would be looking for them here and the chances of running into any acquaintances or colleagues very remote.

Perhaps a little too far out of the way for Bill who lived out of the City. He hadn't minded, however, he *did* need to look at one or two shops pre-Christmas and it wasn't too far by train. People who didn't know him may have speculated about "trouble at home"; it was a big chunk of time out of a weekend, but he seemed to genuinely not mind and wanted to help. Truth be told, he was finding it a little exciting to be in on an investigation so early on rather than just being given a ton of paperwork and told to "get a conviction".

After the intense workload of the past five days, each of them felt the need to step back, to try and see the forest not just the trees. And each of them felt there was something odd with the investigation, something they couldn't put their finger on, like a word that temporarily slips your mind.

Martin was the first to start the serious conversation after the business of ordering food and drinks and general greetings was out the way.

'I thought it might be a good idea to have a weekly "bull-session". Make sure everyone's up to date on the details. A time to look at the big picture. So… meeting outside the office, let our hair down…', a smile from Kasia at that as she looked at Martin's mostly bald head, '…and throw out ideas, even the oddball ones. As for meeting away from our offices… call it a gut thing; I've got this weird little feeling that something's not quite right, I want your input on this as well, but, well…'

He looked down at the table in thought for a few seconds before looking up, this time with his no-nonsense professional face back. 'Obviously we can't discuss sensitive details in public, but…' he looked around. The tables closest to theirs were empty.

'Siobhan', he nodded at the redhead, 'has been shadowing the investigation up to now, but, as of yesterday, is officially part of the team. And with last night's announcement, perfect timing. Perhaps you can lead off?'

Siobhan took up the conversation. 'As you all know late last night, early in the morning in the Middle East, ISIL claimed credit for the attack on Robbins and Trump. I had a chat with the NY Intelligence Centre a couple of hours back and we're not convinced about their claim; the usual pattern isn't in the communique or in the attack itself. I'm going to meet Sharmila tomorrow morning to see if the FBI has any opinions if that's okay with you, Ivan?'

'Oh, sure. No worries there'.

'We're continuing to evaluate, and hopefully some of our overseas assets can help us assign a likelihood, but for now I'd treat this as a low probability'.

'Doesn't help us with the public, though', mused Martin. 'New Yorkers are a little paranoid when it comes to being targeted by terrorists. Definitely going to be more pressure on us to solve this one quickly'.

Bill leant forward, 'Hang on a sec. I'd like to revisit that "low probability", Siobhan. Alden called me yesterday, and US States Attorney's don't call on Saturdays just to chat, he thinks there is "substance" in the idea that the true criminals are foreigners'.

Ivan slurped an oyster and washed it down with a mouthful of stout. 'Interesting. Rafi suggested the same thing on Thursday. Said Murray Allard had a source'.

'Mmmm', Martin interjected. 'NY Intelligence Centre reports to Allard, right?' Siobhan nodded. 'But they said they didn't think it likely'. Again, Siobhan nodded. 'So…' Martin had his thinking face on again, '…if Allard thinks there is something to it, it's not coming from his own analysis team'.

Ivan jumped in. 'You saw who was at the meeting in our offices on Tuesday?' Not waiting for an answer, he carried on. 'Brice Payton. Our not-so-secret CIA cousin'.

'And', said Martin, 'so was Morna MacCallum'. Seeing a couple of questioning faces, he went on. 'Morna's with DoD, NSA, she's a signals analyst. Do you think your bosses may be trying to say they have some information that they can't admit to?'

'Maybe, maybe', Ivan mused. 'Not much we can do with it. Except… Siobhan, when you talk to Sharmila tomorrow, can you at least think of this as a medium, not low, possibility, especially with the other data that's coming in? Thanks. Which, I think, takes us to what Martin and his boys in blue have found, yes?'

'Sure. Except I think you'll find it's more our girl in plainclothes'.

Thumb flick to Kasia. 'Who did most of the work. As you all know we've got a 95% ID on our perp. Name's Jaffar Saqqaf, twenty years old. Kasia interviewed the parents yesterday, got a photo ID, they'll do an official identification of the body tomorrow. The coroner said the body was middle-eastern. If he had to guess he would have said Persian, which means Iran/Iraq. Plenty of them in Syria as well. The boy's clean, no fingerprint matches in our system…'

'Oh, hey', Ivan interrupted Martin. 'Forgot to tell you that we pulled a negative on federal fingerprints as well. Came in yesterday afternoon. Takes us longer to do a country search'.

'Well', continued Martin, 'no surprise. Not an issue either, now we know who he is'.

'So how'd you find him?' Bill asked, draining his glass.

Kasia took over. 'We'd alerted missing persons to notify us if any calls came in matching the description. Round about nine Friday evening they called me with a possible match. I went round to the house yesterday; it's just off Halsey Street in 'little Syria''. I showed them the photo – cleaned up of course. They immediately reacted. They showed me some other pictures of him as well. I'm sure our guy is their son. Seems Jaffar's friend', she took a quick look at her notebook. 'Kino Melki, rooms with Jaffar at college. He hadn't seen Jaffar since Tuesday so he called the parents on Thursday. They called around and finally, on Friday, called missing persons'.

Martin nodded, 'All this matches what FIU said when they examined the clothes, standard wear for someone from around here'. Ivan gave Martin a sharp look. 'It's OK, Ivan, the clothes are on their way now to your CSI people. Old habits die hard and the coroner sent the clothes over to our lab as per normal. The Friday night shift didn't click that the FBI has dibs on the forensics. Soon as I realised what had happened I got them bagged and tagged and sent to Washington. Hopefully no harm done. No unique identifiers on the clothes, but no attempt to remove labels or anything. No personal ID on the body, no wallet, nothing. Typical suicide, and that's what the coroner is putting forward as cause of death'.

'O-k-a-y', Ivan replied, unsure whether to make a deal of the fact that NY looked at the evidence before CSI. Picking his battles, he decided not to and turned to Kasia. 'So what do we know of this… Jaffar? *Are* we looking at some fundamentalist Islam situation?'

Kasia picked up the narrative again. 'Not sure at this point. He seems squeaky clean. Second generation Syrian, no trouble in or out of school, according to the parents at least. Decent student, reasonable grades, no permanent girlfriend, but then he may not have admitted to that; Mr and Mrs Saqqaf are somewhat conservative. He won a few athletic awards in high school, but nothing much. Worked part-time at a baker's nearby. Gene and I will get some uniforms working it; we'll have a much better idea by the end of the week. I'm hoping to see this Kino Melki this evening, he's at work right now'.

'So nothing that shouts, "Ahmed the Terrifying Terrorist", yet?' Siobhan asked.

'N-o-o, but' Kasia had obviously saved the best 'til last. 'Jaffar was a model airplane and drone fanatic. His bedroom was full of magazines, models, spare parts, *et cetera*. Parents said he spent all his spare time taking photos with his own drone', another quick check at her notebook. 'His latest toy was a brand-new DJI Phantom 5, which was in his room, incidentally. He'd submitted quite a few pictures to some online competitions. They showed me a few, some were really good, very artistic'.

A silence fell on the table as everyone processed the ramification of this.

Martin broke that silence. 'Ivan, if it's OK with you, I'd like to keep the lid on this for a few more days at least. The election has left America more polarised than ever, and after Trump's anti-Muslim rhetoric we really need to think about public safety and security; how we're going to release this news. And we *really* need to be sure of our facts as well'.

Ivan nodded agreement as did the others at the table.

'Mind you', Martin continued. 'I'm talking about keeping this from the higher ups as well. No lies – if they ask a direct question, we answer it, but no need to volunteer anything quite yet. The last thing we need is to see Muslims being lynched. Yeah, yeah, I'm being dramatic, but all of us here can make claims to being in a minority and my grandparents would surely identify with what I'm saying'.

'How long for, Martin?' Siobhan asked. 'Seeing as I've just been parachuted into the investigation, Ross is going to want an update and he'd find it pretty odd that I didn't mention a terrorist connection seeing as we are the anti-terrorist task force'.

'Wednesday? Thursday? Perhaps stress what you've heard officially from the Intelligence Centre rather than a Sunday afternoon drinks bull-session? If you feel you should tell him, then do so by all means, but also let him know our concerns about making sure we have a solid handle on the PR side of things first. Ivan, a lot of this will come down on Sharmila, can you brief her and provide assistance if needed?'

'It's covered, don't worry'. Ivan said. 'We may as well talk about the drone now we know Jaffar was interested in them. The original identification as a "Parrot" turned out to be wrong; CSI now tell me they have a very high confidence that it was a KittyHawk Supreme Quadcopter. It's a commercial product, one of the first drones to get FAA approval for delivering stuff, delivered some medication in Virginia last year. Not cheap, around four thousand bucks for this model. Two good pieces of news from this: One, the company that makes it is American, not French, and two, they haven't made that many. We're tracking down all their sales at the moment. CSI also say that they've found signs of some modifications, but hard to tell what'.

'Don't these sorts of drones have lights on them? Especially if FAA approves them for use in built up areas?' Kasia asked.

'Good point, this one has a very bright LED and some running lights. I don't remember any of the Secret Service saying they saw lights'.

'Gene got a hit on some CCTV footage. It's definitely a drone, but dark, no lights on it at all. It flew *down* from the direction of St. Patrick's. We've been scouring tapes and videos from the public since Thursday looking for the launch point, but I don't think we're going to find it'.

'This was at 6:10'. Martin reminded the group. 'About forty minutes after the last security sweep of the roof, but only ten minutes from when the last sweep could have happened, at 6p.m. At that time, the Service and our Critical Response people shut down all access to maintenance areas and the rooftop other than to our own personnel. Again, whoever organised this, and it sure wasn't Jaffar, *knew* the procedures'.

They all fell quiet again as the waitress delivered another round of drinks and cleared away the oyster shells. Afterwards, Siobhan asked, 'Anything from CSI on the explosive device?'

'Definitely Semtex and most likely a US source. Best guess at the moment is it's US military origin stolen from…' Ivan paused.

'Iraq?' Guessed Siobhan.

'Yep. As for the device, CSI are having some difficulties piecing it together, but it looks like it was a pressure trigger. The owl could have armed it when it grabbed it with its talons and it was set to blow with a release of pressure'.

'Homemade?'

'Nope. US military, probably. Again, they're still putting the jigsaw together, and a lot of the pieces simply aren't there, minute pieces missed at the scene, Ivan held his hand up to Kasia. 'No, no. Not blaming your people, millimetre-sized pieces of unidentifiable plastic are impossible to distinguish from the usual dirt and grit on the street. 'sides, some of the missing pieces don't even exist anymore, vaporised by the explosion'.

Siobhan went on. 'What else do we know about this Jaffar? What about that suicide note?'

'Ah, yes', Ivan replied. 'Sharmila recognised it quite quickly, it's a quote by Lawrence of Arabia in his book *Seven Pillars of Wisdom*. Which, for those of us who aren't English majors like Sharmila, was written after the First World War. Some see it as a primer for Arab independence against the colonising British. In other words…' he paused for effect '…exactly the sort of thing that ISIL is fighting for now'.

Bill Ngo had been typically quiet for much of the meeting, listening carefully and trying to "see the forest". 'So we've got a young Syrian, Muslim male who launches an expensive, American drone carrying a bomb made with American parts that is then flown by the Secret Service at the President-Elect, killing the

V-P. He then commits suicide leaving behind a note to "overthrow the usurper". You know how ludicrous that sounds?'

Martin nodded in agreement. 'Which is why we should be focusing on the *what* and *how* rather than the *why* at this point. I think we have a "mystery man"', a look from Kasia, 'or woman to find. Maybe more than one. Someone bought that drone and fixed a bomb using Semtex from Iraq to it. I highly doubt that was Jaffar working by himself. It doesn't fit that he would be able to get owl to fly at Robbins. The answer to that, and an answer to who put dead batteries in the recall device, will go a long way to unravelling this puzzle'. He took a pull at his beer. 'Ivan, how'd your guys do in Holland?'

'Not the easiest of interviews my agents tell me, but productive. No obvious leads, no alarm bells ringing. The fellow out there works with half-a-dozen law enforcement agencies and has been vetted every which way to Sunday by them all. He's clean. It takes months to train a bird. If anyone tampered with the training this fellow, Bart, would either have known or be doing the training. We'll keep checking, but there is absolutely no evidence to suggest anything funny was going on. It would be great if we could interview the Service Agents again, Jean and Tomas, but Rafi tells me that will need to be a formal request… which I'm working on'.

Martin nodded again. 'And I'd like to go over the time before the owl was released with a fine toothcomb with Agent Tomas, he must know something about those batteries. Siobhan', he turned to face her, 'the JTTF may be able to leverage something there. JTTF works closely with Major Allard and *he* talks a lot with Ian Croft, the USSS Deputy Director for New York. Perhaps if you talk to your old boss while Ivan and I talk to ours, we can get those interviews sooner rather than later'.

'Sure thing, Martin. Glad to be of help'. She paused in thought for a second, glancing at her notes. 'What about the gun?'

'We got no hits, it wasn't registered in this state. Ivan?'

'ATF's NTC, the National Tracing Centre, got back to me yesterday; nothing. All that means is that the gun hasn't been reported stolen, and wasn't bought in any of the States that have mandatory registration like New York. We're running it through A2K, the Access 2000 software that traces the gun from when it left the factory. It's a top-down approach that usually works, but does take time. Making things worse is that it's a Sturm and Ruger nine-mil, one of the commonest guns in America, but', he grinned, 'we're the FBI! We'll find it, just give us a few more days…' his grin slipped. 'Providing it was bought in the US, of course'.

'You know what?' Bill suddenly asked no one in particular. 'I've been trying to figure out what to get junior for Christmas. I'm going to get him a drone'. He smiled as he pulled his coat on.

Drinks drained, and the bill paid, the five stepped outside into the sleet.

Martin and Kino Melkin's meeting place was a compromise, and like most compromises, far from ideal.

Kino had been reluctant to have a policeman visit him at the house he shared with four people, *three now Jaffar was gone*, and Martin was reluctant to bring Kino to the station or have *this* conversation in a public place such as a restaurant. Unlike some of his colleagues, Lt.-Commander King still believed the police existed to serve the public and that people were innocent until proven guilty. Given the tensions between police and the community during the hot summer, Martin found this attitude increasingly challenged on both sides. Especially because he was black, he sometimes felt that neither his police colleagues nor the African-American community completed trusted him.

Kino and King met by a park bench in a small park near the Brooklyn bus terminal, easy for Kino to get to, and a 20 minute taxi ride from the wine bar and, later, back to Martin's home. Convenient, yes. Comfortable, no. The sleet had changed to snow as the dull day imperceptibly blurred into night leaving an inch of slush everywhere. Neither of them even considered sitting on the cold, wet bench.

So they walked, the middle-aged policeman wishing he'd brought a hat and the tall, dark and good-looking young man simply wishing he was home.

Martin had put Kino at ease as they had walked laps around the small park. They'd covered the basics, condolences for the (presumed) loss of Kino's friend and the concerns about Jaffar's absence that had led Kino to call the parents on Thursday night. They'd talked of how Kino and Jaffar had gone to the same high school, had gone to the same community college together and their shared love of drones...

'We were always online, checking out the latest news, looking for deals, talking to other geeks like us who built their own drones'. Kino spoke with a slight Middle-Eastern accent that softened his Brooklyn accent a little. 'I like the technical side, I'm always looking for ways to extend battery life or new collision-avoidance software. Jaffar's more into how to use them. He's an amazing pilot and gets some great video clips, but what he really likes to do is take stills and then manipulate them on his laptop'. Martin did not correct Kino's use of the present tense when talking about Jaffar.

"bout a month back, we was surfing *droneonman*, it's a site for dronestans, and saw this comp. Right up Jaffar's street, they wanted urban drone pix. So J submitted a couple of his photos and he won! Two weeks ago he gets a courier package, it's the latest DJI Phantom! No way we can afford one so he was stoked. His name also went in the draw for the main prize. Last week he finds his name came outta the hat. Not first prize, but runner-up; he gets to beta a new

KittyHawk Quad! Man says to meet him at his office in mid-town Tuesday evening. Tells J not to tell anyone as they wanted to blow people away with some cool pix of New York. So J headed into the City right after class… last time I saw him'. Kino's voice got very quiet.

'Then what, Kino?' Martin urged gently.

'When he didn't come home I was pissed, man. I really wanted to know how it went. But then I figured he'd gone onto some other place with the people, mebbe a drone party thing, and crashed. They obviously had money; mebbe they splashed a room for him. Didn't see him Wednesday, but our schedules are different so no big deal. When he doesn't come home Wednesday, I'm figrin' he's got lucky with some rich girl so I send him a coupla texts teasing him, but got no reply. Which makes sense iffun a boy's getting' his end away, right? Thursday comes round, still no answer to my texts. He doesn't answer his phone. Now I'm worried so I call Mister and Missus Saqqaf. Guess you know the rest, huh?'

Martin nodded although Kino probably couldn't see him in the dark.

'Did this man have a name, Kino? Or say where they were going to meet exactly?'

'Nah'.

'You still have the details of that website and the competition?'

'Oh, sure, you wannem?' Kino dug for his mobile, almost happy to have something constructive to do and an excuse to reconnect with the virtual world after talking to this old guy for the past twenty minutes.

'Thanks'. Martin jotted down the details. 'I'll have someone contact you officially tomorrow if it's okay. We'll need you to sign a statement with everything you've said'.

Although phrased as a request, they both knew that Kino had no choice in the matter, so Martin continued. 'You remember what time Jaffar left for the City?'

'Sure, last class on Tuesday ends at four. He was pumped, man, so he just left, practically flew outta there'.

And he was seen entering 630 Fifth just before five-thirty. Enough time, just, to have stopped off somewhere for ten minutes en route. They walked on for a while in silence. Martin was beginning to shiver.

'Did he have anything with him? A backpack for example?'

'Yeah, we both had our school stuff. J's got this beat up old black thing he always has with him'.

'And he'd have his wallet and ID and things?'

'Yeah, I guess. I mean, we don't check one each other like that'.

'Know what you mean. My wife always asks me if I've got my wallet when I leave in the morning. I wish she wouldn't, makes me feel either really old or like a kid'. Again some silence as their feet splashed the slush apart. On the grass, the snow was beginning to settle whitely in the dark.

'This is probably hard, Kino, but I need to ask. Do you know why Jaffar would kill himself?'

A pause. 'No, man. He was good. An' he'd just won a Phantom... life was workin' for us, y'know?'

An even longer pause. This was an important question, but Martin didn't want to scare Kino, but... he made his tone as light as possible. 'Hey, Kino, what mosque did you guys go to?'

His tone must have worked; Kino didn't hesitate. 'Don't go to a mosque, just a masjid up at Gates and Ralph. The imam's a really cool guy, y'know? Does a lot of work with the younger people. Why?'

Day Seven

December 5, 2016

Brice Payton took the first call in the borrowed office that he was currently calling his. An eavesdropper would only have heard his side of the conversation.

'Yes?'

'And good morning to you as well, Senator'.

'Yes, we're well aware of ISIL's claim. It was in the Times and on CNN. The Agency is capable of picking up on clues that way'.

'Yes, we have assets on it, and yes, we are talking to DoD and NSA. As you know, some of the assets we have are... shared. And as you also know, Senator, your call is somewhat irregular. The oversight committee is most definitely entitled to know this information, but in its place, in its time, not by calling a... friend... of the Agency's over a vulnerable line'.

'Thank you for the advice, Senator. I do appreciate the gravity of the situation'.

'Yes. Thank you again. And have a nice day as well. Goodbye'.

Brice Payton took the second call about fifteen minutes later.

'Yes?'

'Ah. Good morning, Mr Secretary'.

'Yes'.

'Well, yes'.

'But he shouldn't...'

'Of course'.

'Perfectly. I understand, but don't you think...'

'No, of course not'.

'Bart Sneiders and Rostam Alinejad. Got it. We could do with more...'

'No'.

'Yes'.

'Major Allard'.

'I will'.

'You too, Mr Secretary'.

Chastened, he left his borrowed office.

Martin had come into the office at nine to find Kasia already hard at work. He hadn't had a good night. The early signs of a cold had kept him awake, and he looked it: red-eyed and runny nose.

'You look like shit, boss'.

'I feel it. Spent an hour wandering around outside last night without my hat'.

He filled Kasia in on his conversation with Kino the previous evening.

'I'm having an office day as much as I can. Try and throw this cold off before it gets any worse. Think you'll have to go to the mosque without me'. From experience, Kasia knew Martin suffered intensely when he had man-flu and was more than happy to have an excuse to avoid him for a while.

'I'll follow up on the website and competition thing with NY Intelligence Centre, go through Siobhan on that one, and, of course, get Ivan and the FBI onto it. You said you saw a new drone in Jaffar's bedroom, yeah? A Phantom something-or-other?'

'Uh-huh. A "DJI Phantom 5" still with packaging lying around'.

'So that part of the story holds up… strange how so many of these people can hide their feelings and thoughts away from even their closest friends. It's always "he was such a nice man", "I can't believe it"…' Martin shook his head sadly. 'I think Kino's clean, but we're going to need to do a full check on him regardless. I'll get that started as well. As for Jaffar, well… it's going to be hard on his parents. They're due here at eleven, right?' Kasia nodded.

'This mosque, masjid, may be where it started. Take some uniformed as backup, huh? You don't want to walk into a jihadist den by yourself. You sure you're going to be alright without me?'

'I think I'll manage, boss. You just tuck yourself up behind your chair. It's toasty in here, you should be able to throw this off within the week if you look after yourself. Want me to bring you something, hot tea? Paracetamol? NeoCitran?'

Martin was impressed by her offer to buy him NeoCitran. Martin had "discovered" NeoCitran when he had been on assignment in Canada. To buy it, Kasia would have to go to a drug store four blocks away that stocked international brands.

'Thanks, Kasia, really appreciate that…' Martin started and then looked at her smile; there was no way she was actually going to do any of that. 'Ah, fugeddaboutit, you look after yourself; I'll be fine here'. He finished with just a slight shiver. Kasia couldn't work out if he was simply being dramatic or actually believed he was going to die from the sniffles.

Kasia had dropped into the police station across the road from the masjid to request uniformed assistance rather than bringing someone with her from Manhattan. *Much more likely to have local knowledge and know what we're walking into.*

The entrance to the masjid was a normal door between two storefronts. Apart from a couple of posters, one flapping idly in the wind - in what Kasia assumed was Arabic there was nothing to indicate that this was a religious establishment. The solid outer door stood open, towards the street and the unlocked inner, metal-bar door opened inwards towards a set of stairs that led up to the next floor.

Kasia and Gabriel went up the stairwell cautiously. It was dimly lit with the sole source of light coming from the street below. Luckily, yesterday's squall had blown over and it was a bright day. Most of the snow and slush had already melted, and there was enough light to guide them.

At the top of the stairs was another perfectly normal door. Kasia knocked and, a few seconds later, a man opened the door.

'Hi. New York Police. I'm Detective Kasia Pasternak and this is Officer Gabriel Montero. Mind if we come in and ask a few questions?'

The man had a full, black beard that covered his neck. He was dressed in an open neck shirt, over which he wore a long smock, jeans and sneakers. He extended his arm in welcome. 'Of course. We are open to everyone here. Even female detectives'. *Late thirties,* Kasia thought, *dark complexion, but he could be Mediterranean or north African as much as Middle-Eastern. A slight accent, but essentially New York.*

He followed them through into a reception room that was half-office, half-lounge. He pointed them to a comfortable couch, which they both ignored, and then introduced himself. 'I'm Abdulrashid, the imam of this masjid. Can I bring you tea?'

'Ah, no thanks', Kasia replied. 'This may not take long. Do you know a young man called Kino Melki?'

'Yes, of course. Very polite young man. Good at school from what I hear. He comes here once in a while'. While courteous, the imam did not quite follow the normal pattern, Kasia thought. *He hasn't asked why we're here or whether Kino's in trouble.*

'What about Jaffar Saqqaf? Know him as well?'

'Kino and Jaffar are good friends. Roommates I think. They often came here together. Are you sure you don't want tea? Or to sit?'

'No, thank you anyway. What is this place exactly, Kino said it's not a mosque?'

'Masjid just means a small mosque and "mosque" isn't always seen as a positive term in America nowadays so we prefer "masjid". It's really just a community centre. We observe the usual religious rituals – Quranic studies, spiritual guidance, daily and weekly prayers – though the daily sessions, especially *fajr* at five a.m. are not well attended. But we also have outings and barbeques in the summer, and a games night for the teens in the winter. We do a lot of outreach in the community, helping people through tight times, some translation services for new immigrants, that sort of thing. Some people would probably say I'm not a good Muslim because I'm not strict enough and believe in interfaith dialogue, but, especially with the new political realities, we need to be... not permissive, but tolerant of individual preferences. I want the second generation to understand the loving and kind Islam, not what is all too often portrayed on television and in the news. And I'm not going to get that if I act like some thundery parent telling people what they can and can't do'.

He paused and then went on. 'We get all sorts here so I also have to be aware of and tolerant of a range of cultures. Despite what many people think, Islam is not a homogenous whole, one faith, but many, many cultures'. *And maybe not even one faith, seems Sunnis and Shias... Shiities? have their differences,* Kasia thought.

Unaware of Kasia's doubts, he continued. 'We have a wide range of people who come here, I'm Pashtun – Afghani, and the majority of men who come here are Bangladeshi, but we also have Lebanese, Syrians, Indians, Filipinos, you name it'.

'Sounds like you're a busy man...' Kasia hesitated, 'What do I call you? Is there an equivalent of the Catholic "father"?'

The imam laughed. 'No, no. Islam isn't hierarchical, every Muslim has their own relationship with Allah. No one is more superior to anyone else. My role is a guide, a mentor, not a position of authority. So you can call me Abdulrashid, or Abdul, or even Rashid, if you like. I'm not fussy. Although I'd probably draw the line at "Rashy"'. He smiled.

Kasia found herself liking this man and disliked what she knew she had to do next. 'I'm sure you're wondering why we're here, but you haven't asked'.

'I reckoned you'd get around to telling me when you were ready. In my culture we often talk, over tea...' *and that sounded like a mild rebuke,* Kasia thought, '...about inconsequentialities before getting down to business'.

She hesitated and then thought of Martin and his sniffles waiting for her back at the office.

'You know what... Abdulrashid... I think Officer Montero and I would like that tea after all'.

She sat down on the couch.

Martin had accompanied Jaffar's parents to the Chief Medical Examiner's office where they had duly identified the body of their son, and understandably and predictably broken into tears. Mrs Saqqaf in particular had broken out into inconsolable sobs and shrieks. Martin, never comfortable with this part of his job, stood uncomfortably by, hoping that his red and watery eyes gave the impression of grief more than the flu. Finally, he had got two female police officers to guide the pair into a patrol car and over to Police Plaza a five minute drive away.

Most rooms in police stations were uninviting, but police headquarters had a few rooms available for public use that were much more amenable. They were set up to handle press conferences, school tours, VIP visits and the like. Martin put Jaffar's parents in a room that would not have looked out of place in an office building. He asked if they wanted to go home first and he'd take statements later, but the father had said that they wanted to get it out of the way so they could concentrate on grieving and informing the family.

For obvious reasons Martin wasn't going to interrogate the pair: He'd spoken to them for a while, but nothing had rung any alarm bells, the parents seemed to be fairly typical New York immigrants and their son a typical second generation American. He left them with a more sympathetic uniformed officer who brought them tea and finalised the paperwork.

Back in the investigation room, Martin was alone with his thoughts for the first time in a while. Then he picked up his phone; he needed to make a lot of calls.

He called Ivan.

NTC had traced the gun to Vermont. Bad news; gun registration was very limited in that State, but Ivan had people on their way to the retailer as they spoke. He also told Ivan he'd send over the video footage that had been compiled so far. "Sorry, slipped my mind for a couple of days".

He called the hospital.

Trump had had another brain bleed and was going into surgery that afternoon. The doctor seemed confident this would finally relief the swelling and they'd be able to bring him out of the coma in a few days. The prognosis was good.

He called Siobhan.

'Had she been able to get anywhere re access to the Secret Service Agents?' She told him that she'd get somewhere if certain people didn't keep calling her to see if she'd got anywhere. She'd call him when and if she did get somewhere…

He called Emery, his C.O.

He explained their need to interview the Agents and the bureaucracy wall that had been put up. Could Emery, or Emery's boss, Nolan Quinn, Chief of Detectives, talk to Murray Allard or Ian Croft and expedite the issue? *See what I can do.*

Finished with his calls, he stared at the walls of the investigation room. Few enough pictures or notes tacked there yet, and most of them unconnected. He was feeling a bit sorry for himself so decided to have another hot lemon tea, do some research on the law firm and the lawyer in whose office Jaffar's body had been found and waited for Kasia to return.

Kasia sat on the couch and sipped her tea. Abdulrashid, sitting across from her also with a cup, had explained that it was a traditional Afghan tea made with cardamom and loaded with sugar. *Not exactly my cup of tea,* she thought.

'Abdulrashid', she began. 'You've mentioned the political climate a couple of times now. How do you and your community feel about Mr Trump winning the election?'

'Concerned, of course', the imam began. Many of the people here are first generation Americans born in different countries, and we don't know what he means by his statements. Mr Trump has always been a bit short on details. For example, what happens if a Muslim, an American Muslim, mind, who was born outside of the USA does something wrong, not even a big something, but something criminal. Will he or she be stripped of citizenship and sent back to a country whose citizenship they have rescinded? In some cases this would amount to a death sentence for, say, shoplifting!

'And what about the second generation, Kino for example, would the same thing apply? Can *I*, an American citizen, attend my brother's wedding in Kabul, and still be able to come home or would I be denied re-entry because of my faith? Can any of my family overseas visit me here in my home? A friend of the masjid is in the Navy. The *US* navy. He sailed out in October and is due back in February or March. Will Trump let him off the boat?'

Kasia leant forward, nodded slightly, encouraging him to continue.

'Here in Brooklyn things aren't too bad, but if I'm wearing my normal clothes and go into the City with my beard and dark skin, I risk getting abused. There are others I know of, particularly outside the State, for whom it is much worse. Some days I fear we may be heading towards lynch mobs, but hope that won't come to pass. I hate to say it, but the tensions between the police and blacks has helped us in a way. The public seems to have forgotten how dangerous we Muslims are. For now, at least. *Insh'Allah*'.

'What's that? Sounds like something ISIL would say'.

Abdulrashid paused to let a momentary spasm of anger at this police officer's ignorance pass without trace on his face. '*Insh'Allah*? It means "as God wills it". We say it in much the same way as you say "bless you" when you sneeze. Just a saying'.

'So Muslims would be happy if Mr Trump would die?' Kasia had caught something on the imam's face. Not sure what, she'd decided to be provocative, see if she could get him off guard.

'Again, it's very common for non-Muslims to think of the Islamic world as speaking with one voice. We don't.

So to ask if all *Muslims* would be happy, no, of course not, just like all *Americans* there will be a wide range of feelings, disgust and horror at an attempt at someone's life, sympathy for Mrs Trump and his children, and, of course, for many, relief., but for now, Mr Trump is still alive, *Insh'Allah*, and all of America waits to see what will happen'.

'But is it fair to say that the majority of Muslims, at least those you know, those who come here to worship, would be happier to see Mr Trump not become President?'

'Yes, probably, but not if the cost is another man's life. None of us could wish that'.

Not even one of you? Wondered Kasia, but kept her silence on that question.

'And what about Kino and Jaffar's politics?'

'Ah. And now you ask me what you came here to ask, yes?'

'Perhaps. Can you answer that question, please?'

The temperature in the room had dropped a few degrees.

'Of course. They were young men. Political, but only in the idealist sense. Not very focused, they talked of how the World could be a better place, but in generalities. They cared about the environment, but also about their job prospects, marriage, career. If I had to guess, I would say that they didn't vote for Trump, but maybe they didn't vote at all. Like many young people, they feel distanced from the political process, getting most of their news and views from John Oliver. Now. I have been hospitable and helpful. I have invited you into my house. I have served tea. Do you not think you owe *me* some answers now?'

'Abdulrashid', Kasia began. 'Jaffar Saqqaf killed himself on Tuesday night. We're looking into a potential connection between his death and the attack on Mr Robbins and Mr Trump'.

She looked carefully at the imam as she said this. As far as she could tell, his shock and grief was sincere and deep. 'I'm sorry', she concluded.

The man looked at her, trying to see the lie, trying to process the reason why a police officer would tell him such an outrageous thing. Failing to see a lie, he looked down as tears welled.

'How... why...?' He stumbled.

'We don't know yet', Kasia said softly, 'but it's why we have to ask these difficult questions. Can you tell me the last time you saw Jaffar?'

Abdulrashid took a minute to regain his composure, taking a sip of now cold tea. 'Umm. Perhaps ten days ago? Kino and Jaffar often come... came... on Thursday afternoons. They finished college early on those days and had a few hours to kill. We have a games afternoon on Thursdays'.

'And was that the last time you saw Kino as well?'

'Oh, no, Kino comes every Friday to prayers'.

'Didn't Jaffar come with him?'

Abdulrashid looked up, puzzled. 'Of course not. He's Christian'.

It was getting dark by the time Kasia had picked Martin up and re-navigated the traffic back to Brooklyn. Unlike Manhattan, on-street parking was not an issue. They parked Kasia's car almost directly outside the Saqqaf's residence. The building was typical of the neighbourhood: a three-storey, walk-up brownstone in a row of similar buildings. Kasia had explained that the building held just three apartments, one to each floor, and that Jaffar had lived on the second floor. Mr Saqqaf answered the door within a minute of their knock.

'I'm very sorry to disturb you again', Kasia said, 'but can we come in for a few minutes? I believe you've already met Lieutenant King?'

Wordlessly, he nodded and ushered them into the dim hallway and into the first room on the right. The curtains were still open, but little light was coming in at this time of day. Martin looked around. The furnishings spoke of the origins and the journey of the two people who lived here, somewhat cluttered with ornately decorated furniture, chintz fabrics, almost baroque mirrors and wall coverings favouring reds, oranges and golds. And photographs. Many, many photographs of people, most of them in Middle-Eastern dress. The overall effect was, to Martin, oppressive; overly warm and overly stuffy.

Mr Saqqaf had entered first and sat next to his wife on a small two-seater couch, gently placing his hand on her back. She was dimly illuminated by a Moorish table lantern, its fretwork casting speckles of light and dark that danced over her face and hands as she moved. She was dressed in a black *thawb* with a few pearls embroidered around the neckline and a black scarf on her head. *Clearly in mourning*, thought Martin. Wordlessly, her reddened eyes downcast, she reluctantly waved the police officer once more into her grief.

As Kasia entered behind Martin, Mrs Saqqaf quickly and almost unnoticeably crossed herself by moving just her forearm and wrist. *There's that woman with the devil-animal eyes again.*

Kasia leaned into Martin and said, *sotto voce*, 'Damn. She crossed herself the first time we met as well, I didn't twig'.

They exchanged greetings and condolences appropriate for the occasion, Martin apologising once again for their intrusion. Mr Saqqaf did all the talking. They were not offered tea.

When he judged the time to be right, Martin asked, 'Why didn't you tell us you are Christian?'

'There are many things we did not tell you. And many things you did not ask. Is it that strange to follow Christ? I understand even some Americans do so'.

This isn't going to be easy, but then it never is. 'But you are Syrians?'

'Yes, but also "Assyrians". We have been in the Levant for over five thousand years… and persecuted for almost as long, ever since the Persians took our land.

"Syria" is a new word. But here in America, no one cares where you're from, we can live our lives without fear. And with the rise of *dhaesh*, America is even more important as sanctuary for our people'.

'How long have you been here?'

'In America? Twenty-six years. Twenty-two of them right here in this apartment. Jaffar lived all his life here…' Briefly, his strong voice cracked.

'And Jaffar? He was happy? He had no reason to want to hurt America?'

'Why would we want to hurt America? The American government recently helped some of his cousins to escape. He is doing well at school. He has, had, a girlfriend; he wouldn't tell us, but we knew, he had', he stumbled again on the past tense. 'Good friends, hobbies, work. Some of his friends are Persians, Arabs, Muslims, even Turks. America breaks down the barriers between us'.

Martin allowed the man time to reflect on his son's life, now ended so unexpectedly. Martin tried to put himself in Mr Saqqaf's place. *So many of his dreams for the future will be gone now. No marriage, no grandchildren.*

Martin thought of his own children, the eldest just six years younger than Jaffar. He also reflected on that last statement, "America breaks down the barriers between us". *For how much longer will that be true? "Give me your tired, your poor, Your huddled masses". Not anymore. Now, we build walls and barriers. We send the huddled masses home.*

Breaking their mutual reverie he asked, 'Do you think I could take a look at Jaffar's room?'

Suspicion, fear and a desire to help resolve his son's death flitted across the man's dark and creased face already made years older by grief. He nodded. 'It's the second on the left' he waved his right arm vaguely, his left never leaving his wife. 'He wasn't here much, but it is his room for whenever he wants'.

The two police officers left the mourning room and almost groped their way down the dark hall to the indicated door. Kasia turned on the overhead light and they both blinked for a few seconds with the sudden illumination.

Martin stood near the door and looked around. Perhaps a little tidier, perhaps a little more conventional than the rooms of other young American men, but not extraordinarily so. No religious books, pictures or icons, Christian or Muslim. A bookshelf with a wide range of topics, again, typical of a young mind casting around for what futures he would embrace.

A couple of posters of bands and sports heroes, no sexy pinups or girl bands - that would probably have been a step too far for his conservative mother. Actually, Martin realised as he stood still, letting his eyes do the wandering, there was nothing to indicate Kino's sexual inclinations at all. *Probably nothing, but worth throwing into the mix at the next brainstorming session*, he thought, *despite what his father said about a "girlfriend", there could be another reason for not discussing his private life with his parents.* He hummed to himself.

'What's that, Martin?'

'Hmm?' He realised he been singing quietly to himself. 'Nothing much. I was thinking of the title of that Bowie song, "Young Americans". Then his other song came into my head, "We are the dead".'

'Aren't you the cheery one?'

'No, no, it's not that. There's a line in there about someone suddenly having a rush of empathy and realising how quick we are to judge people who are different from us…' He continued to look around the room.

Some small trophies on the window ledge and a shelf indicating that the boy had probably been averagely active in sports, but not outstanding. Alongside were a few pictures from those same sports, baseball, soccer and… tennis. An odd choice for this context, thought Martin. There was something… something… about the photographs. The tickling at the back of Martin's mind was now a jangling nerve. What was it?

All of a sudden, it clicked. Martin looked at the boy holding a tennis racquet and the other picture where he was wearing a baseball glove.

'Mr Saqqaf', asked Martin as he returned to the front room. 'Was your son left-handed?'

Day Eight

December 6, 2016

Tuesday morning. A week since the attack and New York City had already put the event behind it. Rockefeller Plaza had been cleaned up, the Christmas tree lights repaired and lit up one night without fanfare. The restaurants, streets and shops were as busy as ever.

The sun had still not cleared the horizon, but the day promised to be bright. *Bright, but cold*, Kasia thought, watching her breath form clouds around her face. *Good if I can get out of the office for a while.* The sidewalks were dry and a few birds could be heard greeting the day above the morning traffic, *sparrows* she guessed; like many city dwellers, Kasia was not good with identifying wildlife. She had dropped Martin home after their visit to the Saqqaf's, he'd have to take the bus to work as he'd left his car at the office. He'd hinted for her to pick him up in the morning "to avoid this flu getting any worse", but she'd pretended not to understand and he had pretended to believe her. *It takes him an extra ten minutes to take the bus, it would add twenty, thirty minutes to my drive to pick him up. And it's only a cold, not flu.*

The two had spent the morning in companionable silence for the most part. Phone calls, colleagues dropping in with updates or questions, and the constant background of papers being read, marked up, stapled, de-stapled, filed and, occasionally, scrunched up with a discouraged sigh and tossed in the approximate direction of a waste can. And, of course, sniffles and sneezes from Martin.

Martin had called Ivan the previous night while Kasia drove him home and gave him the news that Jaffar was both Christian and left-handed. In return, Ivan had invited them to his office for a working lunch. Rafi Matos had been leant on by the FBI director for some progress which meant, of course, that Rafi had leant on Ivan.

They were putting on coats and, in Martin's case, gloves, a scarf and a big fur hat that always made Kasia think Martin was trying to channel the Russian detective in the novel *Gorky Park*, when Martin's phone rang. From Kasia's perspective, it wasn't much of a conversation, more a series of grunts and "uh-huh"s that ended with, 'thanks, Doc. Appreciate it'.

Kasia raised her eyebrows at Martin. 'That was Lloyd Randall over at Mount Sinai. Trump's surgery was successful. They expect to start bringing him out the coma in 24-48 hours'.

'Good news. So we only have one homicide, not two'.

'Isn't one enough?' he said grumpily as he pulled the fur ear flaps down.

Lunch was decent. Ivan had arranged a deli delivery of Thai pumpkin soup and a variety of bagels and wraps. With Rafi uptown, he'd also snagged his boss's with the all-important access to the espresso machine.

Once again, there were five of them, but a different five; Bill was unavailable. Sharmila joined Martin, Kasia, Siobhan and Ivan. Over sandwiches, Kasia brought Siobhan up to date.

'So... none of us have been saying it out loud, but I would think at least a few of us were thinking we had another Tsarnaev', Ivan said, referring to the brothers who carried out the Boston marathon bombing. 'Second-generation Muslim, disillusioned by America, looks for meaning in life, gets radicalised and... boom! He's a terrorist. I know I was leaning that way and it looks like I was wrong'.

'Excuse me being slow', Sharmila interjected in her Indian-polite way and mid-Western accent, 'but what's the fuss over the left-handedness?'

'Ah, that's right Sharmila. I don't think you saw the autopsy report. Jaffar supposedly shot himself in his right temple. And the gun was in his right hand. We were fairly sure there was at least one other person involved, someone who supplied the gun, someone who bought the drone, *et cetera*, but now it seems that other person was in the same room with Jaffar'.

Kasia leaned over to Martin and whispered, 'So we're back to two homicides'.

Ivan continued, 'I got a call from our agents in Vermont. The store owner was relatively co-operative; gave a name and an address with hardly any pressure from the guys. Name's Larry T. Edwards, he bought the gun over two years ago. The retailer says he always asks for ID, driver's licence mostly, but then he would say that, wouldn't he? Either way, it doesn't matter as he doesn't write down any of the details of the ID shown. He did have an address so they went over there, it's a McDonald's. Been there for a decade. We're running Edwards' name in Washington and the names of employees of McDonald's for the past two years, but this is probably a dead end'.

'The gun wasn't reported stolen?' Sharmila asked.

'No. We would have traced it faster if it had been, but that's another reason why this won't go anywhere. Whoever this is didn't care if we traced the gun'.

'You think this Edwards – that name'll do until we get a better ID – killed Jaffar?' This time, it was Siobhan.

'Well, Occam's razor and all that, it's the simplest theory for now. Seeing as we don't know who was in the room with Jaffar anyway, we may as well call them "Edwards" until we have some evidence that there are more people involved'.

'What I'm getting at', Siobhan continued, 'is that Edwards may be the Islamic extremist.'

She ticked her points off one-by-one on her outstretched fingers. 'One. There's the suicide note. Planted by Edwards, it references the same dream of Islamic emancipation as ISIL espouses.

'Two. ISIL have claimed credit. Three. The Semtex came from Iraq. Four. Trump has pissed off a lot of Muslims'.

'Among others…'

'Yeah, yeah'. Siobhan agreed. 'I'm just not ready to drop the *jihadist* angle yet. Martin asked me to see what I could do about getting access to the Secret Service people, so I talked to Ross. He said he'd see what strings he could pull…'

'Exactly what Emery told me', Martin interjected '– "see what he could do", does no-one upstairs want to help?'

'I thought *you* were "upstairs", *Lieutenant-Commander*', Kasia added, smiling.

'…um, I was saying…' Siobhan steered them back on track. 'I chatted to Ross this morning, whoever he's talking to, and it has to be someone very senior, but not official, is convinced this is overseas-sponsored terrorism'.

'Mmm'. Ivan was the first to respond. 'And who, pray tell, would be considered "very senior, but not official"? Our CIA cousins or Secret Service?'

'Could be political'. Martin added.

'Maybe', admitted Ivan. 'We've got some other news as well. Seems KittyHawk, the manufacturers of the drone, aren't just in the US as I said on Sunday. To get their seed capital, they crowd sourced. The bigger donors got sent initial production models. The drone used would have been one of these as they haven't rolled out the line to the public yet. The lab's trying to confirm that. Anyway, the bigger donors are, as expected, mostly in the US, but a fair number come from Europe. Including Holland, where the owl was trained. Plus a few in the Middle East, but preliminary findings have them as US expats rather than locals'. He paused to say, "and-this-is-interesting". 'A particularly large donor is Chinese. Our first investigations into them are proving to be a dead end. The donor's the equivalent of a shell company or however that works in a communist system. The Chinese must be up there with Mexicans in not liking Republicans at the moment. Something we haven't considered? Siobhan, think back, is there anything that Ross has said that was specific to Muslims or Middle East or could it include China?'

'I don't think so. He just said "foreign". And if we going down that route, we should also throw in our allies. Trump's made it clear that he wants Japan and Korea to stump up for American defence. Maybe a few of them aren't happy'.

'I think we may be getting side-tracked here', Martin said. 'I said at the beginning that if we focus on motivation, we won't get anywhere. Way too many people could have motive. Let's stick to what we have. For example, CRC have done a great job in tracking this competition that Jaffar supposedly won. There wasn't one'.

'What?'

'Nope. All the URLs Kino gave us were dead ends. Most of the cached pages have been wiped. As far as CRC can tell it was all faked, only Jaffar and a few of us his friends, like Kino, received invitations and saw the website. There was no nation-wide competition, there was no picture judging. They made it look convincing, but it seems clear that Jaffar was targeted'.

'Very interesting', said Ivan. 'The level of sophistication keeps going up, this has got to be the work of a group of people, and a group with excellent IT skills, hackers? Access to explosives, inside information re Secret Service procedures and, yes, Martin, access to their equipment… or personnel. We could still be looking at a traitor inside the service. Maybe someone being blackmailed'.

'It could still be ISIL', Siobhan insisted, but she didn't sound too convinced herself. 'And we've also got someone feeding info to our bosses at a high level'.

'Actually, we know someone who fits the profile Ivan just sketched much closer to home', said Sharmila.

'Who?'

'You, Siobhan'. Sharmila looked straight-faced at the redhead. Then she laughed. 'Your face! Priceless!'

'Very funny, Sharmila', Ivan said. 'Now if we can get back to business? That just shows that we're still not getting anywhere with "who". I agree with Martin, let's keep plugging away at the facts on the ground. Basic investigative work. We'll dig up something more concrete that will help narrow down the "who" later. Now, I've got a couple more things for you people. Border patrol got back to us', he waved a hand dismissively. 'We forgot to tell them to stop looking. Anyway, they had nothing on Jaffar – no surprises there – but… Sharmila, you talked to them. Tell everyone.'

Sharmila took up the narrative in her sing-song accent. 'Yah. As Ivan said, nothing on Jaffar, but then the officer said something odd. He said they also had nothing on "Rostin Alineeyad". I asked "who?" and there was a bit of a pause and then he said, "oh, nothing, sorry I was getting confused with another case". I pressed a bit, but it was clear that he wasn't going to say anything more. I got the feeling that he wasn't so much confused as trying to cover up a slip. Anyone here looking for a "Rostin"? I didn't get a spelling'.

Shakes of heads all round.

'Rostin Alineeyad. What sort of name's that? Arabic? Russian?' Siobhan asked.

'As I said, he wasn't going to give any more details, and he didn't repeat the name. I could be out by quite a bit, it was all a bit fast and out of the blue'.

Ivan took over. 'I dunno. It could be nothing, but I've got a feeling about some of this. I've asked Rafi to make this a formal request to Homeland Security. We're not talking obstruction of a federal investigation… yet… but I am a bit pissed off with this hands off stuff from the Service. Now this. Whatever "this" is. We really need to give the DA a heads up about the direction this is taking. Kasia, you know Bill Ngo well, yeah? Can you brief him on this? Still unofficial, but good for him to know'.

She smiled. 'Of course. We're overdue for a lunch ourselves so maybe I can catch him after work instead'.

Ivan nodded his thanks. 'Meanwhile, I've a video to show you'. Ivan swivelled his monitor so the others could see the screen. 'It's just before the bomb went off. The lab's done a great job at enhancing and combining multiple videos and slowing them down, but even so… well, watch'.

The video was often jerky, the crowd level sources, all from mobile phones, often had frames blacked out by heads in the way. Light levels fluctuated enormously as cameras adjusted to background lights, but the footage from the television station covering the event was all too clear. The first time Ivan showed it, there were involuntary expulsions of breath from the watchers when the bomb went off and they saw, for the first time in slow motion, the effect of the explosion on humans, bird and structures around them.

Ivan looked at their faces. 'Yeah. I was a bit like that the first time I saw it. We may be used to coming onto a scene after the fact, but seeing it in real life as it were is a bit shocking'.

The screen had frozen shortly after the blast. It was only too clear that Robbins injuries were fatal. The back of his head was barely visible behind a fine cloud of blood, hair, bone and… bits of owl. Secret Service Agent Amy Johnson, Kasia guiltily reminded herself that she was also a victim of the attack and had largely been forgotten, could be seen falling back, one hand reaching to her waist, probably her gun, and the other lifting towards her neck where a large bubble of blood was beginning to emerge. Much of the rest of the image was filled with debris. Trump's legs could just be seen to the left of the screen partially obscured by another Agent's body, presumably the man who had pushed Trump away.

'I needed you all to see that first so you can get the shock out the way. Now I'm going to show you a couple of clips, frame-by-frame just before the explosion. Watch the owl. Watch how it moves'.

The shots were framed around Trump and Robbins posed together at the podium, the giant tree in the background. The owl appeared from the right of the screen as a white blur with a dark shadow beneath it. In some frames it was clearly an owl, in others, just a splash of white. As the frames progressed it came more into focus and was unmistakeably an owl. An owl, carrying a drone, flying towards Robbins.

'Wait! Pause it'. Martin almost shouted, which caused him to cough and then sneeze. It took him a few seconds to speak again. 'Sorry about that. Look at the owl. Draw a line through its body. Assume it's flying in a straight line – it's not flying towards Robbins. At least not his head. Hard to see from this angle, but it looks like it's flying towards the podium'.

'Yep. That's what I thought too. Didn't want to say anything first though'.

Martin nodded for him to continue, eyes focused on the screen. Now it had been pointed out it was clear that the bird was aiming lower than Robbins' head.

More towards his torso, his waist. Frame-by-frame, the owl got closer. Ivan paused the tape.

'At this point, you can see people are reacting. Keep your eyes on the owl, but also on Robbins' right hand. See that?'

'He's holding something'.

'Yeah. What would he be holding at a time like that?'

'It's hard to tell. A microphone? Was he speaking? I can't remember'.

Ivan gave a small laugh. 'Oh, no. Donald Trump may share a podium with his running mate, but he wasn't going to let anyone but him do the talking. He had, if you remember, said something about "being grateful for Mr Robbins' support" and 'letting'' him do the honours of flicking the switch. I think that's the trigger for the lights. Keep watching'.

As the movement on the stage became more frenetic, the images became blurrier, especially fast-moving hands. Even so, they could see Robbins beginning to duck, his right arm instinctively moving up to cover his face. Agent Johnson hit Robbins in the side with her shoulder. As they both fell towards the ground, the owl swerved from its previous level flight, following the agent and the Vice-President-Elect to the right and down. The last frame was a uniform, overexposed white as the bomb went off.

'Let me go back one frame, just before the explosion'.

Ivan did as he said. On the screen, the owl was angled upwards, wings spread wide to slow itself down, preparing to land. The drone was clearly visible, just centimetres away from Robbins' head.

Kasia spoke first. 'It wasn't going for his head. It followed his arm that he brought up to his head'.

'Exactly. Your people bagged and tagged everything in the area, right?'

'Of course. And shipped it all to you'.

'But without an inventory list'.

'No… I don't think so; wouldn't have been time. They bagged and tagged it directly to your people. Didn't they make an inventory?'

'Sure did. Still are as a matter of fact; there's a lot of small bits and pieces that take time to catalogue. I've got them looking for the controls for the lights as a priority now. It's not on our list, but then that initial list isn't exactly detailed, you know how it goes: "twisted piece of metal, grid 12-E, photo ref. 1005". Maybe it was all plastic and blew apart or burnt…'

Martin sat back and rubbed his already red eyes. 'So, Ivan, you're thinking this is how they "subverted" the owl?'

'Could be. I've got IT working on audio. We were told it was an auditory signal. Wish I knew what kind of signal we were listening for. I'm not even sure it's in the human auditory range. Pretty sure birds can hear sounds at a much higher frequency than people, especially owls that hunt at night'.

'Another reason to lean on the service?'

'You betcha'.

'Hi Rusty'. Wilkins' friend from Border Control was on the phone. 'We've found your guy, Rostam Alinejad. He applied for a tourist visa three weeks back. Entered the US at JFK on November twenty-third. Doesn't look like he's left the country yet, but if he drove over one of the smaller border crossings we may not get the records for a few days…'

'Thanks, Terry, that's great. I owe you'.

Rusty Wilkins'' walk was decidedly bouncier than it had been for the past few days. *Now I've got something for Ian and maybe get Allard off my back.*

'Well done, Rusty'. Ian Croft said after Wilkins had updated him. 'It's still our problem, of course. It was our owl, and our procedure, but at least we'll get some credibility back'. *We can also spread the blame a bit, the Service weren't the only ones vetting this guy* he thought to himself.

'We might even get some credit from some of the other countries who also use these birds for giving them a heads-up on a potential weakness in the system. I'll make sure it goes through the right channels; put us front and centre for being vigilant. Time to get Agents Holgersen and Byrnes back here. Get them to make their report on this guy formal. We'll need to share this with the FBI of course, but at least it shows we're also serious investigators'.

Wilkins left the office. Alone, Croft thought back to 9/11. So much information had been known ahead of time, but not acted upon. *This could easily be a second 9/11 in that sense as well. Did we know about Alinejad ahead of time? Could we have stopped him coming here?*

The Department of Homeland Security (DHS) had been created to prevent such a thing happening again, to promote information sharing, but it hadn't worked that well and worse, all the departments involved, Secret Service, Border Control, Immigration… they were all part of DHS. *The Director needs to know about this, maybe even the Secretary.*

With a sigh, he sat up in his chair and reached for the phone.

It was going to be a night for lucky breaks. The sort that detectives the world over admit can make or break an investigation. There were two such breaks, both of them involving Kasia Pasternak. The first happened in a midtown bar.

Bill Ngo had been stuck in his office with casework until past six o'clock. Kasia had had a lot of paperwork as well. They decided to go further uptown for a drink and debrief. Taking FDR instead of her usual Brooklyn Bridge route added maybe ten minutes to Kasia's drive home to her apartment in Greenpoint and the tunnel toll was paid by NYPD. *There were a few perks to being a senior detective,* she thought.

She often drove this route when she and Bill worked late, it saved him having to change trains on his way home to Pelham. They had long established a routine; where to park, where to eat, where to drink. Bill always got the first round. As this was going to be a cheap – for Manhattan – one-hour chat, they decided to go to "their" sports bar in one of the Grand Central underpasses. Decent bar food and drinks at decent prices. Bill would have a couple of beers while Kasia, conscious of still having to drive, albeit less than five miles, would nurse a white wine.

Everything went as expected, Kasia told Bill of the afternoon's meeting and, after determining that he had nothing new on the Robbins-Trump case, they drifted into small talk, what each other was doing over Christmas being the main topic. And then things changed.

Bill saw Morna first. Leaning forward across the table so he could lower his voice a little, he said, 'Hey, isn't that Morna wasshername? The NSA intel woman?'

Kasia twisted around and looked. 'Yep. So? We're not at work anymore'.

'Well, she's a signals analyst, maybe she could help with the audio signal angle. And knowing NSA, she's probably got leverage with the Secret Service, maybe help us open them up a bit'.

Kasia knew Bill didn't drink a lot. A couple of beers didn't make him drunk, but it did make him more gregarious. *And* more likely to act spontaneously rather than his usual very methodical approach. Besides, they'd finished their drinks and she wanted to get home, there had been some very long days recently.

Too late. Bill had already stood, caught Morna's eye and waved her over. She had a "I know I should know you, but I don't" look on her face and didn't seem too eager to join them. Kasia turned around again and then Morna's face lit up with recognition. She picked up her drink, *a cocktail, interesting. Does that mean she's expecting to meet someone else?* Kasia thought as Morna weaved past a few people near the bar. Trade was steady, but not busy on a cold Tuesday evening, most of the after-work crowd having drifted off. *As we should be.* Kasia strapped on a smile, stood and offered a hand. 'Hi'.

The small talk ritual began again. A waiter came over. Bill ordered a beer and another wine for Kasia. *Would be ungracious to sit here pouting without one. And this'll mean two glasses in two hours. What the hell, I'll be fine on the short drive home.* As they talked, Kasia tried to place Morna, they'd only met a few times, mostly in corridors and elevators. Her accent was hard to place, perhaps a hint of the South? It was similarly difficult to place her ethnicity. Despite her name she was definitely not Scottish. Dark skinned with dark hair and deep brown eyes, she was attractive, but not overly so. Not tall, not short, dressed appropriately for midtown Manhattan in winter, she could have been Italian, Mexican, South American, maybe even Native American. *Easy to blend in, perfect for a spook if that's what she really is.*

'Small world, huh? What brings you here of all places, Morna?'

'Kasia told me to come'.

'Huh?' Asked Bill. *Huh?* Thought Kasia.

Seeing their faces, Morna laughed. 'No, not here as in *here*, right now, to meet you guys. Just to this bar. Remember that meeting at Rafi's office last week, Kasia? I told you I was staying at the Westin down the road and wanted a local's advice where to go. Somewhere friendly, but somewhere I wouldn't get hassled if I was by myself, and you recommended this place'.

R-i-g-h-t… I did. And so she isn't meeting someone. 'You said you were in New York for a few weeks right? Hoping to get home before Christmas?'

'That's it. Brice and… well some other folk… wanted to talk to me first-hand about this "second 9/11" angle I'd caught'.

'Uh-huh', Kasia encouraged, trying to catch Bill's eye or at least kick his leg under the table before he denied any such knowledge.

'But truth be told, I've been cooling my heels for a week. Thought Rafi or NYPD would have wanted some information on this. Especially since that "claim" over the weekend'. She waggled her fingers in the air to signify quotation marks.

Alright, I'm hooked. 'Actually Morna… well, I have no idea what you're talking about'. *There. I said it. If it turns out Ivan or Martin "forgot" to tell me, I'll have their testicles off.*

'Oh?' Genuinely surprised. 'I was in New York for something else when the attack happened and Brice invited me to that meeting. Don't know why, no one wanted to talk to me'.

'Why don't you start from the beginning?'

'Sure. It's why I'm still in the City! Although I didn't expect to have this discussion in a bar…' She looked around with a dubious face. 'Look, do me a favour, will you? It may seem a bit melodramatic, but can you both turn your phones off, please? Kasia, you don't carry a police radio when you're off duty, do you?'

'I've got one in the car, but not on me, no'. Belatedly, Kasia realised that this wasn't Morna's first cocktail of the evening. *Perhaps she started in the hotel and got lonely.*

'And I'm not going to be too explicit if you get me'.

Nods, confident from Kasia, a little less so from Bill.

'Right. You know what I do, I'm a listener. One of the things I heard, and I'm giving you the short version, okay? One of the things was about a "second nine-eleven". Definite threats involved, not enough for a general warning, but enough to get people worried. There was also a direct reference to this "second nine-eleven". Thing is, when I got the original Arabic, I thought that the translator may have got it wrong. Maybe it was just the numerals, "two-nine-one-one" or "two-nine-eleven" or even "twenty-nine eleven", meaning November twenty-ninth in the Middle East. If so, we had a definitive warning of an… event… on that date. Lo and behold, we do have an event'.

'How come we didn't hear about this?'

'Beats me. I've been here over a week. I was at the meeting with you guys, but you and Ivan disappeared before I could talk to you. I wasn't sure whether any of the rest were operational enough. I don't just tell anyone; there are enough rumours and theories around. I like to make sure my intel goes to people who can act'.

'Anyway', Morna said, 'I left the meeting a little later figuring that Brice was still hobnobbing with the brass and he could tell them if he wanted. A few days later, I call Ian Croft. You know Ian? Deputy Director of the Service?'

Kasia nodded. *She's connected that's for sure, I can't imagine me, or even Martin, being able to just "call Ian".*

Morna had already continued. 'I told him the same thing and he said it was "very interesting" and he'd make sure the relevant agencies would be told. By that I assumed he meant the FBI at least, perhaps he did and they didn't tell you?'

Kasia laughed, 'No, no, if Rafi knows, Ivan knows. And if Ivan knows, I know'. *And that better be true.*

'Of course, with my job, I'm quite sensitive to nuances and subtleties of speech, I knew what Ian meant by "very interesting". I assumed he meant he'd downgrade it to routine traffic, but not bury it completely. What reason would he have to do that?'

Indeed. Why would he?

Morna carried on, enjoying the opportunity to tell her story. 'Rusty Wilkins called me last Friday. Said the same sort of thing, but at least I knew the info was doing the rounds. Then we get that "claim"', the fingers didn't come out this time, but Kasia could hear the quotation marks, 'on Sunday. It's crap'.

'You don't think…' Kasia didn't want to make Morna nervous and clam up by saying "ISIL", '…those people are behind it?'

'Hah! Not a chance. I thought there was something weird when it was announced. Yesterday I got a chance to look at the source data. Definitely not the *dhaesh* boys. What the signal most resembles is a hasty attempt to make it look as if it came from the supposed claimants, but coming from someone very different. It's good, especially if it was done in just a few days, but, no, my unofficial opinion is that the claim is a fake. When I get back to… to my own place… I'll be able to tell for sure.

Siobhan's not going to be happy, Kasia thought, *she's desperate for it to be ISIL-AQ terrorism and put the Terrorism Task force in the fore.*

'And then, this morning, I get a heads up to check traffic for a 'Rostam Alineyad' on any of the hops in conjunction with this case, especially if connected to any Middle-Eastern traffic. So, if someone up high in DoD, DHS and/or the Agency is still thinking Islam-jihad even if it isn't ISIL, why am I getting the impression that NYPD isn't?'

Good, good question…

'I'm not sure I can answer that, Morna, but I'll do some digging. Meanwhile, thanks a lot. Really, really interesting. I'll tell Ivan and Rafi in the morning – I mean that. Can I call on you in a day or two and swap stories, keep each other up to date?'

'Sure. Maybe over another cocktail. It was good for me to finally talk to someone'.

Kasia had got home past nine o'clock, hungry, but too tired to cook. She scrounged some leftovers from her fridge, caught the late news on the television, had a shower and went to bed. It was sometime before midnight when her phone went.

'Pasternak'.

The voice on the other end was distorted and a little difficult to hear.

'Detective Pasternak. I have some things to tell you about Trump and Robbins. And some things I can't tell you. No, just listen for a minute. You're looking in the wrong place. I know your bosses are saying that there's foreign involvement, but there isn't. It's much closer to home'.

The comment about her bosses got Kasia's attention; she tried shaking off her sleepiness.

'I don't know who you are, but you can't just call...'

'STOP! Don't say *the phrase* or you'll never hear from me again'.

Kasia was fully awake now. It was not common knowledge, even within law enforcement, that certain phone numbers were automatically monitored for certain innocuous phrases that would alert a human being to start listening in and tracing the call. Kasia had one of those phones.

'Okay... you've got my attention. Who are you?'

A distorted gurgle came down the line that took Kasia a few seconds to identify as laughter.

'As if. You can call me Mister White'.

Which is very strange as I think I'm talking to a woman. 'What's that supposed to mean?'

'Think Tarantino', said the artificial voice, still gurgling. 'And it's not just about revenge. It's also about profit, making the best of a situation'. The call ended.

Kasia called the station to get someone onto getting her phone records, she could have done it herself, but she needed to try and get back to sleep. *Which will probably be difficult.* She was right.

Day Nine

December 7, 2016

Martin came into the room about ten minutes after Kasia. 'You'll never guess what happened last night'

'Yeah, I had a doozy as well. What happened with you?' Kasia asked.

'My fever broke, I may be getting better', whereupon he flourished a Kleenex and blew his nose.

Kasia had not slept much and her boss's hypochondria was increasingly annoying. 'For Chrissakes, Martin, strap on a pair! You've had a cold, that's it, just a cold!'

Taken aback, Martin looked at Kasia.

'Sorry. But, well, when you said something had happened to you last night… it'll be easier if I tell you about my evening'.

Martin was silent while Kasia told of her chance meeting with Morna and then her strange midnight call. When she finished, his only response was: 'We need to tell Ivan. Now. In person. And no one else'.

Martin picked up his phone while Kasia listened to one side of the conversation.

'Ivan? Got a few minutes, really important'.

'Yeah?'

'No, that'll be fine, but can we meet in the library first?'

'No, not yours. The public library on Murray. I'll explain when we're there'.

'Great. See ya in ten'.

They put their coats back on. Yesterday's high had continued. It was decidedly chilly under a cornflower blue sky.

As they walked, Martin felt his "detective radar" buzzing. *What was Kasia doing uptown with Bill Ngo? Friends, sure, but why not meet around here?* Out of concern for Kasia, his thinking was not as clear as usual. *He's a nice guy and all, good looking I suppose –, but he's married. And an Assistant D.A. If there was something going on, even a hint of a something, Kasia'd be the one to pay the price.*

The three were an odd looking group. Ivan Biskup caught the eye first, he was a tall man and broad. His winter overcoat made him seem even bigger.

Competing for attention would be Kasia Pasternak. Although her ancestral roots lay close to Ivan's, they couldn't have been more different physically. Slim where Ivan was broad, blonde where he was dark. Clear skinned to his blotchy complexion. Cold, calm expression to his warm exuberance. And those pale grey eyes the polar opposite of Ivan's dark-brown-to-the-point-of-black.

Almost hidden behind these two was short, black Martin King. His balding head wrapped up in his fur hat with ear flaps, he gave the impression of a kindly grandfather a decade older than his true age.

So much for judging people by their looks.

The three walked around the atrium of the building where they could talk, quietly, without intruding on others' peace, but still sheltered from the cold outside.

Martin indicated to Kasia to tell Ivan about her mystery caller. When she finished, Martin said, 'Call it paranoia or call it a gut response from a coupla decades of experience, but I don't like this. Let's take it at face value and assume this... *Mister White* does know our call tracking protocol. Add that to some of the information-without-source that is coming from our superiors. *And* an outstanding hypothesis that there's a mole in the Secret Service. The President- and Vice-President-elect of the goddamned United States of America were attacked. There are some powerful forces behind this... Jaffar's just the end of a long ball of string and when we start pulling, I'm not sure what we'll unravel'.

'So', he concluded, 'I'd like this source to remain just with us for now. And that means no Bill, Kasia'.

'Okay, boss'.

'Sure, Martin, for now'.

'Good. Thanks, guys. I know it's unusual, but so's the case. Back to what the caller said. Two words of interest to me: "Tarantino" and "profit". By Tarantino, did he, she, mean the film maker?'

Ivan and Kasia exchanged a glance. 'You not familiar with "Reservoir Dogs", Martin?' asked Ivan.

'Ah... I think I caught it a while ago'. Seeing their faces, he continued. 'What? I have kids. Nowadays when I watch a movie, it's more likely to be "Zootopia" than some Tarantino gore fest'.

Smiling, Ivan held up a hand. 'No criticism meant, Martin. In that film, there was a gang of... five? People. Gangsters. They didn't want each other to know their real names, need-to-know stuff, so they called each other by colours, Mr Blue, Mr Pink and...'

'Mr White', finished Martin. 'Okay, I got it. And kinda remember as well'.

Serious now, Kasia said, 'Which means *if*, and it's a big "if" for now, Mister White is telling the truth then there is more than one person behind this'.

'Oh, no', moaned Ivan, 'not another *nakazeny* JFK conspiracy'.

'And', continued Kasia, '"Think about profit". What if this is more about Trump-as-billionaire than Trump-as-President? Old business partners with an axe to grind? Wall Street types who've shorted Trump Enterprises? That sort of thing?'

'Huh. I can see why you two want to keep this quiet for a while, there's no way I'm going to officially add this to the investigation or tell Rafi until we've got a lot more to go on. You're not interested in the fact that Mister White knows about your call protocols?'

Martin shook his head. 'Uh-uh. Everyone and their mother must know we have them, it's based on a New York State Homeland Security protocol. The caller may not have known the actual phrase, but there are a few thousand people who know we use them and counted on us not calling their bluff'.

'So how'd you want to proceed?'

'Well, why don't we, NYPD, just keep this little part of the investigation separate from the overall FBI-led investigation for now? If someone questions it, it'll just look like we were doing due diligence by looking into all possible motives. We're also going to put Kasia's phone on constant surveillance. We may, just may, get NSA-Morna in on that aspect for now. Again, unofficially, but Kasia thinks Morna's feeling a bit under-utilised at the moment'.

'Really? I didn't know you knew Morna'.

'Well, Kasia's got something else to tell you and you'll like this even less, but at least this one can be done in your nice warm office'.

From what he had heard on the short walk from the library to his office, Ivan had decided that Rafi needed to hear this as well. The three walked into his office still radiating the cold from outside. They settled in, the FBI men had coffee while Kasia opted for soda water and Martin had a hot lemon tea. Kasia told of her chance meeting with Morna the night before. Ivan and Martin interspersing comments and details where necessary. At the end, Rafi summarised:

'Morna *and* Sharmila, independently, tell us that the DHS, Secret Service, Border Control, Immigration, whoever, have been chasing a lead. A certain Rostam Alinejad, who may be an Islamic extremist, who may be in the USA and who may have killed Mason Robbins, *and haven't informed us?* Moreover, they had access to DoD-NSA information suggesting that a terrorist plan to kill him, and Mr Trump I assume, *existed before the attack?* Jesus Christ, have we learnt nothing in the fifteen years since 9/11?'

The others wisely kept silent.

Rafi picked up his phone. 'Sharmila? My office, now!'

While they waited for Sharmila to arrive the four swapped notes on their attempts to get information from the USSS. Rafi had been in the meeting with Allard and Croft wherein they'd agreed that no USSS agents would be interviewed by the FBI, or NYPD for that matter, without prior notice and Service representation, legal if necessary, present.

'But that didn't mean *no* access. And it *didn't* mean denial of access to physical evidence'. Rafi's anger was growing by the minute. Looking at Ivan, he asked, 'So where is this transponder that Martin has been so anxious to see? With CSI?'

'No', Ivan replied, trying to be as neutral as possible. His boss gave him substantial autonomy, but if Ivan had been late in coming to Rafi, Ivan was going to be on the end of some of his anger. 'It's still with the Service. As is the audio signal itself, I asked for a digital copy last Friday after I got the report from our agents in The Netherlands, but was told it was classified and we needed to go formal on this. I think you signed the request a couple of days ago'. *There, that should show I'm still on top of things and haven't been wasting time.*

Rafi was indeed mollified by this. 'Yeah, I saw that. Thought it was just a formality after the fact. Didn't realise we didn't have a copy yet. Can I assume, then, that the rest of the Service's material, the owl's cage, handler's gloves, anything like that is also not at CSI?'

Glum nod from Ivan, but he was saved from any backlash by Sharmila's arrival.

'Thanks for coming, Sharmila', Rafi said, as if she had actually had a choice in the matter. 'Who'd you speak to at Border Control regarding Rostam Alinejad?'

While Rafi sat at his desk with his phone to his ear waiting to be put through to Sharmila's contact at Border Control, Martin's phone rang. He went into the corridor to take it. When he came back in, Rafi was in full flow on the phone.

Whoever's on the other end is taking a real reaming, Martin thought. He beckoned for Ivan and Kasia to lean in. 'That was the office. They've got results on Kasia's midnight caller. It was bounced around a lot, but they'll give 60-40 odds that it originated here in the US'.

Rafi hung up and indicated he had one more call to make.

'Siobhan? Rafina Matos here. I hear you have been trying to help us get access to the Secret Service Agents on duty the night of the attack?'

'No, not Agent Wilkins, the others'. He snapped his fingers at Ivan with a questioning look.

'Tomas, Gomez, Holgersen and... ah... Stankić'.

'Tomas, Gomez, Holgersen and Stankić'. Rafi repeated.

'Uh-huh. Uh-huh. So, basically, nada?'

'Great. Thanks Siobhan. Talk again soon'.

Again, he indicated silently for the others to stay put while he made one more call. This time, he was more conciliatory, almost jovial.

'Brice! Rafi. How are you?'

'Good, good! Listen, I'm just helping the team out on a few odds and ends on this Trump-Robbins investigation. What do you fellers know about Rostam Alinejad and the "second 9/11"? We're not convinced they're directly connected, what do you think?'

He put his phone back in his pocket and leant back in his chair, hands behind his head, looking at the ceiling. Finally, he rocked forward fast enough to cause the others to move back slightly.

'I don't think Brice or the Agency sees the connection', Rafi began. 'He sees it as tenuous at best; he trusts Morna's analysis that the ISIL claim is bogus, and is reserving judgement – sitting on the fence – on the idea that an Islamist plot pre-existed. That idea is based on just one intercept; an intercept that has different interpretations depending on who's doing the translating.

'Brice gives Morna credit for a unique take on the intercept, but there's been no other traffic or humtel on this; zero confirmation. More interestingly, he got a call from Senator Metaxas a few days back – the Senator's on the Intelligence Oversight Committee. Brice is used to politicians who get a bit carried away with the "James Bond glamour" of the spy world and then cross the line from oversight to wanting involvement in ops.

'Metaxas wanted the Intelligence community to give more credence to the second 9/11 theory, and put more assets on chasing down Islamists, especially one Rostam Alinejad. Somehow, this Senators knew about this guy before we did.

'Anyway, Brice doesn't like people – even Senators from the Oversight Committee – who try to run his operations. He politely put the Senator in his place. "Let the professionals do their work", sort of thing. Rafi looked at his audience to make sure they were still following him.

'Within an hour Brice gets another call, this one from the Deputy Secretary of Defence. High-powered stuff. Brice is told, no nonsense, to put assets on the Islamist angle in general and chasing Alinejad in particular.

'As he said to me, either there are some very powerful people running intelligence without the knowledge of the FBI and CIA or there are some very powerful politicians running scared as to what happens now. I never did buy into the "cigarette man" character in the X-Files. Which only leaves the politicians running scared scenario.

'It's probably tied into what has to be going on in Congress right now. They must be having a huge bun fight to see who's going to be V-P now Robbins is dead. They're probably arguing who gets the presidency if Trump doesn't make it as well. Which, however, I understand won't be the case. Trump's supposedly doing well'.

Rafi's long and uncharacteristically structured speech reminded the others in the room that before he sat in the politicised Director's chair, Rafina Matos had been an excellent field agent.

Rafi wrapped up. 'First things first. I don't know why Rostam Alinejad is so damn important, but we need to find him if he's still in the country. Put out an APB on him; get cops across the country looking for him. Sharmila, get details from Border Control. I think you'll find your contact there to be very co-operative now. The rest of you, keep going for now, but I would hope we can get a bit more out of the Secret Service in a day or two. I'm going to Washington to shake a few trees'.

The others took this as the dismissal it was, put on coats and said their goodbyes. As Ivan was about to leave, Rafi called him back.

'And Ivan, I don't mind you using this office while I'm away, but fill up the Nespresso cups once in a while, would ya?'

Bill Ngo had also started the day by briefing his boss on the previous evening's conversation with Morna.

After Bill had left Alden's office, Alden made a few calls, including one to Senator Marvin Jäger of the FBI Oversight Office. An eavesdropper would have heard Alden's side of the conversation:

'Marvin, it's Alden. We're getting some odd signals over here. I know you've always been helpful, but, well, seems some of your fellow Senators may have crossed the line a bit. Y'know, overzealous?'

'Sure. If I were you, I'd have a quiet word with some of the people on the Intelligence Committee, they may have been whispering into FBI ears, your backyard, not theirs, yes?'

'Oh, it's this "second 9/11" and foreign involvement in the Trump-Robbins case. I passed your info onto Bill Ngo, the Assistant US Attorney on the case here in New York, but now some people are questioning the theory…'

'No, I'd rather not at this point, it's getting a little hot here. Thing is, I'm glad you told me, but we both knew that I'd need something more concrete, sources and all that, before we started putting a trial case together, right? Well, I think we may need to start doing that now'.

'Uh-huh. No, I understand completely. Same at this end'.

'So you can't give me anything at the moment? Fair enough. Any idea when you might be able to?'

'Uh-huh. Okay. Well, thanks anyway, Marvin. Best to Claire and we should catch up when I'm next in D.C'.

'Yeah. You too. Bye'.

Alden Saunders, US Attorney for the Southern District of New York, hung up the phone and looked out of his window thoughtfully.

He was still looking out the window a few minutes later when his phone rang.

'This is Saunders'.

'Hi Alden. Rafi Matos here. I just had a very interesting discussion about the Trump-Robbins investigation'.

'Yeah, me too. Bill Ngo told me about his accidental meeting with Morna MacCallum at NSA'.

'Uh-huh, Ivan did the same for me. I'm not sure it *was* accidental at this point, but Ivan and Detective Pasternak are, so I'll assume that for now. The picture I'm getting is that this was very coordinated and very sophisticated. That it probably wasn't ISIL, but could still be Islamist terrorists. Call that a sixty, seventy percenter. Brice over at the Agency would probably agree with that.

Defence and the Secret Service had a lead on an Islamist terrorist here in the US'.

'*Had* a lead?'

'Yeah. Had. They were trying to "keep it in the family". I'm not happy with the way some things keep pointing to Service culpability. Anyway, it's not their lead now. We've taken it over. We put out an APB a few minutes ago. Why I'm calling you, at some point, we're going to find this guy and we're going to need to hold him on something. No way am I just going to interview him and put him back on the street. That's where you come in'.

'That's crazy, Rafi! Bill told me that Morna didn't even really know his name, it sounded like a hunch and a prayer wrapped in a wish. You pull someone in when we don't have anything concrete on him and we'll be lucky to keep him overnight'.

'And if he arranged a hit on our President and Veep-elect and we knew where he was and didn't act? Can't do it, Alden. Anyway, Bill didn't have the whole picture. Border Control have confirmed they got an official request from the Service to look for this guy, not just Morna's throwaway line. I'm going to Washington tonight to see if I can't loosen some lips. By the time we pick up Alinejad, I'll know why the Service wanted to talk to him and, by extension, what we'll want to talk to him about. What I need to know is if you're with me to act quickly. As soon as I know what the Service suspects, and assuming it's big, will you be able to conjure up a warrant of sorts so we can hold him for a week?'

'There's a lot of ifs in there. Let's just say I'm a hundred percent behind you, if you give me something with which I can invoke the Patriot Act, I'll be able to hold someone indefinitely while you find evidence.

'Thanks. Now… there's something else that doesn't feel right. Let me lay a few facts out, they may look unconnected at first, but my gut tells me there's something going on. Brice gets a call from Senator Metaxas saying the Intelligence Committee thinks this is an Islamist plot. Then he gets a call from the Deputy Secretary of Defence saying the same. Brice also told me he had a conversation with Rusty Wilkins, the Service Agent-in-Charge on the night, and that he, Brice, not Rusty, got the feeling that Wilkins was trying to say that Linda Starr of Homeland Security oversight was trying to send a message. And last week, Murray Allard told me that "higher ups" in Homeland Security had information about Muslims and a plot. So one Senator and one Congresswoman, Metaxas and Starr, who are on both on intelligence-related oversight committees *and* the Deputy Secretary of Defence think there is an ISIL, or someone like them, plot while the field level staff don't see it'.

'Uh… okay, there's a lot of different stuff here, Rafi. Not sure I follow at the moment, but keep going'.

'And Secret Service have been uncooperative with us. Allard and Croft, Wilkins' boss in the Service, are close and both of them are one step away from being "higher ups" in Homeland Security. I don't get it, but there's a disconnect somewhere'.

There was a pause in the conversation as Alden Saunders digested the information.

'Assuming you're onto something, Rafi, there's another bit of information you need. I just talked to Marvin Jäger'.

'Senator Jäger? Of the FBI oversight committee? Isn't he more my line than yours?'

'Technically, yes, but Marvin and I go back aways. I'd heard some of what you've just said and told Marvin that some Senators may be exceeding their briefs. Hinted that they could be interfering in an FBI investigation and to back off. Funny thing is, Marvin then tried to tell *me* that Islamists were behind this. I ask him why he's telling me, not the FBI? He hums and haws. Suggests that I have a good relationship with you and could perhaps "put Rafi back on track". I tell him that it doesn't work like that and he should know better. You and I – Justice and FBI – cooperate but we can't interfere with each other. The FBI figures it all out, catches the bad guys then I figure out what charges will stick and go to court. That's the way it always goes. He backed down, but reluctantly, as if he knew something, but couldn't tell me. He'd tried to tell me the same thing a week back'.

'So now we have *two* Senators, one Congresswoman and the DoD telling us it's Jihadists and our field teams saying it isn't?'

'Looks it. I wouldn't say anyone's close to being confident, certainly nothing I'd build a case on, but, yeah', Alden replied.

'So what now?' Rafi asked.

'Who you planning on seeing in Washington?'

'I've already got a meet with the Director. Hoping Robert may be able to get the ear of his opposite number at the Service. If I'm really persuasive, he may bump it to the Attorney-General which means we may get the DHS Secretary on the line. If the "higher-ups" know something, they need to tell us'.

'Good luck with that! Let me know how you make out'.

'Well, no guarantees, but the main objective is to get the USSS to loosen up and give us access to their agents and the evidence, *now*. I'm pretty confident I'll get that. If I get anything else, like what's the source of all this pressure, that'll be cream on top'.

Deputy Director Ian Croft's intercom beeped. "The Director's on the line, Mr Croft".

Croft was not surprised. Yesterday, he had briefed the Director late in the day on the work the Secret Service in New York had done: The identification of Alinejad; the suspicion that he had trained the bird to carry the bomb to and; helped by Border Control and Immigration, they were confident that Alinejad was still in the country and the Service were giving their files on the matter to the FBI. Damage controlled. He'd also mentioned that Agents Byrnes and Holgersen were to arrive back in New York today for formal statements.

'Good afternoon, Director'.

'Not a good afternoon, Ian. Not a good afternoon at all'.

Croft was stunned by this opener. 'What's up?'

'A lot of stuff is up. I have to attend an emergency session tomorrow morning with the DHS Secretary, Justice and the Director of the FBI. And they're not happy, Ian. They say that the Service has been impeding a Federal murder investigation. And a very high profile one at that'.

'But we're the ones giving them information, we got Alinejad for them'.

'Did you? Did you, indeed? The FBI say they haven't heard from you at all. Tell me you actually did pass over the Alinejad files'.

'Of course we did!'

'Are you sure? Who did you talk to?' Mixing his metaphors, the Director continued, 'I want all bases covered when I'm hauled over the carpet tomorrow'.

'Ah... well, I didn't talk to them directly, Agent Wilkins is in charge of the investigation; he would have been in touch'.

'Check that for me, will you, Ian? I'll hold'.

Keeping the Director on hold was not something Croft was used to doing. Quickly, he called Rusty Wilkins, got the details and was back on the line with the Director in under four minutes.

'Got some bad news, sir. Bit of a miscommunication at this end. Agent Wilkins didn't reach the FBI yesterday. He's on it now, though'.

'I see'. The fifteen second silence that followed felt like hours to Croft. 'Anything else you haven't done Ian? Anything else that I might be surprised with tomorrow? No, don't answer. We'll talk later'. And he hung up. Croft exhaled as he realised he'd been holding his breath.

'Wilkins! Get in here. Now!'

Day Ten

December 8, 2016

Outside the hospital Donald Trump's Chief of Staff introduced Mr Trump's personal physician, Dr. Lloyd Randall, to the media. Like many senior doctors and surgeons, Randall was confident and controlled; being faced with a dozen microphones and cameras did not faze him at all. This was not his first press conference for a high-profile client and he knew how to sound professional and reassuring without being so medical as to confuse the audience.

'I am pleased to announce that Mr Trump is recovering nicely and is out of immediate danger. As you know, Mr Trump received a number of injuries amongst the most serious being a puncture wound to his left lung and multiple contusions. The injury that concerned us the most was a cranial bleed that put pressure on his brain. We operated twice to relieve this swelling, most recently two days ago; Tuesday afternoon.

'This morning, we brought Mr Trump out of his induced coma and he is alert and responsive. He is, however, still in recovery and we will be keeping him here for a few more days to ensure his body is repairing itself before we consider sending him home.

'Mrs Trump is with him at the moment and I understand other members of his family will be visiting later in the day. He has expressed a desire to speak to select members of the media, but it is my professional opinion that we should all wait a couple more days. He is a strong and vital man and should make a full and speedy recovery, but let's not push it', Dr. Randall ended with a slight chuckle.

Francisco Duarte looked around at a couple of dozen people in the room. 'We're agreed, then? Romney has our backing for Veep and our six Electors will write Rubio in as an alternative presidential candidate so we at least have a horse in the race if Donald doesn't make it'.

The listeners nodded in agreement although some were noticeably more cautious than others. Many voices interrupted themselves as several people talked at the same time.

'I'm good with Rubio although the news sounds like we won't need anyone. Trump's doing well according to the hospital, but...'

'I'm still not comfortable with choosing a Vice-President without the President's input'.

'And *I'm* not comfortable letting that asshole choose his own breakfast, let alone a Veep'.

Francisco lowered his head and weakly raised a hand. 'Please. We've been over and over this. It's still our Party, and Donald is just one part of it. We need to put a lot of strong people around him to make sure that he doesn't do anything *too* stupid while in office. It's George Dubya all over again.

'More importantly, it's our responsibility to ensure that the Party's reputation remains somewhat intact at the end of four years. God knows, that's going to be hard enough! *And* a lot of us in this room could be facing tough re-election campaigns in two years if Trump goes off the rails.

'Plus', he continued raising a finger. 'We've got just over a week to get names out to the Electors and make sure they know how to spell "Rubio"! If we wait for Donald we'll never make the deadline regardless of whatever cockamamie decision he'll make. You heard the doctor, it'll still be a few days before he can talk. And notice he said "his *body* is repairing itself" nothing about his mind'.

'Oh, c'mon, Francisco! We can't make too much out of a casual remark like that'.

'You sure a respected doctor like Randall would make a "casual" remark?' Duarte responded. 'I'm not. And I don't want to assume that he *will* be capable of making a rational decision by Saturday. He still needs to be briefed on the situation, and he hasn't even been told Mason was killed as far as I know.

'We simply don't have enough time for him to start sounding people out, doing his own horse trading and getting someone to agree to work with him. We've got to get a name out to the Electors by a week Monday.

'We've got a good, solid candidate in Romney who we can work with. And let me tell you, getting Mitt to even agree to work with Donald was hard enough'. *Just,* he thought, *getting Romney into the same room with Trump was difficult just a couple of months ago.*

'Okay, okay. I'm in the minority here so go ahead, but there's gonna be fireworks when Trump hears what we've done'.

'Sure will. But his hands will be tied; it's actually a great opportunity for the Party to get some control back'.

No one said it out loud, but many people thought: *Almost as if it was planned that way in advance.*

Martin was going through the case notes and material in the investigation room by himself. Kasia was away somewhere. *Don't have to know where she is 24/7*, he thought.

He continued to flick at random through the notes. Occasionally, he'd stretch and get up to study the walls that were covered with pictures, clippings, post-it's and strings connecting apparently unconnected facts. *We've missed something....*

He watched, perhaps for the fiftieth time, the video compilation of Jaffar's movements leading up to the point where he disappeared into 630 Fifth Avenue, never to be seen alive again.

Suddenly, he froze the tape and stared at the screen. He reached for his phone.

'Ivan? Martin here. Jaffar was carrying a black backpack. I don't recall seeing it at the scene; I assume your forensics picked it up, but we've never discussed what was in it. Run it by me?'

There was a silence at the other end broken by the sound of pages turning and typing on a keyboard.

'There's no backpack or contents listed in the inventory, Martin. Why do you think he had one?'

'His friend Kino told me he always carried one and had it on the day he disappeared. It's clear on the video footage that he had it when he entered 630, surprised you didn't catch it earlier'.

'I haven't seen the footage, Martin, you've never shown it to me'.

There was a brief silence on Martin's end. 'Damn. That's what comes from multi-agency investigations, I guess, even when we are cooperating. Didn't realise you hadn't seen it'.

'Wonder what else we've forgotten to share...', Ivan mused. 'Perhaps we can get some people at both our ends to do a cross-check on evidence, and make sure we've both got copies and a record of what the other has at least'.

'Good idea. I'll get Gene onto that here. Meanwhile, we're missing a backpack'.

'Important?'

'Not sure. Could be just schoolbooks, but if it turned out to have residue from the gun or drone controls, that would change our current thinking. Either way, it's a loose end. I'll get Gene on that, have uniformed do a search of the building, see if the caretakers or cleaners found anything. Doubt it'll turn up anything, it's been a week now, but it may even give us a lead on "Mr Edwards". Suppose he met Jaffar in the building, gave him the drone controls, shot him and then took the backpack'.

'Jaffar could have dumped it somewhere or put it down outside the office and it got stolen', Ivan suggested.

'Yeah, but not as likely as our Mr Edwards taking it. I still don't get why Edwards had to go through all that trouble to get Jaffar to use the drone, why not just use it himself, walk away and drop the controls in a trash can?'

'Guess we'll have to wait to ask Mr Edwards himself that question! And you'd better be careful not to start believing that "Edwards" is actually our guy's name and not just a nickname we've given him'.

'Yeah', agreed Martin. 'Easy to fall into that trap isn't it? And on that subject... any news on the real Edwards?'

'Not a thing. Complete blank. As good as a professional job'.

'You suggesting Edwards is a professional?'

'A hitman? Maybe, but I haven't seen anything else suggesting a Mafia link', Ivan replied.

'No, not criminal-professional, spook-professional. Could help explain why some people higher up, including members of intelligence oversight, seem to know more than we do'.

'And explain why Brice Payton keeps popping up!'

'Yeah. But if it is a spook, *whose* spook? Ours? Chinese?'

'Let's not waste too much energy on that right now', Ivan suggested. 'It's an interesting theory, but still a theory for now. As you said yourself, let's focus on finding who did what, the why should follow. Meanwhile, while NYPD uniformed are looking for a metaphorical needle in a haystack, why don't you have your guys go through the video evidence *after* the attack, look for anyone leaving the building with a black backpack?'

'Good idea'.

Rafina Matos had arrived at FBI Headquarters by ten. All too often, he had to get up at an ungodly hour to catch a flight that got him to D.C. in time for morning meetings, but not this time. He'd been more successful than he'd anticipated. Rafi had got the attention of some *very* senior people. The price was that the meeting couldn't take place until tomorrow, Friday. At least he'd be home for the weekend.

He decided to spend the morning and lunch catching up with old friends and colleagues at FBI HQ on Penn Avenue, strengthening old relationships and forging new ones. He also decided to treat himself to a drive down to Quantico in Virginia and spend the afternoon at the FBI lab with the forensics people - CSI. While not quite as dramatic as the television series, the lab was a fascinating place to spend a few hours.

He'd hung around the lab until six-thirty to let the traffic to D.C. die down a little and then headed back to the capital. He had arranged to meet some work-buddies for dinner at eight at a restaurant near his hotel so he could have a couple of drinks as well.

Just before eleven as he was brushing his teeth before bed he received a call: Rostam Alinejad had rented a car in Florida just a week ago. He didn't seem to be covering his tracks in any way. *Probably thinks he's beyond suspicion, foreign, no priors, no apparent connection to terrorists or Trump. If only the Service, or that fellow in Holland, Snieders? - had told us of Alinejad earlier, we'd already have him. Still, we should get him in a day or two now.*

He was confident that the next day's meeting would go well, and slipped off into a deep, dreamless sleep.

This time the conversation was in English. Once again using VOIP rather than cellular networks, rerouted via various VPNs and deliberately distorted.

The first voice said, 'It seems the investigators are having doubts about an ISIL connection'.

Second voice: 'Don't worry Mister Pink. Mister Black told us it was only a delaying tactic anyway, muddy the waters, sow doubt, that sort of thing'.

A third voice, possibly female. 'Well Mister Black isn't that credible at the moment Mister Blue. The job isn't finished yet. And it was meant to be done before the College'.

Second voice: 'We've had this discussion, Brown. Black told us that the original plan was unnecessarily complicated; *that's* what put is in this position'.

First voice again. 'So what's he doing about it? *Is* he doing anything?'

Second voice: 'Of course, but... Black tells me that the second attempt can only happen after... after... *he* is away from his current location'.

First voice: 'Hospital?'

Second: 'Chrissakes, Pink! Try not to use specifics, huh?'

Third voice: 'That'll be too late... but we can probably live with it as long as *it* gets done. Can Mister Black guarantee it will get done, even if it's late?'

'Absolutely. But you may as well know there are other players in the game now'.

First and third together: 'What!'

'Hey, I'm just the messenger, seems some... Pacific... friends have been in touch with Mister Black'.

First: 'Pacific friends?'

Third voice, slowly: 'We don't have any Pacific friends, Blue'.

'Seems we do now'.

Two storeys below ground, the listening post looked much like any other open plan government office. The absence of windows was something people quickly got used to. Nearly all the people working that night were young, mostly in their twenties. College students or graduates who were serving their country by listening in on the world's conversations.

Sitting back-to-back in their cubicles were two such men just starting the night shift. There was nothing in particular that made them stand out from the other young men and women that night. Just a little tidier; clean shaven and well dressed. Both of them were intelligent and Mormon, this position had the huge benefit of being able to go home, at least on weekends.

Their current assignment was, however, quite distinct from the others in the room. These two, merely because they had been the first to overhear a "Tarantino Call", as they were now known, had been assigned to those calls and any "hops", leads, provided by the calls. Unfortunately, so far they had generated zero hops. In addition to their own signal data they were sent digital copies of the recordings of Kasia Pasternak's conversations with "Mister White". Although their line manager was here in the Utah basement with them, their main technical line went through one Morna MacCallum, currently stationed in New York City.

'I think I got something on that crazy Tarantino thing'.

'What?'

'The algorithm for "Mister" and colours flagged a call a few minutes back. Too many cut outs to trace, but I bounced the conversation back into the system to look for matching outgoes rather than ins. Got an eighty-percenter matching one of the sides of the conversation. Probably not as secure as the others'.

'And?'

> It seems the investigators are having doubts about an ISIL connection.
> So what's he doing about it? Is he doing anything?
> Hospital?
> What!
> Pacific Friends?

'Not much to go on. I don't hear any references to Mr Rainbow; why'd'ya think it's a Tarantino.'"?'

'Not much, that's for sure. As for the hit, the algorithm looks for the word "Mister" and then a colour at least twice in a thirty-second clip. It did that, but couldn't unscramble the signal to record it. That's where I stepped in. I told the computers to listen for the scrambled signal, and then match the scrambled pattern to any outgoing signals. It found a couple and one of them had weaker encryption than the others. Got it to focus there. Sure enough, it was able to unscramble that one side of the call. It's how we ended up with this. It's not much I know, but it's something. And, if I say so myself, some pretty slick work on my part'.

'Sure, sure, Mike. You'll get a medal for this. Not sure if it tells us much though'.

'Well, for starters, it tells us that they're not on a unified system. Different callers are using different encryption, probably different hardware. A-n-d... I saved the best for last: Origin of the matched source signal'.

'Oh?'

'Right here in the good ol' USA. Washington'.

'D.C. or State?'

'D.C'.

'Any tighter?'

'No, but you never how this sort of piece fits into the larger puzzle'.

Day Eleven

December 9, 2016

The room would not have been out of place in many boardrooms. There was a large oval table made of thick wood; high-backed leather chairs on swivel bases; a sideboard with coffee, tea, fresh fruit and a selection of breakfast cereals and pastries (but no doughnuts, too déclassé at this level). There was also a large picture window. Unfortunately, the view was nothing more spectacular than the modern buildings of the American University opposite.

They represented a variety of agencies: Rafi from the FBI; Emery McKinley and his boss Nolan Quinn of the NYPD Detectives" Bureau; Murray Allard, wearing his Counterterrorism (New York) Office hat; Alden Saunders from the Department of Justice, also New York; Ian Croft, Deputy Director of the US Secret Service and; Brice Payton, CIA, ostensibly representing the Department of Defence.

Although the majority of them were based on New York, the meeting was being held in the office of the Deputy Secretary of the Department for Homeland Security to emphasise the seriousness of the occasion. It was also expected that various Washington-based people, senior to the people in this office, would want to talk to their subordinates face-to-face immediately after the meeting and may even drop in to see how things were going.

Gender imbalance in power politics is not a new observation so having seven men and no women meet was not that unusual for Washington. As luck would have it, however, the most powerful presence at this meeting *was* female. The Attorney-General of the United States had decided that, while the discussion was important, it didn't justify her physical presence so she was joining via teleconference and it was to her image on the big screen that all seven men aligned their chairs.

She had made her displeasure, and her expectations for the future, clear to all the participants:

'...the better part of ten days has been lost...'

'The DHS was created to stop just this kind of agency-territoriality...'

'...time you gentle*men* stopped your pissing contest and got on the same page...'

It wasn't said openly, but the fact that the Secret Service was in the doghouse was also very clear. US Customs and Borders were not sanctioned for, as she said, '...deliberately obscuring if not withholding important information commissioned by the Secret Service from the FBI', only because they weren't present at the meeting. There was no doubt that the Attorney General would be having a word with *their* Director shortly.

Under such direction, it was no surprise that the meeting started promptly, and that it was amicable, with all of them promising complete transparency and cooperation. All data would be shared, at least upwards to the investigating FBI agents, and perhaps, depending on good behaviour, downwards or laterally with the other agencies as deemed necessary by those same FBI agents.

Ian Croft started to claim that, 'Certain aspects of the Service's procedures need to remain secret for reasons of national security…'

He was cut off by A-G who said that she had had "a frank discussion" with both the Director of the Secret Service and *his* boss, the Secretary of the DHS. They had both agreed that "there was no higher national security imperative than the rapid and successful apprehension of the perpetrators of this heinous crime". *In other words, Ian, sit down and shut up unless you have something that will advance this investigation instead of obstructing it.*

Brice Payton had pledged the full cooperation of the Department of Defence, the CIA and the National Security Agency by saying that they '…would be more proactive in looking for, and sharing, in full, any and all intelligence information they gathered overseas'.

Everyone knew he was more interested in twisting the knife into the Secret Service's wound than actually doing what he said. It was understood that anything the NSA and CIA said always came with the unstated proviso, 'so long as it isn't against what we judge to be national security'.

Brice also said that '…any and all domestic intelligence would be shared. However, the NSA and the CIA don't, of course, have any authority to collect any such information and even if they did, it would only be under such conditions wherein it would be impossible to admit it existed, much less share, without a court order'.

At that point he was reminded that the Attorney General was the most senior law officer in the country. A court order wouldn't be that difficult to arrange…

By ten in the morning, the FBI knew that Rostam Alinejad had rented a car in Florida. By eleven, two FBI Agents had met the Orange County Sheriff. The Sheriff put his Special Response Team (SRT) on alert. He then managed to catch a local judge before an early lunch.

After just ten minutes of discussing the situation with the Sheriff and the FBI agents, the judge signed a court order. Armed with the piece of paper, the three men drove to the car rental agency at Orlando International airport. There was no real need for the court order. The agency was more than happy to help the law enforcement officers, especially if it meant preventing damage to their car. Fifteen minutes and one cup of coffee later, and GPS tracking on Alinejad's car had been turned on and the software app transferred to Agent Briggs' mobile phone. No drama.

The car was less than thirty kilometres away, registering on the app as being stationery in the Disneyworld parking lot. The SRT was told to go to the amusement park on a "ten-minute standby" status. That is, they could relax, but would need to be able to respond to any event within ten minutes of receiving an order to do so.

Phone calls were made to Disneyworld security and, borrowing the rental agencies computer facilities, a scan of Alinejad's passport photo was sent to them with strict instructions to search and observe only; 'Do *not* make contact or approach the subject'.

Briggs then called the Orlando Police Department, asked for a meeting with the Chief and for assistance in calling hotels in the area in case he had registered under his own name. Both requests were granted.

The Agents then drove an hour up highway 15 onto 408 where they met with the OPD Chief at twelve-fifty in the afternoon. After once again checking that the car had still not moved (no surprise there, Briggs had been watching the GPS app constantly while the Sheriff drove) it was agreed that an OPD patrol car would get within visual distance, but no closer, within ten minutes. This would be replaced by four plainclothes officers in two unmarked cars as soon as possible. No police would enter Disneyworld itself at that time, but the OPD SWAT would liaise with, and provide backup as required, to the SRT team at the park.

Back in the car, they travelled south on highway 4 and were at Disneyworld by two in the afternoon. At two twenty-two, Disneyworld security called to say that they had made a positive identification. The subject was in the company of a woman and two children and they were acting like any other visitor to the park. Loath to start anything in a public space full of children, Agent Briggs maintained an "observe only" status.

A little while later, OPD called. A Rostam Alinejad and family had checked into the Shady Beach Motel two nights before. Despite its name, the motel is nowhere near a beach, but it is close to SeaWorld. They were due to check out in two days' time on December tenth. The staff at the hotel couldn't think of anything remarkable about the Alinejads, they seemed nice enough and spoke "good English" with slight accents.

The Sheriff, who by this time was beginning to get bored at the slow pace of the "Federals", was all for searching the hotel room, but Briggs vetoed that. If there had been an indication of impending danger, or flight, or, well, *anything* to suggest that he was dealing with a dangerous criminal, he would have authorised the search, even without a warrant. But there wasn't. Alinejad was acting like any other tourist on holiday. If he *did* have anything to do with the bomb in New York, he was being very cool about it. *Perhaps*, thought Briggs, *he's even inviting us to do something that can later be used to get a mistrial.* For now, Briggs asked the Sheriff if he would move his SRT up to the hotel and called the OPD Chief once more to get an unmarked car to put Alinejad's room under surveillance, but to keep his SWAT at base for now. Asking his FBI colleague to keep an eye on the GPS and to inform him if the car started moving, Briggs stepped out of the car and walked a distance away before using his phone. He didn't want the others to hear that he needed help from New York on this one.

After the Washington meeting adjourned, phone calls were made to subordinates in New York. This was entirely expected and most of the people who received the phone calls had already kept their calendars clear for the afternoon.

With Rafi still in Washington, Ivan had once again commandeered his boss's office. Yet the room still felt cramped with eight people representing five departments sitting in it. Ivan and Sharmila of the FBI were there of course, as were Martin, Kasia and Siobhan of NYPD.

Bill Ngo was also present: Pressing his advantage in having the Attorney-General presiding over the Washington meeting, Alden Saunders had insisted that the US Attorney's office become more involved in the investigation. His main concern was that further inter-agency infighting could lead to lapses in due process that could jeopardise any case that was eventually brought forward. This was readily agreed upon in Washington in the morning.

The seventh person was welcomed warmly, but also with some surprise. Technical Analyst Morna MacCallum of the National Security Agency was now seconded to the investigation. The surprise was not that electronic surveillance and intelligence resources were being made available full-time to such a high-profile investigation. Nor were Morna's capabilities in question. The surprise was who this was *not*.

Homeland Security had its own intelligence department at a national level – the National Protection and Programs Directorate, who often worked closely with the Secret Service. Similarly, the New York State Division of Homeland Security and Emergency Services had its own intelligence officers in the Intelligence and Analysis Unit, that worked with New York Office of Counterterrorism (Murray Allard's purview) and the Joint Terrorism Task Force (Siobhan's crowd). That neither of these departments were represented, indeed, had been usurped by the NSA, part of the Department of Defence, spoke volumes about the current standing of Homeland Security with the Attorney-General and the White House vis-à-vis this investigation.

The last person present in Rafi's office that afternoon was welcomed somewhat reluctantly. US Secret Service Agent-in-Charge Rusty Wilkins was not in either Ivan's or Martin's good graces. And, judging by Morna's presence, the Secret Service as a whole was not in the good graces of the FBI, the A-G or NYPD. Nevertheless, here he was and, judging by Wilkins" attitude – eager to repair the damage to his reputation by being *very* cooperative.

'Alright', Ivan said after the bulk of the first hour had been spent making sure that everyone was more or less up to date with the major developments in the case. 'Now onto new information. Acting on the Secret Service's information', he looked at Wilkins, trying to be non-judgemental, 'and with the help of the Orange County Sheriff's Department and Orlando PD, we picked up Rostam Alinejad's trail in Florida earlier today. Agent-in-Charge Paul Briggs called me twenty minutes ago wanting some direction as to next steps'.

'Next steps?' asked Martin. 'Surely it's straight-forward, get him into custody and up here to New York for questioning!'

'That *would* seem to be the obvious move', Ivan replied, 'but I can tell you right now that it doesn't look right. Either he is the coolest customer we've seen or he isn't who we're looking for. He hasn't been hiding, he hasn't covered his tracks. He's staying with a woman and two children who he claims are his family. The hotel says the IDs were convincing, Dutch passports. Border Control confirms they entered the US on those same passports.

'Alinejad and the family are currently in Disneyworld. We've got them under surveillance, but everyone says they're acting exactly like tourists. The local law wants to kick down the hotel door and do a search, but Briggs has been able to hold them back "while he gets a warrant". Which is to say, ask me what to do. One thing for sure, we're not pulling out a bunch of guns in Disneyworld in front of God knows how many mobile phones to go viral on YouTube in minutes, but neither are we going to give Alinejad a chance to turn this into a hostage situation. We need to know how dangerous this man is and how confident we are in that threat assessment'.

Ivan looked at Wilkins. 'So. Rusty. What do you have on Alinejad?'

Looking decidedly uncomfortable, Wilkins said, 'He's an Iraqi. Spent time in Saudi Arabia training hunting birds, falcons, *et cetera.*, for Saudi princes and businessmen. They're keen on falconry…'

'Yeah, we know, Rusty', interrupted Bill, 'how about we just stick to facts rather than background info'.

Obviously feeling the antagonism in Bill's voice, Rusty continued. '…well, anyway, he spent time in Saudi and about a month ago, after training our owl, but before the attack, he comes here to the US'. He tailed off, perhaps realising how weak this sounded.

Silence while everyone waited for more details.

Bill was the first to voice disbelief when it became apparent that the Secret Service man had finished. 'And on this basis, we put out an APB, line up a Sheriff eager to break down a hotel door without a warrant and detain a man and his…' he held his hand up to stop Rusty's interruption '…fine, his *alleged* wife and two children'.

Ivan asked, 'What did Europol have to say?'

'Ah. Well, we didn't go through official channels so we haven't asked them'.

'Great'. Sarcasm dripped. 'Sharmila – your department?'

'On it, boss. They've probably closed up for the day right now, but first thing in their morning, I'll have the paperwork on their desks. I'll follow it up with a call in the morning, our morning, their lunch'.

'Thanks'.

Turning back to Rusty, Ivan continued. 'What about his movements? When did he come here? Was his "family" with him when he entered the US?'

'Yeah, we've got all that'. Rusty slid a sheet of paper over the table to Ivan.

Ivan looked it over. 'Hmmm…. Not much here'.

Rusty was of the same opinion. 'Maybe Agents Byrnes and Holgersen can tell us more about him. They spent weeks with him in Holland when they were over there'.

This time it was Martin who jumped in. 'And where are these two agents? The ones we've been trying to interview for a week?'

'Downstairs', replied Rusty, 'they came back from intensive training in the Catskills yesterday and are now available for discussions'. He tried to look the picture of cooperation, but Martin still looked at him doubtfully.

'Ivan? Mind if Kasia and I do the first interviews with the agents?'

'By all means, Martin. Other than Alinejad, what's your interest?'

'Those damn batteries. I still want to know how dead batteries got into the transponder. And see if they can tell us anything more about this owl and its training. Even though they were fairly comprehensive on that aspect in the first interview, we may have missed something'.

'Oh…kay… I might sit in on some of that. Rusty', Ivan turned back to the Agent, 'why don't you go down to Washington and work with CSI, they've got all the evidence down there and have been trying to isolate possible audio signals, but it would be *very* useful if they knew what they were looking for. You do have a recording of the owl's recall signal, don't you?'

'Of course. Happy to share it'. After a week of stonewalling by Wilkins, the others in the room were perhaps entitled to say something, but they kept their peace… for now.

'Good. Now, what else…? CSI are continuing to look at Jaffar's clothes, the providence of the drone and the explosives used, they've confirmed that the chemical signature has a ninety-five percent probability of being from US Special Forces stock used in Iraq five years ago by the way, but I don't think we're going to get much more from those'.

'And', Martin added, 'NYPD are still digging into Jaffar's acquaintances, school friends, work colleagues, you know, the usual. We're also investigating the mosque, how the community feels about it, what sort of social work they do, have the neighbours seen anything or anyone odd. Nothing unusual so far'.

Morna had been mostly quiet during the meeting. Now she said, 'DoD's also looking at the mosque, but more from the overseas angle, groups that share that particular branch of Islam, who the founders were and funders are, do they do any cross-cultural exchanges, *et cetera*'.

'Excellent'.

'And', she continued, 'we had a hit on your midnight caller, Kasia'.

Ivan jumped in. 'D'yamind if we shelve that for another time, Morna? Important stuff and all that, but I'd like to keep the meeting on topic. As we said to Rusty earlier, perhaps we should stick to facts for now. That other issues a bit too hypothetical for now'.

Morna looked querulously at Ivan, but said no more.

'Meanwhile', Ivan continued, 'we haven't discussed the elephant in the room. Mister Edwards'.

'Who?' Wilkins asked.

'The registered owner of the gun that killed Jaffar. We've been using his name as a generic for whoever turns out to be behind this. And it could well be more than one person. One or many, the fact remains that we're no closer to identifying them than we were a week ago. And no', Ivan said looking at Wilkins, 'I don't think Alinejad is going to fit the bill. So people, there's a lot of work still to be done. Let's get out there and do it!'

The meeting broke up with people grabbing bags, coats and hats. Sharmila and Siobhan had left together with no need for outdoor clothing; they were going to spend the rest of the day getting in touch with, or at least sending emails to be opened in the morning - with their contacts in Europe.

As they went out the door, Ivan called Martin, Kasia and Morna back in.

He waved his hand at the others. 'Just a bit of admin paperwork to get Morna settled in as part of the team. The rest of you carry on, we'll be done here in half an hour or so'.

Rusty was only too happy to leave, 'I should be in Virginia tomorrow morning, keep in touch?'

Kasia turned to Bill, 'Catch you later for a drink?'

'Not today, tomorrow? Have to get back to the family tonight'.

'Okay. See ya'.

Other than a thoughtful flicker crossing his lined face, Martin stood impassively, in no hurry either way.

Once the door had closed again, Ivan turned to Morna. 'Sorry about that, but the others are not briefed as yet on Kasia's "midnight caller"'.

'Oh?' Morna asked. 'I thought we were all chummy now and sharing everything?'

'Not exactly', Ivan replied. 'The agreement is that people, especially Rusty-type people, the Service, have to share everything with us, the investigators. We still have some leeway as to what we share with others. And I had a feeling that you were about to share something that I'm not quite ready to have go public as yet. You think you got a hit on Mister White?'

'Well, not exactly, but a good probability that it was him…' responded Morna before being interrupted by Kasia.

'Or her'.

Nodding, Morna continued, '…or her. Or associates. Eighty percent chance or higher that we caught a fragment of a conversation that included terms such as "Mister White", "Mister Green", "Mister Red" or some variant'.

'Just a fragment, Morna?' Martin asked.

'Fraid so. Nothing earth-shattering, but some interesting titbits. We don't know how many people were on the call, but we're confident that the speaker we heard was male and that his end of the call originated in Washington D.C'.

That got everyone's attention.

'We're talking domestic terrorism?' asked Siobhan.

'Way too early to be saying it's "terrorism", but at least one person is probably in the US, yes. Interestingly, what we did catch, it was in English by the way, so no translation issues this time, had references to "Pacific Friends", "Hospital" and even a reference to us'.

'Us?'

'Us as in "the investigators". The voice said that we are having doubts about an ISIL connection. Obviously, we're continuing to listen in for more calls. And if Mister White calls Kasia again, we've got a really good chance to pin this down further'.

'So who would be in a position to speak about *our* doubts?' Martin asked the room in general.

Kasia broke the silence. 'Wasn't it you, Ivan, who suggested China may have a hand in this? "Pacific friends"?'

'Yeah, but I was just thinking out loud. We need more…' He stopped, uncertainty written on his face. Changing the subject, he continued, 'Anyway, good work, Morna, keep listening and keep us posted. One way or another we'll figure out who this Mister White is'.

Ivan had kept quiet while the others talked and then looked thoughtfully at Morna. 'Incidentally, exactly *how* are you, that is, the NSA, able to do all this listening?'

'Well, it's complicated of course, and I'm not a techie, I know how to analyse and interpret signals, but collection is a bit beyond…'

Ivan held up a hand. Softly, he asked, 'No, not how you listen *technically, but* how you listen *legally*. As far as I know, none of the NSA, CIA or DHS have the *legal* right to listen in on domestic phone calls. The FBI does, but even we need a judge's consent'.

Morna looked a little, but only a little, embarrassed. 'Wel-l-l-l… there are ways. Much of it depends on the definition of "domestic", but much of it can also be gotten around by changing a US-domestic phone call of interest into a foreign-international phone call of interest. In this case, I believe it was suggested to Wellington that there was a Kiwi involvement'.

Ivan's expression was a mix of annoyance, professional curiosity and straight puzzlement. 'Wellington? As in New Zealand?'

'Yep'.

'But there's been no suggestion anywhere of a New Zealand involvement!'

'And that's the plus! You don't want to involve someone and then find out they have legitimate interests or even jurisdiction'.

'I'm not following you, how does New Zealand come in?'

Morna was more animated now she was talking about the work she loved. 'New Zealand's one of our "Five Eyes" partners, along with Canada, UK and Australia, right? All five countries have the right to listen in on their citizens so long as that citizen is *overseas*. So, if we tell them that we think a New Zealand citizen may be involved in a terrorist incident or plot here in the USA, then NZSIS, their security services, can do the listening. As part of RISP - Reciprocal Information Sharing Protocol, they customarily share what they find with us. In this case, although they didn't find any NZ connection – surprise, surprise – they did hear something which suggested a link to your case: "Mister Pink", "Mister Black" and "Mister Blue" were heard on a conversation'.

'And that gives the NSA the right to listen in on Americans?'

'Oh, no. It gives *you*, the FBI, the right to listen in'.

'Huh?'

'The Foreign Intelligence Surveillance Act of 1978, FISA, and the Patriot Act amendments, especially section 206, gave you, the FBI, particularly your Electronic Surveillance Technology Section in Chantilly, an opening to expand domestic wiretapping including VOIP conversations on a roving, "follow the target" basis without the need for case-by-case permission from a judge. When Rafi registered this investigation as a top priority for national security purposes with the Attorney General, it enabled that section of the Act'.

'Kinda following you here, but I still don't see how *you* have the authority to do this'.

Morna laughed. 'The paperwork for my secondment this investigation went through last night and is coincidentally time-stamped about thirty minutes before NZSIS *officially* notified us of what they had found. In other words, I was the FBI before we got the RISP information from New Zealand!'

Ivan was taken aback, unsure of how he felt about all of this.

Martin broke the tension by laughing loudly. 'Well, all I can say is that I'm glad you're on our side, Morna! Welcome to the team'. As he stuck out his hand for her to shake, he said, somewhat less confidently, 'You *are* on our side, aren't you?'

Morna simply shook his hand and smiled.

After everyone left, Ivan picked up his phone and called Florida.

'Agent Briggs? Ivan Biskup again. Look, we're not entirely comfortable at the moment with our intelligence on Alinejad. Can you keep him under surveillance, but do nothing else for now?'

'Uh-huh. Well, obviously if the situation changes, use your initiative, but I think we have to consider the possibility of mistaken identity and that he is what he seems to be, a Dutchman on holiday'.

'Mmmm. Yeah. I think no matter what, we'll want to have a talk to him, he must be aware that it was "his" bird that killed Robbins so an interview shouldn't be too much of a surprise. Do you think you can keep everyone calm until the morning? Tight surveillance during the night then just the two of you have a friendly meeting over a breakfast coffee? Without the family present if possible. Be good to avoid a hostage situation…'

Martin and Kasia were walking down the stairs to the second floor of the FBI building where Kelia Byrnes and Tomas Holgersen were waiting.

Looking sidelong at Kasia, Martin asked, '*Back* to the family tonight?'

'Huh?'

'When Bill said "no" to meeting you for a drink later, he said, "Not today, tomorrow? Have to get back to the family tonight." Sounds like he doesn't always get back to the family'.

Kasia stopped walking. She turned to face her boss and said, 'Are you trying to say something, Martin?' Although her voice was calm, Martin knew her well enough to know she was angry.

'Well, it's just that you never really say anything about your personal life. We've known each other for three years now, you've been to my place for bar-b-que's and things and not once have you brought a date or mentioned a boyfriend or anything…' He finished lamely, knowing he'd made a mistake, but unsure how to undo it.

'Maybe that's because I'm a lesbian! Or maybe asexual… or an alien! Or maybe, just maybe, it's because I don't want to discuss my personal life, or have it discussed behind my back, at work. You're not my boss out of hours, Martin, and maybe this is none of your business!'

It is my business if it affects your work or my investigation, Martin thought and then was immediately ashamed at his own thought. *And when has Kasia ever given you any reason to think she was giving less than a hundred percent?*

He flipped his hands palm up by his waist. 'Sorry. No, I'm really sorry, Kasia. You're absolutely right. I'm out of place. Sometimes I forget to not be a detective. My wife gives me shit for that as well'.

Her face softened, just a little. She was fond of Martin and had a lot of respect for him as a detective and a family man. It would take more than this to undo those three years of partnership. 'Humph!' She said somewhat theatrically. 'Well. In that case, apology accepted'.

He stuck out a hand. 'Friends?'

She took it 'Friends'.

She is so sleeping with Bill, Martin thought.

He has no idea what I do outside of work, Kasia thought.

'Good evening, Agent Byrnes, Agent Holgersen. Apologies for keeping you so long, no rest for the wicked'. This with a slight chuckle. *Martin can put on the charm when he wants to,* thought Kasia.

'I'm Lieutenant Commander Martin King of the New York Detectives" Division and this is Detective First Grade Kasia Pasternak., but please, let's keep this informal; it's just Martin and Kasia'. He finished with a smile and handshakes.

'Pleased to meet you... Martin' Jean Byrnes stumbled a little on using the first name of a senior officer. The Secret Service was much more protocol-driven. Perhaps because they were confronted on a daily basis with *very* important people, such as the President. 'I'm Jean and this is Mark. And we're not actually "Agents". We're just "Technicians"'.

'Ah. Good to know. Anyway, let's all have a seat and perhaps we can get this over with quickly and we can all get home at a reasonable hour. Do you want anything? Coffee?'

'No thanks. All we've done is sit here and drink coffee. So if we seem a bit nervous, put it down to caffeine?'

'Sure, why not? Why don't you start by telling us what you know about Rostam Alinejad. You spent some weeks with him, didn't you? He's Iraqi?'

'Er... well, he's of Iraqi background, but he would prefer the term "Persian"'. Jean, it seems, was used to doing the talking while Tomas was content to listen. 'Really, he's Dutch. Third-generation, I think. His family lives further north, near Groningen. They have a dairy farm or something'.

'We were led to believe that he went from Iraq to Saudi Arabia where he learnt about falconry and training birds. Are you saying this isn't true?'

'Oh, he was in Saudi alright, but he went there from Holland, not from Iraq. As far as I know, he's never been to Iraq. And he went to Saudi Arabia to teach them... not to learn from them. He did his bachelor's in veterinary science and then went on to do a master's in Amsterdam. Academically I guess you'd call him an ornithologist, but most of what he does training the birds comes from techniques that he's developed. He's considered one of the leading experts in this field. It's why the Saudi's wanted him to help them. He's got a fantastic way with birds; they trust him. Bart's very lucky to have him'.

'Did he spend a long time in the Middle East?'

'A couple of months I think. He didn't really like it, far too restrictive, especially for someone who was a student in Amsterdam!'

'And you spent a lot of time together?'

Tomas decided to answer that question. 'Sure. There's not a lot to do in Apeldoorn, it's a smallish town in the middle of a lot of woods and greenlands. There's a few tourist things like the Ape House and the Queen's residence, but we spent most of our free time in the town, y'know, we'd bicycle in, have a few beers, cycle back out'.

'Did he ever say anything political?'

Again Tomas carried on the narrative. 'Of course, we went out two, three times a week for over ten weeks. Politics, religion, sport, music, movies, we talked about all the regular stuff. I know what you're getting at, though, and no, he wasn't overly political, but neither was he hiding anything. He didn't like Trump, but in Europe that's a mainstream position, not a fanatic's'.

'What did he say about Trump?'

'That he was going to destroy America just like Boris Johnson destroyed Britain and Wilders would destroy the Netherlands if he could, there are many jokes in Holland about those three with their wild, bleached hair'.

'Wilders?'

'Geert Wilders. Far right, anti-muslim, xenophobic, leader of the, the… uh, Jean?'

'Dutch Party for Freedom'.

'And did he ever say anything about wanting to hurt Trump?'

'No. Never. He actually didn't say that much about him. I think he, like a lot of Europeans, see American politics like American football, a weird game with lots of odd rules where the sport is hidden by entertainment, cheerleaders, half-time shows and things like that. When he'd had a few he was more likely to get passionate about the Brexit vote and how that could lead to the dissolution of European peace'.

'And', added Jean, smiling fondly in remembrance, 'that Holland didn't qualify for the 2016 Euros. He seemed to see that as a major failing of the national character'.

Kasia decided to try a new line of questioning. 'Did you know he was coming to America? Didn't he want to meet up?'

Jean answered. 'He told us he was coming over though I don't think he'd fixed the dates when we were there. His kids really wanted to see Disneyland, "Course he took them to Disneyworld, cheaper, but they won't care about the difference. As for catching up, we swapped email addresses, but Tom and I aren't always available and Rostam was with his family. We aren't close friends. I gather he has a lot of work-visitors like Tom and I. While he's friendly enough and enjoyed going out with us, we were also "work". So, no, I'm not surprised that we haven't heard from him'.

'And', Tomas added, 'given what happened to Hedwig, he may not have wanted to meet us, he probably associates us with her death'.

Kasia blinked at that. 'He would be concerned about an owl? What about Mr Robbins?'

'Well, he knew and loved the owl. He didn't know Robbins'.

There was a knock on the door and Ivan came in. 'How's it going in here? All good?'

'Not really', said Martin, swivelling his chair around to look up at Ivan. 'Doesn't look like we've got the right guy. You're just in time for the big question'. Martin waved Ivan to a chair and then turned back to the Secret Service officers. 'Do you think that Rostam could have had anything to do with the attack on Robbins and Trump?'

Jean and Tomas answered simultaneously.

'Not a chance'.

'Absolutely not'.

'Even indirectly like helping someone train… Hedwig to carry the drone and bomb?'

Jean laughed lightly. 'Of course he did help someone train Hedwig. Us! That's why we were there. And the whole point of the training is to get the birds to carry a drone, and any payload, away. The only puzzling thing is why she went towards the podium instead of the recall signal'.

Martin turned to face Tomas directly. 'And, Tom, I think that's a key question. What happened?'

Tomas Holgersen reddened, clearly uncomfortable with the question. 'I've asked myself that a million times, sir'. Martin let the word pass as Tomas continued. 'My signal didn't go off. Yet it had when I'd tested it before we set up'.

'What time was that?'

'Around five, five-fifteen. There's a lot of gear to check up and it's best to check the transponder early before Jean brings the birds out, it can agitate them'.

'And you're sure it worked?'

'Very sure. Not only do we have a checklist that I never deviate from, I quite clearly remember testing it'.

'And how do you test it?'

Tomas gave Martin an odd look. 'You listen'.

'It's audible? I thought birds heard much higher frequencies than humans'.

'Some do, but owls don't. Their hearing range is quite limited. Superbly adapted to the sounds they need to hear for hunting, but nothing outside that'.

'So the batteries were working then. Any chance it could have been left on and drained the batteries in the hour or so before the attack or the batteries were old?'

'The protocol says to always use fresh batteries for live operations. I opened the pack myself. As for leaving it on, no way; it's loud and annoying. Everyone in the area would have noticed'.

'So. Fresh batteries. Device working. Then an hour later, batteries are dead and device doesn't work. What happened in that hour, Tomas?'

He looked down at the floor and almost visibly squirmed in his seat. Jean leant over to him. 'C'mon, Tom. We talked about this. It's what happened. You need to tell them'.

Taking a deep breath, he looked up at Martin. 'Normally, everything is in my possession or sight from the time it's checked to the time the operation is closed'.

'Go on, Tom', Martin encouraged gently. 'That's the normal procedure. What was not normal that night?'

'The birds draw a lot of interest. We often have VIPs wanting to see this new approach to security'.

'And that night you had a visitor?'

'Yes'.

'Who was it, Mark?'

'Linda Starr'.

'Congresswoman Linda Starr', Ivan interjected, 'of the House Committee on Homeland Security?'

'Yes. It would have to be someone with that sort of security clearance, not everyone gets access to a Service Protection Detail'. Everyone could hear the capitals. 'Even then, it was only after the perimeter agents got clearance directly from Director Croft that they were allowed in'.

'They?' Kasia asked.

'Uh, yeah. Congresswomen are rarely by themselves. There were three or four others, all men, with her. I assumed they were either Service Agents, I don't know everyone in the Service, or her admin assistants, chief of staff, that sort of thing'.

'But you don't know how many?'

'I was busy trying to get set up. I don't like these sorts of interruptions and no one expects me to be a tour guide. They ask me questions; I answer. So, no, I wasn't paying attention to how many. Probably four. Yeah, four'.

'And', Martin couldn't help himself leaning forward, 'did any of these people, the Congresswoman or any of her entourage, handle the recall device?'

Tomas' face twitched. 'I can't be sure, but... yeah, maybe. There's a lot of equipment around, everything from things for the birds, treats, the cage, arm bands, that sort of thing, plus there's stuff to deal with whatever might be on the drone. I have to wear PPE, Personal Protection Equipment, and I have to be able to deal with possible explosives, biological weapons, radioactive material, anything. There are bomb-disposal personnel and others with NBC trained who can get called in of course, but I'm the front line'.

Martin allowed Tomas to ramble on for a while, knowing it was his way of dealing with the stress, but Martin was also getting a little stressed. *So close.* 'I'm sure it's a tough job, Tomas. You were saying about someone handling the recall device?'

'I didn't see someone actually touch it, but a movement caught my eye, maybe some of the Christmas lights reflecting off the metal surface.

So I turned and looked. I'm sure the transponder was moving slightly. It's a cylinder, and it was rolling a bit. I didn't think much of it at the time, maybe I thought the wind had caught it. Maybe the wind *had* caught it. But there was a man walking away from it. Somehow I thought that he wasn't one of the four that had come in with the Congresswoman. I can't tell you why, just a gut thought'.

'You didn't recognise him? Could you describe him?'

'I only saw his back. Remember, it was dark there, I'd intentionally chosen the darkest corner I could find. Hedwig doesn't… didn't like flying into bright areas. Another thing I can't understand about what she did'.

'About that. Why *would* Hedwig fly towards the podium?'

'There's only one thing that would make her fly in any direction' Jean answered, 'particularly towards an area full of people and lights, the recall signal'.

'And it had to be *the* recall signal, the one you use?'

'Absolutely, it takes months to properly instil that response'.

'Huh'. Martin turned back to Tomas. 'You're sure it was a man you saw walking away?'

'Uh, yeah…' Tomas paused to recall, '…yeah, definitely a man. Dressed in a nice suit with an expensive topcoat'.

'Where did he go afterwards?'

Again a pause while he searched his memory. 'Not sure', Tomas said slowly, 'but now I think about it, he was angling away from the Congresswoman and her party. Maybe that's why I feel he wasn't part of her group'.

Martin, Kasia and Ivan exchanged looks, *Congresswoman Starr?* Then Ivan said, 'Well, Tom – and Jean – I think that's probably it for now. Thanks so much for staying late on a Friday night. You will be staying in town for a while? Just in case we have a few more questions'.

After the two Secret Service officers had left, the three of them sat quietly for a while, digesting what they'd heard. Ivan decided to go first.

'Let's deal with the easy stuff first, shall we?' Without waiting for an answer, he continued. 'Looks like Wilkins jumped the gun a bit on Alinejad. I'll have Agent Briggs have a chat to him in the morning, but that looks like a closed lead to me. Agreed?'

Nods of assent from Martin and Kasia.

'As for Congresswoman Starr…' Ivan exhaled loudly. 'She could be perfectly legit. As Holgersen said, he gets a lot of visitors. Or she's involved somehow. We know some higher ups have been trying to tell us something, maybe she was there to try and *stop* something happening; something she couldn't tell the Service about directly'.

'And our mystery man?'

'Hell, Martin, you know full well that Holgersen could have been mistaken, or that it *was* one of Starr's entourage, or that someone had brushed against it, or that the wind *had* caught it and that person was just putting it back'.

'And yet, Ivan, the batteries were dead. Maybe someone smart enough to know about explosives and Secret Service protocols and such is smart enough to know a Congresswoman's itinerary and attach themselves to the group temporarily before slipping away again'.

'Yeah'. Another sigh. 'Don't think I could convince you to question a sitting member of Congress?'

'Fat chance, Ivan', Martin said with a smile, 'you're the top dog on this investigation, this one's yours!'

'Not sure what I'm more worried about, her or the fact that I'm going to have to call Rafi late on a Friday night. For sure I'm going through him on something like this'.

'Yep, and I'm going to call Emery, but I'll do that in the morning. Good luck, Ivan, don't forget to get some sleep tonight!'

Outside the FBI building, Martin and Kasia both hunched deeper into their coats. It was a clear and cold night, well below freezing and in this corner of New York, relatively dark for Manhattan. Both of them had left their cars at Police Plaza; they set off at a brisk walk with Martin struggling a little to keep pace with Kasia's longer legs.

Ten minutes later and they were at their cars in the now mostly empty police parking lot. As Martin unlocked his car, Kasia called out to him.

'Do you wanna go for a drink, Martin? Or do you have to get "back to your family" tonight?'

'Oh, I should…' he stopped as Kasia's laugh drifted over to him.

She got into her car and drove off.

Day Twelve

December 10, 2016

The King's lie-in ritual had been established when the kids were younger; one parent looked after them on Saturday mornings, the other on Sundays. Now they were teenagers there was no need for that level of parenting; they were perfectly capable of getting dressed and preparing breakfast by themselves, but the ritual continued.

Saturday was Martin's turn. He'd tried to doze, but his mind was too active. Clattering noises and the smell of toast and coffee coming from the kitchen had become too much and by nine he had joined his family. *Amazing how the kids are so active on weekend mornings when it takes us everything we've got to get them out of bed on schooldays...*

After breakfast, he called Kasia. Yes, she was happy to meet him in town so long as she got away by lunch. She wanted to do some shopping and meet friends in the afternoon... and so long as Martin brought along some bagels.

He called Ivan and found him already at his office, sounding as if he'd spent the night there.

Martin hopped in his car, stopped at the deli on his side of the Bridge, and made it into the City within half an hour. The weather had turned grey and wet, not cold enough for snow, but a drizzle that threatened to turn into a steady light rain later. Added to this was a gusty cold northerly that rattled down the Avenues. He decided to put up with the hassle and expense of paying for parking at the FBI building as a guest instead of parking at his office.

Ivan was using Rafi's office yet again. On the phone, he waved vaguely in the air as Martin walked in whether in greeting or an invitation to help himself to coffee and a chair or both, Martin couldn't tell. Kasia had yet to arrive. Martin grabbed a coffee and bagel, offering one to Ivan who took it with a silent thanks, and plopped himself down on the couch with a handful of files from the investigation. Sometimes, it was good to flick through notes at random, letting strands of ideas percolate and intertwine, connecting and falling apart without the restriction of planned thought. Kasia, he knew, abhorred this loose form of lateral thinking, but Martin found it helped to step back once a week or so and let it all flow...

Martin frowned and turned back to the files, now searching more methodically. When he found the Scene-of-Crime report for Jaffar's murder (no one put much credence into the suicide theory anymore), he slowed and then stopped. He then spent a few minutes on his smart phone. 'Well, I'll be...' he muttered to himself.

'Hey', Martin called over to Ivan. 'The owner of the handgun. His middle initial was "T" right? That wasn't "T" for "Thomas", was it?'

Ivan checked through his notes. 'Yeah', he replied, 'how'd you know?'

'Lucky guess. But it could mean we've just stepped into the twilight zone…'

Kasia arrived shortly afterwards, looking quite "stylish" Martin thought. She was definitely dressed more for going out in Manhattan in a knee length black dress than another day in the office. She grabbed an herbal tea and bagel and settled in on the couch next to Martin by kicking off her heels and folding her long legs underneath her. Ivan pulled a chair up around the coffee table and joined them.

'So I talked to Rafi last night', Ivan began, 'for about an hour. I told him about Mister White. He wasn't too happy that we'd kept that fact from him for three days, but he got over it. Then I told him what Tomas had said about Linda Starr. He was very interested in that…'

Ivan adjusted his bulk in his chair and took a big pull on his coffee.

'Didn't get a lot of sleep last night so bear with me, and jump in if I'm not being clear. Yesterday Tomas tells us that Starr and her entourage were present on the night. Then Rafi tells me that Brice Payton said that Rusty Wilkins said that Starr was one of the "higher-ups" who have been pushing us to look at a foreign involvement'. Seeing Martin and Kasia's looks across the table, he held up his hands. 'Yeah, I know, third hand gossip, lots of "he said that he said", but…'

'Anyway', Ivan continued, 'Brice also told Rafi that he, Brice, had had a call from Senator Markos Metaxas also saying the attack was by Islamist fundamentalists. When Brice downplayed that, he got a call from the Deputy Secretary of Defence telling him to listen to the Senator. Remember, Starr is on the Congressional Homeland Security Committee and Metaxas is on the Senate Intelligence Oversight Committee. These are connected people'.

'When did this happen, Ivan?' Kasia asked.

'About a week, ten days ago now. Rafi said that this had been confirmed by Allard…' He didn't quite use his fingers to waggle imaginary quotation marks around the word, "confirmed".

'Murray Allard? Of NY Counter Terrorism?' asked Martin.

'Yep, that Allard. He'd also talked earlier about higher ups in Homeland Security. Could be Starr'.

'*Could* being the operative word…'

'Yeah, Martin, I know; all very circumstantial at present. But then Rafi tells me that Allard and the Deputy Director of the Secret Service, Ian Croft, were the ones behind the stonewalling we got earlier from the Service. Protecting themselves?' Ivan asked and, answering his own question, continued. 'Maybe, but after last night, I'm not sure they have that much to worry about, maybe some small errors in judgement, but nothing seriously culpable that I can see'.

'You think they were protecting someone else? Like Starr?' Martin asked.

'It's a possibility. Or maybe some *quid pro quo* thing going on. Croft is very much part of Starr's oversight responsibilities, but there's more. Alden', Ivan looked at Kasia, 'Bill's boss, had been told by Senator Marvin Jäger that fundamentalists were responsible. And, before you ask, yes, Senator Jäger is also on an oversight committee, this time ours. The FBI's I mean. He's the chair of the Senate FBI Oversight Committee'.

'Holy crap!'

'Not very ladylike, Kasia'. Ivan admonished. She flipped a finger at him.

'What did Rafi suggest, Ivan?'

Ivan looked Martin straight in the eye. 'Rafi thinks we need to have a *talk* with some sitting members of Congress. And for that, he needs to go to the Director. Says he should be able to do that first thing Monday'.

'Wow'.

'Yep. Wow. Martin, you were always concerned about those batteries. You were right. It seems they've indirectly opened a whole new avenue of inquiry for us. Not one I'm keen to pursue. I don't want to think about the possibility that our Government may have been involved in this attack'.

'You *have* been busy, Ivan. I talked to Emery last night and he also wants to bump it up a level. I've got a meet with him and the Chief on Monday, but as far as I can tell they just want to be kept informed. Still making sure we don't tread on FBI toes'.

'Appreciate that, Martin. And appreciate all the help both of you', he swept his arms wide in a gesture of inclusivity and almost spilling his coffee in the process, 'and of the Department. Great help'.

'Glad to be of assistance. It happened on our patch so we feel some responsibility. Which is why, in case you've forgotten, when The Donald gets released from hospital today, we will have a *lot* of personnel on the streets'.

'Right! I had forgotten. And that reminds me of something else I've forgotten to update you on. Agent Briggs met up with Alinejad this morning. All very civilised, no issues at all. He sent the kids off with their mother for breakfast and they had a good chat. Briggs is absolutely convinced he has nothing to do with the attack. On the day they were upstate. Kids had wanted to see Niagara Falls. He had receipts and photos. Briggs is verifying all of it of course, but it seems genuine. As for the bird, Alinejad was most emphatic in agreeing with Byrnes, there *had* to have been a recall signal to convince it to fly towards Robbins. It did *not* have to be the signal that he had used when training the owl. Said there'd been enough time since it had been sold to the Secret Service for them to have trained it with a new signal. In fact, he says that's the recommendation from his firm exactly for these sorts of situations. They don't want to know what signals their clients use'.

'And was it a new signal?'

'CSI is waiting for confirmation from Sneiders in the Netherlands, but, no, it doesn't seem so. I talked to Byrnes again last night and she says that they didn't want to add too many new factors into a pilot project so just went with the signal the bird was used to'.

'And they didn't see that as a security risk?'

'Sneiders' firm probably has a higher security clearance than Byrnes and Holgersen – I guess they trusted the signal was secure. I also got a confirmation from Europol this morning. They confirmed that Sneiders and Alinejad and the whole firm have been vetted multiple times and cleared. They also hinted that they wish we wouldn't keep asking them the same question. Seems between the Service, us and some "unidentified others" – maybe some other intelligence sorts from the embassy – we've been told this half-a-dozen times already'.

'So…' Kasia said, '…assuming that it was a signal coming from the other end of the square, and that is what everyone is telling us it must have been, whoever got the signal could have got it from the Service *or* from the Netherlands. Both of them are supposed to be secure, but the signal came from somewhere'.

'Worse than that', said Ivan. 'The signal used in training is a generic one. Many birds are trained with the same signal, definitely all the owls have the same signal. Anyone who has a bird trained by them would know the generic signal. It's the equivalent of leaving the PIN on your mobile set to "0000"'.

'Damn. Once again, nothing we can use to pin down who's behind this'.

'Not without a *lot* of legwork, and most of it overseas to boot, no'.

The tagline running across the bottom of the screens across the country shouted:

TRUMP OUT. "TRUMPHANT" DONALD LEAVES HOSPITAL.

The video clip was short, but clear. Donald Trump walked, without assistance of any kind, but with his wife on one side and one step behind, out of the main doors of Mount Sinai Hospital. He smiled and waved confidently at the crowd, especially the photographers, and got into his limousine.

He looked pale, but that could have been the pale winter light and the glare of cameras on this grey, drizzly day. His distinctive hair was covered by an uncharacteristic Fedora beneath which a few white bandages could be seen. He also had a bandage on his neck. There were a few other signs of superficial trauma, some bruising and cuts, but they were mostly healed by now.

Also visible was a very strong police and Secret Service presence. No doubt there were more agents and officers less visually obvious scattered in the crowd and along his route, but there were enough visible to send the intended message: "Not a second time".

Day Thirteen

December 11, 2016

The five who had met in the wine bar a week ago, Martin, Ivan, Kasia, Bill and Siobhan, were now six with the inclusion of Morna MacCallum. It was a remarkably similar afternoon. Yesterday's drizzle having turned to sleet overnight and continuing through the day. Once again, the dark wood interior was warm and comforting. Drinks had been ordered, but no food this time. The demands of the festive season meant that all of them had engagements involving food later and most of them had also had lunch with friends or family before coming here.

Ivan was looking even more bearish than usual, he had not shaved since Friday morning and had not had more than four hours sleep the previous two nights. He started the proceedings by repeating his conversation with Rafi and that Metaxas, Jäger, Starr, Allard and Croft were all now "of interest", but with the utmost of respect ('for now!') and any discussion of this was definitely on a "need to know" basis.

He looked at Kasia and Martin across the high table from him. 'Apologies for having to sit through all that again - thanks for your patience. Now for some things that no one has heard before. I think most of you know we'd identified the type of drone used and that it was sort of a prototype; only two hundred were made. We've been tracking all of them down which, for the most part, hasn't been too difficult, some of them hadn't even been shipped. So far, we've physically seen all of them that were sent to US customers except for one, that one was sold on eBay and it's a bit harder to find. Seems it was sold on a cash and buyer-picks-up basis. There's also a dozen or so overseas that we still haven't traced. But', he held up a finger, 'if we're really lucky, we'll trace all but one and that one will be the one used in the attack. Hopefully, we'll know within a week'.

He took a sip at his Brooklyn Stout. He was pacing his alcohol this afternoon, dinner was likely to be boozy. 'We've also had a chance to examine the transponder that is meant to broadcast the recall signal. It's clean except for Tomas' prints. No signs of tampering or damage. However, the batteries had definitely been swapped. They're from a different manufacturer than the ones Tomas always gets from stores. And very definitely drained flat'.

'Why swap batteries at all?' asked Morna. 'Surely that meant more time to be caught, better just to take the existing ones out'.

'We can't be sure of course, but one good reason would be to keep the weight the same in case Holgersen picked it up and had time to notice. And now, Martin seems to have been keeping some sort of surprise for us. Yes?'

'If you're referring to what I found in your office yesterday just before Kasia came in, then yes. I wanted to do a bit more digging on Google before mentioning, but... well, this is just plain weird.

If you recall, Sharmila identified the suicide note as a quote from Lawrence of Arabia, "All men dream" and all the rest'. General nods around the table. So far, so good.

'And Ivan's people identified the owner of the gun as "Larry T. Edwards" although that's almost definitely fake. I assume nothing new has come from that, Ivan?'

A shake of the head, another sip of stout.

'The "T" stands for "Thomas". "Larry Thomas Edwards". Lawrence of Arabia's actual name was…'

'Thomas Edward Lawrence!' Siobhan shouted eagerly.

'Yep. Bit of a coincidence, huh? And it *could* be a coincidence until I vaguely remembered something else. T.E. Lawrence was an officer during World War One, serving in military intelligence. After the war he became a "diplomat"; a nicer word than "spy". There is evidence that he was with the British Secret Intelligence Service, the SIS. The SIS is better known as MI6, equivalent to our CIA; MI5 is like the FBI'.

The five faces looking at him showed varying degrees of interest and puzzlement. Seeing this, Martin hurried on. 'Stay with me, this story is actually relevant to our case. In the *Second* World War, the British started another intelligence service, the SOE; Special Operations Executive. This was a joint task force that included members of MI6 and MI5. The SOE set up shop here in New York, completely with the knowledge and blessing of the US Government; indeed, the FBI and the OSS, predecessor of the CIA, worked closely with the SOE here. And guess where their office was?'

Generally blank faces all round.

'No one knows their New York history, huh? The office they used was number 3603 in 630 Fifth Avenue'.

Blank faces suddenly lit up with understanding.

Kasia was the first to say it. 'And Jaffar's body was found in room 3306, 630 Fifth'.

'Yep', Martin nodded. 'Along with a gun registered in the name of a long-dead British Secret Service agent'.

'And what the fuck is all this supposed to mean?' exploded Ivan. 'This case is difficult enough! You're not suggesting we're looking for a ghost?'

Laughing gently, Martin said, 'No, no, Ivan. There's lots of different explanations, but the one I ended up liking the most last night is that our killer thinks he's the smart one. They often do. So he's left this little "calling card", y'know how the Joker used to leave a playing card for Batman to find. It fits with what you heard from Rafi. There's a connection somewhere with intelligence services'.

Bill was already on his second draught beer of the afternoon; he could take the train home. '*British* intelligence?'

'No, I don't think so. It's not as if he wants to identify himself… or herself, but this strikes me as a macho-stoopid thing to do so I'm staying with "him"… but he does want to play games. *If* I'm right, and the coincidences do seem too much, then the clue tells us he's connected to intelligence and/or military, but not which one. Could be DoD, CIA, DHS, even FBI… no, Ivan, I'm *not* suggesting that. Could be foreign'.

Martin looked at Morna. 'You do realise that this puts you in an awkward position?'

'Yeah, I got that'.

'Just remember that at the moment, as you pointed out yourself the other day, you're FBI, not Department of Defence, NSA or whoever you usually work for'.

'You know who I usually work for, Martin!' Mock outrage reinforced by a mouthful of sauvignon.

Martin looked thoughtful. 'Mmmm…. who the "NSA" reports to tends to be a little fuzzy around the edges, but we'll let that slide for now. That said, your knowledge of Defence and experience with working with spooks could be just what we need. Think back over the case, but look at it from a CIA-perspective; anything change?'

Morna sat back, glass in hand and thought for a minute while the others did the same. Martin's story had opened up many new ways of looking at the case even if there wasn't any actual new evidence.

Morna leant forward onto the table. 'There are a few things. One, the set up and attack was technically complex, used sophisticated methods and a careful timetable. All hallmarks of a special forces type of operation. Two, having intelligence personnel involved, especially if they were insiders, would go a long way to answering our questions about access'. She paused as a thought came to her. 'Did any of the people with Starr that night have intelligence links?'

Ivan answered that. 'As I mentioned, it's something we hope to ask the Congresswoman, but we need the Director's approval first'.

'I could…'

'No, Morna, we really need to go by the book on this. Shortcuts could lead to shortening of careers. I mean that'.

'And', Bill added, 'blow any chance of building a case. If this does lead to high-profile individuals, rest assured they'll have lawyers digging through everything. One lapse in procedure and the case gets thrown out'.

Rebuked, Morna said, 'Fair enough. And there's another connection with DoD, those explosives. We know they were US military'.

'Actually Special Forces. Does that mean they could have been used by the CIA?' Kasia asked.

'Not sure, but I know who would be able to tell us', answered Morna. Turning to Ivan, she asked, 'I know we want this kept close to our chests, but how would you feel if I bounced a few things off Brice Payton? I trust him, but even so, I don't need to tell him everything. Just see if he has any ideas about how those sorts of explosives could end up here or if knows of any ops-guys hanging around, that sort of thing?'

'Okay, Morna, but keep it short and make sure he knows that it's unofficial and confidential'.

She nodded.

Kasia turned to Ivan. 'Do we know what countries the unaccounted-for drones are in?'

'Yes. It's not that the records are incomplete, it just takes time when working in foreign countries. Luckily, we don't need to be official, all we need to do is have someone physically look at the drone and check the serial number. Everyone has been happy to cooperate so far. In a couple of cases I understand they did it over Skype-video. So the ones we still haven't seen are in the places you'd expect, Gulf States, China and Russia'.

'Are we still considering Islamists?' Siobhan asked.

'I don't think so. It's possible, but then so is everything else at the moment. Put it this way, we've got no evidence to suggest Muslim extremism, but nothing to discount it. However, the majority of what we have, which isn't much, admittedly, does seem to point to something closer to home'.

'But Kasia's got a point', Martin added. 'For example. Jaffar wasn't an extremist, wasn't even Muslim for that matter, but he, and anyone else involved, could have been influenced or coerced by someone else and that someone else could be ISIL'.

'I thought you were the one who said that we shouldn't get bogged down in theorising about who and why', laughed Ivan. 'But sure, it's all possible. After all, we still don't know why Oswald shot Kennedy and whether Castro or Khrushchev or the CIA was behind him!'

'Aw, shit, Ivan, please don't even suggest that this case will end up like that one, I don't want to spend the rest of my life being interviewed by PBS on various conspiracy theories. Let's all keep believing we can solve this one?'

'Sure, sure, Martin. However, in my experience, a lot of cases never get satisfactorily resolved'.

'That's the FBI! At NYPD, we like to close our cases properly'.

'I think, Martin, if you look at the actual numbers on successful case closures…'

'Boys, boys!' Kasia interrupted the jokey-but-somewhat-serious interagency banter. 'Something you said, Martin…. Something about "coerced"… Let me think without you two bickering for a second'.

She took a sip of pinot noir and closed her eyes. Suddenly, she shot forward, eyes wide. 'Got it! Remember Michael Sandford? The British tourist who tried to shoot Trump in June. Out West. California, I think. At the time of his arrest his father said he must have been "coerced". Any connections? Maybe this isn't an isolated event?'

'Nice one, Kasia', murmured Ivan. 'I think that's another one for my people to look into. We'll let you know'.

The conversation drifted into comments about Trump's release from hospital, the weather, the ridiculous gifts children wanted and the even more ridiculous prices being charged. They wound down as drinks were finished and everyone wandered out of the bar.

Martin waved a cab down on the same side of the street as the bar; he was taking a short trip south and home for what was left of the day. Across the road, he saw Kasia and Bill get in the same taxi to head north. *Stop it,* he thought to himself, *none of your business.*

As he got into his own taxi to go home, he found himself humming a Jagger-Richards song that David Bowie had also sung, "Let's Spend The Night Together".

He chuckled to himself and told the driver, 'Crown Heights'.

The call came in the early morning. Kasia had to lean over the body in the bed next to her to grab her work mobile.

Sleepily, she answered. 'Pasternak'.

'It's White. I can't stay on long. There's going to be another attempt now that he's out of... he's out'.

Waking up, Kasia asked. 'Is the intelligence community involved in any way?'

There was a brief silence. 'I won't say'.

Now fully awake, Kasia replied, 'Okay. Last time we talked, you said we should look at "profit", is it China?'

Even through the distortion on the line, Kasia could hear frustrated anger. 'No, no. You're still looking in the wrong place. You're still looking outside. Look inside. Political profit, not financial'.

Kasia tried throwing the caller off balance. 'Who killed Robbins?'

'Mr Black'.

'Who's Mr Black?'

'I don't know'. A pause. 'I really don't'.

And the call ended.

'Damn. New routing methods. Still think it's domestic, but can't swear to it. How'd you do on content?'

'Better than you I think. I may be able to get a voice pattern out of this once I strip away the distortion'.

Day Fourteen

December 12, 2016

The Monday morning commute was miserable. Yesterday's sleet had turned into wet snow overnight, coating New York in a thin layer of grey slush. Cars slipped on the greasy surfaces, forcing everyone, including yellow cabs, to go slower than usual. A slew of fender benders compounded delays and everyone's mood turned as grey as the sky.

Ivan was in his shared office, Rafi having reclaimed his office after returning from Washington. Ivan's desk was next to a window and usually had a good view of the southern tip of Manhattan. Today the view was obscured by low cloud and freezing rain that flung itself angrily at the panes. *A good day for working the phones and catching up with paperwork,* he thought to himself.

He called Martin only to find that he was in a meeting with his bosses. As he hung up, Ivan's phone rang. It was *his* boss. Rafi had had made some discreet calls over the weekend and early this morning. The consensus was that the FBI should, diplomatically of course, interview Congresswoman Starr and her staff.

However, everyone also felt that the velvet glove needed an iron fist inside it. As such, nothing would happen until the Attorney-General and Alden Saunders had prepared various subpoenas, search warrants and indictments that could be signed if necessary. It had been felt that there was insufficient evidence to interview Senators Jäger and Metaxas, but that the Director, Rafi's boss, would have a quiet word with Jäger and the Secretary of the Department of Homeland Security would do the same with Metaxas. Should either of them be dissatisfied with the conversation then either or both of the Senators could be elevated to interview status. With luck, the go-ahead should be given by the end of the week.

Ivan had questioned why the head of the DHS would talk to Metaxas. Rafi said that the brass were having reservations about the USSS. Ian Croft or his boss, the Director of the Secret Service, would be the obvious choice to talk to the Senator, but the Secretary felt it "prudent to limit the Service's involvement at this time". The same thing went for the New York Governor's office. And *that* meant the NY Office of Counter Terrorism, Murray Allard's group, was to be side-lined for now. In neither case was there any evidence of wrongdoing, but small alarm bells had been ringing in peoples' heads.

Hanging up, he saw he had missed a call from Martin. Ivan called Martin back, but he was on the phone again. Ivan left a message himself.

Ivan had just got into a rhythm of his overdue expenses claim when Martin called again.

'Finally! How are you on this miserable morning, Ivan?'

'Not so bad, not so bad. Beats being on the street. You?'

'bout the same. Listen, Kasia got another call from Mister White last night'.

'And?'

'I'm going to courier the transcript over to you. I don't want to use mail for this, but neither am I stirring out of my office unless I have to! There's not much to it, but he/she seems to refute any Chinese involvement; hinted that it could be politically motivated here in the US'.

Ivan stared at the splats of wet snow splattering against the window. 'And that would tie in with a Congress-Senate connection' he said, softly now, his back to his colleagues more from habit than real concern. 'And it looks like others agree', he continued, 'we should be getting the go-ahead to interview Starr by the end of the week'.

'Yeah, I know. Nolan was in on that call this morning and Emery and I listened in. It's where I've been all this morning. Something else interesting in Kasia's call'.

'Yeah?'

'Yeah. White said that a certain "Mister Black" killed Robbins'.

'And who's Mr Black when he's home?'

'No other details. You'll see when you get the transcript. Ever since then I've had that nursery rhyme running around in my head'.

'What nursery rhyme?'

'There's a lot of verses and I don't remember them all, but it goes something like:

> Who killed Cock Robin?
> I, said the Sparrow,
> with my bow and arrow,
> I killed Cock Robin.
> Who saw him die?
> I, said the Fly,
> with my little eye,
> I saw him die.
> Who'll dig his grave?
> I, said the Owl,
> with my little trowel,
> I'll dig his grave.
> All the birds of the air
> fell a-sighing and a-sobbing,
> when they heard the bell toll
> for poor Cock Robin.

'There's a lot about birds in the poem and that bit about "my little eye", there were a lot of 'little eyes" on mobile phones that watched Robbins die, and that the *Owl* will dig his grave…. Weird, huh?'

'I'll admit that your intuition got us somewhere with the Lawrence of Arabia-spy connection, Martin, but this? Sounds a bit far-fetched, my friend. You seriously trying to suggest someone murdered Robbins because of a nursery rhyme?'

Martin laughed down the connection. 'No, no! Sometimes it's good to let the mind wander, make connections deep down. I don't take it literally, but I do wonder if there isn't something my subconscious is trying to tell me. Just found it funny, is all'.

'Alright. So long as NYPD isn't running around Manhattan picking up all the pigeons for questioning! Now it's my turn to give you some good news in terms of progress: Once CSI got the digitised recall signal from the Secret Service, they were able to search the audio from the night. They'd already isolated a lot of possibles so the search went quickly, they found it!'

'What? Found what?'

'There was a second recall signal. A strong one. They've triangulated the source from a bunch of different recordings and it definitely came from the podium area. They're giving it a sixty-percent confidence that it was from the switch used to turn on the Christmas lights'.

'The one in Robbins' hand!'

'Exactly. They're now digging through the physical remnants, see if they can piece together what's left of that switch and see if it was rigged'.

'Great stuff! Now all *we* have to do is work out who had access to that switch. See if anyone on Starr's staff was there?'

'When we get the go-ahead it'll definitely be a line of inquiry'.

'And I've got something for you, Ivan, but nowhere near as exciting. We, well, Gene found the backpack'.

'What? That's great news, Martin!'

'Nah, not really. It's definitely Jaffar's, got his school books and things in it, but nothing else obviously incriminating. We're sending to Virginia so your lab can take it apart. I'm not holding my breath'.

'Where was it?' Ivan asked.

Martin gave a soft, self-deprecating chuckle. 'Lost and found... 630 Fifth has a cleaning service; they hold onto anything they find lying around in the building, but they don't keep records of *where* things are found, not even on what floor. All we can say is that it was found in a common area, hallway, elevator, stairwell, toilet, that sort of thing. We're trying to find who's been working in the past week. See if they remember finding it'.

'One last thing, and this is better news', Martin continued. 'As you know, Kasia's phone is set to auto-trace and record now. Seems White's call was protected using unfamiliar encryption-slash-protection so they weren't able to get much of a location fix, but they do think they've got enough now for a preliminary voice pattern. I was planning on asking Morna if she wanted to check this against Linda Starr, but perhaps you want your Virginia boys to do it?'

'No, Morna'll do fine. Let me know what she finds'.

Morna was sipping tea in the restaurant in her hotel. She was happy to follow Martin and Ivan's example and not step foot outside if she could help it.

Brice Payton walked into the lobby. He shuddered his coat free of snow and scuffed his boots free of slush. A yellow sign in the lobby warned that the floor was slippery; a cleaner in a white jacket mopped constantly and ineffectually at the water brought in by guests.

He walked over to the restaurant, spied Morna and slid into the seat opposite her. It would be a short discussion: Brice declined to order anything.

After a few minutes, Morna had sketched in some of the broader aspects of where the investigation stood. Brice knew he wasn't being told everything, but was professional enough not to take it personally. Need-to-know was something he faced on a regular basis.

'Could the CIA get access to Semtex if it's provided to Special Forces?'

'You mean the stuff used in the attack traced to Iraq? Sure. That's almost a Standard Operating Procedure for covert ops'.

'Have you heard of anything, anything at all, that could suggest that we, Defence, NSA, CIA, are running anything domestically, anything political?'

He leant forward, conspiratorially. 'Very off the record, and strictly between you and I... no. Not that I know of'.

'But you would say that, wouldn't you?'

Brice laughed. 'Of course!' He continued more seriously. 'Remember when I got that call from Senator Metaxas and I told him that he was full of shit when he kept saying it was ISIL? I did that partly because of your analysis, Morna. You're good at what you do, and I trust you. So what was he talking about? I don't know, but it sure isn't coming from anywhere in the Agency. Bottom line: Do I think someone, somewhere is running something? Yep. But not us'.

'It's just there are some... aspects... which suggest Agency involvement. Possibly not your group though. Could be foreign. Could be some other domestic group'.

'Ah... can you give me anything tangible here?'

'Well, someone had access to those explosives, Brice. And someone was able to get close to, maybe even interfere with, a Secret Service protection detail. And someone is leaving us... clues... that refer to espionage people, historical espionage. We're not sure what it all means yet, but there's no doubt someone with good field craft and internal access is involved'.

'I can sniff around if that's what you're asking, no guarantees, no one likes a snitch and I won't comment on anything classified, but if someone's making the Agency look bad or using the Agency for illegal domestics... Anywhere specific you want me to start?'

'Congresswoman Linda Starr and her team'. Morna said, bluntly.

'A Congresswoman?' Brice looked surprised. 'No wonder you're being circumspect! Let me see what I can do'. And with that, he got up and went back out onto the depressing streets.

'Hi Frank'.

'Hi Steve'.

'Thought I'd let you know, as far as we can ever be sure of these things, we've got seven Electors who're going to write in Stevens'' name and eight who're going to write in yours. That should mean Hilary still gets two hundred and twenty-one'.

'Thanks, Steve, appreciate that. Not that it looks like it'll come to that; that bastard seems to have recovered nicely. Still, give the country four years of him and they'll be ready to swing back our way'.

'And as you said earlier, it's always good to cover all the bases. If something does happen to Trump, at least we've got three horses in the race now'.

When the Director of the Federal Bureau of Intelligence meets a Senator, especially one who is on an Intelligence Oversight Committee, go for lunch, they don't go to McDonalds. The Blue Duck Tavern is one of a select few restaurants in the city where the movers and shakers deign to meet, greet and eat.

The Tavern's outdoor dining patio is one of its many attractions, but not today. Washington was being subject to the same weather front as New York. A cold drizzle had fallen all morning and there was no sign that it was going to stop any time soon.

Inside, the décor is modern, almost Spartan. Long bench seating stretches along one wall. The small tables can be easily moved to accommodate different party sizes. Not the sort of place one talks about sensitive subjects yet a certain privacy can be found simply because so many conversations were ongoing at the same time. Anyone who is overheard probably meant to be.

The Director had calculated that the restaurant would be seen as casual enough to indicate an informal discussion between colleagues who had known each other a long time. At the same time the BDT was enough of a part of the Washington "power circuit" to indicate that this was still business.

They walked the length of the restaurant, exchanging greetings with other colleagues and acquaintances until they reached their table. The Director slid onto the bench seating facing the rest of the room leaving the Senator with his back to the other patrons.

Their conversation was long and wide-ranging: polite inquiries into families and mutual friends; the merits of this restaurant compared to others; the miserable weather; comments on the dishes they ordered; respective plans for Christmas; recent policy shifts and trends and the like.

Mid-way, the Senator detected a slight shift in the Director's body language. *This* was what the lunch was really about.

'Marvin', the Director began. 'A week or so ago you told Alden Saunders that you felt that the attack on Robbins and Trump was the work of Islamist fundamentalists'.

'I suggested as much, yes', the Senator agreed, cautiously.

'Other people also "suggested" the same thing. These other people are all here, on Capitol Hill. Normally, politicians don't know more details about homicide cases than the Agency or other law officers'.

'Sometimes politicians are in a position to see a bigger picture. We talk to a much wider range of sources than your average detective and are used to putting together hypotheses based on less exact information. After all', he lifted his tone and smiled. 'We don't have to put together a case that holds up in court'.

The Director paused before saying, 'I suppose it's who these "other sources" are, and why they weren't made known to, or didn't contact, the FBI that intrigues us. Care to enlighten me, Marvin?'

Still being jovial, he replied, 'Well, I didn't actually say that this was the case here, now did I?' Seeing no returning smile, he added, more seriously, 'The reason they didn't contact you was that they don't exist. There were no mysterious sources hiding in the shadows'.

'So you and the others just came up with this theory yourselves?'

'Basically. I wouldn't discredit our capabilities quite so off-handedly, though'. He seemed completely unaware that he had fallen into the Director's trap. *So... they* are *all in it together. Or at least some of them. Not just a coincidence. Organised.*

The Director smiled gently. 'Of course, Marvin. You do see that there's a fine line between floating theories and', his tone steeled, just slightly, 'conspiring to influence the course of a federal investigation?'

The Senator's face flushed a little, at the use of the word "conspiring". 'I don't think a member of the FBI Oversight Committee needs a lecture on the limits and constraints of legal procedure, Director. It seemed to us that the investigators were downplaying the possibility of an immediate danger by plodding along, that's all. It doesn't take a genius to see the man's upset Muslims everywhere. It's also clear that Muslims have a tendency towards violent solutions'.

'Actually, Marvin', he interrupted. 'That's a dangerous stereotype. Well over ninety-nine percent of Muslims are not violent'.

'But that one percent, when they get violent, they are really violent'.

He held up a hand to stop the conversation there. *This is a topic that'll get us nowhere. He* is *a Republican.* 'But if it's obvious that Muslims are violent and hate Mr Trump', *with good reason,* he didn't say, 'Why would the Bureau need your help to see the obvious?'

'We had additional information, some from State, but mostly through our own contacts here and abroad'.

'Ah... so there *was* a secret source of information that wasn't made known to the Bureau?'

'Don't be obtuse! You know what I mean. There was nothing specific. Just a lot of minor things that added up to a feeling, a sense of the degree of antagonism that exists "out there"'. He waved his hands vaguely in the air.

'Alright, alright'. Once again, the Director sought to calm the Senator down a little. He was beginning to enjoy himself; it had been a long time since he'd had to interview anyone, but the old skills came back quickly enough. *Keep them off balance; dictate the flow. Anger then calm. Logic then emotion. Clarity then chaos, but never, never, anything that can be used as grounds for dismissal or harassment.*

'So what you're saying is that you all thought that there could be a Muslim fanatic wandering around New York; that the Bureau needed to be more aware of this threat, but because you didn't have any specific information, all you could do was to hint and suggest'.

The Senator leant forward, almost stabbing the Director in the chest with the pan-seared scallop on the end of his fork. 'Exactly. Exactly'. Mollified, he sat back in his chair and popped the mollusc into his mouth.

'And who, exactly, are we talking about when you say "we", Marvin? Other Senators, perhaps?'

The Senator stopped chewing and looked carefully at the Director. 'I'd rather not say. And I'm not too comfortable with where this conversation is going. You say those other people contacted you. Go and ask them yourself'.

'Part of the nature of a conspiracy is the need to keep the names of co-conspirators secret, don't you think?' He asked the question as if it was part of an academic discussion, knowing full well its true incendiary nature. He wasn't disappointed by the response.

The Senator leant forward again, face close to his plate and hissed, 'There was no conspiracy!' He said this much louder than he had intended and this, along with the theatrics of his movements, only served to catch the attention of a few other diners nearby. The Director looked each of them direct in the eyes with a completely blank expression. They turned back to their own conversations without comment. He then delivered the conversational *coup de grace*.

'No, of course not, Marvin. It's just that there are some indications that some "people", people who move in your circles, maybe even people who shared your group's concerns about an Islamic plot, may have gone a little further than just talking'.

The Senator almost spluttered. Indeed, an errant morsel of mollusc found its way onto his lower lip. 'What are you saying? This sounds very much like an accusation without foundation, and given our respective positions, could even be seen as an attempt to intimidate a member of the Oversight Committee. Perhaps *you're* the one who is doing something untoward!'

Gotcha! Thought the Director. *It's when they go on the offensive that you know you're getting close to the heart of it.* 'Not at all, Marvin. Like your group, I have "nothing specific, just a lot of minor things that add up to a feeling"'. *Now let's see if our listeners hear a change in tone the next time they listen in.*

The rest of the meal was finished in silence, uncomfortable on one side, almost smug on the other.

'Well! A full house today'.

'Not quite, Mister Blue, Mister Black hasn't joined us. Again'.

'I told you when we started this. Mister Black, as operations, prefers to keep some distance. For your protection as much as his'.

'Huh! Operations - that's one of the issues for this call Mister Blue. Since the first… event… we haven't seen much in terms of "operations". I thought we'd decided that it must all be over by the end of this week. Seeing as Mister Black only wants to talk to you, perhaps you should remind him of the terms of his contract'.

'Actually that's one of the reasons *I* wanted this call. Mister Black told me that it's all in place; it'll all be over within a week'.

'Not "within *a* week", Mister Blue, by the end of *this* week. That's just three days away!'

'Don't lecture me, Mister Pink. I'm fully aware of the deadline and it *isn't* this weekend, it's Monday. Black is confident it'll all be over by then'.

'Our man… he'll be… terminated?'

'Careful of the terminology, please Mister White. To answer your question, it's highly likely that our man will no longer be here'.

'Highly likely? Not certainly?'

'Likely, yes. But even if he's still with us, it won't matter. The nature of the… event… is such that our man will never be seen publicly again. And that will suit our purposes as much as a more permanent solution'.

'How do you mean?'

'Well, Mister White, someone who is very vain is unlikely to want to be seen without a face. The "event" will be… disfiguring at the very least'.

'Does anyone else feel that we may be going a bit far? Or is it just me?'

'Mister Yellow was happy with the thought of disfiguring when we last talked'. There was a silence.

'Hmmm. Might be a little late to be having second thoughts… On another topic Mister Blue, do you think Mister Black may be double-dipping? There's some evidence that he may be selling the same product to multiple buyers. For example, those "Pacific friends"'.

'I can't say one way or another myself, Mister Brown. I can ask him next time we talk. Personally, I don't care if he is so long as we get our objective met'.

'Call terminated. I couldn't get a thing! They've got access to some really good encryption. You?'

'Nada. Best I can say is a call happened. No idea what was said, but I can say there were multiple people on that call, four to six. I've got some metadata; maybe we can unscramble it over the next day or two'.

Day Fifteen

December 13, 2016

The new office of the Republican National Committee in Queens was not fancy, just a regular store front on a regular street in one of the "most ethnically diverse neighbourhoods in the country". It had been decided some time ago, even before Donald Trump became their candidate, that the Republican Party needed to do a better job at engaging with minorities hence the decision to open this new office.

Once the decision was made at a national level, internal politics became an issue. The New York State and the Manhattan Republican Party Committees saw it as an intrusion on their turf and an indictment of the effectiveness of their own community engagement activities. That the high-profile event of Trump's return to the public eye was being held in this small office rather than one of the more spacious offices of the local Committees was seen as yet another slap in the face.

We're used to divisions in this Party, thought Francisco Duarte, *and never more than this year. Still, we all need to present a unified front… somehow.*

The Chairman of the RNC stood in the new office flanked by Dina Accardo, the Co-Chair of the RNC. The rooms were chaotic, desks and floor space buried under piles of envelopes stuffed, and waiting to be stuffed, left over campaign posters, leaflets and other sundries after a successful campaign.

It was also packed with people, steaming and dripping onto leftover posters from their brief time in the inclement weather outside. It was uncomfortably warm and humid, and there was no space to hang overcoats; most people still had theirs on, adding to their discomfort. *Just like the man not to give any consideration to other people,* Francisco thought to himself. Donald Trump had decided that his first public appearance should be humble, a homage to the "God who saved me so I can make America great again…'. *Makes me want to puke. Just another facile grab for personal adoration. Now he thinks he's some kind of Christ figure raised from the dead.*

Francisco and Dina had flown in from Washington earlier that morning and had gone straight to Trump's private residence, navigating a series of security checkpoints to do so. There, they had been treated to a full-blown "Trumpertantrum". *The Vice-President is* mine *to decide, not yours!* He'd thundered. *And Romney of all people! You do remember what he said about me during the primaries, don't you? He called me a racist. He said I wasn't smart. He said….*

Francisco and Dina had allowed the storm to rage over their heads and finally trickle away. Nothing was going to change. The College was six days away. The Electors had been told who to vote for in place of Robbins and most, if not all, had agreed to do so.

There was no way Trump would be able to reach all the Electors, especially as Francisco had no intention of making the list available to him, and then convince them to change their vote to some other person who hadn't even been identified yet.

When Trump was cautioned about the possibility of upsetting the apple cart so much that he ended up with a Democratic Vice-President instead of Romney, the storm rose up once more and became a tempest. Once again Francisco and Dina faced Trump's rage and waited for the storm to abate to a squall and then whimper to a close. At the end, Francisco reminded Trump that, *yes, you are our President, but we are also your party. Neither can exist without the other. Accept the lesser of the two evils gracefully and let's pull together.*

A foolish thing to say under the circumstances, perhaps, as it drew another five minute tirade, but after that the pair were able to withdraw, the conversation having ended in a draw.

As they left Trump Tower for Queens, Dina turned to Francisco. Casually, she asked, 'He's looking good, don't you think?'

'Same old, same old. He still looks odd if that's what you mean by good'. Francisco replied churlishly. He always begrudged the time he spent talking to the President-Elect. He felt he had better things to do.

'Seriously, Francisco', Dina continued gamely, 'for someone who's in New York in winter and was in a coma a week ago, he's looking quiet refreshed and… tanned'.

'Huh. You're right. So used to seeing him like that, I guess I didn't think anything of it. Guess he's back at the spray tan, sun bed, carrot pills or whatever he uses'.

'And did you notice his hair?'

'You can't help, but notice his hair! I always notice his effing hair!'

'Didn't he just have brain surgery? Don't doctors have to shave the scalp to do that? What about stitches? A scar? See any of that?'

'No… You're not trying to suggest that this whole thing has been faked, are you?'

Dina laughed. 'No, Francisco. Just pointing out that he's got some good make-up people on his team. They've done a great job'. She paused for a while as they got into their limousine. 'That's a good thing for us, you know, he is literally the face of the party'.

And it also tells us a lot about his priorities, he thought to himself.

Now they were alone in the limo and the driver was sealed off from them, she turned sideways and looked seriously at her boss.

'Listen, Francisco', he hated being called Frank, 'what if something were to happen to Donald before the inauguration?'

'What do you mean, "happen"?' He had also become serious, giving her his full attention and mirroring her mood.

Dina spoke slowly, measuring her words carefully. 'I think some people, people in the Party, may not be one hundred percent behind him'.

'C'mon on, Dina. "#NeverTrump"'s behind us now. Sure, a lot of people think he's a sonofabitch "but he's our sonofabitch"! We've got the whole team pulling in one direction now, and a lot of that is because of your hard work, Dina'.

'Fancy Francisco Duarte quoting a Democrat!' Dina joked. Both of them sensing that they stood at the lip of a very dark discussion and both hesitant to go into it. 'But seriously, what if some people weren't completely convinced? That this is a huge mistake, it'll take the Party decades to recover from a Trump Presidency; there's a lot of Senators and Congress…men who are worried about their jobs'.

'That's where Romney came in, a check-and-balance to The Donald's excesses. The last of the doubters were won over by that, surely? It's Dubya all over. Donald may be prone to gaffes and rubbing some people the wrong way, but a lot of people like him. With good advisers and the public on side, we'll make this a great term, you'll see'.

Dina looked out of her window, her back to him, staring at the grey streets sliding by. 'Perhaps. And perhaps there's a few who still think they can do something about it'.

'What? With less than a week to go before the College? They think they can influence the Electors? Same argument we just used with Trump, too late'.

'Maybe not at the College'. She still kept her back to him.

'What? Afterwards? Announcing some great scandal before the inauguration that disqualifies him?' He kept up his light tone, but her body language made it difficult.

She turned back to face him. 'Yes. Something like that. Something that would mean he can't be President'.

'I'm surprised at you, Dina, that's PoliSci 101! "In the case where the President is incapable of performing his duties", and "incapable" includes "unable" and "unfit", "he is succeeded by the Vice-President". Again, one of the reasons we chose Romney as Veep'.

'Actually, it's not that clear-cut, if he's… let's say found "unfit"… for his duties between the College and the count, it's possible that the House will have to choose from the other candidates'.

'Yeah, yeah' he waved his hand dismissively, moving confidently into "mansplaining" mode. 'And that's why we've got a few Electors writing in Rubio's name'.

'I suppose I'm just not sure that Rubio's the right choice. This whole campaign, election, assassination attempt…' once again, she turned to the window. It sounded to Francisco that she could be struggling to keep her voice steady. '…has been so divisive and upsetting.

Some good people lost their jobs at the election, Francisco. Maybe…' she turned to face him again, '…and I'm just throwing out ideas here, maybe the House, even some of our Party, won't want to put in someone who is almost as controversial as Trump after all that's happened. They may want someone who can help them get their jobs back at the mid-terms, not see more seats lost'.

'You not telling me something?'

'No-o-o'. She drew out the word in clear denial of his question, looking him in the eyes. 'Just saying it wouldn't hurt if we had one more name in the hat just in case. Someone more centrist like Paul Ryan. He's already third in line so it's not as if he hasn't thought whether he was capable of it or not'.

He searched her face, but couldn't find any more clues. Reluctant to delve into that dark pit, he backed off. 'Okay, Dina. Not sure exactly what's going on, but I can have a word with Sam, he's already agreed to write in Rubio. I'm sure he'll be happy to write in Ryan instead. There. Happy?'

She made no reply, turning back to the window, looking at the grey river below them as they crossed the Queensboro Bridge, leaving the City behind them. 'By the way, I'm going to Montana over the weekend to see my parents before Christmas'.

The sidewalk outside the Fresh Pond Road building was equally crowded, but with security personnel as opposed to the politicos and party faithful inside. Properly dressed for the weather, the US Secret Service, FBI and NYPD personnel were more comfortable than those inside. Outside this ring of protection was a ring of media, and outside them, a final press of members of the public eager for a glimpse of their soon-to-be President… for better or worse.

Kasia Pasternak stood near the door to the office on the outside, enjoying the cool air on her face. She wasn't enjoying the slush that had splashed over the tops of her boots and inside; her feet were wet and cold. *Always happens. Doesn't seem to matter how carefully I walk.* The RNC office was not far from Kasia's apartment in Greenpoint so she had volunteered to be the investigation's eyes and ears. Eugene Marchetti was the senior Detective on duty; he and Kasia had chatted for a while about security, neither could see anything that needed addressing, everyone was particularly motivated to make sure this event went safely, if not smoothly.

Trump had given instructions regarding media access, wanting to make sure he came across as strong and fit on television screens across the country later that day. The Secret Service and NYPD, in a rare act of cooperation, had quietly vetoed those instructions. The President-Elect wouldn't get the media coverage he wanted, but he *would* be kept safe.

Sealed off from the weather outside in the Case Room, Martin relaxed back in his chair. There wasn't much for him to do at this point. He was waiting for others to get back to him. Waiting for approval to expand the investigation to include Starr. Even then, there wouldn't be much for him to do, interviews with Congress-women were FBI territory, not a job for "run of the mill policemen" like him. *I really should be upstairs in my office. There's work to be done there.* The thought was hardly one to motivate him, but he couldn't stop himself listing all the outstanding chores. *There's a pile of performance evaluations to go over, staff roster over the holidays, that new workplace safety policy… what happened to just being a detective?*

Earlier, Morna had told Martin that she had run the voice sample against Linda Starr's voice. No match; it wasn't her. Martin had called Ivan to tell him. In return, Ivan told him that CSI had confirmed that the audio signal had come from the switch used by Robbins to turn on the Christmas lights. Audio and physical evidence backed it up. Ivan had also told Martin that, so far, the lab had found nothing unusual about Jaffar's backpack. It was a college kid's backpack, that's all.

And that had reminded Martin to tell Ivan that Gene had talked to the cleaner who had found the backpack in the first place, fairly certain it had been left hanging up in a cubicle of the men's toilets on the thirty-third floor. He was dusting for prints, but a week late, it was unlikely anything would come of it.

By the time Kasia got to the office from Queens it was gone lunch. She found Martin upstairs, in his office, dutifully, if not eagerly, going through piles of paper. 'It's why you get paid the big bucks, Martin', she smiled.

He glanced up, putting on a mock scowl, grunted, and went back to an inventory discrepancy report.

A few hours later, as the grey skies outside their windows started to slide almost perceptibly into night, Kasia's phone rang.

'It's me'.

'White?' Kasia said it loud enough for Martin to catch. She also stood up and waved frantically at him to make sure she got his attention.

'Listen. There's going to be another attack, within the week, probably in the next couple of days. I was told it will be "disfiguring". That he "won't have a face". It's horrible'.

'What do they want, Mister White?' Kasia asked.

'It's what they didn't want that matters'.

'Who's telling you this?'

But she had already hung up.

Kasia and Martin looked at each other. 'Disfiguring? No face?' Repeated Kasia. 'An acid attack?'

'Dunno'. Martin replied. 'But I guess I'd better call Ivan again. And whatever our differences, the Secret Service Protection Detail need to know. I'll call Agent Wilkins right after I've called Ivan'.

'And what was that about "It's what they didn't want that matters"?'

Martin scratched his head. 'Maybe she was saying that "they", whoever they are, didn't want it to become disfiguring? She did say it was horrible'.

'Could be, but did you notice the odd phrasing? Sometime in the past "they didn't want" something to happen in the future. With that past tense, it could mean that they got what they wanted – it's no longer "what they don't want". It's happened; "what they didn't want." And it's a negative, you know, like they did this thing to stop something happening rather than making something happen'.

'You're losing me…'

'I'm looking at motive. This is all political, right? No matter who did it, the targets are politicians. Everything we've got so far says the motive was probably political. All this year the political messages have been negative, vote for me, not because I'm good, but because I'm not the other guy. It hasn't been about making anything positive happen, it's been about not having something negative happen. So what if the same thing was going on here? The people behind it didn't have a specific outcome in mind; they just wanted something *not* to happen'.

'Like Trump *not* becoming President?'.

'Exactly. And who didn't want that?'

'Dammit Kasia, we're back where we started! Millions, billions of people didn't want Trump to become President'.

'Not millions of politicians'. Kasia said quietly.

'What?'

'*If* we agree this is political, then White's remarks about "inside" and "profit" means the people behind this are political, even politicians. So what *politicians* didn't want Trump as President?'

Martin took a deep breath in and let it out slowly. 'Pretty much all Democrats, but also a big chunk of the Republican party… people who signed up to the "#notrump" campaign for example'.

'Yep. And from what I remember, Starr was pretty vocal against him at the time. That said, there *are* other types of "negative political" motives, importers who want to stop him ripping up trade agreements for example…'

'…or Senior Department of Defence who don't want to be put into the position of having to choose between implementing illegal orders and disobeying orders from the Commander-in-Chief…'

'…ambassadors and people at State who'll be the ones trying to explain and justify Trump's foreign policy to world leaders…'

They looked at each other and laughed. 'Okay'. Kasia said. 'Maybe it didn't give us a short list after all, but it *is* nice to have a working hypothesis for motive, isn't it?'

'For sure! But now I think I have to leave the airy-fairy theories behind and get on to some real police work – like getting on the phone with Ivan and Ian'.

As she turned back to her own paperwork, she could just catch some words Martin was singing softly. She was sure it was another of his Bowie favourites:

There's danger in the wind
You're safe with me darling
But sometimes I'm not me
There's danger in my mind

Walk with me along the shore
I think we'll find
There's acid in the breeze
There's danger in my mind

Outside the nondescript grey concrete building, the weather was better than in New York or Washington. Cold, but not severe. It would only just go below zero that evening, clear and still. Inside it was always a comfortable nineteen degrees; the only wind the occasional soft sigh of an excellent ventilation system.

'Have you noticed the times? The Tarantino calls are all made between seven and eleven Eastern Standard. That's one to five in the morning European time, not great for them, but not bad for someone in Asia or Australia; it'd be their morning. So we can at least give that feedback, a small downtick against Europe. Not that there was much to indicate a European involvement in the first place...'

'But think about what that means here in the US. It's a perfect time slot for people who work nine-to-five on the east coast and want to talk after work. This is the best time to talk in private, but not have to get up in the middle of the night'.

'Okay. So they don't have to work shifts like us saps. So what?'

'It could mean that they're all in the EST zone; there's an overlap with office hours on the west coast'.

'Bit of a stretch...'

'Bear with me for a bit... what if we assume that the calls *are* all coming from the east coast? It'd make sense to retarget some of our assets and allocate more processing to east coast signals for a while. See if we can crack that crazy encryption and bounce they're using'.

'Okay – why not? Worth a try at least'.

There were three voices on the call.

'You know who I met yesterday. It didn't go well. He suspects something'.

'You think you had a bad meeting, Pink? I had a call from…'

'No names, please Mister Orange'.

'…from, well, the head of the… group I'm supposed to oversee. Mister Blue… she knows about us! Said they have a source who told them there may be another attack on… on our man. She gave no details of course, doubt if she would know them anyway, but she said "she"'.

'She said she? What's that supposed to mean?'

'Dammit, Pink! It's not easy to explain with all these restrictions Blue insists on'.

'With good reason, Orange, it's for all of our protection. Try again. The first "she" meant the person who called you?'

'Yes'.

'Good. And the second "she" was said by the first "she" to indicate who the information is coming from'.

'Yes. That's it exactly!'

'Excellent. Which also explains why Misters White and Brown are not on this call, correct Mister Orange?'

'Uh-huh'.

'Wait! You're telling us that White or Brown may have leaked?'

'No need to panic yet, Mister Pink. I think what Mister Orange is telling us is that there *may* be a leak. It's also possible that the top lady got her pronouns wrong. Or she was fishing. Or she was referring to one of the open conversations we've all had. Even if there was a leak, it may only have been one and accidental at that. So let's not run off half-cocked, hey?'

'Okay, okay, Blue, but I'll be glad when this week's over and we can drop this stupid "Mister Orange" and "Mister White" crap!'

'I think we'd all agree with you there! None of us thought our arrangement would need to go on for so long. Meanwhile, I'm going to courier some new hardware and instructions to you'.

'Just to the two of us?'

'No, Mister Pink. First that would mean that we *do* suspect our colleagues when there is no proof. And second, if one of them is leaking, that would be a sure way to tip them off. No, we all get new instructions on how to contact each other. Each of them will be slightly different though. It'll make it even harder to crack'.

'Wow! For a, butt-ugly dude, you can sometimes have good ideas. I got three positive hits, all in the US. Two definitely in the Washington, D.C. area, one somewhere in lower New York State. Probably the City, but could also have been Jersey. What did you get?'

'A lot!

> ---unintelligible--- You think you had a bad ---unintelligible--- had a call from No ---unintelligible--- Mister Orange from, well, the head of the ---unintelligible--- oversee. Mister Blue - she knows about ---unintelligible--- another attack on... on our man. She gave no details ---unintelligible--- know them anyway –, but she said "she" ---unintelligible--- Dammit, Pink! It's not easy ---unintelligible--- Blue insists on. With good reason, Orange, it's for ---unintelligible--- try again, the first "she" meant the person who ---unintelligible--- And the second "she" was said by the first "she" to indicate who the information is coming from. Yes. That's ---unintelligible--- also explains why Misters White and Brown are not on ---unintelligible--- No need to panic yet, Mister Pink. I think what Mister ---unintelligible--- may be a leak. It's also possible that the top lady got ---unintelligible--- she was fishing. Or she was referring to ---unintelligible--- one and accidental at that. So let's not ---unintelligible--- I think we'd all agree ---unintelligible--- thought our arrangement would need to go on ---unintelligible--- I'm going to courier some new hardware and ---unintelligible--- No, Mister Pink, first that would mean that ---unintelligible--- proof and second, if one of them is leaking, that would be a sure ---unintelligible--- get new instructions on how to contact each ---unintelligible--- slightly different though, it'll make it even harder ---unintelligible---

I'm sending this through to Morna now'.

Day Sixteen
December 14, 2016

As if someone had turned on a switch, the weather had suddenly improved. A strong warm southerly had hit New York just after sunrise. The wind died down a few hours later leaving blue skies and balmy temperatures. By eleven o'clock most of the slush had melted. A few fragile piles of grey ice remained from the drifts left by snowploughs; and these piles were melting rapidly, the honeycombed ice sparkling in the sun.

No one in the windowless Case Room could admire the fine weather. The room was a little claustrophobic with five people, but no one minded.

Ivan had asked Martin if he and Sharmila could meet Martin and Kasia at NYPD Headquarters instead of at the FBI building. Ivan would be bringing Morna. The reason for the change in venue would be clear once they got there. No, he didn't want to say anything else over the phone.

Morna started by unfolding a small box made of copper mesh. She asked everyone to put their mobile phones into it and then proceeded to do a sweep of the room for listening devices. Although this room was meant to be somewhat safe from eavesdropping, it had never been intended to be used as a vault: a room completely isolated and protected from visual, electronic and audio surveillance. After this ritual, Morna pronounced it safe and they could get down to business. In parts intrigued, amused and fascinated to have a glimpse into the darker side of NSA procedures, the others sat themselves around the table and waited for her to begin.

Morna passed copies of last night's transcript to everyone. She didn't need to say that each copy would need to be given back to her and no notes taken. Everyone knew the drill, even if was just from watching spy movies…

She gave them all some time to read and think and then said, 'Issue number One. They, whoever they are – I'll get to that later – know there's a leak. They aren't sure who it is, but they believe her to be female. As there seems to be only two females in the group, our "Mister" White is in some danger. We need to warn her. Do we have any way of contacting her?'

Kasia shook her head, 'No'.

'Alright, second best is to tell her the next time she calls. It's your operation, but that's my recommendation. Second point', Morna continued. 'They mention a second attack, presumably on Trump. Whether this is real, or them reporting what the leak has said to us isn't clear'.

'Isn't that the same thing?' Asked Sharmila.

'Not at all. For example, it's possible that White was told that there would be another attack to see if we get told that. Then if they find out that *we* think there'll be a second attack, they'll *know* Mister White is their leak'.

'And how would they find that out?' Kasia asked, a little frostily, 'From one of us?'

Ivan stepped in. 'No. Not from one of us in this room. Or at least, I don't believe so. But we have to assume that these people are getting their information from someone. There's a on both sides. Now it's just who can find their leak first. It's the reason why we're having the conversation here. I'm not sure that our offices, the FBI's, are clean. So that's one question we need to answer today: Who knew about Mister White?'

Martin started. 'From our side, there's obviously Kasia and myself who've known from the beginning. Emery and Nolan...', seeing Morna's quizzical look he expanded, '...sorry, Assistant Chief Emery McKinley and Chief Nolan Quinn, my boss and *his* boss'.

Ivan took up the list. 'In the FBI, we have me and Sharmila, our temporary agent, Morna, here', he smiled at her. 'My boss Rafina Matos, who told the FBI Director. And, as of yesterday, Bill Ngo, Deputy U.S. Attorney and his boss, U.S. Attorney Alden Saunders. Alden said he'd be talking to the Attorney-General herself who may or may not have told the Secretary of Homeland Security. Who these people talked to is anyone's guess, they were told to keep it quiet, but...'

'Yeah', Morna smiled grimly, 'too many people. This intercept came in around eight-thirty last night. Can I presume that all these people who were told yesterday knew about it before then?'

Nods. 'Told before lunch, most of them', added Ivan.

Kasia sat up quickly. 'Wait a minute! Martin, after White called me yesterday, you said you'd call Agent Wilkins: Secret Service', she added to the others in the room, 'did you tell him where we got the information from?'

'Damn... can't remember what I said exactly. I wouldn't have said "Mister White" that's for sure... He did ask me how we knew, and I think I said "a source". Not sure if I identified the gender'.

Morna looked thoughtful for a minute. 'Alright. I'm not sure we can do much to isolate the leak, but we can try and stop anything more coming out. If White is right, we only have to do it for five, six days. There'll either be another attack in that time or they're won't. Don't suppose this will make much difference to security precautions around the man?'

Ivan, Kasia and Martin all shook their heads at the same time. 'We could give a heads up, especially to the Secret Service Protection Detail. Tell them to look for anything like acid that could be thrown'.

As the others started to nod, Morna held up a hand. 'Hang on. There's nothing in the intercept about acid. That's exactly the sort of detail that could have been given to White, and White alone, to help identify her. Uh...', she scanned the transcript, '...for example, everyone is told they'll be a second attack, but White is told acid, Brown is told a gun at short range, Orange a sniper, Pink a car bomb, that sort of thing.

How much extra protection will it get Trump if the Detail is told to watch out for acid? I assume that they aren't going to let anyone get close enough to do that even if they aren't told'.

An uncomfortable silence from Martin and Kasia. Alongside the USSS, NYPD shared the responsibility for Trump's security. Withholding details from field personnel was not something they were used to do.

'Okay', Martin said grudgingly, 'we'll hold back on that, but...' he looked directly at Morna, 'I'm going to tell Detective Eugene Marchetti, he's in the field and has a right to know. Maybe he'll see something odd and that knowledge will give him the extra few seconds he needs'. He paused. 'I'll have a think about talking to my counterpart in CRC - Critical Response Command of the NYPD Counterterrorism Bureau. They're not officially part of the Protection Detail, but they'll be out there'.

'Good'. Morna continued to run the conversation. 'Another fact from the transcript, we're dealing with at least six people. There were three voices on the tape, we're relatively confident they're all men. Two of them are probably in Washington. That'd be Orange and Pink. The third, Blue, seemed to be in charge and he's right here in New York. They talked about White and Brown, both presumed Female. No location on Brown though our listeners have a gut feeling she's also here on the East Coast. As for White, her first calls came from Washington, but the last one didn't. It was very short and protected as usual, but we think it may have come from somewhere near here, New York again. Finally, White talked about a Mister Black at one point. We've never caught a reference to him outside of her call to Kasia that once'.

'Six'. Martin repeated, nodding to himself. 'But so far, only one person actually fingered as the perp; all the others are, at best, guilty of conspiring to murder'.

'Still a major offence', noted Ivan.

Kasia had been re-reading the transcript. 'What do we make of "head of the", seems to refer to a female, and "the top lady". Is that Brown? Is that *Linda Starr*?'

Morna answered. 'It could be. It could also be the Attorney-General. Or the head of the cleaning crew. Not enough evidence yet. More importantly from my side is the last bit. Looks like they're going to change their communications protocols. It may be that they'll stop using phones and just meet in person. Our intel could lose some quality over the next few days'.

'Just when we need it most', Ivan said unhappily.

'Yep', Morna agreed. 'As it is it looks like they've been using military-grade encryption, just not all the time. Almost as if only a few of them have the right equipment or are using it properly only half the time. Note that we never actually get to hear Pink's voice so we're less confident of his gender. Now!' She perked up. 'Something less depressing. I talked to Brice and he's got a name for us, could be interesting. Dan Kendall. Occasionally works on Linda Starr's staff. Sort of a minder-cum-investigator-cum-bodyguard. Brice knows *of* him, seems to have a vague recollection of having met him once. Anyway, Brice says he's got a mixed background. Did a lot of analysis work for the CIA in Asia fifteen, twenty years back. Then he did something classified in the Middle East. Ostensibly for DoD, maybe Special Forces, but could just as easily have been a continuation of his Agency work. Brice also says he's no longer fully *persona grata* at the Agency. Some black mark somewhere. No one wants to give details, but no one will recommend him for Agency work either'.

'Right', Ivan wrapped up. 'If he's part of Starr's staff, he's part of our mandate. Let's find this Dan Kendall, see where he was on the Twenty-Ninth'.

Before Ivan could hang up, Morna said, 'One more thing, Ivan'.

'Yeah?'

'Brice also said that he remembered that Rusty Wilkins called him out of the blue on December second. Wanted to go for coffee. Brice was convinced that Wilkins wanted some information through the back door, but, well, you know Brice, he's a good poker player'.

'I do know Brice. How is this relevant?' A touch of impatience.

'Brice says Wilkins suggested that Linda Starr would be grateful if Brice cooperated'.

'I don't even want to think about why a Congresswoman would be grateful for someone interfering in the investigation of the murder of a Vice-President-Elect. You have any ideas?'

'Not really, but interesting, huh?'

Yeah. Great. I could do with less "interesting" and more clarity.

Day Seventeen

December 15, 2016

Outside, the weather remained warm and clear. The high settling in across the entire eastern seaboard. Hatless heads, smiling faces and open coats showed that many New Yorkers felt the weather more like spring than winter.

Inside Ivan's office, it was also calm, but an enforced calm. Rafi was back in Washington, but Ivan stayed at his own desk working away at a profusion of overdue routine work, both on and off the Robbins-Trump case. His mind wasn't on it – it felt like the investigation had suddenly run into sand. Progress was slow and tiresome.

He looked out the window. His office faced east towards the Supreme Court building and, standing, he could look down onto Foley Square where a number of people were sitting on benches or strolling around, enjoying the sunshine after the past week's depressing conditions. For a moment, he thought he saw Kasia Pasternak down in the park. The woman had her back to him, smoking a cigarette and talking to... *huh! That's Bill Ngo. It probably* is *Kasia. Not surprising, their offices are both around here.*

He felt a pang of envy. *Much nicer out there than in here.* Sighing, he lowered himself into his chair, which creaked softly under the load, and picked up yet another report on yet another mundane topic. He looked at his mobile phone sitting on the desk. *C'mon, Rafi, get us approvals to go interview some people, what's the hold up?*

Ivan had gone out for lunch. Unable to find anywhere to sit outside and reluctant to sit inside a restaurant on a day like this, had settled for take-out and a short walk before returning to his office. Sharmila found him at his desk munching on a sandwich. Characteristically, she was immaculately dressed; her small stature contrasting strikingly with Ivan's bulk. In her normal sing-song Mid-Western accent, she updated Ivan.

'I've been working on the emails between Edwards/Lawrence and Jaffar. I've also looked at the website and any other traffic I could find. They show a similar pattern to the communications we've been intercepting, lots of cut outs and shells. The website that Jaffar accessed had a "dot-biz" suffix, but is actually "dot-tv"'.

'Tuvalu?' Asked Ivan, naming the small Pacific Island nation that made a significant amount of its export earnings from selling internet URLs with the useful ".tv" suffix.

'Oh-yah. More likely not where the original was hosted. There's bursts of heavy traffic comparable to site editing and updating coming from... wanna guess?'

'Right here in New York?'

'Nope, but maybe just as good: China! But that's where we lose it'.

'So we have another China link?'

'Not necessarily. Could have been re-routed through there, but it's a smart move. It's hard for us to track traffic that goes through China. We're looking for patterns, but the amount of data is huge. Even with supercomputer access, which we don't have, it'd probably take weeks to sort through the world's metadata. Even assuming the data is still there. Most of this sort of history gets wiped after thirty days'.

'Another dead end', Ivan muttered.

'For now, perhaps, yah', replied Sharmila, much more upbeat. 'I've also been chasing the money, harder to hide'.

'What money?'

'Well, someone paid Tuvalu for that URL'.

'And?'

'And… it was paid for by a shell company. Actually an onion ring of shell companies, we're still digging, but each layer results in at least a dozen different trails that need to be investigated. It'll probably result in more than a thousand leads, but given time, it's doable'.

'How much time, Sharmila? I'm getting the feeling that everything is taking more time than we have'.

'Oh… a week? Two?'

Ivan looked out his window. He wanted to shout, "*Chyort! We don't have two weeks!*", but shouting at Sharmila wouldn't do any good at all. Besides, he wasn't even sure if there was a time issue. *Sure there's a time component to do with the possible second attack, but in terms of solving the case… the media were hounding the PR department, that was it. Even the Governor and other politicos who usually lean on us are being reasonable. Hmmm… wonder if there's a reason for that? Maybe some of those people are involved. It'd explain why they're keeping a low profile…*

Ivan glimpsed a reflection in the window he'd been looking through while he pondered. Realising the reflection was Sharmila and that she was still standing there, he turned around sheepishly.

'Sorry. Wool-gathering. Two weeks, huh? Well, see what you can do, would be good if it was sooner than that'.

'Oh, sure. And about them there drones. I checked in with Gavin, they've narrowed it down to two. All the others have been verified as still flying, except for two that have already been crashed, but we've seen the parts and they sure weren't in an explosion!'

'Sharmila, please'. Ivan looked tired. 'What are the two we don't know about?'

'One's the one that was sold on eBay. Still looking for the fella who bought that one. We've got ads in local papers and the local police are on the lookout. Seems reasonable to assume someone who bought it in person at least lives in the same State, no?'

'Unless they're deliberating trying to hide something'.

'Yah. But if we look locally first then maybe we can rule it out faster'.

'Uh-huh. And the other one?'

'Oh! You'll like this. It's the one sent to China. They're not being very cooperative'.

'*Chyort!*' This time, Ivan couldn't help swearing out loud. 'China again. Everywhere we look, there's China. Not doing anything wrong, exactly, just lurking in the background. Are they involved or not?' he asked rhetorically. 'There'll be hell to pay if they are and Trump finds out'.

'Yah. And, boss?' Sharmila got Ivan's attention. 'Something else for you. Just thought it interesting, is all. You remember that lady reporter on Fox? The one that Trump got into a fight with? Megyn Kelly?'

Ivan knew from experience that Sharmila often needed to take the long way round to get her news out. Any attempt to speed her up simply flustered her and slowed things down so he simply nodded and grunted.

'Well… yesterday, when we were talking, something rang in my head about "Dan Kendall". So I did a search, Dan Kendall is Ms. Kelly's ex-husband. Have we got motive?'

Ivan looked blankly at her for a couple of seconds, then: 'Well, crap! Get onto that! This could be the break we've been looking for!'

As Sharmila left, Ivan looked out of the window again. Inside suddenly seemed to be as warm and sunny as outside.

The President-Elect was watching the late news before calling it a day and heading to bed. He'd started to feel tired and achy an hour back. *Probably been overdoing it a bit.* He put the back of a hand to his forehead. *Feels warm. Should grab a couple of Tylenol before bed.*

Day Eighteen
December 16, 2016

Friday morning. The end of the week and a glorious weekend was promised. On the downside, it was not looking good for anyone dreaming of a white Christmas.

Ivan was back at his desk, significantly cheerier than the day before. This was partly due to the weather, sunshine always has an uplifting effect on him, and partly due to news he'd got around ten-thirty. He'd received an official notice stating that certain people who may have "knowledge relevant to an ongoing investigation" could be questioned. Such questioning should be conducted "in a restrained manner", but, and this was the part that made Ivan happy, "if subjects were unduly recalcitrant", they could be "invited" to FBI offices for the questioning and any complaints or refusals should be "referred to either the Attorney-General of the United States or the Director of the Federal Bureau of Investigation or both, *in person*".

The people who should be approached "in the first instance" were Congress-woman Linda Starr, Dan Kendall, Senators Marvin Jäger and Markos Metaxas. Further individuals were identified as being approved for questioning *if, and only if,* they were mentioned as being possibly relevant to the case by one of the four primary individuals. These others were Deputy Director Ian Croft of the United States Secret Service and *any* other USSS personnel mentioned and Major Murray Allard Deputy Commissioner for Counterterrorism, New York Governor's office and any other individual within the New York State Division of Homeland Security and Emergency Services, but *not* anyone from the Federal Department of Homeland Security without further authorisation.

Questioning would take place under the supervision of the Deputy United States Attorney General. Those authorised to conduct questioning were U.S. Attorney Alden Saunders, Deputy U.S. Attorney Bill Ngo, FBI Special Agent Ivan Biskup and NYPD Lieutenant-Commander Martin King. At their discretion, they could co-opt others to be present, but at least one of these people had to be with the interviewee at all times.

Ivan called Martin with the good news. Martin was less than impressed, almost grumpy. 'Great. Just before the last weekend before Christmas. A lot of these people will be flying home, would have been so much better if we could have caught them all in Washington'.

'C'mon, Martin. At least we've got something! We can get to work now. One way or another we need to show that Starr either did or didn't have something to do with the attack'.

'I guess. I just dunno. White told us there was going to be another attack and nothing's happened. Trump's booked some "time with his family" this weekend,

I understand that was a consequence of some strong suggestions by the USSS and others. Anyway, he's going to be holed up in Trump Tower until Monday and that place is on lock down. I just don't see anything happening. Kasia and I are beginning to think that Morna may have been onto something; White was fed a line to try and smoke out their leak. There may not be a second attack'.

'You may be right, Martin. Our job, however, is to solve the attack that *did* happen. Others are in charge of making sure another one doesn't happen'.

'Oh, I'm just feeling like we got derailed somewhere. I'll be fine. On another note, we started looking at videos again, see if we can put together a movement plan of Starr and her group on the night. Now we've got the go-ahead, that'd be the first thing I want to ask her, a full list, preferably with photographs, of who was with her and where they went, make sure it all jives with the videos'.

'Good work. I'll start teeing up interview times. You want to come to Washington with me?'

'No, no… I think I'll stay here. I'm sure you can handle it without me holding your hand!'

'Hah! That'll be the day when I need hand-holding from a street cop! Rafi's still down in D.C. I'll ask him to see if he can get that list for you'.

'Thanks, that'd definitely make our job a bit easier. Talk to ya later'.

'Yeah, and have a good weekend if I don't talk to you before'.

Amazingly, within an hour of Rafi's request, a helpful aide had produced everything they needed: a list of everyone who was with the Congresswoman on the Twenty-Ninth of November, their itineraries and copies of their staff badge photos.

Rafi sent them to Ivan who distributed them amongst the team.

A little later, Sharmila dropped by Ivan's desk again.

'Those photos you sent round? Helpful, but not. That Megyn Fox connection? Doesn't fit. *Doctor* Dan Kendall isn't the Kendall in the photos. Doesn't look like him at all. I made a couple of calls as well? Initial reports have him in Washington on the Twenty-Ninth. Well, actually, Virginia, he works at a pain clinic there. He did a couple of procedures that afternoon. The log book says he didn't finish until past five p.m. I can continue to look into…'

Ivan shook his head. 'No… that's fine, Sharmila. Good idea, it's important to keep thinking outside the box like that and "no" is sometimes as good an answer as "yes"'.

'And…', she continued, 'same thing for Michael Sandford'.

'Who?'

'You remember. That English tourist who wanted to shoot Trump way back in June? Kasia thought there might be a connection and you asked me to look into it'.

'Oh, yeah…' *Think I asked her; can't remember now. So many loose threads to pull on…*

'Well, yeah, you did. And so I did. Anyhoo… not getting anything there either. Other than the fact that he doesn't like Trump, there's no connection I can see. I'll keep the post-it note on the board to dot "I's and cross "T's'.

One door opens, two close. That's got to be progress of a sort, Ivan thought.

Across town, as Sharmila and Ivan finished their conversation, three large black cars pulled into the emergency entrance of Mount Sinai hospital. The first car swept around the curved drive, turned sharply and stopped, blocking the exit. The third car performed a similar manoeuvre at the entrance to the drive. The middle car, a limousine with blacked out windows stopped directly opposite the hospital double doors. They seemed to have been expected; a body was hustled out of the limousine, onto a waiting gurney and thence into the bowels of the hospital itself.

It took less than a minute. There were no casual passers-by to catch a glimpse of that notorious blonde hairstyle on the gurney.

Doctor Randall trotted alongside the gurney, listening to the medical staff surrounding his patient as they headed directly to Intensive Care.

'Pull his case files, we're all familiar with the patient, but best to have information at our fingertips…'

'Currently febrile, temperature is thirty-nine point seven. Pulse is rapid, but strong'.

'I want bloods, stat!'

'He reported having general aches last night, becoming progressively focused into the head area. He admits to having taken a number of Tylenol's last night…

'…masking the symptoms, and lowering the fever so he felt okay until today. Damn, I hate late presentations…'

They entered an elevator.

'He now reports intense pain around the site of the craniectomy we recently performed and behind his right eye'.

'There *is* some swelling and mild inflammation in the area, but it's not commensurate with the degree of pain being reported'.

'Get some swabs of the area. And get this damn hair out of the way! How'd it grow back like this?'

One of the interns looked closely at the offending hair as they exited the elevator. 'I think he may have had hair extensions…'

'I don't care! Just get it shaved off!'

Two Secret Service Agents had followed the gurney. One of them objected. 'He won't want that, Doctor'.

The hospital had become used to their presence the last time the President-Elect had been admitted, but could be occasionally confused as to who had authority in some areas. Managing the interface between the medical staff and the Secret Service was one of Randall's responsibilities. He said, 'and he damned well won't like dying either. The hair goes'.

They turned into an ICU room and carefully transferred the man onto the bed. Randall ensured himself that the Agents remembered the protocols established last time. They did; they made no attempt to enter the ICU.

Trump was fully conscious, but obviously in a lot of pain and didn't care how he was man-handled. The well-organised team went smoothly about their business, hooking the patient up to various monitors and inserting an IV line.

Meanwhile, the medics around him continued to issue instructions.

'I need a CT in the next twenty minutes people, and see when we can get him into the MRI. May not need it, but I want a slot open at a moment's notice'.

'I want ten mil morphine, four grams Zosyn, a thousand mil vancomycin and five hundred clindamycin. Come on, people. This is the President-Elect, don't even think about overuse of antibiotics creating resistance right now'.

Day Nineteen

December 17, 2016

The medical team had worked through the night, sleeping when they could. Doctor Randall had stayed with them, usually observing from the gallery, but occasionally – suitably attired, of course – entering the operating theatre itself.

Initially, Trump had seemed to brighten as the morphine kicked in, but alternating bouts of vomiting and diarrhoea soon had him weak and shaking. He even managed to look pale under his tan. He had put up a small fight when the nursing staff started to cut his clothes off of him. *Do you know how much those pants cost? Probably more than you earn in a year!* But his heart wasn't in it. And it was his heart that the doctors were initially most worried about.

The sudden strain of fighting the infection coming so soon after surgery had tested Trump's body's capacity to fight back. He became confused, calling a blonde doctor by his wife's name, and then screaming curses at an empty corner of the room where, to Trump's mind, Francisco Duarte stood taunting him.

This period didn't last long before he sagged back into his pillow, silent and still. Despite the high levels of antibiotics and fluids being pumped into him, his blood pressure had suddenly dropped as he went into sepsis shock.

After an hour, the medical team had stabilised him and work on diagnosing and treating his infection could continue.

Once Trump's head had been completely shaven, the extent of the infection became clearer. The CT scan had shown infection and tissue damage within the cranium and into the brain itself. By this time, the right side of Trump's skull had swollen and blistered. Under physical inspection, some of the blisters ruptured and a thin, grey liquid leaked out. The scalp had also started to discolour, the red of infection giving way to a deep violet. Confirmation from blood tests that he had a severe infection seemed superfluous.

Initial lab results had ruled out bacterial meningitis, the commonest serious post-craniectomy complication. That had narrowed down the possibilities, but they still didn't know exactly what they were dealing with. The medical team decided that a small surgical exploration would give valuable information while they waited for an MRI.

This was delayed as Randall first tried to get consent for Trump himself, and then, when it was clear that he was temporarily *non compos mentis,* Randall had to explain to Mrs Trump and the Secret Service Agent in Charge what they planned on doing. It wasn't until close to eleven o'clock that he got authorisation to proceed.

As Randall was going to assist the neurosurgeon, he dressed himself as if he was entering an operating theatre for his own protection. He knew that Trump hadn't travelled recently, but the Ebola outbreak was still recent enough to make all of them take stringent precautions until they were sure of what they were dealing with.

The neurosurgeon started by giving the patient a sedative through the intravenous line and anesthetising the area around the epicentre of the infection. With Trump barely conscious, the doctor cut a small hole in the tissues of the skull, exposing the bone. He turned to Randall.

'I'm going to have a feel around', he said, holding up a gloved finger.

'Seriously?' Asked Randall. 'You're going to stick your finger in his head?'

'It's the best way to diagnose necrotising fasciitis. You must be thinking there's a chance that's what we're dealing with, just as I am'.

'It crossed my mind, but… highly unusual to find it on the head'.

'It is at that', the surgeon agreed. 'Let's find out shall we?' He inserted a fingertip into the hole. After less than a minute, he withdrew his finger and shook his head at Randall. 'I think it is NF. You have a feel'.

Randall took the surgeon's place. Rotating his finger inside the incision, he was unpleasantly surprised to feel little resistance. The flesh, connecting tissue, muscles, blood vessels, everything, felt like warm, soft peanut, butter. Randall couldn't stop himself thinking, *the crunchy kind with bits of peanut scattered through it.*

Even worse, the bone around the small hole they had made ten days ago to relieve the bleed was soft. It had a texture like that of wood that had been infested with woodworm. He could feel it giving even with the slight pressure of his finger. As he withdrew his finger, he noted amidst the general fluid and tissue small splinters of bone adhering to his glove. *Not good…*

This was the moment when the complaint was officially diagnosed as necrotising fasciitis, the "flesh-eating disease" of public imagination. The flesh wasn't really "eaten"; there were no tiny monstrosities like those seen in pictures by electron microscopes chomping away. It was better to talk about "flesh-dissolving". The bacteria release toxins that break down the cells and tissues into a formless mush.

With that diagnosis, both men knew a long night lay ahead. It wasn't a common morbidity, but the treatment protocol was well-established. Aggressive use of antibiotics, which they had been doing ever since Trump came into the hospital, and debridement; cutting away of the dead and dying tissue as fast as possible to prevent the bacteria from spreading.

The surgeon took over, collecting fluid samples and cut away small pieces of flesh, carefully sealing them to be sent to the lab as soon as he was finished. He folded the right ear forward to better access the scalp. As he did, he saw that the skin at the base of the ear where it attached to the skull had turned black. He turned to Randall.

'Get him into a theatre, now!'

In theory, the surgery is not difficult; cut away everything that is infected and burn it. The difficult part is in keeping the patient alive. A secondary consideration is to minimise the damage and subsequent disfigurement. This was not an easy task as the small exploratory surgery that Randall had just performed would need to be repeated in different areas of the patient's head and face to ensure that all infected areas were identified and removed. Patients afflicted by the disease who survive – and the mortality rate is high – usually end up with massive wounds that need multiple skin grafts. It was often necessary to amputate limbs, but amputation was obviously not an option in this case.

Randall booked an OT and asked the senior theatre nurse to assemble a team and prep the theatre. He got another team working on preparing the patient while he made some calls. Trump may be under for many hours, but Randall wouldn't be. A variety of specialists, particularly from neurosurgery, dermatology and plastics were going to be required.

Saturday. Martin King's day to lie-in. Although he hadn't slept much later than usual, the house was quiet. His wife had said something about going to the beautician's in the morning, and the kids were still asleep.

Dressing himself in his usual weekend attire, he followed his Saturday routine. Macchinetta coffee. The *New York Times*. Toast with peanut butter. The crunchy kind.

His work mobile rang.

'King'.

Ivan was on the other end.

'Hi Martin. Sorry to disturb on a Saturday… again. Trump's in hospital'.

'What! What happened? There's nothing in the paper'.

'No, it's being kept quiet. He was re-admitted late yesterday afternoon. He's got a really bad infection. The Service Agents with him reported to Ian Croft, who called Rafi, who called me and now, I'm calling you. It's quite possible that, other than the hospital staff, that's the sum total of who knows about this'.

'So what is it?'

'The doctor says it might be something called, ah…' Ivan was obviously reading a note. 'Here it is… necrotising fasciitis. I think I pronounced it right'.

'What's that?'

'Another name for it is "flesh-eating disease". It's nasty: Attacks the flesh and it simply disappears. After going all red and black and crap like that first. And here's the kicker: It's on his face…'

'So White was right, what was it she said, "It would be horrible, disfiguring and he won't have a face"? Something like that?'

'That's the one'.

'How'd he get this thing?'

'Kicker number two. Doc Randall has no idea. It does happen, but it's very rare. Of course, he may be trying to cover some malpractice, this is the sort of thing you pick up in hospitals. I don't think so though, partly because we were warned that this sort of thing was going to happen'.

'Does Randall know that?'

'Nope. And Rafi and Croft agree that we keep it that way. Croft says the Agents on duty don't know about White's warning. He told Rusty Wilkins and Rusty decided not to tell anyone else at this point'.

'Any theories? Anything at all?'

'The doctors are, of course, looking at purely medical issues, not foul play.

They say it's bacterial, that it enters the body through breaks in the skin. No surprise that it seems to have got in where he had surgery, that the bacteria are fairly common, but that most people fight it off before it even starts to get a hold. They think maybe Trump's immune system was low after surgery or even something called immunoageing. I think they mean he's old'.

'So where does that leave us, Ivan?'

'Not much for us to do really, the Protection Detail are still there in case of anything else and the hospital is doing what it can for him. I wanted to chat to you first, but I think we should get Rafi and Ian to extend our investigation and allow us to bring Doctor Randall up to speed. He's probably our best bet for figuring out how this infection could have been the result of an intentional act. This is the "second attack" for sure, Martin'.

'Totally agree. Too much of a coincidence otherwise. Just a thought, I think we also need to tell Kasia, just because she does the thinking for the both of us, and Morna. I think Morna actually has a lot more knowledge, even experience, of the darker Agency arts than she lets on. If necessary, we could even ask Brice. Attack by bacteria is a little out of our league.

'Yeah. Could be right. Sort of thing the Russians do isn't it?'

'I think they're more into poison, but yeah, definitely got the whiff of spook activities'.

'Before we tell Morna or Brice, maybe we should push the "pause", button. We know that we have a leak somewhere, right?'

'Yeah, but I assume that came from just too many people, "loose lips sink ships" stuff'.

'What if it wasn't? What if this is a clandestine-espionage sort of attack? We do have at least two people in that business who are privy to most of the details of the investigation'. Ivan sounded worried.

'What? Morna? I can't believe it'.

'Buddy, when have you ever not been surprised when you solve a case and find out who did it and for what trivial reason? The depths that people will sink to always comes as a surprise'.

'Likely that we'll need someone who knows biological weapons to help us figure this out eventually, but, alright, let's tell Kasia, but hold off on Morna. At least until the doctor can give us some idea where it came from. You never know, maybe he got it when he washed his face at the hospital, y'know a dirty washcloth'.

'Unlikely, he said the symptoms start within hours of infection...' Ivan tailed off as both men suddenly came to the same conclusion. 'Crap! That means...'

'…he picked up in his house!' Martin finished. 'Call Rafi and Ian now. Double-check with the Service that he hasn't left the apartment in the last twenty-four hours and get them to get Mrs Trump and anyone else in that apartment out of there. That's a crime scene now. I'm going over to Trump Tower; with luck Kasia'll be home and I can pick her up on the way. Can you get a CSI team there today or should I have our FIU do it?'

'No, I can get CSI there. Especially if we're dealing with biologicals, they probably have more training on that. I'll also call CDC. The doctors wouldn't have done that, it's not that contagious by itself, but if someone has weaponised it, that's a different picture altogether'.

'Done. Let's keep in touch and hey…'

'Yeah, Martin?'

'What was the last thing you said to me yesterday? "Have a great weekend?" Thanks a lot, pal'.

Day Twenty

December 18, 2016

Dina Accardo left her parents' house early Sunday morning. She planned on being back in D.C. in time to have a little "Dina Time" to unwind before getting ready for a small, but important, dinner party. She and her husband had agreed that this weekend would be the best for seeing their respective families before the Christmas. This year they were expecting just two of their four children to come home, but that would be busy enough once the three grand-children were included.

She was looking forward to hosting them, just as she was looking forward to tonight's dinner even though it was more Party business. As co-chair of the RNC, she rarely attended any social function that didn't have some work component. She didn't mind. She liked her career and enjoyed the networking and social side of it.

Still, after the stress of the previous week, she needed some time to herself. Even the visit with her parents hadn't been easy. They were both in their eighties now and their decision to remain in the small town of Hamilton was not the most practical decision. Yet they had lived there most of their lives, where else would they go? On the plus side, the mountain scenery and air was enchanting no matter what the season.

She had deliberately left earlier than absolutely necessary. Dina's husband wouldn't get home until Monday which meant she had the day to herself until dinner. The early start on a Sunday almost guaranteed that she wouldn't see another car on the fantastic drive from Hamilton to the airport in Missoula.

If this was summer she would have been tempted to pull over at one of the small picnic spots and walk along the mountain stream that ran adjacent to the road for much of the way. But with the temperature still well below zero, she was happy to stay in the warmth of her rented Mercedes. The small, but powerful car stuck faithfully to the road as it curved and dipped down the valley. At times she felt like a bird swooping through the forests on either side, the firs cloaked silently in brilliant white snow. *Enjoy it while I can still afford it, these imports are going to cost a lot more when Trump starts ripping up trade agreements. Still, my Lexus will probably be jump in resale value now…*

The road itself was mostly in shade, but above her the mountains were dazzlingly white against a soft powder blue sky without a cloud in sight. Brilliant shafts of sunshine occasionally cut through the trees, temporarily rendering the windscreen frostily opaque. Despite this, she went fast enjoying the power and stability of the car. She knew this road well having driven it many, many times when she was younger. It was a good road and had been ploughed and gritted since the last snowfall.

As she came around a bend, a sunbeam blocked her sight for a split second. Having seen the light ahead she had anticipated the momentary blindness. She hadn't anticipated suddenly seeing a man standing in the middle of the road when her windscreen cleared. A man pointing a rifle at her.

Time slowed down. Instinctively, she pulled the steering wheel to the right to avoid the man. At the same time her windscreen shattered into a million stars and she could no longer see the road. She thought she heard a sharp crack. She felt the back end of the car slide to the left and she steered into the skid as she had done many times before. Learning to drive in the mountains of Montana meant plenty of practice in driving on snow and ice. There was a heavy thump to her left and the car lifted up on that side, throwing her towards the passenger side. Just as quickly, the car righted itself and, just for a second, she felt that she was *really* flying. Through the shattered windscreen she saw a dark vertical line that rapidly grew thicker. Dina's last thought as the branch smashed through the screen and into her chest was a mundane, *it's a tree.*

Conscious of leaving footsteps, the man stayed on the ploughed asphalt as he examined the wreckage below him.

The Mercedes' engine had stalled on impact, but the wheels were still turning slowly. Unlike in the movies, cars are not so fragile that they immediately burst into flames when they crash. This one didn't either. The branches supporting it started to creak and groan. With a harsh crack, one large limb suddenly gave way and the car fell backwards into the snow. It stood on its tail for a second and then tilted forward, its front end bouncing up and back down as it fell. Slowly, it started to slide forward, catching the tree trunk enough to turn it slightly, but not enough to stop its descent.

The car gathered speed, scattering snow as it went, until it splashed into the river with a gout of water on either side. It sat there at a forty-five degree angle, front end submerged in the water up to the doors. Anyone inside would be at least half immersed in the icy water.

The man stood there a bit longer, watching for any movement. There wasn't any. Satisfied, he turned and walked down the road to where he had parked at a rest stop that bore the wheel tracks of a number of vehicles before he added his own.

Crown Heights, Brooklyn, New York

The securing of Trump's home yesterday had gone remarkably smoothly. He and Kasia had met the Secret Service Agents the day before and, after some argument, managed to get Mrs Trump and their domestic staff out of the apartment. It was then sealed off in anticipation of the FBI's Crime Scene Investigation Unit. That it was a penthouse was of great help in maintaining secrecy. No other tenants on the same floor, exclusive-use elevators and private below-ground exits had meant that the operation went off without a hitch and without anyone, especially the media, the wiser. The first CSI team had arrived late in the afternoon and started their work. Mission Accomplished.

Martin had dropped Kasia in town; she'd been meeting friends again. Martin had then driven himself home to spend the afternoon with his family, but that was yesterday. Today was Sunday. And Sunday was Martin's wife's turn to sleep-in.

His two teenagers had breezed through the kitchen earlier saying something about going into the City together as they went out the front door. Now, the house was quiet. Martin could just hear his wife's slow, deep breathing from the bedroom. Occasionally, the furnace would turn on and the house would breathe in synchronisation with his wife.

It was peaceful, almost meditative. Martin was enjoying the quiet kitchen. Once again dressed in his weekend uniform complete with robe and slippers, he was able to make up for the past interrupted weekends.

Pity the paper's all over the place. Chiding himself for picking the one negative on an otherwise sunny morning, he prepared his customary coffee and toast, collected the paper's sections and settled in at the counter.

The surgical team had worked on their patient through the night. It had been extremely stressful. Not only were they cutting near essential blood vessels and organs such as the jugular veins, carotid arteries, right ear and eye, but they were also acutely aware of the importance of the man on their table. To make matters worse, the wounds wept significant fluids and emitted foul-smelling gases, a result of gas gangrene that often made the medics gag.

Around three in the morning, they were forced to excise part of the retromandibular vein and put in a temporary by-pass. It was likely that the patient would have difficulty eating and talking if he recovered.

Potential damage to the brain remained a major concern. The bacteria had attacked the meninges, three layers of tissue under the skull that cover the brain itself. The doctors would only be able to tell what cognitive or motor functions had been impaired when the patient woke.

Which happened just before seven on Sunday morning. The anaesthesiologist's concerns had grown as the hours wore on until finally the team decided that the risk of keeping him under general anaesthetic was too high, and they decided to bring him around, albeit still heavily sedated.

The surgeons had been aggressive in surgically removing all the necrotic tissue they could find. Areas suspected of being necrotic, but had yet to be debrided had been cross-hatched with a scalpel and a collagenase-based salve applied. The enzymes in collagenase would continue to break down any necrotic tissue while he woke up; the surgeons could then revisit the sites after the patient was awake and continue surgical debridement under local anaesthetic. The wounds would be left open requiring the patient to be kept in an aseptic environment until further notice.

While the patient emerged from anaesthetic, the surgical team could take a break. Some of them, such as the theatre nurses and anaesthesiologist had been in the theatre the whole time, but could now go off duty. Quite a few of them pulled off their gowns and masks as quickly as they could and made hurried beelines to the nearest washroom. They hadn't been able to relieve themselves for many hours...

Others on the team had been able to take breaks during the operation as different specialists took their turn. Some had even managed catnaps between their shifts, but none of them were fully rested. Despite their tiredness, there was still much work to be done, notes to be made while still fresh, cultures and lab reports to assess, instructions for post-op care to be given. All of these things, and more, were taken care of between more personal needs, breakfast, showers, coffee, and phone calls home.

Doctor Randall skipped a shower for now, but did get himself an herbal tea; he avoided caffeine on shifts like these. Then he faced the task of making some difficult phone calls, and an even more difficult discussion with Mrs Trump and why it would be best if she didn't see her husband right at this moment.

Rafina Matos flew back from Washington on Saturday and was home before dinner. He spent a quiet night with his wife and had gone to bed early. He suspected that he wouldn't be having a quiet Sunday.

He was right. The first phone call came close to midnight.

'What was that?' His wife asked sleepily after he'd hung up.

'Donald Trump's had a relapse, he's back in hospital'. He spared his wife the preliminary diagnosis of a "flesh-eating" disease. After confirming that there was nothing for him to do, he fell into a light and troubled sleep.

Despite his restless night, Rafi had got up at six as usual; even on weekends he couldn't sleep in. He watched the news while having his first coffee of the day. He was relieved to see that there was nothing about Trump's illness nor about the work that was ongoing at Trump Towers.

The headline had been a car accident in Montana. The Co-chair of the Republican National Committee had died the previous day. Police did not suspect foul play, skid marks on the road suggesting that she had suddenly swerved, probably to avoid a deer or other animal, lost control and left the road.

At seven-thirty, his phone rang. It was Ian Croft.

'Good morning Rafi, sorry to have to call so early on a Sunday'.

'Don't think about it. I've been up for a while. Waiting for your call, actually. How is he?'

'I just got off the phone with Lloyd Randall. It's not good. They confirmed it's… necrotising fasciitis', he pronounced the words slowly and carefully. 'It spread very fast, but they think they may have got most of it overnight. They'll monitor constantly and cut away anything suspicious as soon as they see it'.

'So they've had to cut some skin off?'

'My god, Rafi, it's not just "some skin"! It's awful. Randall told me they've cut off his right ear and eyelid and all, *all,* the skin and flesh down to the bone between them. *And* over most of the right side of his head and even onto the neck'.

'Jeesus…' whispered Rafi.

'Yeah. They're not sure they can save his right eye. They've cut away a lot of the cheek and eyebrow around the socket. The eye itself is untouched for now, but it's kinda sitting there all by itself, just bone around it. Like a hallowe'en skeleton mask. He says if the bacteria don't breach the outer layers, the eye may survive. But here's the thing; it got into his brain.

'Normally, the doc says, the bacteria doesn't attack bone, but after the surgery last week, there were weaknesses and it got through the holes in the skull that hadn't fully healed and into the brain'.

'It's eating Trump's brain?' Rafi said incredulously. 'Sounds like a bad science fiction movie'.

'I know, it does, doesn't it?'

'What does it mean?'

'There's a layer of tissue beneath the skull that the brain's wrapped in. A final layer of protection that keeps bacteria out. Sort of like using Saran wrap for leftovers. *Meninges* he called them. Anyway, in this case, instead of keeping bacteria out, *this* bacteria likes the stuff, eats it'.

Rafi made a groaning sound. He wasn't sure he should have had muesli for breakfast.

'So, the bacteria gets through the bone and finds a layer of meninges and goes wild, munching away like it's candy. Now the bacteria is spreading between the skull and the brain, moving around the whole head. The only way they could catch it was to lift the bones of the skull'.

'Huh?'

'Yeah. They sawed a big circle in his head. Had to be large to ensure they got everything. Then they cut the circle into triangular flaps and peeled back the entire freakin' right side of his head so they could cut out all the damaged *meninges*. He said they're confident they got it all, but medicine is never one hundred percent'.

Rafi let out a big sigh. 'Anything else?'

'fraid so. While the bugs were going ape shit, eating the meninges', Croft was obviously proud of having learnt this new word, 'another set of bugs decided to chomp on the brain itself. Doc says it's right at the junction of…', he paused to read out the terms, '…the right parietal, temporal and frontal lobes. They had to cut some of it away'.

'They've cut out part of the brain?'

'Yep. Amazingly, he doesn't think they'll be too much impact, won't kill him, but they'll need to do extensive tests later. The worrying thing is damage to the frontal lobe, but so far that's minor. He could develop speech problems or even behavioural changes'.

'Not good in anyone, let alone the Commander-in-Chief'. Noted Rafi.

'Precisely. Randall says it's relatively superficial at the moment and he still hopes for recovery. Note that he's talking about recovering as an individual, not as a potential President. When I pressed him for details on what sort of damage we could be looking at, he used a couple of medical terms. I wrote them down…', his voice trailed off momentarily as he looked at his notes, '…constructional apraxia and contralateral neglect. What it all adds up to is that Trump may be alive, but he may also have problems washing himself, making his breakfast, and have difficulty understanding verbal instructions and be in denial of anything he doesn't agree with'. He paused, but couldn't help himself from adding, 'Not that the last two would be different'.

Rafi laughed and Ian joined in. They both needed a bit of temporary relief.

When the laughter stopped, Ian carried on. 'Listen, Rafi, we got off to a bad start on this investigation. And some of that is my fault, I wanted to protect the Service and my Agents and made some bad calls. I hope we can move on from that. We have a serious issue here and we all need to work together'.

A little surprised to receive what amounted to an apology from the Deputy Director of the Secret Service, Rafi managed to say, 'No worries, Ian, exactly my sentiments as well'.

'Great. Obviously, it's still the Service's responsibility to protect Trump and equally obviously, we have failed in that duty a second time. I see this as a reflection of the capability of the attacker or attackers and even perhaps of the interagency conflicts we experienced at the beginning'.

Of course you would, Ian. Anything except incompetence of your Service. Still, we do need to work together now.

Unaware of Rafi's scepticism, Croft carried on. 'Now, however, we can be sure that this was the second attack that your people got the warning about', Rafi decided not to correct him; the warning came from NYPD, not FBI. *Close enough, I guess, and he's still trying to spread responsibility for this mess as far as he can.*

'Which means', Croft continued, 'while the Service is still on duty, it's now up to the FBI to find out who's doing this. And I can assure you of the full cooperation of the Service'. *Sure, now the shit's hit the fan, we get to pick up the pieces.* 'The hospital is still liaising with us. Of course, I'll keep you in the loop, Rafi, but I think you and I need to get onto the same page on a few decisions'.

'I'm listening', said Rafi, non-committally.

'I need to brief the Director', he meant of the Secret Service, 'and possibly the DHS Secretary, but maybe the Director will want to do that himself. I'm also going to call the Speaker of the House and the Vice-President. That takes care of the White House and the Senate at the same time. Who they want to tell is up to them, of course, but we're going to need to formulate a common statement, we're not going to be able to keep this from the public for much longer. I suspect that the Republican Committee is going to need to do some very quick reshuffling'.

'Which', Rafi said, 'is going to add to their problems, you saw the news?'

'What news?'

'The RNC co-chair, Accardo, died in a car crash yesterday'.

'My God! It just keeps getting worse! No foul play?'

'No'.

'Well, that's good. I'm not sure the Service can provide Protection for many more people, we're already stretched trying to cover anyone who might become POTUS or the Veep which, as you may have realised, is no longer clear cut.

'As far as the FBI's concerned, I don't think you should make any announcements until the politicians have had a chance to say something. I suspect the White House will have a press conference tomorrow. Once *that* happens, though, the FBI and NYPD are likely to be swamped by requests for news and interviews. Might be a good idea to get your people prepared for that'.

Great! Now he wants to tell me how to run the Bureau. 'Of course, Ian, thanks for the heads up'.

'But the big decision is something you and I have to decide'.

'Go ahead'.

'I haven't told the doctor about the warning that the second attack would be disfiguring. I think we need to, but… your call, your investigation'.

'Mmmm. I agree, it may help him in the treatment. Do you think he might be able to help us in return?'

'He may have done so already. He told me that one of the complications he's facing is that the disease is very complex. From the cultures he took, they can see that the infection is a mix of type one and type two bacteria', another pause for note-reading, '*clostridium* and *streptococcal*. He also said that the real problem was that there were traces of… methicillin-resistant *Staphylococcus aureus*, MRSA, that doesn't respond to antibiotics. Thing is, this MRSA stuff is found in… *monomicrobial* necrotizing fasciitis'.

'Which means what, Ian?' Interested as he was, Rafi was also anxious for Croft to get to the point so he could get on with his own phone calls.

'Which means it's rarely, if ever, seen in conjunction with other bacteria. Randall says he's never seen anything like it, talking about writing a journal article about it later. Seriously, Rafi, what's *wrong* with these people? A man's dying and they're thinking of embellishing their CVs'. Without waiting for a response, Croft carried on. 'In other words, Randall is saying that this combination doesn't happen in nature'.

Even though Ian couldn't see him, Rafi nodded slowly in agreement with Croft's unspoken conclusion. 'It's been weaponised'. He said quietly.

'Yeah. And now *you've* got to find out how it got onto Trump's face'.

Day Twenty-One

December 19, 2016
Electoral College

Across the country, five hundred and thirty-eight men and women, Electors of the Electoral College named on one of fifty-one Certificates of Ascertainment, met in their respective State capitals. In a process proscribed by the Twelfth Amendment to the US Constitution, each Elector cast two votes, one for the President and one for the Vice-President of the United States.

After all the Electors in a State (or, in the case of Washington, the District) had voted, they summarised the results onto six identical pairs (one for the President, one for the Vice-President) of Certificates of Vote, and sealed them into signed envelopes along with their State's Certificate of Ascertainment.

The next day six envelopes were sent, by registered post, to six different officials. Each of fifty-one envelopes was duly placed in a locked, fireproof filing cabinet in six different offices where they would sit until January sixth.

One of those offices was that of Joe Biden, President of the Senate and Vice President of the United States where he joked with his Chief of Staff about "Schrödinger's Cabinet".

And so, from that day, until January sixth when the envelopes would be removed from the cabinet and counted at a joint session of Congress, Donald Trump was both the President of the United States and not the President.

Whether he was alive or dead on the Sixth was another matter altogether and of no relevance to his status as President or non-President.

They had laboured all through the previous night and day. Realising that the bacteria was not responding to the antibiotics and was still spreading, the surgeons decided to put the patient under general anaesthetic once again. Chemical and mechanical debridement techniques were introduced alongside surgery.

At two in the morning, the patient lost his right eye.

At seven, his nose and right cheek were cut away, exposing his jaw and teeth on that side. In any other case, the doctors would have stopped at this point, allowing the patient to die. This wasn't any other case.

By midday, the top of the skull had been completely removed. The brain was seventy percent exposed, sitting in a bowl of bone with one side gone. They kept the patient's head tilted to his left to stop the brain from sliding out.

The right side of the brain now had a visually discernible scoop missing. Then, almost fast enough to see, the carotid artery started changing colour from its customary bright red. First it deepened to a dark red then became purple and finally black as it died.

Doctor Lloyd Randall stood back from the bed, looked at the surgeons, then over to the monitors above the man's head and then finally coming to rest on the clock on the wall.

'Time of death; fifteen-fifteen'.

Ivan Biskup and Bill Ngo met Linda Starr in her office. The conversation was cordial and the Congresswoman was cooperative. Her Executive Assistant stayed present throughout and took notes. The two men expressed their condolences for the death of Mrs Accardo. Starr thanked them; she had been "a good woman, trusted colleague and a faithful friend". Which was one reason why she could not spare them a lot of time on this visit; she had to attend, well, not a wake as such, but an informal remembrance for Dina at the Capitol Hill Club later.

Starr was not surprised by the visit. Indeed, she expressed surprise that it had taken them so long. After all, she *had* been at Rockefeller Centre on that awful night. Was she so intimidating that even the FBI needed permission to talk to her?

No, she hadn't been there when the actual attack had occurred. The President-Elect was due at a Party dinner later than night and she had gone there early to meet some people. Who? Party officials and some lobbyists if you must know. Jens, her EA, can give you a list.

She said that "of course" she knew Senators Jäger and Metaxas, they were colleagues of hers. Just because they were Senators and she was in the House didn't preclude contact. On the contrary, she often had to talk to fellow senior Republicans in both houses to ensure they were all on the same page. No, she didn't know where they had been on the Twenty-Ninth, Washington, she presumed. Easy enough to find out.

She wasn't sure if either of them knew Dan Kendall. Ask them. Why didn't the two men come over to the Club later? The Senators would surely be at the Remembrance... if they were in the capital, that is.

Yes, Dan was with her in New York on that night. She often took him with her as part of her security detail when she travelled. He's a very "versatile man with initiative". No, she wasn't sure where he was at the moment. He's not part of her permanent staff, more of a "consultant". She hadn't anticipated needing him until the New Year so hadn't asked him about his plans.

Why did she visit Secret Service Technician Holgersen that night? Wouldn't you, simply out of curiosity? What a fascinating idea to use eagles and owls to intercept drones! We tend to be enamoured of technology and sometimes forget that Nature can supply us with equally good solutions at lower costs. On a professional level, she had been one of the advocates for the program and had facilitated its funding.

While she had them here, there was another matter she wanted to briefly discuss and then she really had to be going...

Ivan and Bill found themselves a bench outside the Capitol Building. The weather was still warm for this time of year, but the sun was losing its strength ahead of nightfall. They were both grateful for their coats.

'What did you think of that last bit, Bill?'

'Possible theft of Party funds? I'm not a forensic accountant, no idea. Would have thought it would be more up the Agency's alley'.

'Oh, sure. I'll be passing the information on to CID'. He was referring to the largest department in the FBI, the Criminal Investigative Division. 'I was more interested in why mention it to *us*? Why *now*? Was she deflecting?'

'You really are a suspicious sort, aren't you Ivan? I didn't get that from her at all. Look at it from her side, she thinks there's a chunk of cash missing. Half-a-million may be a lot to you and me, but compared to the amounts she signs off each day it's probably peanuts. Annoyingly small peanuts. She's coming out of a difficult election period, she needed to get re-elected, remember? And has just lost a colleague. All of a sudden, bam! The two agencies responsible for investigating just this sort of thing walk through her door. Hell, if I was her, I'd probably have brought it up sooner, get it off my plate as soon as I could'.

'So you think that's it, taking advantage of our visit? Just seemed to me that *if* she was somehow involved in a contract killing… well, there'd be a need for some money and this is a good a way as any for laundering it'.

'Possible, but, call it my legal training if you want, you're bypassing the presumption of innocence. Once you decide she's guilty, then anything she does can have a guilty explanation. Why don't we pass it on to the people who handle this stuff in our respective organisations and then we're shot of it. Do what Starr did: Report and move on to more important things'.

'Okay. What about the rest of what she said?'

'Again, no alarm bells for me. I'd like to talk with Kendall though. We should get a list from Jens there of when Kendall has worked for Starr, dates and places, *et cetera*'.

'And how he got paid'.

'Of course'.

'Nothing else?' Ivan was pushing and both men knew it, he'd taken three days away from his office at a crucial time in the investigation and wanted something positive to come out of the trip. Both men were also rattled with the news about Trump's infection although neither of them knew yet that he had died.

'Not much. C'mon, Ivan. We weren't expecting a confession! We're down here to sniff around. Throw our weight around, get a few people nervous, see if we can scare up some birds. Her reasons for being at the Center sounded reasonable. We can go through this' he patted an inside pocket where he had the Congresswoman's itinerary for the past six months, 'but from first glance, she seems to have done a lot of these on-the-ground visits. Linda Starr likes to get her hands dirty in the field, get her information first hand, just like we're doing'.

'Alright', Ivan sighed. 'Want to go to this "Remembrance"?'

'Not really, but may as well. It's a good a place as any for us bird dogs to panic some turkeys'.

'Why do I get the feeling you don't hunt, Bill? Nice try, anyway'.

Capitol Hill Club, Washington

Despite being less than a week away from Christmas, the atmosphere was not festive. On top of the news of Dina Accardo's death, many people in the room would be unemployed in the New Year. There was a hint of desperation in some of the conversations.

Francisco Duarte stood in the middle of the crowd in the Eisenhower room. The Capitol Club staff had done wonders to put together a reception at very short notice. The others in the room, and there were well over a hundred people already with more coming in, treated Francisco almost as a bereaved spouse, shaking his hand and quietly extending their condolences "for his loss". And perhaps that was not so far-fetched; Duarte had worked closely with Dina Accardo for over a decade and it was likely that they had seen each other more often than their spouses did.

Always the consummate politician, he accepted their sympathies gracefully, but still used the occasion to ask about a few key bills, remind people of votes, check loyalties, and the like. When there was nothing politically pressing, he would ask questions about their families or make other personal, but unobtrusive, inquiries. He was very much an elder statesman in his element.

Beneath the veneer, however, his stomach was churning almost as much as his thoughts. He'd been informed by Paul Ryan, Speaker of the House, about Trump's death just an hour prior. For now, they were keeping the lid on it. Ryan was meeting with the Vice-President, who was also the President of the Senate, now. Francisco would have to excuse himself from this gathering as soon as appropriately possible and join the summit in progress. The news would have to be broken tonight in time for both the late news and the morning papers. He understood the major Nationals and networks had already been given a heads-up that there would be a major announcement in the next few hours and they may want to keep front pages and headline slots clear.

He leant over to an aide and whispered, 'Keep 'em happy for a while, would you? I need to make a quick visit to the washroom'. He walked purposefully through the crowd to the bar for a refill, fast enough to discourage conversation, but not too fast as to seem rude. He deliberately chose a route that took him through early arrivals with whom he had already talked. Picking up a new glass, he then left the room and headed to the washrooms. Doing this bought him as much as ten minutes to think.

Duarte's mind was churning. First Dina's death, now Trump's. And Trump's death meant a lot – *a huge lot* – of work in the next couple of weeks, all without Dina's help. Overriding all of that, however, was a suspicion that there was more here than the eye could see.

He kept running over one of the last conversation he'd had with Dina. It had been in the car leaving Trump's "coming out" party in Queens. She'd told him she was going to go to Montana. He knew her parents were there, he knew she liked to drive herself. He also knew that roads up there could be icy and *accidents do happen*. But in hindsight he knew she'd been trying to tell him something that day, but he hadn't caught it. He caught himself from drifting into self-recriminations. *Time for that later if need be.*

She'd asked him what would happen if Trump were not fit to be President in January. He'd thought she was hinting that she'd heard about some kind of scandal or was worried that there man was going to make yet another gaffe, one so serious that he couldn't take the oath. It had never occurred to him that "something" could mean "death".

What else did she say? Something about people inside *the Party. Did she know he was going to die? How could she? The doctors say he contracted a severe post-surgical bacterial infection. How could she know that in advance? Was she referring to the attack in November? No… she kept referring to a future event "what if…" something happened. Didn't she say Trump was a huge mistake, that there were Senators and Congressmen who had lost their jobs and others worried for their jobs in two years' time. That they "would do something" to stop Trump? Something that didn't rely on changing College votes? That's it! She said, "Something that would mean he can't be President". She didn't say he'd be dead, though. What if this was planned and Dina found out about it? And then someone found out that she had found out. And that someone killed her? No! Too many suppositions. "If you hear hoof beats, think horses, not zebras". Trump got an infection after a long surgery. Dina died in a car crash. Shit happens.*

He found he'd been washing his hands for well over two minutes. He turned off the tap, dried his hands and prepared to re-enter the crowd, but he couldn't stop one more thought: *If Dina did get killed because she knew something, what happens if "they" know she told me? Are those people in this room?*

He'd left his drink in the washroom so went back to the bar, now blocked by a press of people. The crowd parted for him, however, and the bartender already had his drink ready. *One good thing about being tall!* He turned and went back towards the door. Most newcomers would be found near the entrance or crowding around the bar. So long as he managed to shake hands or say hello to ninety percent of the people who came here tonight, he would have done his duty and get over to the White House.

Two men Duarte didn't know stood uncertainly just inside the doorway. One was a large man, both in height and breadth, with a definite dark five o'clock shadow. His companion was of Asian descent. Smaller, not much shorter, but slightly built. Neither had drinks in their hands. *May as well start with those two,* Francisco thought.

'Hi. Good of you to come. Not sure we've met…?'

The smaller of the two held out his hand to be shook. 'Ah. Good evening Mr Duarte. Terribly sorry to hear about…', "your loss" seemed inappropriate, '…Mrs Accardo. I'm Bill Ngo, Assistant US Attorney, New York'.

Ivan extended his hand. 'Ivan Biskup, Special Agent with the Federal Bureau of Intelligence. Also New York'.

Duarte was nonplussed. 'We-e-e-ll', he drawled, emphasising his Southern accent for the two Yankees. 'Welcome to the Capitol Club. You folks ever been here before?' They both shook their heads. Covering his inner concern, Francisco asked, 'And what brings you-all to D.C.?'

Francisco noted that they exchanged a quick glance before Ivan said, 'We're with the Trump-Robbins investigation…'

'Surely you don't think there's a connection with Dina's tragic accident?' he asked, belatedly realising that he'd been too fast asking.

'Oh, no', Bill said smoothly. 'What makes you think there would be?'

Recovering his composure, Francisco put the ball back in their court, hoping to regain the initiative. 'Oh, I don't! Jest assumed if that's what you're working on, that's why you'd be at a Remembrance for Dina? But where are my manners? The bar's over there; paid for by the Republican Party!'

Francisco felt back in control. The dismissal was obvious, the intimation that the two were here because of free booze subtle, and the suggestion that they were probably not Republicans masterful.

The two bid their farewells and headed to the bar as suggested. Bill knew a few of the people in the room by sight, if not by name. Although Ivan was no stranger to D.C., he knew no one here. As they reached the bar Ivan asked, somewhat doubtfully, 'Not on duty are we?'

'I won't tell if you won't!' Replied Bill. Ivan noticed that Bill ordered a ginger ale with ice *after* he had ordered a Budweiser.

'What did you think of Mr Duarte, Bill? Think we "scared up a turkey" there?'

Bill considered his response. For a prosecuting attorney, he had an odd tendency to believe the best in people. 'He's obviously under a lot of strain. Mrs Accardo was a long-time colleague of his. Probably friends. And', he held up a finger, 'it's quite possible that he knows Trump is back in hospital…' Another pause. 'Still… yes, I think we may have done. Might be worth having a conversation with Mr Duarte before we head back to New York'.

They circulated for a while, not straying too far apart and rarely engaging in anything more than superficial introductions. Linda Starr had arrived and was making the rounds, but her body language discouraged further conversation. Disappointingly, neither of the two Senators on their list made an appearance and Duarte had disappeared. They didn't stay for a second drink.

The official announcement of Donald Trump's death was made by President Obama at eight forty-five in the evening. Time enough for the networks to do some basic editing for sound bites before the nine o'clock news.

The President stuck to the facts; it would be hard for him to praise a man that he so clearly disliked. The President also mentioned the "tragic and untimely" death of Dina Accardo and the "double tragedy" that had befallen the Republican Party. His short statement was reminiscent of so many he had had to give during his tenure after mass shootings: Condolences for all affected; prayers and best wishes for the families; more prayers for the well-being United States of America in general and for strength and wisdom for the Republican Party in the days and weeks to come.

There was no mention of foul play in either case nor were the grisly details of Trump's last hours discussed.

Holiday Inn, 6th Street SW, Washington

The bartender of the Holiday Inn bar had turned the volume up without asking. A couple in the corner had objected briefly, but were quickly shut down by the rest of the patrons. They left shortly afterwards.

Bill and Ivan watched the news along with everyone else. Unlike everyone else, however, they had both received phone calls beforehand and knew what was coming. Yet it still felt more real somehow to see it on television, broadcast so everyone, not just a select few, knew.

That his death happened on the same day as the Electoral College was a great opportunity for the networks to segue to the implications of a second death of an "elected" official. There hadn't really been enough time to put together anything that was both coherent and informative. Instead, there was a series of "talking heads" who dispensed wisdom as indiscriminately and as voluminously as the draught beer taps that Ivan now nodded to, he didn't have to drive anywhere and he was damn well owed a beer after the last few weeks. Bill joined him, but at roughly half the bigger man's pace.

Day Twenty-Two

December 20

Head thumping just ever so slightly, Ivan called Martin even before he had left for the City.

'What've you got, Martin?' Ivan had asked the detective to talk to Doctor Randall in Ivan's absence. Now Trump was dead, the Secret Service were no longer responsible. This was a second murder investigation, FBI and NYPD territory.

'I told Doc Randall about the warning. Gave him the whole Espionage and Patriot Act spiel about talking to anyone, but he's cool. He tells me that the bacteria don't live long outside the human body, but that it could be weaponised, my term, not his, if it was kept frozen or in deep pressure for up to a few weeks. Upon thawing or releasing, the life span of unprotected bacteria would probably be less than a day'.

'So you could get it from toilet handles, but unlikely?'

'Yeah, much less if there was ultraviolet, that is, outdoors, or antibiotics or disinfectants or a whole bunch of other environmental factors'.

'Why do I get the feeling you've already worked through this Martin? Cut to the chase - what's the likely transmission method?'

'Huh! Spoil my fun. Okay. Other than the possibility that Trump washed his face in ice cubes or was using cold packs on his neck that had been coated with bacteria, we're looking at something he probably sprayed on himself'.

'Cologne?'

'Nope, nothing with alcohol. Ditto for cleansers. And before you say it that also rules out shaving cream'.

'So, what... crap! Spray tan!'

'Yep. That's what I came to... only thing is, there isn't any in the apartment. CSI have gone over it with the proverbial toothcomb'.

'Funny word that. "Toothcomb". Wonder where it comes from. Sure as hell I've never combed my teeth. Brushed "em, sure, but not combed'.

'Focus Ivan, focus! For your information, a "toothcomb" is a set of teeth that can be used to groom − comb - hair. Hyraxes have them. I think some other mammals do as well'.

'Huh! I guess that's why you have Kasia, she does all the logical stuff while you pack your head full of trivia. Where'd you get that from anyway?'

'David Attenborough. I got into the habit of watching late night television when the kids were teething and then carried on as a way to decompress at the end of the day'.

Both men paused for a minute until Martin continued. 'Drifted off topic a bit… Guess we're both not focusing, huh? Early in the morning and not a lot of time off recently. As I was saying. Aerosols. Spray tan. None in Trump's apartment'.

'So his colour's natural? Amazing!' Talking about the man in the past tense would come later.

'Doubt it', laughed Martin. 'And we know his movements. He didn't visit a tanning salon. He has a sun bed in the penthouse, but his wife says he didn't use it, caused some pain after the surgery. I'm sure the doctors told him not to as well, but he may not have listened to them'.

'So what's left?'

'Precisely, my dear Ivan! Although I do the exact opposite of Sherlock Holmes, fill my mind full of irrelevant trivia, I do believe in the great detective's aphorism: "Once you eliminate the impossible, whatever remains, no matter how improbable, must be the truth." Trump must have used a cosmetic service. Tracing them down is top of my to-do list today'.

Voice one: 'Where's Mister Blue?'

Voice two: 'Don't think he's coming, Pink. Just the three of us'.

Voice one: 'So we start without him?'

Voice three: 'He told me he was going away for a while. Didn't think he meant he couldn't log in'.

Voice two: 'Where did he go Mister Brown? Montana?'

Voice one: 'Crissakes, Orange. No specifics, remember?'

Voice three: 'While we're at it, let's stop with this "Mister Brown" crap. Stupid idea in the first place'.

Voice one: 'But he's got a point. Did Blue, did *we*, have anything to do with White?'

Voice three: 'Don't know, why would we?'

Voice one: 'Because of the leak'.

Voice three: 'What leak?'

Voice two: 'Someone's been talking. Someone female. Blue said he'd tell Black. It seems Black cleared you…'

A long silence.

Voice one: 'You there, Brown?'

Voice three: 'Yeah, I'm here. And not sure I'm believing what I'm hearing. *You* suspected *me*? After all I've done. And now I'm hearing that we, you, may have had White… And this, the way it ended, sickening. No, don't say anything. I definitely do *not* want to hear anymore. Now. Not ever. Probably best if both of you don't let me even *see* you for a while!'

Voice two: 'Hey, Brown, don't forget Blue's *your* boy. And yeah, it was sickening, I heard some of the details, but we didn't tell him to do anything like *that* or anything to White. Maybe you did for all we know. As for who may have actually *done* something, that'd be Black. Whoever he is. Maybe we should ask him. How come he's never on the line?'

Voice three: 'Blue said Black'd only work through him. Called it a "cut-out"'.

Voice one: '*You've* never met Black? You don't know who he is?'

Voice three: 'No. And I don't want to know. Same as I don't want to know how Black *knew* our man would get sick'.

Another silence.

Voice two: 'So is that it? Is it over? I sure hope so'.

Voice three: 'Not quite. There's still compensation'.

Voice one: 'After what happened? Screw that!'

Voice three: 'Blue also said that Black doesn't like "dishonourable finishes", we're vulnerable'.

Voice one: 'Exposure? So is he'.

Voice two: 'I don't think he was talking exposure, something more final?'

Voice three: 'That's the impression I got, yes. And we don't even know who Black is'.

Voice one: 'Do we even know he exists?'

Voice two: 'Well, whodya think's been doing this crap?'

Voice one: 'Maybe Blue. Blue always does the talking for Black. Maybe he *is* Black'.

Voice three: 'I can't believe that of… Blue'.

Voice one: 'And I can't believe what's been happening, *I* sure as hell didn't say to… to… when I heard, I wanted to puke'.

Voice two: 'Too late for that, Pink. We're in this together. Now we just need to get out. Brown, is the… compensation prepped?'

Voice three: 'Yeah. I've got that covered'.

Voice two: 'Then let's go ahead so we can wrap this up. Maybe you can ask Blue at some other time about Black and White…., but if I was you, I'd just let this fade away'.

Voice three: 'Right. Then we're done with this. Even if this isn't what we thought would happen when we started, it is what it is. Don't forget we got what we wanted. Someone else gets the top job. Destroy everything Blue gave you'.

'Wow! They said they were going to a new system and how! I couldn't get a handle on anything. Very slippery. Looks like they were doing microhops across SIMS, even across networks and media on top of their normal encryption. In the middle, it almost looked like they split the signal over a peer-to-peer network. And used end-to-end encryption; maybe even something as simple as WhatsApp: I got diddly squat'.

'You're loss is my gain! Lots of noise, but I got the whole conversation, word-for-word'.

'Great! Enough for voice analysis?'

'Don't think so... I think they may have been using real-time voice-to-voice transcribers; not their real voices. It was like listening to three robots talking to each other'.

'Still, good stuff to send up the line, yeah? Anything interesting that you could see?'

'Don't know enough about what they're working on, but I'm sure Morna and the gang'll find it fascinating. There were two things for us, though'.

'Oh?'

'Yep. One, they've stopped using "Mister"-plus-colour. That's going to make it a lot harder for us to pick up'.

'Ah, we can do it, just needs a new algorithm and a load more computing power. This project's got top priority so we'll have no trouble getting it'.

'Well, yes, but it probably doesn't matter. The second point is that they're calling it quits. I think that was the last call they're going to make'.

Day Twenty-Three

December 21

There was a definite buzz in the New York air; one could almost hear everyone talking about the events of the past month. The headlines, both on-screen and on paper, had moved on from the hard facts onto speculation. Stories and rumours were already seeping out from the hospital. CSI agents in bio-hazard suits had been seen at Trump Tower. How could this have happened, was there a conspiracy? Were the Secret Service involved? Was it another terrorist attack? If so, by whom? Russians? Muslims? What did it mean for America? What had happened at the Electoral College? There were questions as to why the College was allowed to go ahead and calls for a new College to be held before the Congressional count. Never mind that there was no legal basis or process for that. And what about Dina Accardo? Coincidence? I think not!

Surprised no one's mentioned Aliens or made a connection to Oswald somehow, Martin thought sourly. His car was in the shop for a minor rattle so he had taken public transit today. It took about the same time to get to the office, but being face to face with his fellow city-dwellers distracted him from his normal morning reverie.

He was already off-balance, unsettled, feeling as if he had turned up late for work. As he walked into the building, along the corridors, waited for an elevator, he was bombarded by discussions, questions, theories, some directly at him, but most just wrapping around his head like cotton wool, stopping him from thinking. The rumour mill seemed to be even more intense inside Police headquarters than on the streets.

Martin went to his office, quickly scanned for messages, reports, files that had been put on his desk in his absence and then almost ran down the emergency stairs to the case room. Closing the door behind him, he plopped himself down in the nearest chair with an audible "phew!"

'Madhouse, huh?' Kasia asked.

Martin hadn't even seen her sitting in the corner when he came in. He jumped. 'Don't do that!'

'What, say hello?' she asked, innocently.

The rest of the morning had been spent discussing events with colleagues, briefing superiors and saying as little as possible to the media. Just before lunch Siobhan, Sharmila and Morna came by.

Ivan was still in D.C. with Bill. Morna had sent a copy of last night's transcript via secure NSA internal mail to Washington and then had a printout hand-delivered to Ivan. She was still concerned about leaks. They were both due back tonight and could be brought up to speed in the morning.

After distributing copies of the transcript of yesterday's call and explaining the technical issues regarding voice analysis and tracing, Morna started the meeting.

'There's quite a lot here. First we can be sure that Brown and White are female, the others are male. The reference to Montana, the absence of White and other comments suggest that White may have been Dina Accardo. I've asked the techs to try voice matching Kasia's calls to her. Should get results soon. Next, it's clear that Blue has gone AWOL, but that there is still a payment to be made. If we can somehow trace that, we'd have some tangible evidence. There is a definite threat of violence in the air. It seems only Black, possibly Blue, are the ones to use violence, so they'll be our murderers. Finally, they're closing down. This may have been one of the last, if not *the* last transmission, no more data'.

'Thanks, Morna', Martin said. 'Any ideas how we could trace that payment?'

'Not really. I suppose if we're still thinking about Starr, Metaxas and/or Jäger we could watch their accounts or subpoena them?'

Martin sounded doubtful. 'I'll let Alden and Bill make that call, I'm not sure we've got enough to pull a Congresswoman's personal bank accounts. That said, any payments made outside *personal* accounts, say from a slush fund, and would probably be a matter of public record. We just need to know where to look'. He paused. 'And have reasonable cause to do the looking. I'm not sure that these transcripts will be acceptable to a judge as a basis for a Grand Jury indictment. The lawyers are going to have their work cut out for them trying to get them admitted in a trial given their providence'.

Kasia added, 'And I'm not sure that there's anything indictable on the tapes at all; they have all been very careful in not being specific. There's a lot of circumstantial evidence, but nothing that a good defence lawyer couldn't dismiss as pure coincidence. That said, if they *were* talking about Trump or Accardo, none of them sounded happy. Perhaps we could get one of them to roll over?'

'Perhaps', Martin agreed. 'It'd be great if we could find Mister Blue and Mister Black. And Dan Kendall, especially if they turn out to be the same person. Any news on him Sharmila?'

'No. Ivan told me yesterday that Starr said she didn't know where Kendall is. He's not a permanent member of staff. She did confirm, however, that he was with her on the night of the Twenty-Ninth. We're not ready to put out an APB, but we have started some inquiries. Including with Ravalli Sheriff's department, they cover Hamilton, and Montana Highway Patrol. We're also getting a couple of Agents out there to "assist" in the accident investigation. Nothing yet, but you never know'.

'Alright. Any other news?'

Sharmila continued her briefing. 'We found the eBay drone. Very much still in one piece. That means the only drone that's missing is one that went to China. *That's* got to be our murder weapon'.

'Mmmm. That sort of thing, negative evidence rather than positive, "here's the knife in this bag, your Honour", evidence can get thrown out. Do we know *who* it went to in China?' Kasia asked.

'No… the crowd-sourced money came from an SOE, a State Owned Enterprise, called China Universal Exports. The payment was authorised by a Mister "Chang" or "Zhang". Before you ask, there are over a hundred million people with that surname. And I can't confirm that "China Universal Exports" even exists, at least as anything more than on paper. And, yes, I am aware that "Universal Exports" is the fake company name that James Bond uses'.

Martin sighed. 'So more silly spy stuff'.

Even though it wasn't a question, Sharmila answered anyway. 'Yah. But maybe it's not so silly. Maybe it's meant to look silly, even comic. Make us think that we're dealing with amateurs'.

'Which', Morna added, 'we are one hundred percent not; the encryption used so far, especially last night is state-of-the-art'.

'Yet', mused Kasia, 'Mister White's was not'.

Martin was thoughtful. 'Maybe it's both. Maybe the amateur façade wasn't for us, maybe there were two games being played'.

'How'd you mean, Martin?' It was Siobhan's first contribution to the discussion.

Martin looked at the four intelligent women with him in the room. 'One of the most basic mistakes to make in the detective field is to assume that everyone is as smart as you are. Think about what Kasia just said. When White was by herself she was nowhere near as careful as when she was with the others. And then look at last night's call. Even without the actual voices, the inflections, I get the impression that there is a little panicking happening. A feeling that these three are a bit rudderless. Anyone else get that?'

Morna nodded. 'Yeah. At least compared to some other conversations we heard. Brown, who is most likely *not* a "Mister" from what was said, seemed to be somewhat in control, but the others were floundering'.

'And', Kasia said, excitedly, 'this is the first call without Blue!'

'Uh-huh. And Blue has often been calling the shots'. Said Martin. 'What if Blue was having a small joke to himself with this cloak and dagger stuff? We've been told that Black did the deeds. And Black only works through Blue'.

'But Blue and Black could be the same guy!' Siobhan added. 'Blue's been playing both them and us'.

'That's certainly one interpretation', agreed Martin. 'It's also possible that we're barking up the wrong tree, completely, but I don't think so'.

'There's more you know…' Sharmila said mildly. That got their attention.

'I had CID, our fraud squad, working on those payments I told you about, the ones for the website'.

'The ones in Tuvalu?'

'Yah. As I said earlier, the closest I could get was that the money may have come from China. No identifying details, but then CID said that when they trawled through the metadata, they found "CUEL" – all in caps – used in a way that suggests it could be the originator'. She paused, waiting for someone to make the connection.

'An anagram of "clue"?' Martin added, tentatively.

'Well, it is… not what I was thinking about, though' said Sharmila.

Quietly, Kasia said, 'China Universal Exports… Limited?'

'Possible, hah? So… on a hunch, I thought, "where does funny money come from?" and asked CID to look through the Panama Papers. They found a "CUE Limited". Registered in British Virgin Islands. CUE transferred twelve thousand, six hundred US dollars late October twenty-eighth'.

'To?'

'Don't know. That's as far as we can get. However', Sharmila's face lit up, 'it caught CID's attention because it's so small. Most transfers from these sorts of places are in the hundreds of thousands or millions. And it caught *my* attention because on November first that's exactly how much the webhosting company in Tuvalu got paid!'

'Excellent work, Sharmila! Excellent!' Martin said. The others all added their congratulations.

'CID may be able to get a bit more on CUE, they're still working on it'.

'Anyone got anything else?' Martin asked. 'No? Alright, I've got just one thing, but first I'd like to say that I'm proud of what everyone *has* managed to do. *And* that we're all talking about evidence that will stand up in court, not just theories. We may not have found our murder, or murderers, yet, but we are getting somewhere. We know how murders number one and two – let's not forget Agent Johnson – were done and have the remains of the weapon. We've got a good idea on how murder number three happened, and trust me, we'll find Trump was murdered, that was no accidental infection. Gene tracked down the cosmetics service that Trump uses. They got CSI to load up anything that could even have come *near* Trump in the past week. It's all in the lab in Virginia now'.

Day Twenty-Four

December 22

Over three weeks had passed since the initial attack, Christmas was coming and, more importantly, so was a presidential inauguration. The bosses needed an update.

Six men met in Rafi's office. Martin and his boss Emery took the couch. Bill and *his* boss, Alden, sat in armchairs at either end of the coffee table. Ivan pulled up the last armchair and squeezed it in between the table and Rafi's desk. Rafi himself preferred to half-stand, half-sit propped against his desk facing them all.

Ivan, as the chief investigator, gave a quick overview in bullet points:

- Robbins was killed by an explosive device on a drone carried by an owl.
- The Secret Service, Rostam Alinejad and Jaffar Saqqaf had been exonerated as innocent pawns who had been manipulated by the real killer.
- This killer showed signs of military and/or intelligence training and had left clues behind that suggested intelligence more than military. The presumption was that this had been done for egotistical purposes
- Trump's infection had been caused by a deliberate attack using a biological weapon: "Earlier this morning, the lab was able to confirm that an aerosol used for the application of cosmetic tanning to Donald Trump's face contained the same unlikely combination of bacteria that led to his demise". Once again, the modus operandi suggested someone with both access to, and training in, military-intelligence assets.
- Dina Accardo's death was seen as suspicious even though local authorities felt it to be accidental. This was primarily based on the fact that Detective Pasternak had received a number of "Deep Throat" style calls that provided valuable information about the case. "Yesterday, I was informed that lab-comparison of the voice on those calls with the voice of Mrs Accardo resulted in a ninety-five percent probability that they were the same person". Mrs Accardo's calls had led us to an NSA-led listening operation which eventuated in the strong suspicion that all of these murders were a consequence of a conspiracy between five or six people. Mrs Accardo had originally been one of those conspirators, but had changed her mind and tried to stop the attacks *after* the first.
- The motive for these murders has still to be determined, but there is reason to believe that they were politically motivated. Based on this assumption, we have tentatively identified the conspirators to be Mrs Accardo, Congresswoman Linda Starr, Senator Marvin Jäger, Senator Markos Metaxas and Mister Dan Kendall. At present, we do not know the whereabouts of Mister Kendall and it must be stressed that we have no concrete evidence to link any of these people, except Mrs Accardo, to the crimes as yet. The evidence, while strong, is circumstantial.

- There is an, as yet unconfirmed, possibility of a link to China, whether the Government or other groups within that country cannot be determined at this time. Note that the existence of one motivation does not preclude the other; there is a possibility that the murderer himself, assumed to be Dan Kendall with or without an accomplice, may have been playing a double game, acting as a mercenary and selling his services to two parties simultaneously, both of whom gained by Trump's demise. Mr Robbins death may or may not have been part of the original objective.

'Moving forward, I recommend that we formally question one of these people, presenting copies of the transcripts of the calls they made and other evidence with the intent of compelling a confession or similar verification of our suspicions. I would recommend one of the Senators as, if it is them on the calls, they have appeared to be the less committed and, perhaps, less culpable than the Congresswoman and thus more open to plea-bargaining. Even better would be to bring both of them in at the same time and present them with the classic "Prisoner's Dilemma". Meanwhile, efforts are being stepped up in the search for Dan Kendall.'

The three senior officials thanked Ivan for his succinct and informative account. They then subjected Ivan and Martin and, to a lesser extent, Bill, to a long and intense grilling on the details.

The meeting ended at five-thirty. Everyone was tired, but satisfied. Alden, Emery and Rafi thanked the men again for their hard work, their honesty and their patience during a long day. *As if we had a choice,* they all thought. 'Now, the three of us are going to put on our thinking caps and consider your recommendation. Good night gentlemen'.

As they waited by the elevator, Ivan said to the other two, '*Chyort!* I could do with a drink. Anyone with me?'

'You know, for a Slovak, you swear a lot in Russian...'

'Huh!' Ivan snorted.

'Coincidentally', Martin continued, 'I called Kasia at lunch. Told her that we might be wanting to do precisely that and if she wanted to join... Turns out it's Morna's last day in the City and the girls had already thought going out. Morna's heading home for the holidays now it looks like her part in the investigation may be over. Sounded like a good excuse for a pre-Christmas drink to me. Kasia said she'd try and get Siobhan and Sharmila to join'.

As the elevator doors opened, Ivan said, 'Fat chance, getting Sharmila to join. She never socialises with people from the office'.

'Kasia also said that Morna wanted Brice to join so maybe we'll have to watch what we say'.

'And what we do. He'll probably have mini cameras all over the place!'

They rode down to the ground floor, each of them feeling a weight lifting off their shoulders. A social gathering with like-minded people would be a very fine thing.

'I suggested we meet at "our" wine bar in Brooklyn, but Kasia suggested a bar in midtown near Central, just up from Morna's hotel. Said you know where it is, Bill?' Martin asked, innocently, but antennae fully out to catch any inflections in Bill's voice or manner.

'Oh, sure. Kasia and I go there occasionally'.

If there had been any guilt, Martin didn't catch it. He said, 'I came in by train today - my car's still in the shop. I know you take the train Bill, so this'll be easy for you to go home from…' Martin stressed "go home" slightly while looking closely at Bill. *Nothing. Maybe there is nothing, Martin. Drop it, you're no longer being concerned, you're being creepy.* 'What about you Ivan, drive?'

'Well, I did, but I think I'll leave the car here overnight…'

A Vietnamese, African-American and a Slovak walked into a bar…

Morna, Brice and Siobhan sat on one side of a long table. Opposite them sat Kasia and…

'Sharmila!' Roared Ivan. He grabbed the small woman up and gave her a big hug that Sharmila was almost completely hidden in. While they hugged, Bill scooted in next to Kasia while Martin grabbed a chair and stuck it at the far end of the table. Releasing a somewhat embarrassed Sharmila who sat back on the bench, now next to Bill, Ivan copied Martin and sat in a chair at the other end of the table.

A waiter appeared. Orders were placed. Drinks arrived. A toast was made to Morna. The evening started auspiciously. Office and personal chit-chat flowed. Brice, Kasia and Siobhan were ready for another. Ivan and Martin drained their glasses quickly, 'Just to catch up to you!' Laughed Ivan.

Sharmila leant forward. Never a loud speaker, she wasn't going to raise her voice in public, but neither could she hold in her news any longer.

'While you boys were having fun in the executive offices, I was slaving away, yah? I've found Kendall'.

The few who were still whispering to each other stopped.

'What? Where?'

'He flew to Japan on Sunday night. Just past midnight on Monday, actually. All Nippon Airways out of LAX. He'd flown to Los Angeles on Delta out of Salt Lake City'.

Ivan asked, 'Salt Lake City? Why? Surely there are direct flights to LA?'

Martin said softly, 'I think Sharmila's going to tell us that *was* a direct flight'.

Sharmila nodded. 'Uh-huh. *If* you were in, say, Idaho or *Montana*, Salt Lake would be the closest airport for you to then get to LA. And if you'd been near…'

'…Hamilton?' Asked Martin.

'Yah. You've got that one, Martin. If you were near where poor Mrs Accardo died on Sunday morning, you'd only have twenty miles or so to drive to Missoula where you could catch a flight to Salt Lake, there were a few that day. Or you could *drive* straight to Salt Lake, takes about seven hours. Enough time to catch Delta 4764 at five forty-five to LA'.

'Do we have records of him catching a flight out of Missoula or renting a car anywhere?' Ivan was much more serious than just five minutes previous.

'No, but I can keep looking tomorrow'.

Brice interrupted. 'Could easily have used another name. I didn't realise you were still looking at him. I'm not sure I'm supposed to say this, but then again, I'm not sure I'm not supposed to say anything, "withholding evidence" and all that. Dan Kendall isn't his name'.

'What?'

'Kendall's a 'legend''. The name, the background, everything, was put together by the Agency years ago. He can drop it any time he wants. Probably even has nested identities'.

'So what's his real name?' asked Ivan.

'Beats me', Brice said with a shrug. 'Way above my pay grade. It's possible that when I first met him it was another name, that's why I wasn't sure whether I had met him or not, but there's no guarantee that would have been his real name even if I could remember'.

'Crap'. Ivan leant back. 'And from Tokyo, it's a single hop to Shanghai'.

'Well, yah, that's what I thought. I didn't think it was so important to know *how* he got where he got, more important to know *where* he got. Was. Is. Whatever'. Sharmila's face was already a touch flushed. 'So I've been in touch with Narita airport security. Lovely people, they are. Very helpful and very organised. I sent them Kendall's photo, or whatever his name is. They've got some fantastic face recognition software there, we really should get some, eh?'

'Sharmila…', groaned Ivan.

'Oh. Yah. Sorry, boss. So they found him. In Narita. And then he wasn't there. Their software automatically tracks people as they move from one camera to another, interpolates between blind spots. Anyhoo, Kendall walked into one of those blind spots and never came out. Airport security really were very helpful. They manually ran the films. Easy to spot. Tall *gaijin*, light rain jacket, *et cetera, et cetera*. Walks behind a row of shops where they're doing some renovations. No cameras at the moment. There are three ways out of that blind spot when you include going back out the way you go in. He doesn't come out, they ran the tapes for an hour past the time he went in'.

Brice said, 'Probably took off or reversed his coat, took off/put on a hat, changed his walk. Basic counter-surveillance. He knew where the blind spot was and knew what he was doing'.

'Shit!'

'Oh, yah. Shit!'

The party mood had definitely diminished.

Then Sharmila, who was always upbeat, said. 'Oh, hey! I forgot. Got some good news as well! You remember I talked about them Panama Papers and getting CID on it? Guess who they found associated with CUE Limited? "D. Kendall" and "L. Zhang"!'

'Wow, Sharmila, sometimes I think you do more work than the rest of us put together!'

'Does that mean a raise, boss?' She asked, sweetly.

The party broke up an hour later, it *was* a school night and none of them had had dinner yet. Martin was so deep in thought about the day, the week, the month that he forgot to notice if Kasia and Bill went in the same direction.

Day Twenty-Five

December 23

Outside, the high had finally moved on. It wasn't particularly cold, but the sky was overcast and the sunshine that had given the city a patina of cheerfulness had slipped away, revealing the grimy reality.

Inside his office and looking out at the dreary day, Ivan felt the case slipping away from him. Rafi had told him that no one wanted to be seen grilling Senators just before Christmas and "while the country was mourning" unless there was a *very* good chance that the interviews would lead to an arrest. An arrest of the person who did it, not just conspirators.

'Hell, we don't have enough jails to hold everyone who said they thought it would be a good thing if Trump died or who benefited from his death. We need to arrest the murderer. Then we go for the conspirators', Rafi had said while Ivan thought, *but the conspirators are the only ones who'll lead us to the murderer.*

He went through the papers on his desk perfunctorily, approving things without thinking about them. Half-finishing reports before starting on another.

Mid-morning, his mood was lifted momentarily when Martin called. NYPD had found a clear picture of Dan Kendall entering 630 Fifth Street, the building that Jaffar's body had been found in, at four o'clock on the twenty-ninth. Although there was no contradiction with Linda Starr's records, they merely said that Kendall had met her and her staff at five, there was no known explanation for him to have gone to that building at that time.

On the other hand, there was no record that he had gone *back* to the building after Jaffar had activated the drone to kill him. In fact... Ivan searched through all the case notes until he found... *Sooksin!* Starr's records show Kendall with her from before six until after nine at the dinner function. This could be checked, of course, maybe the records were wrong, maybe he had slipped away... *for long enough to get back across time, murder a boy when the whole plaza was in panic mode and a major security shut down starting, get out and back without anyone seeing him? Helluva pee break...*

Ivan looked out the window. *"A major security shut down". So never mind how he got there, how the hell did he get away at all? If Jaffar had got the drone airborne...* he pulled up the records describing the events of that night...*it was only up for, at most five minutes. The Service said they spotted it almost immediately, as it was climbing. So... Jaffar's in room 630. Say seven o'clock to make it easy on me. He starts the drone. Maybe Kendall's already there, OK. He waits until the drone gets snatched by the owl. Say seven-o-five. Now he can shoot Jaffar, leave the note and the gun, pick up the backpack... no, say the backpack had already been left. Maybe it was an accident. Jaffar was excited. Needed a pee. Forgets his schoolbooks. So Kendall can shoot and start to leave immediately, but the owl took less than a minute to fly across the plaza.*

Even running down the corridor and stairs, Kendall would have needed, seven, eight minutes? Secret Service and NYPD were all over the place by then, but in the panic… he's got no gun, no one's looking for him… maybe he's just another screaming civilian trying to get away. Then there's the alibi…

He gave up and called Martin. Explained what he'd been thinking.

Martin said, 'Remember what I said last time, Ivan? "Once you eliminate the impossible, whatever remains, no matter how improbable, must be the truth". If Kendall couldn't get back to kill Jaffar, then he didn't'.

'We have another killer? Is it the Mister Black and Mister Blue thing?'

Martin hesitated. 'Possibly. Hadn't thought about that. I was going simpler. Maybe Jaffar was already dead. The coroner's report couldn't be that specific about time of death. What if Kendall entered 630 at four and killed Jaffar as soon as he arrived. Left the gun, the note, the controls. Then he's free to be with Linda Starr all night'.

'Then how did a dead Jaffar operate the drone?'

'Again, if he couldn't, then he didn't. So what else do we have?'

'Someone *else* operated the drone', Ivan concluded with wonder in his voice, *now, the case was getting solved!*

Martin burst his bubble with a chuckle. 'Y-e-s. Possible. But unnecessarily complicated. These drones are designed to be operated at a distance, yes? So why not at a temporal distance as well?'

'What? Martin, you're losing me'. *And my patience…*

'Can drones be operated on a timer?'

Ivan got off the phone with CSI. *Could the KittyHawk operate automatically on a timer? Oh, sure. For basic stuff like hovering, very easily. Some of the newer ones are fully programmable.*

And just like that, Ivan thought, *an alibi is broken.*

He was heading for lunch when he got a call from the FBI Agent in Montana. The Sheriff department's now treating the Accardo accident as suspicious. The accident investigators took a closer look at the windscreen. The shatter pattern is a little odd. Looks like there could have been a spot fracture prior to the accident; a bird, a stone… a bullet.

Ivan ate alone in the deli down the road. It was half-empty. A couple of days before Christmas and people were: a) already off on holiday; b) going out to "nice" (expensive) restaurants as befitted the season; c) scrimping and eating brown bag lunches; d) working through lunch to get out early.

It started to rain as he left the deli.

By three o'clock, his office had emptied and he began to ask himself what he was doing here. He'd done plenty of overtime recently. His phone rang.

'Agent Biskup, here. How can I help?'

'Ah, yes, Agent Biskup. Francisco Duarte. We met in Washington a few days ago. I'm…'

'I know who you are Mr Duarte. Very kind of you to call. How can I be of service?'

'Well, I'm not sure where to begin. It's about Dina Accardo and her accident. You see, I think, maybe that it wasn't an accident'.

'We are beginning to think the same thing, sir. Perhaps you could tell me why *you* think that?'

Day Twenty-Six

December 24

Martin sat in the Case Room, reluctant to head out into the steady rain that had settled in for the holiday. He was alone. Kasia had headed off at midday. Ivan had filled him in on Duarte's phone call.

'Duarte thinks a small group of Republicans, maybe even some Democrats as well got carried away', Ivan explained. 'Bunch of reasons. Some just couldn't accept that Trump had won, some concerned that Trump would bring the Party into disrepute, and some because they had lost their re-election campaigns because the voters in their States found Trump too much. Whatever the reason, they all wanted Trump out and their man in'.

'But the man has no proof, doesn't know names, doesn't know how many in the group. It's pure supposition'. And then Ivan had dropped the bombshell. 'The Director of the FBI called Rafi. There'd been a very high-level discussion that included the Cabinet and the leaders from *both* Parties. Maybe the President himself. They're all worried about security. There's been a loss of faith in "the system" this past year. Not just the brutality of the campaign. They see a connection between political posturing and polarisation and social issues like the police shootings and #BlackLivesMatter. Seems they've been putting pressure on the media since the very beginning to tone down the rhetoric and speculation. The press are terrified of being denied access to briefings so they're happy to play along. And if someone doesn't like the carrot... we've got all these shiny new anti-terrorism and Homeland Security laws to use as sticks'. Ivan's voice was flat, he had been working long hours and for what?

'The Attorney-General reversed herself on the decision to interview the Senators', Ivan continued. '"Insufficient Evidence", she'd said. "Prejudicial to Further Indictments". It's a political decision, Martin, they're scared what's going to happen when those ballots are opened in January. They want to minimise further disruption; time to start rebuilding that faith before it gets out of hand and there are massive riots. They've decided that the leadership needs to show a unified, steady and dignified front. Going after Starr and the rest would look too much like the Democrats having one last swipe at the Republicans out of spite. Besides, the A-G also said that she'll be out of a job under the new Administration whatever happens. Far better to leave it for her successor to handle'.

Martin absorbed all of this for a minute before commenting. 'And what's the likelihood that a Republican Attorney-General will want to prosecute three high-ranking Republicans on purely circumstantial evidence? Are they asking us to drop it? What about Kendall? There's been four murders, Ivan! We don't just walk away, do we?'

'No, they want the public to see "Justice In Action". To make them feel safe again. Give them surety, no grey areas', Ivan replied. 'So the line will be that Kendall did it. The White House press secretary will be making a statement that "A warrant for the arrest of Mr Daniel Kendall, US Citizen has been issued and all countries, *especially China,* are asked to cooperate in bringing the suspect to justice." We'll be given credit, Martin. Me, you, the team. "Thanks to the hard work and dedication of the FBI and the New York Police Department…" that sort of thing. Footage of Kendall in Japan "on the way to China", another Snowden fleeing the land of the free into the hands of, if not "the enemy" then certainly not "our friends"'.

'Not Snowden, Emmanuel Goldstein'.

'Huh? What's that Martin?'

'Emmanuel Goldstein. He was the villain in Orwell's *1984.* Whenever the powers in charge felt the need to tighten their grip on society, they'd dream up some new villainy that Goldstein had supposedly done. Then the nation would pull together in fear of the outsider; there's safety in numbers. Thatcher and Bush did the same with the Falklands and Saddam'.

'Maybe you're right. But you and I aren't pulling the strings. I got the feeling that they're confident that explanation will satisfy the public until Christmas, after which bad weather, and New Year's Eve parties and New Year's Day hangovers means it'll all fade away for the majority. Sure, there'll be a minority who will push conspiracy theories for decades. Experts yammering on TV and dozens of books like after the JFK assassination. Maybe one will even be titled after your poem, Martin, y'know, "Who Killed Cock Robbins?" Do ya know what the real kicker is?'

'Sure. Hit me while I'm down'.

'We don't know if Kendall is guilty at all. We know that isn't his name. Precious little on him at all. We ran the Tokyo photo up to the gun shop in Vermont, "Yep. That'd be the Larry T. Edwards who bought ma gun, a'right", he'd said. And then he'd added "I think. Fella I sold it to may have been older. Different hair 'n' all". How about that on the witness stand?'

'What're you going to do, Ivan?'

'We'll keep the case open, but Rafi'll start reallocating resources over the next week; we've always got more work than staff. I'll have a quick meeting with the case team. Tell 'em we're cooling the investigation down a bit over the holidays. Make a light joke about allowing them some time off. Then I'll go home and have a few stiff ones. It's over'.

The two men shared a companionable silence over the phone. They'd both experienced the slight depression that comes from an unresolved case before.

Ivan sighed heavily. 'Nolan Quinn was in the meeting. He's probably briefed Emery and Ross Benbow by now so I wouldn't be surprised if Emery calls you soon. Ross'll break the news to Siobhan. Alden was also in the meeting so Bill probably already knows. Don't think it'll hit him hard. He wouldn't've got emotionally invested until closer to trial. Ditto for Morna, I think she saw the case more as an intellectual challenge. She said goodbye to it the other night over drinks. That leaves Kasia. She'll take it hard, it's been a lot of work for nothing'.

'You're right. She'd be okay if it hadn't worked out. If we'd been unable to get any leads or the evidence didn't stack up… hundreds of cases don't get closed. But this… this is *wrong*. We were close, so close. Kasia will go ballistic when she hears… or maybe not'.

'What're you thinking?'

'Something she said when she left, "see you in a few days", normal enough, but thinking back, perhaps she already knew this was coming. Smart cookie our Kasia. May not be that surprised after all. Still, I'm not looking forward to telling her…'

They said their goodbyes, wishing each other a "Merry Christmas" *sod departmental "Happy Holidays"*, regards to their respective families, and so on. And then Martin was alone in the windowless room.

He looked around the room. All the files, photographs, reports. Everything fits, but we had no hard evidence. Even Duarte's statement is just hearsay and supposition. Our only witness is dead and Starr and the gang are protected by privilege. Starr gets to walk away. Glumly, he recalled Bowie again:

> She was a psycho killer
> He was a shadow
> They opened doors
> They slipped through cracks
> A trail of confusion
> A trail of death
> Forcing our faces to the mirror
> It shatters as innocence falls to the floor

And was that it? Was this one more blow to our faith in the system, our faith to each other? One more step down the inevitable spiral of the decline and fall of the American Empire? The summer had shown what happens when parts of "The System" lose public respect and trust: Blacks shoot police, police shoot blacks. *Both of which are my people. Blacks and policemen.* Martin shook his head. *God, you're being pessimistic today. Don't take it personally; you win some, you lose some.*

He looked at the computer screen. It showed a clear picture of Dan Kendall at Tokyo airport. *Edwards, Kendall, Lawrence, whatever the hell your name is. Are you a spook? A monster? Or a victim of circumstance? Were we looking too hard in the wrong place? Part of me wants you to be innocent. Then I could sleep at night knowing you got to walk away. Maybe you really are just a "fixer" for Congresswomen. Maybe you're in Tokyo to see old friends. Or maybe you're a murderer. A killer for hire, and we'll never know who paid you.*

Lies and rumours
Suspicion and distrust
Stealth and stories
Daylight exposes vicious thoughts
Meet in dark alleyways
Never say why
Let the others worry
Let the others die

Meanwhile, Martin knew, the real powers-that-be had already moved on. They were thinking about January Sixth. The Constitution and its Amendments were not specific on what happened next. Both candidates who'd won the popular vote were dead and who knows what the Electors did when they cast their ballots The House, the Senate, the White House, even the Supreme Court were pre-discussing various scenarios and what compromises were available: Donald Trump's death was old news; 2017 was a new year.

Martin knew he should go home. He hadn't been spending enough time with his family. Not that the teenagers really noticed, but they would remember when they got older. And his wife needed him. *No, we both need each other.*

Martin looked at the picture again. *Sharmila's right - the Japanese really* do *have good technology.* He continued to stare at the screen, trying to feel the man, not just the image. *Did you sell us all out just for some money? Are you Bowie's "Man who sold the World"?*

From a recess in his memory, he recalled Mearns' poem that had inspired Bowie's song:

Yesterday, upon the stair,
I met a man who wasn't there.
He wasn't there again today,
I wish, I wish he'd go away...

When I came home last night at three,
The man was waiting there for me
But when I looked around the hall,
I couldn't see him there at all!
Go away, go away, don't you come back any more!
Go away, go away, and please don't slam the door...

Last night I saw upon the stair,
A little man who wasn't there,
He wasn't there again today
Oh, how I wish he'd go away...

Well, he'd gone away now, hadn't he? Linda Starr bought you a get-out-of-jail free card to protect her own ass. Helluva Christmas present, Lawrence.

He sighed, turned off the monitor, stood up and started to pack up for the long weekend.

Suddenly, he realised why he'd been thinking of Bowie so much. The musician had been in a film set in Japan. Bowie had played a soldier. *Military intelligence? Can't remember. What was the title? Oh...*

'*Merry Christmas, Mr Lawrence*' Martin chuckled as he turned off the lights.

Epilogue: January Sixth, 2017

On January 6th, Schrödinger's Cabinet was opened.
The joint session of Congress opened the ballots and announced the count.

President		Vice-President	
Donald Trump (R)	269	Mitt Romney (R)	261
Hilary Clinton (D)	240	Tim Kaine (D)	256
Frank Haden (D)	8	Mason Robbins (R)	17
Marco Rubio (R)	7	Ted Cruz (R)	2
Calvin Stevens (D)	5	SPOILED	2
Paul Ryan (R)	1		
Ted Cruz (R)	1		
Linda Starr (R)	4		
Jeff Johnson (L)	2		
SPOILED	1		

The count itself was almost as meaningless as the votes the American People had cast in November.

Previous conclusions by House Committees had stated that all must votes count, even if they are for dead people. However, this was never passed into law and there is room for Congress to debate whether those votes should be counted or thrown out. The same holds true for spoiled ballots.

If the votes for Trump and Robbins were treated as spoiled and spoiled votes discarded, this would mean that the total votes cast for President would be 268. Votes cast for Clinton would easily meet the new simple majority threshold of 135. In the Vice-presidential election, a similar decision would mean that 275 votes would count and 138 would be the majority threshold: Romney would be the Vice-President Elect.

Neither party would be completely happy with the idea of a Democrat President and a Republican Vice-President, but the Democrats would definitely be the happier of the two.

If, however, Congress decided to keep the spoiled votes in the total number cast, then no candidate got a simple majority of 270. In this case, the law is that the House of Representatives, controlled by the Republicans, would be obliged to choose a President from the top three vote winners, two of whom were Democrats. They would want to choose the only Republican, Marco Rubio, but would the American People (or the Supreme Court) stand for a President who only received seven votes and wasn't even on the ballot in November?

Similarly, in the Vice-President vote, the Senate, controlled by the Democrats, is obliged to choose from the top two vote winners. They would obviously lean towards Tim Kaine even though Romney received more Elector votes.

A long January of bitter negotiations loomed ahead...

Acknowledgements

Many, many thanks go to the people who proof read the manuscript: Gail, Guilia, Judy, Kirsten, Penny and Stef. Any errors that remain are, of course, the fault of the author.

Thanks are also owed to those who responded to my Facebook request for help in deciding on the jacket cover and synopsis. There are many of you; you know who you are! In particular I'd like to thank Jo, Kirsty, Laura, Lauren, Reshma and Sarah.

This book was written in Queenstown, New Zealand and Longreach, Queensland, Australia – a long way from New York. So thanks are also due to the anonymous workers behind Google, Google Earth and Wikipedia! I spent substantial time on those sites ensuring that directions, places, flights, *et cetera* were credible.

It would not have been possible without the hard work, love and support of my partner with whom, one Saturday morning, the whole project began.

Aimer, ce n'est pas se regarder l'un l'autre,
c'est regarder ensemble dans la même direction.

For further information and author's notes, see

www.amazon.com/author/adamchilds

www.ingramcontent.com/pod-product-compliance
Lightning Source LLC
Chambersburg PA
CBHW072206170626
46813CB00003B/818